Is it possible for a Chines[e]
the open door to radi[cal]

# THE
# BLU
## PHENOMENON

AN ASIAN ADOPTEE.
AN OLYMPIC CHALLENGE.
AN EPIC DESTINY.

## CATHERINE PIKE PLOUGH

THE **BLU** PHENOMENON
By Catherine Pike Plough
Copyright 2015 by Catherine Pike Plough

Published by White Stone Publications
P. O. Box 2983, Matthews, NC 28106

Design and production by SPARK Publications
www.SPARKpublications.com

All rights reserved.

No part of this book may be reproduced, stored in a retrieval system, or transmitted in any form or by any means without the prior written permission of the publisher, except in the case of brief quotations embodied in critical reviews and certain other noncommercial uses permitted by copyright law. For permission requests, contact the publisher.

Printing History
First edition 2015, ISBN 978-1-943070-14-5

Library of Congress Control Number: 2015916982

JUV013010   JUVENILE FICTION / Family / Adoption
JUV001000   JUVENILE FICTION / Action & Adventure / General
JUV001000   JUVENILE FICTION / Action & Adventure / Adoption


www.TheBluPhenomenon.com

# Dedication

This book is dedicated to adoptees and their families that journey together into futures and purposes yet to be revealed.

# Endorsements

"This story portrays how China's democratic movement might be globalized as a result of adoption and Chinese emigration. Using an inventive story as her vehicle, the author of The Blu Phenomenon conveys a hope that the people of China will yet dream of "change." It is a hope shared by those of us at the Laogai Research Foundation as we seek to educate the world of ongoing human rights atrocities in China. This story is crafted to be both personal and global in its impact."

— **Harry Wu,** Founder & Human Rights Activist
The Laogai Research Foundation

"An engaging read for all young adults ... In particular, Asian and transracial adoptees will find that the cultural complexity presented will resonate with them in a deeply personal and profound way."

—**Susan Soonkeum Cox,** Vice President Policy & External Affairs, Holt International

"As a teacher and a parent, I highly recommend this book for young adults. Beyond the engaging tale of international intrigue, The Blu Phenomenon touches on relevant topics, from cross-cultural adoption and Chinese history to technology, sports, and friendships."

—**S. Dence,** Gifted Education Teacher

"This well-written mystery kept me in suspense to the very last page. I can't wait to read other books from this author."

—**E. Clodfelter,** Student, 14

# Prologue

Cal was only seven at the time. As night fell and exhaustion pressed on him like a leaden quilt, he closed his bright blue eyes and released the day. Then the nightmare began.

He stood alone waiting to meet with someone he did not know, someone important. What he knew with all certainty was that his world was about to change. In the thick blackness of the scene, Cal heard a door close and strained to make out a figure or a face but was met instead with a cluster of brown eyes, blinking, watching. In his dream state, he was aware that his own Asian eyes were no longer blue but dark brown—the way he'd always wished they would be, the way they should be.

When the voice behind the constellation of eyes spoke, it gave Cal an assignment of sorts. The boy resisted.

"Why me? Why do I have to go?"

"The time is coming for you to do your part."

"But how will you find me again?"

"We will give you blue eyes!"

*"No, please! Then I won't be like them—or you! I won't belong anywhere!"*

*"If you have blue eyes, we will be able to find you, and when it is time, we will bring you home."*

Cal awakened trembling. Though the fantasy his mind conjured in sleep was gone, Cal believed the dream reflected something of his own story and, perhaps, hinted at his future. He had, after all, been adopted away from China, his place of birth. And his eyes were, in fact, blue—not brown. From that moment forward, Cal feared he might, someday, be stolen away from the only life he could remember, the one he now lived in Visalia, California.

For many days Cal refused to leave his room, and his parents began to worry.

# PART I

# 01

Cal arrived at Crestwood Park soaked with sweat. Already he felt self-conscious, knowing that Lilli would arrive shortly and emerge from her mother's white SUV, looking like a fresh-picked flower. Cal had pedaled his too-small bike the four miles to the park—managing to dodge cars and also hang on to his soccer ball. There, he pulled off his helmet, grabbed his water bottle, squirted his face with water, and attempted to smooth back his straight black hair. He adjusted his sunglasses, locked up his bike at the rack by the gravel lot, and carried the ball to the bench where they agreed to meet.

Much of the summer had slipped by without Cal seeing his best friend. He tried not to blame Lilli for her commitments to dance, piano, and whatever else crowded her schedule. It was to be expected, he supposed. They were thirteen now. Life was changing. He was changing. And while he resisted the thought of the two friends growing apart, he guessed Lilli had changed too. Just how much he was about to find out.

At the bench Cal juggled the soccer ball from foot to foot to knee to head. It felt good to know he could still do it.

While swimming had become his primary sport, Cal knew he could walk on to any of the top soccer clubs in California if he wanted to. But he didn't.

Five Latino teens headed his direction. The boys spotted the Asian kid with the impressive moves and hoped they'd found a sixth player for a pick-up soccer game. Cal decided to take his show to the next level. He kicked the ball high in the air, caught it between his shoulder blades, let it roll forward over his head and down his extended right leg to his foot, where he sent it up again and caught it. The move was one of his all-time top crowd-pleasers.

A minute later, a stocky boy with dark curly hair stood in front of him. He looked to be Cal's age. The boy tipped his head toward the goals on the mostly-dirt soccer field. It was an invitation.

"Messi! Messi!" the others began to chant, flattering Cal by evoking the name of Argentine soccer legend Lionel Messi.

He hadn't meant to play soccer today, just to show off a little. He glanced back at the parking lot. Still no sign of Lilli.

How would it feel to play again?

"Fifteen minutes—that's all," Cal made his intentions clear. They nodded in agreement.

Ten minutes later, from the corner of his eye, Cal saw Mrs. Cohen's SUV pull in then out of the parking area. Lilli was there.

. . .

Lilli settled on a bench content to enjoy the game. She had few opportunities to see Cal show off, fewer still to spend time alone with him without his sidekick, Levi, and virtually no opportunities just to sit. Even in the summer, her dance schedule was relentless.

A dog barked, and Lilli turned. A few yards away, a man with a large golden dog with a black snout stepped from the walking path into the grass. The man wore dark sunglasses and crouched down on one knee, absorbed in the soccer game. The dog, which Lilli thought looked like an overgrown pug, pestered the man with a stick, but the man paid no attention. Clearly he was not there to exercise his dog. The man's hair was jet black, and his coloring was like hers and Cal's. The watching man, Lilli knew, was Asian.

Fear ran through Lilli's frame. The scene reminded her of something Cal told her once, years before. He described a nightmare, a memory of terror that left him with a fear of being watched or taken.

Since that conversation, she was the one Cal came to on the occasions when he felt someone was watching him, when he suspected that something was about to crash his small safe world. Cal's heightened awareness of his surroundings was also one of the qualities that made him a great athlete. She returned her attention to the game. How was it that Cal was genuinely having fun with these strangers? Why wasn't he afraid?

Then she saw it. He wore sunglasses. With his blue eyes hidden, Cal could relax among the brown eyes on the field. He belonged, if only for the length of a pick-up soccer game.

Lilli looked around now. The man and his dog were gone. She wouldn't mention the man to Cal. What did she know about him anyway?

...

Cal finished off the game—and his opponents—sending the ball into the goal with a showy bicycle kick. Whoops and groans followed, and the group dispersed. Exhilarated and pink with heat, he jogged over to Lilli.

"Am I in trouble?" Cal took off his sunglasses to look at his friend. Lilli wore denim capris and layered tank tops—hot pink over white. The colors looked nice against her shoulder-length black hair and brown skin. With the exception of Cal's blue eyes, the two could pass for brother and sister. Both were Chinese. Both athletic. Both adopted.

"It was fun just watching. Lucky you didn't lose those shades, huh? Pretty awesome."

"Right? Hey, can you keep a secret?"

"Probably."

"Not only do these make me look like a superstar," Cal dropped his voice to a whisper. "They also give me a super power."

"Is that right? I'm just guessing, but do they make you super cocky?"

"Nah, I get that naturally, but they do protect people from my creepy zombie eyes. Perfect for starting at a new school, don't you think?"

"I don't know. The only time I'd be scared of you was if I met you on the soccer field."

"Not even then, I bet. You're pretty much good at everything. I do know that if I tried a pirouette it would definitely be scary."

"That I don't doubt," Lilli conceded at last, and the friends laughed together.

Cal sat down in the grass by the bench and leaned back against his soccer ball. "But enough about me," he said. "Don't see you much. How's your Chinese calligraphy coming?" It was a reoccurring reference to the class where they met when they were only four. Cal and Lilli had been among the dozen or so adoptees signed up for the summer class at the nearby Chinese Cultural Center. The two hit it off, trying to outdo each other with their attempts at Chinese characters. Countless play dates followed.

"Better than yours will ever be," Lilli taunted.

"Guess we'll see who's better than whom when I get over to Valley Oak Middle School, huh?"

"In case no one mentioned this to you, we read books and write papers in public school too. You won't be Headmaster Vandiver's kid there, and you're gonna have to work it!"

"Really? Really? Just watch how I can work it, Tina the ballerina!" Cal jumped to his feet and juggled the ball knee to knee a few times before he kicked it high and caught it behind his right knee. He laughed when Lilli pretended to hide a yawn.

"Shoot, tell me who else you know who can do that—and with sunglasses on!" He dropped down on the bench.

Lilli smiled openly. "This is going to be a fun year, you know, eighth grade. Top dogs. I don't know about Mount Whitney High though—"

"You'll be great there too," Cal assured her.

"Who says I'm worrying about *me*?" she teased. "You're the one who can't sit still!"

"Not to worry." Cal slid his shades down and looked at her. "They'll be back for me by then."

Lilli sat up suddenly. It was the unspoken topic. "Where'd that come from?"

"Saw it myself." Cal pushed his glasses back in place to escape her worried gaze.

"Tell me."

"There was some guy I've never seen before walking a seriously weird-looking dog in the neighborhood. He was watching. I could tell."

"So—"

"So then he just disappeared. I ran the neighborhood three times looking for him."

"Are you worried?" It was the first time Cal admitted to *seeing* a watcher. Until that day, he had only sensed eyes following him.

Cal scanned the horizon. "I'm always worried. You know that. That's why I run so fast."

"You aren't going anywhere!" Lilli redirected the conversation. "Not until after high school graduation anyway. Class of 2024! I want to see you walk across the stage to get your diploma wearing those sunglasses!"

Cal was relieved that he and Lilli could still have a good time together. Around her, he felt relaxed. Safe.

A little later, when Mrs. Cohen arrived in her SUV, Cal

walked Lilli to the gravel lot. "Put a swim on your calendar?" Cal suggested, hoping they could fall into a routine of hanging out more often.

"I'll try to squeeze it in."

"It's important, you know. Even dancers need some exercise."

"Wow. Thanks for the tip," Lilli returned with playful sarcasm. Just as Lilli waved good-bye and was about to close her door, a dog barked. Cal noticed Lilli freeze for a moment and wondered if she had a fear of dogs that he had forgotten.

# 02

As much as Cal loved soccer, he felt most at home in the Olympic-sized pool at the Foskett YMCA. Most weeknights, he and Levi walked the mile to the Y together.

The routine rarely varied. At the pool, Cal paced along the side while Levi swam a few laps. Then the two swam together. After a few laps, Levi sat at the pool's edge while Cal got down to the business of out-swimming his imaginary opponents. Levi held the stopwatch ready. When Cal nodded, Levi yelled, "Go!" and Cal was off.

For 400 meters—eight laps of the pool—Cal focused intently on the rhythm of the swim as he powered through the water. He knew intuitively when he neared his finish. But beyond touching tile and ending his pain he wanted to know—was it enough?

"Time!" Cal demanded even before the water cleared his face.

"Four minutes, ten seconds," Levi reported back, smiling. "If you'd been swimming for Mount Whitney High on Saturday, you'd have taken first place in the 400-meter freestyle!"

Cal grinned, satisfied with his swim time. Pulling off his goggles, he noticed Levi staring in the direction of the preschoolers, or "guppy" swimmers, finishing up across the room. Cal pulled himself from the pool, giving the guppies a glance. Nothing seemed out of the ordinary.

The friends often laughed together as they watched the tiny swimmers empty the pool to meet their California "yuppie-guppy" moms, as they called them. The name emerged after Levi and Cal watched lipsticked women clicking past them in high heels across the wet tile to collect their toweled tots.

Outside the water, the two boys were unlikely—even comical—companions. As they strode to and from the locker room, Cal's compact muscular physique and sleek golden-brown skin stood in stark contrast to his fair, long-limbed buddy. Though Levi stood nearly a full head taller than Cal, his height gave him no physical advantage. Not over Cal. Not even in basketball.

The two had met in guppy class and happily discovered they lived just three blocks apart. By the sixth grade, the boys were inseparable and began walking the mile from the Windswept neighborhood to the Y together. After dark, a family member arrived to drive them home.

Through trial and error, they determined that the best time to swim laps at the Y came about seven o'clock in the evening. Both boys liked the quiet that fell over the facility after tired, hungry kids were hurried home for dinner and the after-work crowd had checked exercise off their to-do lists. Even when Cal and his buddy weren't in the water, they spent lots of time at the Y, where they shot hoops in the gym, raced on the stationary bikes, or played foosball. On swim meet weekends, when the facility was fairly bursting with bodies, the boys ran the quarter-mile track in front of the building until their legs were spent or their water bottles ran dry—whichever came first.

Levi Price came to the Y to escape a frenzied household with four siblings, including one recently returned and jobless college dropout. Cal Vandiver had reasons of his own.

Being an only child, Cal didn't particularly look forward

to being at home. There was no one to play video games with and no one there who enjoyed watching sports on TV. During the school year, he'd return home after seven stifling hours of sitting in class only to engage in equally uninteresting attempts at conversation with his parents.

And Cal felt cramped when he was home—or indoors, in general. For this reason he seized every possible opportunity to spend time in places with lots of space, whether in the pool, at the gym, on the running track, or on the soccer field.

The boy's parents were equally ill at ease. The road that brought together a thirty-something Caucasian couple together with an Asian son had been a bumpy one. As his dad told it, Cal arrived from Hong Kong as an infant with the energy of something nuclear-powered, the appetite of a grown man, and—even more surprising—stunning blue eyes. In short, Jamison Calhoun Vandiver, named after his parents' fathers, was a handful. His mother and father never considered a second child. Not even a pet.

Cal loved the feel of the hot dry evening air that met them outside the Y. The Prices' car, parked at the curb, could only be sadly described as faded gray, four-door, and "compact." With damp towels still hanging around their necks, the two boys threw their gym bags into the back seat and grudgingly climbed in. Cal sighed loudly. Neither was ready for the day to end.

"Five minutes late." Mr. Price's observation served as his hello. "Worn out?"

"Nah," Levi answered, laughing. "You know, the star here has to take a few extra minutes with the fans." Levi gave his buddy a good-natured shove. Cal reached into his bag and, with maximum drama, pulled out his new sunglasses and slid them on.

Cal found his reflection in the rear view mirror. "Smokin' hot!" Turning to Levi, he asked, "Whatcha think?"

"Everybody at school is seriously going to think you're a celebrity or something."

"Maybe at first," Cal said, "but after a day or two, I'll just be the quiet new kid with a light sensitivity problem."

"Sounds like you have a plan."

"Always."

As the boys buckled up, Levi complained loudly. "You know what, Dad?" He squinted at the sunset on the horizon. "I might have a similar disability. Can I have some shades too? Oh! And those fluorescent lights at school, you know, very distracting."

"Especially the ones they never fix, so they blink, like, all year long," Cal added.

"Right?" Levi agreed with mock exasperation. "I'm sure I'd get better grades with some shades."

"And I recall you were also convinced that those ridiculously overpriced shoes you bought with your birthday money were going to make you a better basketball player," Mr. Price joked back. "How'd that work out for you?"

"These shoes are amazing!" Levi kept the game going. "I seriously shut out the celebrity here on the court earlier."

Cal jumped in. "By 'shut out' you mean that you dropped your pride on the court and let me stomp it into dust, right?"

"Good try, son." Levi's father was aware that even a professional basketball player would likely meet his or her match on the court with Cal.

Before pulling out of the Y, Mr. Price swung his arm over the seat and looked at Levi. "Speaking of trampled pride,"—he bit his lip—"your brother didn't get that job with Nerds On Call. Might not want to bring it up."

Levi groaned and muttered not so quietly under his breath, "Sounded like a perfect match to me."

"Just a minor setback," Mr. Price promised.

"Minor to you." Levi seized the opportunity to blow off some steam. "Not for me. Not only is my brainiac brother suddenly home from college at the start of his senior year, but I also have three other numbskull siblings to deal with."

"Careful, Levi." His father threw him a warning glance.

"Celeste is making me crazy with her 'heartbreak' thing …"

"I get that," Mr. Price sympathized.

"Then there's Victor and his pre-delinquent friends at the house playing video games, like, all the time …"

"I'm with you there too," his dad conceded again.

"And Jana is just a little pain with her constant tattling."

Mr. Price sighed. "Someday Celeste will no longer be sixteen, Victor will make us all rich developing video games, and Jana will be working overseas as a spy. See? It's all in the way you look at it." Cal always appreciated that Levi's dad had a sense of humor. His sure didn't.

"So," Levi rattled on to his friend, "can you hang out tomorrow?"

"After I mow the lawn."

"Cool. Hey, did you see a new coach at the pool tonight?"

Cal looked over the top of his sunglasses. He stared at Levi warily, "For real?"

"I'm not sure." Levi tried to sound nonchalant. "For a second I thought I saw a guy—an Asian dude—hanging by the guppies."

"The Foskett Y doesn't have any Asian swim coaches." Cal sounded more annoyed than he meant to.

"I know, dude. Just thought I'd mention it."

"Let me know if you see him again?" Cal's tone turned contrite.

"Sure."

"Want me to drop you at home?" Mr. Price offered. But Cal wasn't ready to be home. He was feeling nervous and needed to run.

"Thanks, but I'll just hoof it." In the Price driveway, Cal slipped on his running shoes, grabbed his gym bag, and was off like a shot. "Later!" he called back to Levi.

"See you tomorrow!" Levi yelled as Cal disappeared in the darkness.

Cal was relieved to be alone with the sound of his shoes on the pavement, his mind temporarily free of the reasons he ran. He surveyed the Windswept neighborhood as he sped passed. Like Mr. Price's car, it was blah. These were not the California homes shown on television. He thought of the pen pal he was assigned in fifth grade, Trevor, from South Carolina.

"Are you a movie star?" Trevor wrote to Cal.

"No," Cal responded. "This isn't Hollywood." Then he added, "But I play wicked soccer." Apparently Trevor wasn't impressed. The exchange of letters was short lived.

Cal did think he looked very "California" in his new shades though. He had his mother to thank for them. With some effort, as she liked to remind him, his mom succeeded in getting a "light sensitivity" diagnosis from the optometrist. A note from the doctor would allow him to wear his shades in the classroom "as needed." This meant Cal would be able to start at his new school without being bombarded with questions about his blue eyes, which according to the doctor—citing the laws of genetics—were highly improbable. And yet, there they were.

"Are you Chinese?" the question had been put to him again and again by students, teachers, and parents.

"Yes."

"But you have—"

"I know. They just are."

He'd so had enough of the questions.

Cal pushed thoughts of school aside and focused on his run. Working his body felt like getting lost in a movie. He watched his heart pound, felt his muscles stretch, and willed oxygen to the aid of his tired limbs. Did other athletes *see* inside their bodies this way?

A few strides short of home, Cal slowed himself, and as he did, his panic resurfaced. Who was the man Levi saw? To calm himself, Cal conjured the feeling of water moving over his face and around his body. He needed to be okay for everyone behind the front door, especially his artist-mother who had an uncanny ability to read worry on his face like a stroke of paint amiss on canvas.

# 03

"There he is!" Cal heard his mother's too-bright greeting from the kitchen just before she made her appearance. The front door of the small-framed ranch opened to a living area that extended to the right and included a couch, Mr. Vandiver's recliner—complete with Mr. Vandiver—and a coffee table. Bookshelves lined the far wall. Also visible from the entrance was the dining room off the back of the house. This was the only space big enough for a table and was used for all the family's meals, as well as Cal's school projects. The left end of the house included three bedrooms, one of which was used as Mr. Vandiver's study. A door off to the right of the dining room led to the kitchen. Behind the kitchen, an oversized mudroom served as his mother's art studio.

With the exception of the mudroom-turned-studio, which the resident painter "let go" to achieve what she called a "creative feel," the Vandiver house was neatly kept. For this Cal was grateful. He much preferred the sparse, colorless space of home to what he perceived as the noisy clutter of the Price household where he and Levi were happy to pass much of their time sitting on the front porch or in the garage.

Even by the time Cal rolled in from a nighttime workout, his dad still looked the part of headmaster, dressed in suit and tie, which never failed to unhappily remind Cal of school every day of his summer break. "Good workout?" he asked, from his lounger, laptop open.

"Yes, sir," Cal replied.

"I think we're ready then." Cal's mom set a casserole dish on the table, completing the banquet-sized meal that awaited the small family. "Let's see if we can fill that hollow leg of yours."

Food was always out at the Vandiver house. One meal seemed to run into the next. For Cal, breakfast typically consisted of leftovers from dinner the night before. Then there was a three-sandwich lunch, followed by a high carb mini-meal late in the afternoon, hearty enough to hold Cal over through his end-of-day workout. That meant the family meal was usually served late, around eight-thirty. It was a solution that allowed all three Vandivers to share a meal together and for Cal to get the physical activity his parents knew he required every bit as much as eating, sleeping, or breathing.

Kimberly Vandiver tried not to resent living life around Cal's constant need for consumption, though it was certainly not the preferred life of her artist within. When she did happen upon a block of time, she ducked into her studio and took up her art the way some people kept a journal, her thoughts somehow more easily expressed on canvas. When time was short, she sat at her computer and searched out new recipes. Or she continued the research she began thirteen years before on incidents of full-blooded Chinese children being born with blue eyes. So far, she'd amassed an impressive collection of dinner selections. Nothing more.

"Looks good, Mom." Cal complimented the chef, his mood brightening as he piled his plate high with turkey breast, green beans, and mashed potatoes with gravy. There was cranberry sauce too. The kind that came out of a can just the way he liked it. And rolls, of course, bread being a staple at every meal.

"I always get to thinking about Thanksgiving foods when school starts up." Cal's mom watched as her son inhaled his meal. "I get turkey on the brain."

"Just glad I'm here to 'gobble' it up!" Cal's joke drew a chuckle from his dad.

In Bruce Vandiver's experience, the family dinner was likely to be his most enjoyable time with Cal. An appreciation for a hot meal was one of the few things, if not the only thing, he had in common with his son.

"Let's hope that cleverness translates to schoolwork." The headmaster's failed attempt at humor successfully killed the relaxed mood. "One week left of summer vacation. Is that right?" Cal's father looked forward to the new school year the way some dads anticipated the start of football season. "Still set on moving over to Valley Oak Middle for eighth grade?"

It had been quite a blow to Headmaster Vandiver when his son announced that he wanted to attend the public middle school for eighth grade rather than Visalia Academy. After all, he'd been at VA since kindergarten. But Cal made it clear he was done with being the headmaster's kid and feeling like his every move was scrutinized. In class he was expected to sit extra still, be extra quiet, and work extra hard at his studies. Essentially, he'd failed on all accounts. There was also more pressure than ever to join the school sports teams. That wasn't going to happen either.

Cal lasted only two years playing on teams for the Visalia Community Sports Association, VCSA. It quickly became painfully clear—to everyone—that even though Cal was an astounding athlete, he wasn't cut out for either teamwork or camaraderie.

In kindergarten he'd started with the t-ball team. For a while, both father and son enjoyed going to practices and games, watching baseball together on TV. The problem was that Cal was a natural. He learned by watching the pros then applied what he learned at the ballpark.

That was the beginning of the end.

By the third game, Cal had figured out how to chase every wobbly ball that came hurling his direction. The bat became a weapon in his hands, and when in the field, there wasn't a ball that he couldn't miraculously intercept. His teammates caught on to the fact that they could pretty much sit back and relax. In the meantime, players for the opposing team feared they'd be struck dead by one of the "Asian" kid's killer hits or be trampled as the same kid bolted around the plates.

The next year it was VCSA soccer. It seemed the perfect sport for Cal, with lots of running and kicking—and no bats. By then though, sports had become more than just a way to burn off energy for Cal. Winning had become his obsession. As might be expected, the other seven-year-olds on his community rec team didn't share Cal's life-or-death approach to soccer. He was merciless with teammates—"Were you taking a nap when we learned how to pass the ball, Maloney?"—who failed to maneuver the ball into the "too-big-to-miss" net for a score. Headmaster Vandiver fielded complaints from team dads at the office. His wife couldn't visit the produce aisle at the grocery store without being confronted by the mothers of other players. Going to a restaurant was out of the question.

The Vandiver soccer scandal lasted two seasons. With Cal making virtually every score, the team moved into the number one spot in the league. In the end though, protests about the boy's "unsportsmanlike" behavior prevailed over his ability to bring home the trophy.

At the time, Cal didn't even understand what the upset was about. What was unsportsmanlike about winning? If he shouldn't care about winning, he wouldn't play. So he didn't.

By middle school, however, the headmaster was inundated with calls as to why his son, whose skills were legendary, wasn't participating in sports at Visalia Academy. What's it going to be next year, Cal? The question came almost daily from VA parents and staff. Soccer? Tennis? Rugby, maybe? But Cal was ready to just be lost in the crowd. At Valley Oak he would be able to blend in alongside his best friends, Levi and Lilli.

"You know, graduating from a private school like VA looks good on a college application."

Cal, who was going in for his third helping of mashed potatoes, suddenly lost his appetite. "Can I get through eighth grade before we start with the college stuff?"

Attempting a good-natured chuckle, the headmaster added, "Just saying—a smaller school is a great way to get a good education and also get noticed."

"I'm a straight C student, Dad. And, as we know, I don't play well with others."

His father reached over and touched the frame of the sunglasses that rested next to Cal's dinner plate. He was aware of their purpose. "Why put yourself in a position that clearly makes you feel *uncomfortable*?"

Cal looked up at his dad. There was weariness in his voice. "Dad, I've been *uncomfortable* for a long time, even at VA. Please, this is something I have to do."

# 04

It was Saturday afternoon, and Lilli convinced her mom to drop her off for class at the dance studio a little early. But her agenda for those few minutes of alone time didn't include extra practice. After her mom pulled out of the parking lot of the Visalia Ballet Academy, Lilli sprinted across the street to the Chinese Cultural Center.

This was where she first met Cal. As preschoolers, the two made attempts at Chinese calligraphy under the patient instruction of Sarah Lu. Later, during her elementary school years, Lilli came with her dad on occasion to say hello to Sarah or to enjoy an exhibit. More recently she came alone, slipping in for a few minutes before or after dance. Here it felt okay for her to be Chinese.

Inside, just beyond the exhibit area, from the back classroom, Lilli could hear young students—four and five-year-olds, she guessed—being taught Mandarin. She recognized Sarah's firm, energetic voice leading the drills. Many of the words Lilli still remembered.

Learning the language of her native country never interested Lilli much. However, she always enjoyed the exhibits that came through, including the short films presented on Asians of influence, including artists, inventors, and historical figures. The featured film for the month was the life and work of Chinese artist Ta Yang, a master of brush paintings and calligraphy. A couple years before, Sarah had given Lilli a newspaper clipping about the artist.

In the small viewing room, the film was running on a loop. Lilli watched the film, captivated. In particular, she was excited to learn that Yang often wrote a short poem or thought in a corner or along the side of each piece. Purposefully placed in exquisitely drawn Chinese characters, the writing seemed to complement and complete his artwork. Lilli made a mental note to ask Sarah to translate the writing on her favorites.

The man was both artist and poet, Lilli mused. She too was dualistic, in a sense. She wasn't just an American; she was also Chinese. At home though, Lilli felt that the two sides of her weren't allowed to coexist.

When the film ended, Lilli reached into her backpack and scrounged around until she found a pencil and a scrap of paper. In the emotion of the moment, Lilli tried to express herself in something of a poem. Like Yang. She wrote:

> Before you knew me, I was.
> Before I knew what I left, it was taken.
> Could it be that in the rush
> You might have left
> Some part of me behind?

Lilli wished Cal was there with her. Had they both left something behind—something across the ocean that separated where they were born from where they were now? Would either of them ever feel whole?

"Good film, huh?" Lilli looked up, startled. It was Sarah Lu.

"Beautiful." Lilli's eyes shone. "Sarah, why do you think I like this stuff? Cal doesn't care anything about it."

Sarah laughed. She knew both teens and their histories. "You should be glad you are interested in your heritage." She touched Lilli lightly on the hand. "Cal, you know, had a different experience."

"What do you mean 'different'?"

Sarah searched Lilli's puzzled face. "Cal didn't spend any time in China—didn't you know?"

"He wasn't born there?"

"Yes, of course. But Cal was never in an orphanage."

What? How was it that she didn't know this about Cal?

Just then the film began again, jarring Lilli from her thoughts. She swung around to look at the small round clock at the back of the theatre. She was already twenty minutes late for her lesson!

Lilli dropped her face in her hands.

"Are you okay?"

"No," Lilli answered, her body suddenly trembling. "I'm not feeling well."

Within minutes, Lilli's father arrived on the scene and walked his daughter to the car.

"I'm sorry, Dad."

"No problem, honey. Stuff happens." Lilli doubted her mother would be as sympathetic.

On the ride home, Lilli thought about the story her father had told her about their family. She was still very small at the time. In the years since, she had pieced together the gaps he'd left in the telling.

A former Miss San Francisco, Linda Cohen miscarried a child—a girl—before Lilli joined the Cohen household. Interviews with the well-known beauty queen were carried in the most popular women's magazines at the time.

In an attempt to make his beautiful wife happy, Lilli's father, Michael Cohen, who also managed his wife's career, was the first to suggest adoption. Meetings with adoption agencies and lawyers followed, but Linda Cohen worried that the process would take years and that a birth mother in the U.S.

could decide to keep her child in the end. The possibility of another loss terrified her.

Soon after, overseas adoption was suggested. As it was explained to them, thousands of infant girls born in China—where boys are preferred—were in desperate need of homes. Because of the government's "one-child policy," many couples giving birth to a girl chose to abandon them in hopes of producing a boy on a second try. Further, the Cohens were elated to learn that they could adopt from China far more quickly than in the U.S. and without the risk of the birth mother backing out of the deal.

But even the months of waiting for her Chinese daughter took a toll on the anxious mother-to-be. Linda Cohen became depressed, giving up her frequent talk show appearances, even missing deadlines for her Finding Your Beautiful You newspaper column.

Meanwhile, Michael Cohen, with no celebrity to manage, went to work with a public relations firm near Fresno. And the little girl that was Lilli went into a Chinese orphanage.

It was almost a year before the paperwork was completed and Lilli was finally able to join the Cohen family.

...

"You missed dance today," an angry Mrs. Cohen confronted Lilli when she emerged from her bedroom at dinnertime.

Lilli's mother stood at the kitchen island, a glass pitcher in hand, filling three glasses with herbal tea. The dining room table was already set, complete with fresh flowers in a vase, a covered casserole dish, and a bowl of fresh fruit. No doubt the work of Juan, the energetic culinary student who did such things for her mother.

Compared to the homes of Lilli's friends, the Cohen's was, by far, the most expansive. And, with the help of a maid service, it was kept pin-neat. After the addition of Lilli to the family, Linda Cohen went on to revive her celebrity status, picking up her weekly Finding Your Beautiful You column and, more recently, hosting a video blog by the same name. Such being the case, Lilli's mother dressed each morning so as to never be caught looking less than her best for a drop-in visitor—or an unexpected media opportunity. She also insisted that her husband, who resumed managing her public career, be likewise prepared. For Lilli it felt like living on a TV set.

"I didn't mean for it to happen, Mom." Lilli responded, though not so contritely as her mother would have liked.

"You *never* miss dance! Mrs. Russ called me from the studio—very concerned. Did you know that? Imagine how I felt when I couldn't even tell her where you were!"

"How difficult for you."

Lilli's sarcasm wasn't lost on her mother. "So where were you?"

"I went to the Cultural Center." Lilli swallowed hard.

"What?"

"I wanted to see a film they were showing on an artist." Lilli skipped the details, knowing that her mother had no interest in Asian culture or any clue as to why her China-born but California-bred daughter just might.

"It was the last week it would be shown and—well, I spent more time there than I expected to, and then—"

"I guess so!" Lilli's mother interrupted. "And you just *lost track* of time, did you?"

"Yes! I was running late—but then I felt sick to my stomach!"

"But you're all right *now*?" Her mother's voice was accusing.

"No!" Lilli erupted. "I'm not 'all right'—I *am* sick! Sick of not having any time for myself. Sick of feeling like there's something wrong with me if I don't think just like you. And," she hesitated before striking her final blow, "I'm sick of dance!" Mrs. Cohen's face registered utter horror. Lilli turned and stomped up the stairs, leaving her parents to enjoy

Juan's lukewarm vegan casserole without her.

In her room, Lilli brooded over her mother's reaction to the events of the day. The ugly exchange confirmed what she already knew: her mother expected Lilli to see the world just as she saw it, to deem as important only those things her mother also deemed important. She was, in fact, expected to be a replica of the former Miss San Francisco, with the exception of her mother's all-American good looks—the thick strawberry blonde hair and just right spread of freckles across the nose. When it came to acknowledging the two sides of Lilli, the teen felt a vast and impenetrable wall, like the Great Wall itself, separating mother and daughter.

...

Lilli was finishing up her homework when she heard a knock at her bedroom door.

"Can I come in, honey?" It was her mother.

"Sure."

Mrs. Cohen entered cautiously. "Want to talk?"

Lilli shrugged and cleared her homework papers to make a spot for her mom at the end of the bed.

"I'm not sure what that was about." Her mother made reference to Lilli's earlier outburst. When Lilli didn't immediately respond, she probed further. "Were you doing research today on a school assignment—something like that?"

Ah. Lilli saw her mother's ploy. To put a fast, tidy end to the matter of the Chinese artist, she was giving her an easy out: school. But Lilli refused to play along.

"Believe it or not, it's just interesting to me." Lilli thought of the poem that was still folded in the back pocket of her jeans. "Ta Yang does a lot of Chinese calligraphy, like what I did with Cal when we were little. Remember?"

"Of course, I do." Her mother was curt. "But you are a dancer now."

At this Lilli dropped back onto the bed. "And I love dance. You know that. It's just that I'm so bored of the routine." She sighed deeply and stared at the ceiling. Mrs. Cohen nearly cried with relief.

"I just feel like there's so much more for me to learn, even about myself."

"What is it you need to know, Lilli? Tell me."

"I want to know why I had to go to an orphanage and Cal didn't."

The question took Mrs. Cohen's breath. "How did you know that?"

"Sarah Lu mentioned it to me. She thought I knew."

Lilli thought her mother's face paled. "I've asked that question a thousand times myself." Her mother's words carried long-held, unresolved hurt. "Just a few weeks after he was born, Cal was able to be at home with the Vandivers."

"But how?" Lilli demanded. "Dad told me there was all this red tape and stuff!" Lilli felt her face go hot. She hated that her mother knew this about Cal and she didn't. She hated that the adoption history she thought she shared with Cal never existed.

"I don't know, really." Her mother's tired voice suggested she had, in the past, deliberated the question to exhaustion. "Mr. Vandiver had connections, I suppose." With this, Lilli's mother was up and headed for the door. "Excuse me, honey. I have to get ready to shoot my vlog in the morning. You get some sleep, okay?" She closed the door behind her.

Clearly her mother was done with that conversation. Clearer still were her mother's feelings of being cheated somehow. Lilli felt robbed too. And guilty.

Lilli reached into her back pocket and pulled out the poem she had written earlier, smoothing it out before her. She wondered if there was anyone with whom she could share it. Not Cal. Not now. Using a pencil, Lilli attempted brush strokes around her words like those she'd seen in Yang's art. As she worked, emotional and physical exhaustion fell heavy over her. Lilli found a quick escape from the day in sleep.

It would be a long while before an unnerved Linda Cohen would find such escape. Memories flooded her like a tsunami: the loss of her unborn daughter; the interminable waiting for Lilli who was growing up without her; the nights when her arms ached for her babies, both untouchable—past and present.

# 05

Cal didn't sleep much the night before the first day of eighth grade. Just as he was about to turn in, Levi sent him a text message: "Welcome to Valley Oak Middle!"

Instead of getting Cal jazzed for his first day, as intended, the text stirred up doubts about his decision. Did he really want to change schools, or was he doing it just to distance himself from his parents? For the millionth time, Cal pondered his motives for leaving VA, where he could have stayed through high school graduation.

Visualizing another first day at VA was a no brainer. He knew who would be there, how it would look, how it would smell, how he'd feel—like a loser. For sure, it would be another year of trying to measure up to everyone's expectations. This was his answer. Cal knew, beyond a shadow of a doubt, that this was his time to explore the greater world as an unknown—with the welcome exceptions of Levi and Lilli.

From the time his radio alarm went off on Monday at 6:15 a.m., Cal was running on adrenaline. With every decision he faced, the teen was struck by how little thought he'd given to the practical points of starting a new school. What should he wear? For eight years, beginning with kindergarten, he had worn a uniform. What did Levi tell him about the cafeteria? Should he pack a sandwich?

Blending in was the goal, which would require serious sacrifices. Cal needed to look more like an honor student than a middle school jock. That meant all athletic wear was out, including his titanium sport necklace. In his dresser drawer, Cal discovered a pair of new but unworn khaki shorts. In his closet he found an equally stiff button-up plaid shirt his mother bought him for occasions that called for "something a little dressy." The store tags were still attached to both. His new sunglasses would draw some attention, but Cal knew that was still preferable to flashing around his freakish blue eyes.

In the bathroom mirror, Cal came face to face with what he felt sure was the biggest dork in too-small clothes ever. His shirt pulled at the buttons. The waist of his shorts cut into his mid-section. Remembering he could now wear his shirt untucked helped—but not much.

There was another problem. Shoes. Cal only had one pair of shoes, his new running shoes. He had no choice. They'd just have to do for now.

"Look at you!" his mother greeted an embarrassed Cal when he appeared for breakfast. "Is this the look you're going for—prep meets jock?"

Cal looked down at his shoes and shook his head. "What I was going for was invisible." He raked his hair. "Obviously, I didn't think that all the way through." Giving the hem of his shorts a yank, Cal stated the obvious: "Unfortunately for me, I'm going to need more nerd-wear. Just bigger." Then he added, looking apologetic, "I'll need new shoes too."

"We'll figure something out."

The headmaster was already gone, and Cal was left alone at the dining room table. It felt weird. He'd never had breakfast on a school morning without both his parents. But

Cal was pretty sure he had avoided a last-ditch effort by his dad to pressure him to return to VA.

Lucky for Cal, his mom prepared way better for the day. The piled-high plate of eggs and sausage she put in front of him convinced him he might make it after all. Even if the button on the waist of his shorts didn't.

Before leaving, Cal brushed his teeth twice, grabbed his backpack—was this a cool backpack?—then, most importantly, slipped on his sunglasses.

His mother's offer to drive Cal to school was intended to ease Cal into his day peacefully and in plenty of time. The ride, however, was anything but relaxing. First-day school traffic stopped the Vandivers' decade-old, blue, four-door heap one mile short of the school entrance. Cal fought the impulse to climb out of the car, backpack over his shoulder, and run the rest of the way.

By the time Cal finally stepped out of the car, the front of the school was crowded with students. How would he ever find Levi? Since cell phones weren't allowed at school, he was on his own. Cal made his way to the grass and stood, watching the flow of bodies. It looked as though a sort of unruly line was beginning to move through the double glass doors at the school entrance.

"Dude, there you are!" Levi surprised him from behind. "I'd have never found you if it wasn't for the sunglasses." Cal moaned inwardly at the suggestion that he stuck out like a sore thumb. Levi nudged him toward the glass doors. As they were pushed along, Levi noticed Cal's radical wardrobe change. "What are you *wearing*?"

"It's the new me." At that moment, Cal was more worried about being trampled than his buddy's opinion of plaid.

"No kidding."

Inside the door, just past the school office, Cal saw students moving through two standing metal detectors. A security officer monitored each detector and visually inspected students as they filed in.

"Really? Metal detectors?" Cal looked behind him at Levi, incredulous. "You didn't tell me!"

"Sorry, dude. I don't even think about it anymore. You didn't bring your cell, did you?"

"No," Cal said. "That you told me. Any other surprises you want to warn me about?"

"Nope, you're good." Then a second thought struck him. "Oh, except for the fact that you got Mrs. Holden for homeroom." Levi shook his head in empathy. "Not good."

The week before, when school schedules arrived in the mail, Cal was disappointed to find that he didn't share a single class with either Levi or Lilli. Not even homeroom with Mrs. Holden, a fate Levi made sound life threatening. Still, he knew they'd be together at lunch.

Cal stepped toward the metal detector. No alarm. Just as he was thinking he was free and clear, a burly school security guard intercepted him.

"No sunglasses during school hours," he barked.

Panic seized Cal. "Wait—" He dove into the front zippered pocket of his backpack where he had tucked away the doctor's form that explained his "condition." He fumbled to unfold it. "Doctor's orders," he managed to get out. "Light sensitivity."

With a mocking laugh, the guard grabbed the doctor's form and gave it a quick glance. "Well, look at that," he said and stepped closer to Cal. Shoving the form back into the boy's chest, he looked down over Cal's sunglasses. The blue eyes that stared back at him took him by surprise.

Suddenly Cal felt brave. "So you see, Mr. Officer—sir—I have a disability." Cal pushed his sunglasses up coolly. "May I go to class now?"

"Out of here," the guard mumbled.

In the hall Levi caught up with him. "That was close. I thought you were toast." But Cal hardly heard him. He was looking over his class schedule for the millionth time that morning.

"Take a breath." Levi understood his friend's confusion with the form that appeared to be printed in secret code. Levi explained it to him again quickly. "Look, the teachers' names—here; subject—here; room numbers—here. Remember, all eighth grade halls are orange and blue. Holden's in 110, over there." Levi indicated the hallway with blue walls on the right. "Look for the room with the fire-breathing dragon," Levi joked. "Enter if you dare!"

"A big help you are," Cal said. "Where're you headed?"

"Orange hall. We'll meet up at lunch, okay?"

"Dandy." Cal didn't feel ready to walk the blue hallway alone. To make matters worse, Cal heard snickering behind him as he headed for homeroom.

"Nice shades, but—whoa—you might want to hide those knees!"

Three boys in long-cut beach shorts and tees passed Cal on the left. The speaker was freakishly tall for an eighth grader, and his shoulder-length hair was pulled back into a ponytail. Cal wondered if maybe the kid had decided to hang around middle school a few extra years.

To his great distress, Cal realized his plan to blend in had failed. He stuck out by not sticking out. After roughing his hair a bit, he gave his too-short shorts another downward tug. It was no use. Cal followed the beach bums to Room 110.

Despite Levi's description, Cal didn't think Mrs. Holden looked any scarier than the ancient teachers he'd faced everyday at VA. Cal guessed she was fifty-something. Her chin-length gray hair was thinning. Under stringy bangs, thick brown-rimmed glasses hung on the end of her nose. Her face was deeply creased, and she didn't bother with make-up. Cal smiled at the thought of bringing her a copy of Lilli's mom's column, Finding Your Beautiful You.

The teacher sat at her desk, staring hard at her roster. Cal guessed she scanned the last names, looking for those she recognized from the past. Occasionally, she looked up to connect a name with a face.

He would have to be in room 110 at the beginning and end of every day. If Cal was going to pull off his plan to bypass everything that made school unbearable for him in the past, it had to start there. It was imperative to him that no one gawk at his blue eyes, question him about his nation of origin, or expect him to be even remotely interested in school sports. If he had failed to think through every other decision about the day—his hair, his clothes, even his lunch—Cal felt confident that his plan was solid and ready for execution.

The late bell rang. Cal dropped his backpack down next to his seat in the middle of the classroom and Mrs. Holden stood to her feet. Everyone looked up briefly from his or her conversation. The words—Mrs. Holden's Homeroom—were written in large letters on the white board behind her desk. Apparently she felt no need for further introduction.

"Attendance," she announced. Groans followed. Cal knew kids dreaded having their full names announced to a classroom of their peers. He was one of them.

"Bens, Kaitlyn?" The ancient woman scanned the room. A "here" followed by a giggle escaped the middle of a circle of girls at the back of the classroom.

It took Cal by surprise to see girls out of uniform at school. Instead of white collared blouses and knee-length shorts or skirts in blue or khaki, there were tank tops, capris, denim skirts, and short shorts in purples, pinks, and various shades of neon.

Mrs. Holden continued her excruciatingly slow process of calling out names, working her way to the letter V. If there was no Wilson or Wood in the class, his was often the final name called.

"Vandiver, Jam—"

"It's Cal!" he interrupted.

After a pause meant to reprimand the new kid for holding up role call, Mrs. Holden repeated the name and studied the face. "Cal?" She asked loudly enough to draw every eye to the new kid. "Did I get that right?"

"Yes, ma'am." Cal kept his tone respectful. "That's what I go by."

Mrs. Holden folded her thin arms and cocked her head to the side—dragonlike.

"Something wrong with your eyes this morning, Cal?"

Cal maintained his posture of politeness. "Light sensitivity." He looked down at his desk long enough to appear slightly embarrassed. "I have a doctor's note."

Apparently Mrs. Holden had come to the end of her attendance sheet and decided to extend her inquisition of the new student until the bell rang for first period.

"I see." The classroom of students held their breaths, watching to find out if the new student was going down. "And where are you from, Cal?"

There it was. The question. And Cal was ready for it.

"I'm from right here," Cal answered with a smile. "I'm Cal from California." Snickers followed the remark, which Cal knew solidly placed him on the fine line between "entertaining" and "troublemaker."

"Mr. Vandiver, what I'm asking you is"—the woman leaned across her desk toward him in an attempt to be intimidating—"what is your heritage?"

"Oh!" Cal sat up in his seat and looked as if the question both surprised and confused him. "Well, ma'am, according to my dad, the name Vandiver originated from Norway, so ..."

Mercifully, the bell rang, interrupting Cal and putting an end to the painful exchange. Mrs. Holden had a do-you-really-think-I'm-buying-this look on her face as Cal rose to leave, but he was pretty sure he was off the hook. Any more questions regarding his "ethnicity" might be construed as inappropriate by public school standards.

As he headed for the door, Cal made sure he caught Mrs. Holden's eye, smiled, and nodded a polite good-bye. Cal congratulated himself. It looked very much like the quiet, light-sensitive kid of undetermined heritage just slayed the dragon.

"Dork." The comment came from the kid with the ponytail, who gave Cal a flat tire on his left heel as he passed him in the hall.

"Good one, Nick," remarked one of his tagalongs.

With homeroom successfully under his belt—more or less, Cal went on to enjoy obstacle-free first and second periods. Neither Mr. Ferris, Cal's algebra teacher, nor Mrs. Carpenter, his English teacher, raised any concerns with the "light sensitivity" issue. And no further inquiries were made into Cal's heritage. In fact, Cal was enjoying smooth sailing right up until third period, healthy living. Here Cal hit a snag. The teacher was Coach Bailey. The problem: his shoes.

To Cal's surprise, a number of students were already seated in Room 124 when he arrived for healthy living. Apparently they'd had their previous class in the same room. Cal was forced to find a seat in the front. While he was painfully aware that his shoes were suspiciously mismatched with the rest of his I'm-all-about-books ensemble, there was no way to hide them.

"I'm Coach Bailey—you can call me Coach B—and this is healthy living class." The man had a half-doughnut ring of white hair and basketball-shaped belly and paced as he spoke. "For those of you who don't know, I oversee the Wildcats sports program. It's my job to make sure the name 'Wildcats'—whether it's basketball, soccer, volleyball, or whatever—strikes fear into the hearts of our opponents this year!" Coach B seemed to be scrutinizing his classroom of eighth graders, those most likely to populate his athletic program.

Cal thought the moment was right to hand his form to Coach B. "Excuse me, I have to give you this." Coach B gave the paper a cursory glance and handed it back. Did he even read it? Surely he'd stricken the new kid from the list of potential Wildcats.

"Starting in the back," Coach B ordered loudly, as if leading a basketball practice in a gymnasium, "give us your name and tell us your sport of choice." Cal's heart skipped a beat, and he started to sweat.

Finally, Coach B's gaze landed on Cal.

"Next!"

"That's Cal," offered one of the beatniks from homeroom.

A second voice explained, "That's because he's from California." Cal turned to see Kaitlyn Bens, smacking her gum and giggling.

"This your first year here?"

"Yes, sir."

"Clearly you like sports." The man nodded at Cal's expensive running shoes. "So what sports do you play?"

Cal determined to keep his reply short and uninteresting to the man who was obviously posing as a teacher in order to scout players for school teams. "I swim." Swimming, as a competitive sport, wasn't offered in Tulare County Schools until ninth grade.

"And you run." Coach B finished Cal's answer.

"No, really," Cal gave his shoes a glance. "I just wear these 'cause they're, you know, comfortable."

"So you don't play *any* other sports? Is that because of your eyes?" Coach B came at Cal again, convinced he understood Cal's problem and was ready with a solution. "There are ways to get around that."

"No, sir, I just don't—"

Coach B interrupted Cal again, "You should try out for a team here at Valley Oak. Tryout times will be posted outside the cafeteria." Cal thought the suggestion sounded more like a command.

When the bell rang, Cal was stuck waiting behind classmates all hurrying to get on to the next, most important, period of the day: lunch. Slowing progress was Coach B, manning the door, handing out blue sheets of paper.

Coach B resorted to his gym voice again to get the attention of his students who were getting louder by the second. "Be sure to take this permission slip for sports before you leave! I need the signature of a parent or guardian. Return it to the office tomorrow!" At last, Cal took his blue sheet, tucked his head to avoid eye contact with Coach B, and hurried out.

Cal was hungry and glad for the break. But even lunch held its challenges on day one at Valley Oak Middle. First and foremost, he didn't know if he would be able to eat what was being served in the cafeteria. Why hadn't he stuck a protein bar in his pocket at least? Secondly, he would, in two short turns of the hallway, stand in the midst of the lunch mob, once again searching for a familiar face.

Students were pooling into the crowded common area just outside the cafeteria when Cal heard it: "Messi! Messi!" Cal's mouth suddenly went dry. It had to be a kid from the soccer game in the park. Up on his toes, Cal looked all around. He couldn't connect the voice with a face. What were the chances? Would the kid blow his cover?

Once inside the cafeteria, Cal tried to make sense of the massive, noisy space. Fortunately for him, the walls were lined with windows, which reminded him of all he had to look forward to at the end of the day. Running. Sun. Solitude.

Eventually, Cal identified two distinct lines, each moving to a separate serving station. The first offered hot entrées and sides; the other was reserved for cold selections such as salads, fruits, and ready-made sandwiches. As was his preference, Cal gravitated toward the hot lunch options. That was until he caught a glimpse of all that awaited him: overcooked Salisbury steak with globby gravy and a choice of greasy hash browned potatoes or watery squash casserole. It only took a second for Cal to move toward the less threatening peanut butter and jelly sandwiches in the second line—taking three. Then he grabbed an apple, along with two cartons of chocolate milk.

Cal scanned the table-filled room again and again before finally spotting Lilli's distinctive super shiny black hair, which she had pulled softly to the side in a ponytail. He made his way through the maze of bodies to where she sat by the window.

"Hey, move it, girlie. I have to eat now," he growled from behind her, "or somebody's going to get hurt."

"Wow, look who's already fallen in with the wrong crowd!" Lilli laughed and made room next to her for her friend. Actually seeing Cal at her school felt surreal for Lilli. Though she looked forward to seeing him at her school, it surprised her now that the day had finally arrived. Doing a double take at Cal, Lilli blurted out, "What is with the clothes?"

Before Cal could comment, Levi dropped down opposite them at the table. "The new guy is eating cafeteria food—really? I know I forgot to tell you about the metal detector," he admitted, "but I know I warned you about that stuff." Reaching into his book bag, Levi pulled out one plastic bag that held a badly mashed sandwich, a second bag with the crumbled remains from a box of Cheez Doodles, and a bottle of water.

Cal bit into his sandwich and made a face. "No joke! I didn't think it was possible to mess up a peanut butter and jelly sandwich! This bread is seriously stale and, like, they forgot to put anything inside!"

Now Lilli, unable to stop staring at Cal's wardrobe, turned accusingly at Levi. "Did you tell him he had to wear this? Did you punk him on his first day?"

"Didn't have anything to do with it," Levi defended himself. "Looks a little like Derek, don't you think?"

"Perfect!" Cal was genuinely pleased to be compared to Levi's super-smart older brother. "If I wanted everyone to know I was a jock I'd of worn—not this!"

Cal took another bite of his sandwich just as Kaitlin Bens, still smacking her chewing gum, hurried up to him and leaned over his shoulder. Her gum smelled like strawberries. "There's a spot over here with us 'Cal from California' if you want to meet some of the other jocks."

Cal was taken off guard by both the offer and the unmistakably flirtatious delivery.

"Hey, that's cool, thanks." In a half whisper he attempted to explain his situation. "I'm not really a jock though. The shoes, you know—"

"Yeah, you wear them because they just 'feel' good. I heard that." Now the girl looked at his lunch plate of sandwiches and gave him a knowing look. "And you burn off all those carbs by walking back and forth to the library, right?" She stood up. "If you change your mind, you know where we are."

As she walked away, Cal stole a glance at the girl whose muscular legs were impossible to miss in her jean shorts. Kaitlyn, he decided, was definitely a runner.

"Did she call you 'Cal from California'?" Lilli was miffed that a complete stranger—who was also happened to be a girl—talked to Cal like they were old friends.

Cal made light of the exchange. "Yeah, well, I decided it wasn't anyone's business where I was born—you know how people are asking all the time—so I introduced myself as 'Cal from California' all morning. Worked like a charm!"

"How are the shades going over?" Levi also eyed the girl as she took a seat at the jock table.

"I got a little grief from my teacher in homeroom."

"Leave it to Holden the harra-ssss-er."

"So let me see if I've got this right," Lilli pressed. "You are no longer the Cal that *we* know. Instead, you're a dork from California with no ethnicity, no fashion sense, and no interest in sports?"

"My next step is to get rid of these shoes. These were all I had today."

"Are we even still your friends, or are you going to move over to the table with the chess club?"

Cal looked up at an incensed Lilli.

Levi spoke up. "It's okay, Lilli. He can be whoever he wants to be."

"Can he, really? It's okay to pretend you're someone you're not?"

Cal was now on his third sandwich in spite of his

complaints. "You could be 'Lilli from California,' except it doesn't have quite the same ring."

"The last thing I want to be is 'Lilli from California'!" Suddenly standing, Lilli picked up her tray to go.

Cal didn't want her to leave. Not like this. He looked up at her pleadingly, "You know why I have to change things up here—"

Lilli leaned in close to Cal like the other girl had done and dropped her voice to a whisper. "You know what I think?" Cal was afraid to hear what was coming next. "I think they already came to get you 'cause I don't know who you are."

Levi and Cal watched an angry Lilli make a beeline out of the cafeteria. Suddenly Cal's sandwiches felt like lead in his stomach.

"You gonna eat that apple?" Levi eyed Cal's lunch remains.

"Go for it." Cal's shorts were pinching him mercilessly, as was his conscience.

# 06

The catchy presentation of his name went over so well in his morning classes that it made introductions a breeze for Cal the rest of the day. In every class, a handful of students knew the bit and anticipated the call of the roster. When they heard "Vandiver," they were ready and waiting, answering in unison, "Cal from California!" Cal only had to raise his hand, innocently.

Even at the end of a taxing first day for both students and teachers, Ms. Delgado, Cal's sixth period Spanish teacher, laughed when the students introduced the new kid.

"Are you any good at speaking Spanish, Cal?" the young Latino teacher asked him in her heavy accent, brushing her long dark hair behind her shoulder. Before he could answer, a distinctly Latino voice called to him from the back of the room.

"¡Buenas tardes, Cal!"

He was here! Cal looked around and recognized the curly-headed kid from the soccer game at the park. Now he knew who had recognized him in the midst of the lunch mob.

"And your name back there?" Ms. Delgado looked over and around heads to identify the speaker.

"Miguel," he answered.

"Buenas tardes, Miguel," Cal returned the greeting.

"¿Quieres jugar fútbol después de la escuela?" Miguel made the game harder.

"And how would you respond to Miguel, Cal from California?" Ms. Delgado prompted.

Cal was momentarily stumped. He knew the word fútbol—Spanish for soccer—and he knew he was being asked a question. Likely the question had to do with when they would play soccer again. Searching the walls of the classroom, he located a colorful laminated poster of the days of the week in Spanish.

"¿Domingo?"

"Ah, soccer game on Sunday, huh?" The teacher nodded approvingly, pointing out the word "Sunday" on the poster for the class. "And I thought you were more of a chess kind of guy."

After the final bell rang in homeroom, Cal stopped by his locker to grab the accumulation of first-day forms. Wedged into the side of his locker was a note. He pulled it out and unfolded it. It read:

Can you meet me at the park at 4:00 today? Lilli

Cal sighed. More than anything he wanted to run off the stress of his first day with Levi. But a run would offer no relief as long as he knew Lilli was upset with him. It had been three hours since lunch, and he couldn't even remember what had gone so wrong.

Among the pile of papers was the blue one Coach B gave him. Cal dropped the athletic permission form in a trash can on his way to the parking lot. He didn't want to give his parents any ideas that school sports were in his future.

"Sure you won't be needing that?" It was Nick, the pony-tailed beach boy and, apparently, the resident bully. The question hit its target: Cal's ego. Nick laughed as he climbed into the passenger seat of a bright red sports car idling behind his mom's comparatively anemic vehicle. Cal kept moving without acknowledging the insult. At least one person was convinced he was serious nerd material.

...

On the drive home, Mrs. Vandiver was full of questions about Cal's first day. She was desperate for details of every class, every teacher—basically, of everything he was, at that moment, trying to forget.

"Did you see Lilli?" His mother prodded, eager to fill in the gigantic holes Cal had left in his account of the day.

"Only for a few minutes at lunch." Cal decided to skip the part about how he'd somehow managed to send his friend fuming from the cafeteria. "If it's okay with you, I think I'll try to meet up with her at the park or something."

"That's fine. But if you're going to go all prep on us, don't we need to do some shopping?" She pointed out the obvious. "Those are the only Spandex-free clothes you own."

"Oh, man!" Cal lamented aloud. How could he give up what remained of his day to shop for clothes he didn't really want to wear?

"Hey, I have a great idea!"

"What?" Cal sounded hopeful.

"You go ahead to the park."

"Huh? But you said we had to go shopping! What am I going to wear to school tomorrow?"

"Oh, did I forget to tell you?" His mother feigned surprise. "Senior moment! I already *did* the shopping, while you were in school!"

"That's awesome!" Cal felt his whole body relax. Both smiled. Cal was free to meet Lilli, and his mother succeeded in reminding her son that he still needed her sometimes.

"Got nerdy stuff, right?"

"You are going to be so handsome."

"That goes without saying."

At home, Cal made a quick change into his black athletic shorts and a gray compression shirt, thankful to be free of his school clothes at last. After inhaling a bowl of microwave noodles, Cal sent a text to Lilli that he was on his way and another to Levi to let him know he'd stop by later.

It was a beautiful day and Cal lamented spending most of it indoors. The tree-lined sidewalk that picked up at the entrance of the Windswept neighborhood and continued the entire four miles to Crestwood Park made for an easy run. Cal drew the air deeply into his lungs and breathed out his day. The worries that had been pressing at his brain were gratefully released as he lost himself in the sound of his breathing, the rhythm of his stride—his place of recovery.

Behind him a car horn sounded. Cal felt his heart jump. He hadn't noticed the vehicle that followed alongside him. He did, however, recognize the commanding voice that called to him. "Looking good, Cal. I'll see you at tryouts next week." It was Coach B, his voice boomed out through the passenger window of the white minivan that he undoubtedly used to haul Wildcats back and forth to basketball games. With that, he waved at Cal, rolled up the window, and sped down the road.

Cal slowed to a walk. The surprise-induced adrenaline rush left his head and heart pounding. It was only the first day of school and Cal already felt like he was being stalked. One thought calmed him: When he failed to show up for tryouts, it would put an abrupt end to any hopeful waiting—and watching—by Coach B.

...

Cal spotted Lilli sitting under the biggest valley oak tree in the park, near the pond. Branches soared above her, blanketing Lilli with a checkered pattern of sunshine and shade. Dropping down next to her, Cal took a minute to catch his breath and join her in savoring the late afternoon sunshine.

"Good first day?" Lilli's tone was cool.

"Yeah, I guess." Cal stretched to touch his shoes. "I feel like I had a major brain workout, and school hasn't really gotten started yet! How 'bout you?"

"I looked forward to lunch all morning—"

"I know! Then I got that gross PB and J sandwich! What's with that?"

"Not done."

"Sorry."

"So I looked forward to lunch all morning and then you—" she stopped then threw up her arms in frustration, "—you didn't show up!"

"Um, I'm pretty sure I remember that sandwich."

"But you changed who you are!"

"For real? Just because I wore sunglasses and found a way around the 'where were you born' question—which, frankly, isn't anyone's business—you're mad at me?"

"It's not what you did to yourself," her words came softer now. "It's what you did to me."

"What did I do to you?"

Lilli hugged her knees to her chest. "Try to understand," she said. "You think it's fun to pretend you're not Asian, like you hate it. What does that mean you think about me?"

Cal wondered how a conversation with a girl could wind him more than a four-mile run at top speed. "It's not like that," he tried to explain. "I don't think of you as Asian. You're just Lilli."

"Well, I am Asian!" Her voice rose now. "I have straight black hair and brown eyes and brown skin!"

"So what? If you were green you would still be Lilli, and you would still be my friend!"

A tear escaped the corner of Lilli's eye, but she continued. "If I pretend it doesn't matter where I'm from, like you do—like my own mother does—" she added with disgust, "I feel like I'm lying, like I'm trying to forget something that's important."

Cal rubbed the back of his neck with his hand, as he tried to understand Lilli's words.

Lilli fidgeted with the silver cursive "L" that hung on a delicate chain around her neck. "I don't mean to sound like a brat. I know I have—a lot. But I'm still Asian. And I want to understand what that means."

Cal didn't know how to respond. He couldn't relate. "It's not like that for me, Lilli," Cal apologized. "I have blue eyes; I speak English; and I play soccer like a Latino. I don't feel any connection to China. I had no idea I hurt you. I'm sorry."

Lilli finally smiled weakly. "Guess it makes sense, if you think about it."

"What makes sense?"

"My mom says you didn't spend any time there. Didn't even go to an orphanage before coming home." Lilli unknowingly shared new information with her friend. "Since you came right home, maybe you didn't have time to miss anything."

"You were in an orphanage?" Cal couldn't remember having this conversation before.

"Of course. It's how things go for kids there without families—well, not for you, obviously. I was there about a year." She looked at him curiously. "I thought you knew."

"Probably did," Cal appeared to shrug off the news. "Just forgot, I guess." But Cal didn't think it was information he had forgotten. He didn't remember his parents ever mentioning anything about his adoption, about how his story differed from Lilli's. Was this why he felt no connection to his country of birth? Why he even tried to hide it?

"I'm glad that for whatever reason you didn't have to go to an orphanage." Lilli smiled. "You really are Cal from California." She gently pulled off his sunglasses and met his eyes. "And that's okay. Know why?"

"No idea."

"Because," she said, eyeing Cal's glasses, "whatever they call you, or whatever dork clothes you choose to wear, I will always make better grades than you!"

"Ah!" It was Cal's turn. "And do you know why?" He took his shades from Lilli and nodded knowingly.

Lilli eyed him with suspicion. "Why?"

"Because they had time to dump that Asian smart juice into you, and I obviously missed out."

They heard a vehicle pull up to the gravel lot. They looked up to see Mrs. Cohen waving for Lilli.

"Yikes, I've got to get home for my piano lesson." Lilli jumped from her place.

They exchanged good-byes and Lilli disappeared into her mother's SUV and back to her routine. The disagreement between them was officially over. For Cal, however, plenty of questions remained.

...

Hearing the front door open and slam closed, Cal's mother called out to her son from her studio, "I'm back here."

"Hi, Mom." Cal entered the kitchen and opened the snack cabinet in search of—something, anything.

"Everything okay?"

Cal stepped into the doorway of the studio where his mother was seated behind her huge paint-spattered art table that had served as a teacher's desk in another life. Wrapped in her painting smock with her reading glasses propped on her nose, she sorted the tubes of paint in the top drawer.

"Fine," he answered, tearing into a protein bar. "I'm going to Levi's until dinner, okay?"

"Okay." She responded without looking up, pulling out tubes of acrylic paint in blues and grays.

# 07

Letting himself in the Price's front door, Cal stepped over piles of clothes, books, and toys to get to the inside garage entry, where he nearly toppled on Jasmine, Jana's cat, who guarded the door like a watchdog. As usual, he could hear Victor and his friends playing video games upstairs and a close-to-tears Celeste on her phone nearby.

Relieved to close the door behind him, Cal greeted the two oldest siblings of the Price clan.

"What's up?"

Of the four Price offspring, the two brothers looked the most alike, with matching long lean frames topped with the same shade of untamed dirty-blonde hair. At 21, Derek, however, had the added distinction of spotty unshaven hair on his chin. And, as Levi tells it, his brother had worn the same pair of knee-torn jeans since his high school graduation.

Derek was seated at a desk with a computer and an array of parts strewn about it. He worked intently, examining each piece in turn—the small, smaller, and the miniscule—as if working a puzzle. To the far right of the desk were new parts, still sealed in clear plastic bags. Levi sat in a metal chair at a card table situated near Derek's desk, his physical science book open in his lap and a notebook and pencil on the table.

The two grunted a return hello. Cal sat down on the secondhand loveseat that had disappeared when Derek left for college and reappeared recently, along with Derek and the stacks of still-packed plastic tubs.

Levi looked up from his book. "Everything okay with Lilli?"

"It's all good." Cal gave Levi a thumbs up.

"How's it going, Derek?" Cal admired the intense concentration Derek brought to the task before him. It had been a long-held belief of Cal's that Derek was the smartest of the Price offspring. While Levi regularly made the A-B honor roll, Cal knew he worked harder to earn those grades than Derek who sailed through high school, graduating at the top of his class. Attending California State University, Fresno had always been Derek's plan. Cal wondered, along with the entire Price family, why Derek the brainiac returned home a year short of finishing his degree in information technology.

"Not too bad for a guy with a little time on his hands and a house full of broken stuff."

"Whatcha doing?"

"I'm upgrading this dinosaur for us to use out here in the garage."

"It's the latest of his fix-it projects since he *dropped out* of school." Levi took a verbal jab at his brother. "He's fixed the clothes dryer, the toaster, something of Victor's—"

"The modem for the computer in his room was fried," Derek interjected.

"The squeal in Mom's car—"

"Worn belt," Derek mumbled.

"And now this. You'd think he might want to use his time looking for a job or something."

At this, Derek looked up and spoke in a low growl, "Drop it."

"Where'd you get these parts from anyway?" Levi asked accusingly. "Did Dad buy them for you?"

"Not everything has to be bought with money."

"What, you into stealing now?"

"You don't know anything." Derek opened a plastic bag and examined the part closely. "I traded some of my old comic books for what I needed."

Levi was secretly impressed at his brother's resourcefulness. "How?" Levi asked.

"Ever heard of The Groundhog?"

"No."

"That's because you're a stupid little kid." Derek didn't look up from is work.

"So tell us already."

"It's a student-run website at Cal State. You can find about anything you need there. People can buy, trade, or barter services to get stuff."

The idea intrigued Cal, who was always looking for a deal on athletic shoes, which he either outgrew or wore out every couple months. "Is that legal?"

"Sure," Derek turned towards Cal, "as long as the IRS—you know, the Internal Revenue Service—gets any taxes owed. Like, if I agreed to build a website for someone in exchange for a flat screen TV, I'd have to report the value of the TV as income. Oh—and you can't buy or sell illegal stuff. That's the black market."

"What kind of illegal stuff?" Cal wished he could learn cool stuff like this in school.

"Like bootleg music or movies or drugs—or people."

"Buying people?" Cal repeated, stunned. "That happens?"

"It does, believe it or not." Derek tore into another plastic package. "It's more likely though that people are looking for babies. That's big business from what I hear." Cal was speechless at this revelation. But Levi insisted on bringing the topic back around to his brother's situation.

Levi slapped his textbook closed, and his brother turned at the sound. "So you trade for parts and you fix the computer. Then what, Derek?"

Derek set the part in his hand down carefully, leaned forward on his elbows, and stared at his brother. "You're not going to leave this alone, are you?"

"Can't." The anger was gone from Levi's voice. Only worry remained. "Going to college was your dream. I just don't get it."

Derek sighed. "There's not a lot I can tell you right now, bro." There was uneasiness in his voice. "All I can say is that I haven't dropped out of school—exactly. I'm going back. It'll just be a while. There's something I have to do first."

"Can you tell me?"

"Soon." Derek turned back to his work. "In a few weeks, if everything goes as planned, I'll be out of here. And when I'm gone, this little piece of paradise will all be yours, okay?"

"You got a Plan B?"

Derek paused. "I guess I don't." He worked a tiny screwdriver deep in the bowels of the computer. "Will you let up on the school thing though? Just let me fix stuff for now."

...

At dinner Cal shoveled in a few forkfuls of baked Ziti then shared highlights from his first day. He began with a description of morning traffic and followed with details of the metal detectors at the school entrance. Then there was the tale of the surprised security guard who insisted on looking behind Cal's shades.

Cal's mom added her own first-day story: "And you didn't see what Cal wore to school this morning." The three had a good laugh together about Cal's too-small clothes matched with his high-end running shoes.

Cal went on to describe the dilemma created by his shoes in healthy living class as Coach Bailey launched his recruiting campaign for Wildcat sports. Cal drew a rare belly laugh from his dad when he confessed to telling Coach B that he didn't really run, but just liked to wear "comfortable" shoes. Next was a recap of his first meal in the Valley Oak Middle

School cafeteria and a mention of Miguel, the Latino in his sixth-period Spanish class, who remembered Cal from a soccer game in the park.

"Ah! Now you have an excellent tutor for Spanish class!" commented his father, always the educator.

For the most part, his dad was quiet through dinner. Cal figured he was preoccupied with the demands, pressures, and unexpected events of his own first day of the new school year at VA. Thankfully, he didn't pester Cal with questions about his classes, or even bring up how uncomfortable it had been for the headmaster to tell teachers and students at VA about his son's decision to change schools.

By the time his mom ducked back in the studio and his dad retired to his study, Cal decided to do a little research on his own. The news Lilli unknowingly shared haunted him. Somehow he escaped a stay in an orphanage. How had that happened? Had her experience really made her different from him? A couple searches later, Cal confirmed the truth of what she said: most Chinese adoptees went to an orphanage for as long as a year while an adoption was finalized.

Black market. The brief discussion in the Price's garage opened up a whole world of possibilities around how he ended up a Vandiver. He always felt like there was something unusual about his circumstances—about him. Was he a black market baby? And what did his eyes have to do with it, if anything? As much as he hated to admit it, Cal wanted—no, needed—more information about the first part of his life, just like Lilli.

Cal decided to begin his investigation with his mother. Since they were alone together during the drive to and from school, Cal considered her his most accessible source of information. Whether or not she would be a willing source was yet to be determined.

...

After a night of tossing and turning, Cal heard his alarm sound at last. It was the second day of school. It was also the start of his fact-finding mission.

In the shower Cal remembered with a fair amount of concern that he forgot to preview the clothes his mom purchased for him. Minutes later he pulled on a new striped button down shirt and black shorts. At least everything seemed to fit. Then he reached for the shoebox on top of the dresser. Under the lid, Cal found leather top-siders, the kind worn without socks, the kind he saw on high schoolers who hung out at the coffee shops. They were terrible—but perfect.

In the bathroom, Cal looked at himself. He was certain that no one would mistake him for a jock today. His transformation to dork was now complete, from head to toe.

"Oh, honey, you look so grown up!" His mother pulled out her phone. "Can I take a picture?"

"Let's not." Cal would not let his nerdy mug appear on his mom's Facebook page.

With that crisis averted, Cal dove into his pancakes and bacon, complimented the chef, gave his mom a rare hug, and was in the car ahead of schedule. It was the perfect set up for snooping into his past.

"Something going on this morning, Cal?" The obstacle-free morning, paired with an amiable son, had raised his mother's suspicions.

"I can breathe, for starters."

Cal happily filled his lungs, confident that he was on track for the heart-warming "mother-son chat." After they hit traffic, Cal made his move. He began with a compliment. "So, Mom, I thought you would be the best one to ask a question."

"What's that?" She smiled, thrilled to be consulted.

"I was thinking about Lilli." His mother's favorite topic. "Yes?"

"Remember when you were telling me about how hard it was for the Cohens while they waited for Lilli to come home?"

"Understandably," she responded. "Every adoptive family

is anxious to bring home their child."

"I got home pretty fast though, didn't I?" As casual and charming as Cal was trying to be, his mother's expression turned guarded.

"Yes, thankfully," she answered. "We worked with a fine adoption team." Unnerved by the question, Mrs. Vandiver took a sudden and concentrated interest in the cars creeping alongside them, checking and rechecking her rear and side mirrors.

"So was it the same agency that Lilli's parents used?"

It was a question that his mom struggled to answer. "Well, yes—in the beginning. But—" she stopped, unable to find the words to explain the events that she didn't completely understand herself.

"But what?"

At a red light, Cal's mother worked to regain her composure. Then she continued, "We were contacted by another agency, and in the end, they were able to bring you home to us—sooner."

"So somebody called *you*?" Cal repeated to be sure he heard his mother correctly.

"Uh-huh."

As they neared the school entrance, a young driver in a rumbling muscle car broadcast his music while honking his horn at friends. Between honks, Cal managed to ask, "Did it cost more for you guys to do it that way?"

His mother looked at him, stunned. "Are you thinking we adopted you through some illegal means?"

"Not illegal, no—" Cal stammered. "I just wondered, you know, if there might have been another way for Lilli ..."

Mrs. Vandiver braked hard in front of the school, jostling loose change in the drink holder and sending a long-lost, mostly-empty water bottle rolling across the floor behind Cal's seat. "Son, if there's something more you want to discuss, we'll do that at dinner, with your father."

In other words, Cal hit a dead end, and any further

questions would have to go to the parental committee. Why? Was it too hard for his mother to discuss? Or did she and his dad need to collaborate stories?

# 08

It was hard for Cal to sit still in class. Reviewing syllabuses always left him feeling overwhelmed. His chest tightened as he thought about papers, projects, and exams scheduled over the course of the semester. His healthy living class would be the only break in his otherwise intense school day. Even there he felt the scrutiny of Coach Bailey, who frowned at the sight of Cal's spiffy new top siders.

"Up here, Vandiver!" Coach B called to him at the close of class, as students packed up their belongings.

Cal approached Coach B's desk warily. "Yes, sir?"

"Let's talk about yesterday afternoon." The round man sat with his hands folded. "I have to say—from the standpoint of a coach of many years—it looked to me like you actually run quite a bit."

"Were you spying on me or something?"

"Nah," Coach B looked at him knowingly. "Just happened to be in the neighborhood."

Cal's secret was out. All he could hope to do was give the school coach a logical reason as to why he wouldn't be at any tryouts. "Sir, I think you need to know that my parents want me to focus on my studies this—"

"By the way," Coach B interrupted, "the office called to let me know they got your APF this morning."

"My APF?"

"Your Athletic Participation Form. You know, the blue form you apparently left at home?" Then Coach B directed his comments to the entire class. "Thank goodness for parents who watch out for you numbskulls, or I'd never get paperwork in and never be able to pull together any teams at all!"

Cal felt a rush of adrenaline hit his bloodstream, and his heart began to race. Just then the bell rang, and students were up and pushing their way to the door.

"There may have been a mistake," Cal told Coach B, trying to keep his voice steady and his knees from collapsing. "My parents made it clear that I wouldn't be participating in any sports."

Coach B was on his feet, readying his classroom for the next period, straightening desks and picking up errant pieces of paper on the floor. "I wouldn't know about that. Just saying your form was turned in." Without looking up, he added, "Decide on a sport, and I'll see you at tryouts."

In his dazed state, Cal didn't remember moving through the lunch line, or picking up two hoagie sandwiches, or finding his way over to the table by the window where he'd met up with his friends the day before. Levi and Lilli were already there.

"He told you *what*?" came Lilli's shocked reaction when Cal repeated the conversation with Coach Bailey.

"Probably just got the name wrong in the front office," Levi concluded, dismissing the APF crisis. "Coach B didn't say he'd actually *seen* the form, right?"

"Unless he forged one for me."

"Why would he do that?" Levi asked. "You don't look much like a sports dude!"

"Yeah, well, he pulled up beside me while I was running yesterday."

"Are you kidding?" Lilli was becoming more alarmed by the second.

"He can't forge a form for you, Cal. Coach would get in big trouble. Unless—" Levi was thinking out loud.

"Unless what?" Cal demanded.

"Unless he didn't think you'd check it for yourself." Then Levi immediately dismissed his own theory. "No way! Listen, last year the office put me in an English class for the wrong grade!"

"You're right," Cal conceded. "Stuff probably gets mixed up all the time."

"Still," Lilli suggested, "you better stop by the office before you leave today. No telling what they might sign you up for next."

"Good idea."

"Hey, maybe I can meet up with you guys later," Lilli proposed. "I don't have anywhere I have to be."

"Bring an extra pair of leotards in case the office puts Cal in ballet class!" Levi stretched his arms overhead ballerina-style.

Just as the bell rang Cal realized he hadn't touched his hoagies. Levi eyed them, but Cal shook his head, wrapped his slightly stale treasures in napkins, and stuffed them in his backpack. "Not a chance, dude," Cal said. "I'm going to be starving after school."

"Ew," remarked Lilli.

. . .

When the bell rang after Spanish—his final class of the day—Cal hurried down the hall to Mrs. Holden's room to ask permission to go to the office.

In the school office, two administrative staffers were standing at a counter that separated visitors from the desks, file cabinets, and workstations beyond. Each of the women at the help counter manned a computer and was involved with disgruntled students. Cal slipped in line behind a short kid who slumped despairingly. At last, he stepped away from the counter, paperwork in hand, shaking his head and muttering about having too many classes.

Cal was next. The office assistant was a young woman. Glasses rested on top of her dark short cropped hair, and she wore an expression that suggested she was already looking forward to the last day of school. Her nameplate read: Ms. Oliver.

"Can I help you?" she sighed.

"I'm Cal Vandiver. Coach Bailey said that someone dropped off an Athletic Permission Form for me today?"

Ms. Oliver slid her glasses down from atop her head and looked at him closely. Squinting, she appeared to be pulling up information from hours before. Suddenly her eyes brightened.

"I did see a form come in." She turned to the older woman who sat at the desk behind her. The gray-haired lady was busy stamping the day's date on various forms and filing them in her drawer. "Sue, do you have that APF we got for Van-di-ver this morning?"

As she thought, the woman checked the state of her hair that was pulled up in a bun. "I believe so."

Cal questioned the woman seated at the desk directly. "I'm sorry, but do you know who brought it in? Um, I'm just wondering if there might have been a mistake in the name."

"No mistake," the graying woman answered over her stack of papers. "Your father brought it by. Asian gentleman."

"Oh, yeah," Ms. Oliver agreed, nodding her head. "Now I remember."

Cal felt his chest tighten. "Can I see that form, please?"

The woman at the desk let out a big sigh and pulled open a file drawer. A minute later she had retrieved a single blue paper.

"Ms. Oliver, I have the form here."

The young woman laid the blue sheet in front of Cal and pointed at the top right corner where it had been stamped earlier that day. "This came in just before lunch."

Cal's eyes dropped to the bottom of the sheet. The name Bruce T. Vandiver appeared in stiff script on the line designated Parent/Guardian. It was, in fact, his father's name—even the T for Thomas—but it was most definitely *not* his father's handwriting.

"Guess you forgot it, huh?" Ms. Oliver asked rhetorically. Then she added, "He said you'd be playing soccer."

Cal was now trembling slightly. He managed a final question. "So did he introduce himself?"

"Nah. We were swamped this morning. I do remember he looked just like you though," she chuckled. "Right down to the sunglasses." Cal felt another student step into the line behind him. As Cal moved toward the office door, Ms. Oliver called after him. "Good luck with that soccer."

Had he stepped into an alternate universe? Was he dreaming? Only his mother's familiar blue vehicle in the school parking lot reassured him that he had not gone completely mad.

It was a quiet ride home. As best Cal could guess, his mom was still recovering from the unfinished conversation between them that morning, and he certainly didn't feel like talking. The radio filled the void of sound.

Cal skipped his after-school run to meet Levi. He was anxious to talk. A quick change of clothes, two hardened hoagies, and a banana milkshake later, Cal was jogging to the Price's house. There, Levi sat on the front steps, a soda can beside him. Inside the glass storm door Cal saw a roaming Jasmine the watch-cat. Cal dropped down next to his friend.

"No run today?"

"This couldn't wait."

"Uh-oh. What's up?"

Just then Mrs. Cohen's SUV stopped at the driveway, and out jumped Lilli. "One hour!" Mrs. Cohen reminded Lilli.

Lilli waved back.

"You made it!" Cal was pleasantly surprised.

"Barely. I had to tell my mom you were having a hard time adjusting to Valley Oak."

"That's not embarrassing."

"Sorry."

"Glad you worked it out—especially today," said a wary Levi. "Something's definitely going on."

"So?" Lilli prompted Cal for information.

Cal took a deep breath and raked his hair back nervously. "You guys ready for this? Seriously, you're not going to believe what I found out!" Both Levi and Lilli sat, literally, on the edge of the steps. Cal took a visual sweep of the area to be sure no one else was within earshot.

"So did you go by the office?" Levi got right to the point.

"They had the form!" Cal blurted out the news. "I threw mine away, so I don't even know where it came from!"

"And your name was on it?" Levi asked.

"Yeah, it was my name—and it had a parent's signature!"

"What do you mean? Who signed it?" Lilli pressed for details.

Cal looked from Levi to Lilli. "It was my father's name, Bruce T. Vandiver, but it definitely wasn't *his* signature. And it wasn't my father who brought in the form."

"Who then?" Lilli asked, indignant.

"It was someone I don't know. At least, I don't think I do." Cal paused a moment, then added, "He was Asian."

Levi jumped to his feet. "What? How do you know?"

Cal dropped his face in his hands and lowered his voice almost to a whisper. "They told me we looked just alike—including our sunglasses."

Lilli groaned.

A rapping sound started on the inside of the storm door. They looked up to see Derek standing there, dressed in his California State t-shirt and his ripped denims. He stepped out and stared at each person in turn.

"What? You guys see a ghost?" When no one responded, he tried again. "Okay, spill it. Who's in trouble?"

Levi looked over at Cal, as if to ask permission to let Derek in on the mystery. Cal met his eyes and nodded. "Cal is," Levi answered ominously. "This is a discussion for the garage."

Derek led the crew through the house to the kitchen then into the garage. Besides the sound of the vacuum cleaner running upstairs, the house was uncharacteristically quiet.

"Celeste took Jana and Victor to the pool," Levi answered Cal's unspoken question. Once all were in the garage, Derek closed the door behind them.

"Please, step inside my office," Derek said, gesturing toward the slightly leaning card table and chairs that also served as Levi's study space. The "dinosaur" on Derek's computer desk was mostly back together with only a few stray parts remaining.

Cal thought Derek had a way about him that invited confidence. In spite of his derelict exterior, he looked smart, as if the wheels of his mind were perpetually in motion.

Each took a chair at the lopsided table.

"So what's the deal?" Derek prepared to dig in to the problem at hand.

Levi broke the news: "Somebody's been tailing Cal, an Asian dude."

"You sure?"

"We've all seen him," said Lilli. "And Cal has proof that this guy was at our school today."

Cal's heart skipped a beat. He stared at Lilli. "What do you mean we've *all* seen him? You saw him too?"

Lilli's cheeks went hot. "Yes," she admitted. "I saw an Asian guy with a big dog watching you play soccer at the park." She felt Cal's eyes bearing down on her. "I didn't want to worry you!"

Feeling a fresh wave of anxiety, Cal stood up suddenly, sending his metal chair clattering to the floor.

"Just stay calm," Derek took control. "Now everybody here knows the situation. Going forward, there can't be any secrets between us." He looked directly at Lilli. "Can we all agree on that?"

"Agreed," each responded.

"Okay, Cal," Derek continued, "start at the beginning."

Cal began pacing as he repeated his story for Derek. "Until now I've just had a *feeling* sometimes like I was being watched. But the other day, when I was running, I actually *saw* someone watching me." Cal stopped and took a couple deep breaths before finishing the tale he knew sounded crazy. "And then today, the guy went to my school and handed in an Athletic Permission Form for me, posing as my father!"

Even Derek needed a moment to recover from this revelation. "Did he say anything that you know of?"

Cal was recalling the pick-up game in the park and glanced at Lilli. "He told the lady in the school office that I'd be playing soccer."

There was a lull in the conversation as this new information sank in.

Lilli dropped her head in her arms and muttered, "I should have told you."

"You couldn't have known something was up," offered Levi.

"So how does this guy know you—and your family—when you don't know him?" Derek thought aloud.

"And who would dare go to my school and do something that only a parent is allowed to do—to give permission for me to play sports?" Cal felt panic building.

"Tell him about how your adoption was—different," Lilli suggested reluctantly.

Cal knew that Lilli was referring to the fact that somehow he'd gotten home in record time, never entering an orphanage.

With a shrug, Cal turned to Derek to explain. "I don't know if it's connected, but I was able to get through a bunch of red tape somehow and be with my parents less than a month after I was born."

"It took me a year to get home," Lilli pointed out with a sulk.

A surprised Derek sat up in his seat.

Cal continued, "After you mentioned the black market the

other day, I started wondering if you were describing what happened to me. So I asked my mom about it."

"What'd she say?" asked Levi.

"She acted all insulted that I thought they might have done something illegal. I guarantee it'll come up again tonight when my dad gets home."

"Let's wait and see what you get from your parents; then reconvene," Derek suggested. "If they're willing to talk, maybe you'll get some clue about who this guy is. It's a start."

After Lilli went home, Cal and Levi decided a run was in order. Together they ran until Levi called for a break. Then they sat and talked, exhausting every possibility as to the identity of the mystery man and what he wanted with Cal. Then they ran again. When the sun dropped below the tree line, Cal looked at his watch. It was time for dinner.

When he arrived home, Cal was glad to find everyone busy. A light was on in his dad's study, and he could hear his mother moving about the kitchen. The house was full of food smells. Cal welcomed the sameness of it all and looked forward to the comfort of a big meal.

"Is that you, Cal?" His mother called to him.

"No, it's your other son," Cal joked. "Though I'm not nearly as smart or as handsome as Cal."

"Good!" Mr. Vandiver's voice came from down the hall. "That means you're also not the son who eats enough for three. Hurry! Let's have dinner before he gets home. I'm really hungry."

"What the deal, Dad?" Cal teased as his dad loaded a double helping of lasagna on his plate. "I'm not going to have any leftovers for breakfast."

"Sorry, son," his dad apologized. "I didn't get out all day. Missed lunch altogether."

Cal thought about the signature on the APF. "Really? You didn't leave the school all day?"

His father shook his head. "I'm not sure I even looked out my window. When I wasn't on the phone or in a meeting, I was tracking a shipment of science textbooks for seventh grade. You know Mr. Alexander doesn't like it when his books are late." Cal's dad cracked a smile. "Without them he can't give any homework."

After finishing up dinner and listening to the breaking news from Visalia Academy—the arrival of the latest addition to the Wilmer Family, number nine—Cal stood to help clear the dishes.

"Let's get those later," his father suggested. "I understand you have some questions for your mother and me. If you don't have homework or anything, this might be a good time to talk."

"Okay." Cal felt both anticipation and anxiety.

"Fine, let's move to the living room."

His parents perched themselves stiffly on the couch, while Cal took a seat on the floor by the coffee table that held piles of papers he hadn't noticed when he came in for dinner. Some looked official. Among them were some photographs and a small notebook, possibly a journal.

For the next two hours, his parents attempted an explanation of Cal's unusual adoption.

Later, lying in bed, Cal tried to piece the story together again, so he could retell it to his friends. He hadn't been prepared for what he'd learned. While the explanation given answered a good many questions, Cal thought it generated at least as many more. And, to his disappointment, he came away from the discussion without any clues as to the possible identity—or agenda—of the man who seemed to be slowly working his way into Cal's life.

# 09

"Hey, dork!" Nick delivered the unwelcome wake-up call that jolted Cal to attention in homeroom.

"Here!" Cal blurted automatically.

Next came Mrs. Holden's equally unwelcome voice: "That wasn't my question, Mr. Vandiver."

"I'm sorry?"

"Let's try once more. Shall we?" The teacher was again determined to discover something new about the last and most evasive student on her roster. "Will your parents be attending the school's open house next week?"

Mrs. Holden stood, arms folded, staring at him. There were snickers from Nick's circle of beatniks in the back.

"Uh," Cal searched for a plausible response. Holden the Harasser was prying again, and Cal determined to not give in an inch. "Actually, both my parents travel a lot. They may not make it."

"Probably shopping for more plaid shirts." Nick's comment elicited more laughter at Cal's expense.

. . .

It was nearly lunchtime, and Cal was wondering how to put off telling his friends what he'd learned from his parents. It felt too soon to talk about. He needed more time to process the news, and he was worried about how it might affect Lilli.

Levi sat alone at their sunny lunch table when Cal arrived. His friend was devouring his deviled ham sandwich, which Cal could smell well before he set down his tray of greasy tacos and refried beans.

"Dude!" Levi spoke, mouth full. "I couldn't find you this morning."

"I got in a little late." It was true, but only because he wanted to avoid the questions he knew Levi would unleash on him that morning. "What's going on?"

"What's going on?" Levi was incredulous. "The question is, what's going on with *you*? Get any information from your folks?"

Cal looked around for Lilli. "Uh, yeah—well, kind of." Cal lifted a forkful of beans. "Where's Lilli?"

"She's not coming. Told me she had to go to a 'Lunch and Cheer' thing in the gym the rest of the week. After school too."

"Lunch and Cheer? For real?"

"Yep. It's like an orientation for anyone thinking about trying out for the Wildcats cheer squad, I think."

Cal searched his brain and came up with nothing Lilli ever said that suggested she was remotely interested in becoming a cheerleader.

"Doesn't sound like Lilli." Cal attempted to maneuver the soggy taco from the plate to his mouth. When it crumbled in his hand, he let out a loud sigh of frustration.

"It's Lilli's mother's idea. She thinks Lilli needs some new friends."

"Ah! That sounds more like it!" said Cal. Poor Lilli. With a pang of empathy, he imagined his friend on the gym bleachers surrounded by giggling girls who passed on lunch because they're watching their weight.

"So what's the story?" Levi tried again.

While Cal hated to disappoint his buddy, he saw Lilli's absence as his way out. "Nothing earth shattering, really." Cal gave up on trying to hold the cracked taco shell and attacked his meat with a fork. "Gross," Cal said, making a face as he chewed.

"And you are surprised once again." Levi gave him a don't-say-I-didn't-warn-you shrug.

"Dang," Cal said, "I'm going to starve."

"So no news you can tell me?"

"Maybe we should wait until Friday. Then I can tell everybody at once." Cal avoided Levi's disappointed gaze. "That make sense?"

"I guess." Levi slurped his straw along the bottom of his drink pouch. "Did you at least tell your parents about the guy?"

Cal shook his head. "No way. My mother would have a freak and call the police. This has to stay between us for now." Cal adjusted his shades. "We'll just have to keep our eyes open."

...

Friday couldn't have been any slower in coming. Questions about his adoption plagued Cal at all hours of the day and night. At the same time, he had other concerns: watching for the fake Mr. Vandiver; wondering how he'd get out of tryouts the following week; and attempting to squeeze in a workout as well as homework each day.

By three o'clock on Friday, Cal's muscles were screaming for exercise. Before meeting up with his friends, he knew he needed a hard run. At home, Cal changed clothes quickly, ate, and hit the pavement. As he ran, he fantasized about spotting the mystery man and chasing him down.

Meanwhile, three of the foursome assembled around Derek's make-do worktable in the Price's garage. By the time Cal arrived, Lilli and Levi were sipping on red-colored sports drinks. A third sat on the table for Cal. In front of Derek was a glass of his beverage of choice—iced coffee.

Cal arrived, mopping his brow on his sleeve.

"Getting ready for tryouts?" Levi wisecracked.

"Hardly," Cal returned, still breathing hard. "Just hoping to run into—or over—a certain someone." Cal looked around the room, "Thanks for being here, guys."

"You know, I could be spending my time with debutants or practicing some cheers, but, well, I put my blossoming social life on hold for this," Lilli played.

"Are you really going through with this cheer squad thing?" Cal asked.

"No way! My mom knows I don't have time in my schedule for cheering, not with piano and dance. She just wants me to be more popular with the girls."

Cal wished Lilli didn't have to endure such pressure from her celebrity mom. "Lunch was brutal without you," he complained. "Just me and Levi with his smelly sandwich."

"It wasn't by choice," she shrugged. "But if I do what she wants, I'm more likely to get to do what I want—occasionally. It's a trade off."

"Okay, enough middle school drama." Derek was already in problem-solving mode and impatient to move on. "We pick up here with Cal, who—we hope—had an enlightening chat with his parents earlier this week."

With a where-do-I-start expression on his face, Cal shifted in his chair and tapped his drink bottle.

"You were holding out, weren't you?" Levi read the strain in his friend's face. "You really *did* find out something important!"

Cal looked sheepish. "I just needed some time to think. I don't know if any of it's important."

"So let's think about it together," Derek pressed.

Cal glanced over at Lilli. "You okay with this?"

"We agreed to be honest with each other, right? It's fine." Lilli held her knees to her chest protectively.

"Here goes," Cal began. "So when my parents started the adoption process, there was a kind of trial program going on between the Chinese government and an organization called the U.S. Center for Adoption."

"What does that mean?" Levi asked.

"The Chinese government wanted assurance that adoptees were placed in 'quality' homes where kids would go on to college. So the 'center' agreed to pull the names of couples looking to adopt who were also educators. My dad was a teacher before he was a headmaster, so my parents ended up on the list."

Cal was aware of the rapt attention of his listeners. Derek scribbled notes; Levi rubbed his neck; Lilli chewed her fingernails. Cal continued, "My parents were contacted and invited to meet with a lawyer dude—an American—who told them they had been picked for this special program and were eligible for a child—a newborn—immediately."

"So if one of my parents had been a teacher, I could have been brought home as a baby?" Lilli's asked wide-eyed, disbelieving.

"I don't know. I guess it's possible."

Lilli seized the moment to vent. "Wow, so somebody figured out that adoption as an infant was way better than letting a kid sit in an orphanage for a year. What a concept!"

Derek spoke up. "That would also mean that someone had to track these kids."

"Exactly!" Cal continued. "My parents thought they might have to pay a lot more money to be in the program, but they didn't. But they did have to agree to complete a survey for the center about me every three years through age 18. That way they'd know how I was doing in school and if I was going to college."

Spurred on by caffeine and new information, Derek was ready to get down to work. "So there are a number of possibilities regarding our mystery guy. Let's brainstorm and put them all on the table."

"You start, Derek. What do *you* think?" Levi asked.

Derek looked at his notes. "The guy could be connected

with the center. The Vandivers would have completed a survey last year, right? So, maybe, this guy came to check the facts firsthand."

Levi picked apart his brother's reasoning. "And he would sign Cal up for school sports, why?"

"Or," Derek flashed his brother a look of contempt, "he could be a college sports recruiter—Cal being an athlete and all."

"But Cal hasn't been playing sports," Lilli pointed out. "I think he's pretty much been banned. Oops, did I say that out loud?" She covered her mouth.

"Ouch!" Cal pretended to pull a dagger from his chest.

"I could see that," Levi considered the theory.

Cal shook his head. "Sorry. No colleges are looking for a C student."

"That's it!" Levi jumped in. "What if there's something in the agreement with the center, in the fine print, that says that if a kid isn't on the honor roll—clearly the case, here—then they can, like, step in?"

"That was harsh, Levi," Cal remarked.

"And do what?" Lilli asked. "Drag him off to a school in China?"

"Hold up," Derek interjected. "There's another possibility."

"What?" asked Cal.

"What if this guy is your birth father?" The room fell quiet at Derek's comment.

Levi finished the thought, "Then he might be planning a kidnapping."

Derek scribbled some more. "Or he might just be returning for Cal. He obviously knows about the Vandivers. Maybe this was the plan all along."

Lilli spoke up, "It doesn't sound like any plan the Vandivers would have gone for."

Derek scratched his fuzzy chin. "Yeah, well, maybe they didn't know they had a 'parachute' kid."

"A what?" The three asked in unison.

Derek looked from Cal to Lilli. "Don't you two keep up with news from the Asian world?"

"Quit trying to be a know-it-all and just explain what you're talking about," Levi demanded.

"I'm just saying," Derek shot back defensively. "So here's what happened. Starting in the early 1980s, U.S. immigration laws were relaxed, and there was an influx of Asian kids from rich families whose parents brought them here, so they could eventually go to a U.S. college. Most came to California 'cause it's closest, right? Some parents made living arrangements for their kids then returned to Asia to work, visiting occasionally."

"No parents around?" Levi relished the thought. "That would be awesome!"

"Yeah, well, maybe. Sometimes these kids became targets for kidnappers looking for a big ransom check from absent parents."

"But I have a family right here," Cal argued the point.

Derek was clearly working to connect the dots. "But don't you think it's interesting that your family was kind of 'selected' for you?"

Lilli picked up on Derek's line of reasoning. "You mean, like, the Vandivers might have been chosen to raise Cal, but his birth parents may be keeping up with him through the center?"

Derek shrugged. "If so, that would mean someone planned to come back for Cal eventually."

The words "come back" triggered Cal's panic button, reminding him of his childhood nightmare. The presence. The blue eyes. The promise to find him. Cal stood and began to pace.

Cal stopped suddenly and said what he knew everyone was thinking. "We have to talk to him."

"Too dangerous!" Lilli insisted, twisting her ponytail.

"This is the deal. I'll *go* to soccer tryouts on Tuesday after school. He'll be there—somewhere."

"We'll just have to find him and confront him," posed Levi.

"On Monday, we should meet again," Derek suggested. "Bring ideas about how to get this guy to talk. And Cal," he added, "don't go out alone." Cal readily agreed.

...

Saturday afternoon, Cal pulled out his pre-algebra textbook, but he couldn't focus. His thoughts were racing. What was his part in the plan to confront the watcher? If the man showed up, he would be busy playing soccer. Then there was the whole business of even going to tryouts. His chest tightened at the thought of it. In the past, he'd been consumed with the need to win. He didn't want to be that guy anymore.

Cal resisted the urge to throw down his books and take a run. No, he knew going out alone was a bad idea. Instead Cal determined to push through homework and promised himself a swim later that evening. The first swim meet was still weeks away. Maybe Lilli could come too, he dared to hope. He shot off texts to Levi and Lilli:

Swim tonight at 9? Who's in?

Halfway through his math assignment, both of Cal's friends responded, agreeing to meet up at the Y. The day was looking up.

That evening Levi and Cal walked together to the Y. The parking lot was clearing out, and the boys dodged the stream of exiting cars. While they waited at the entrance for Lilli, Cal and Levi played their favorite game: taking turns guessing which vehicles would pull out of the Y then—two blocks down the road—pull into the drive-thru at the Wok2China. Vehicles driven by slender thirty-somethings or the silver-haired set were likely to pass the restaurant's neon sign. Cars driven by teens or parents in vans that hauled multiple kids, however, were almost a sure bet.

After fifteen minutes, it was evident that the ever-punctual Lilli wasn't going to show. Cal felt uneasy. Was she safe? Or was this her mother's attempt to keep Lilli from "the guys"?

"We better get in our swim while we can," Levi suggested. Cal conceded. The two walked to the pool area, hung up their towels, and sat down on the side of the pool. They had less than an hour before closing.

Cal was desperate for the serenity he only found under the water's surface. He longed for the resistance of the water that called on every muscle in his body to work and the relief from worries put temporarily on hold. Unhappily, his mental escape was disrupted by Lilli's unexplained absence.

As night fell, the boys made their way to Mr. Price's car. They found Derek at the wheel. "Lilli got a ride?" He checked out the cars around them.

"She didn't show," his brother informed him.

"Huh. Nobody called the house."

"I'll catch up with her when I get home," Cal promised.

"Hey, any one want to make a stop at the Wok2China?" asked Derek. The question was followed by laughter in the backseat.

...

Cal let Derek drop him off at his house. He was anxious to catch up with Lilli. Inside, a light shone in the back of the kitchen. Cal stuck his head through the studio door. On a stool, his mom sat with a drawing pad in her lap and a pencil in her mouth. She stared at three rectangular canvases, each resting on its own easel, as if in series. Clearly, she was in brainstorming mode.

"Mom?"

His mother jumped.

"Sorry to interrupt. Did Lilli call here earlier?"

Taking the pencil from her mouth, Mrs. Vandiver emerged from her artist's daze. "No, son. Didn't hear from her. Is everything okay?"

"Must have gotten our wires crossed. We thought she was

meeting us at the pool. I'll check my email."

"Okay then." She took up her trance-like pose again.

In the hall, Cal heard his father's voice. "Good swim?" Cal knew his dad sat in his big leather chair watching TV—something educational.

"Good swim." Cal stopped at the doorway of the study, waiting for the question he knew would follow.

"Set any Olympic records?" Mr. Vandiver asked on cue.

"Tomorrow's the day!" Cal smiled and continued down the hall. It was a frequent, non-school-related exchange that Cal actually enjoyed.

In his room, Cal opened his inbox to find one new email—from Lilli. The subject line simply read: "Call me tomorrow." There was no message. At least he knew she was safe.

# 10

It was Sunday morning, and Cal was up early. Typically he'd be off for an extended run, but he remembered Derek's instructions. Instead of venturing out alone, Cal decided to spend the morning doing what he could indoors to ready himself for tryouts, now just days away. For Cal, that meant learning by watching. Once he'd devoured what leftovers he could find for his breakfast, Cal took over his father's study, specifically the TV and soft leather chair. Turning on the soccer channel, Cal settled in to study the plays and the players.

Why did this mystery guy want him to play soccer? He watched the game as if looking for clues. Why not track? Even though he wasn't super tall, Cal knew he was faster than anyone on the school track team. He had to admit his love for soccer though: the speed, the footwork, the strategy. The longer he watched his favorite players, the more Cal started feeling pumped about the big day.

Just after one o'clock, Cal called the Cohens.

"Hello?" Lilli's mom answered.

"Hi, this is Cal. Is Lilli available?" There was a pause, then a flustered response.

"Oh, hi, Cal. Let me think. Lilli is not here right now, and to be honest," she gave a little nervous laugh, "I'm not exactly sure where she is. She probably told me, and I just missed it."

"No problem." Cal wondered what Lilli's mom had on her mind that was so important that she lost track of her only daughter. "I'll catch up with her later, thanks anyway."

"That'd be great. Bye now."

Mrs. Cohen was clearly distracted, and Lilli was not at home. There was only one place she would be. Cal was almost out the door when he remembered he was "grounded." He'd have to ask for a ride.

"Meeting Lilli? That's fine, where?" His mother was happy to oblige.

"The Chinese Cultural Center."

Ten minutes later, Cal and his mom spotted Lilli by the picnic tables behind the building. She had spread out a blanket in the grass and leaned back on her strong brown arms. The two had been to many gatherings there: Lilli to play, Cal to eat. Even now, Cal knew this was the place Lilli came to get away, to think.

"Hi," Lilli greeted her friend with a smile. "Thanks for coming."

"You know, I'm not really all that good at reading minds. I could have been way wrong about you being here."

"No, you couldn't. You knew," Lilli responded, looking grateful.

"What happened to you last night? I got a little paranoid when you didn't show up at the pool."

"Sorry, I had a really weird day yesterday."

"What kind of weird?"

"Well, weird thing number one was when my dad insisted on taking me to breakfast, right? He knows I go to dance at one o'clock, so he wants us to get up early. So—whatever—I go."

"Sounds pretty good to me so far." Cal imagined a plate piled high with his mother's pancakes.

"So, weird thing number two, my dad starts saying that stuff will be changing at home, that my mom's going to be really busy. I'm thinking my mom's going to write that book she's been talking about for a while—the whole former beauty pageant, miscarriage, depression, adoption thing. Then she'd be in demand again for talk shows and stuff, which she'd love, of course."

"But that wasn't it?" Cal was trying to decide if the story had a happy ending or not.

"Uh, not hardly! So my dad takes me home, and as we turn on to our street, I see all these cars parked along the curb and people going into our house, like there's a big party going on!"

"What?" Not a fan of surprises, Cal was almost afraid to hear what happened next.

"Yeah! I have no idea what to expect. So I go in, and I see some of our neighbors and people my mom and dad work with. They're all smiling and patting me like a puppy, right? Then I hear my mom say, 'It's Lilli!' and next thing I know she's telling me, 'I have some really special news! Ready? You're going to be a sister!'"

Cal's jaw dropped. "No way!"

"At first I thought she was trying to tell me that she was going to adopt again, but that's not something you just *spring* on your family. Then it hit me: she was actually pregnant!"

"Your mom is pregnant?" Cal struggled to picture a super-slender Mrs. Cohen growing plump and round.

"Can you believe it?"

Cal still couldn't tell how Lilli was taking the news. "So—was this good news, I mean, for you?"

"Well, I can tell you I was fit to be tied with how she broke it to me. Sheesh! I mean, all those people knew before I did!"

"But do you *want* to be a sister?"

Lilli paused, clearly still sorting through her feelings on the subject. "I guess it's cool that I'll have a brother or sister. Seriously though, we won't grow up together. But—" her voice trailed off.

"But what?"

She smiled slyly. "But that also means the pressure's off me to be, you know, just like them. Lilli sat up and wrapped her arms around her knees. They'll get their freckled redheaded star of stage and screen—or whatever—and I can finally be who I want to be, right?"

Curious now, Cal dared to ask what he knew the Cohens would not, "Tell me, Big Sister, what is it you want to be?"

Lilli twisted her hair thoughtfully then answered Cal in her very best valley girl imitation: "Like, I want to be on cheer squad, of course!"

"What?" Cal took the bait.

"Kidding!" With a laugh Lilli jumped up, ran to the overgrown bushes at the side of the building, and reached under to pull out a soccer ball she'd hidden there. "But you're going to be a Wildcat soccer phenomenon. So you better get in some practice," she ordered playfully.

"Whatever you say, coach!"

Cal and Lilli followed the sidewalk the four blocks to Crestwood Park where they found they had the small soccer field all to themselves. Even without a team, Cal got more of a workout than he could have hoped for with Lilli.

"Kick the ball and hit the crossbar ten times in a row!" Lilli barked at Cal. After every order, she belted out an accompanying cheer, choreographed with some of the moves she picked up at the Lunch and Cheer:

> Hit the bar
> You'll be a star.
> And when you're done
> You're number one!

When Cal showed signs of slowing, Lilli had a cheer to remind him to pick up the pace:

> Moving fast
> Wildcat mean

> District Champs
> Cal's on the team!

After a solid hour and a half of practice, Cal collapsed on the field, unable to think of a time when he had worked—and laughed—so hard. Lilli lay down next to him.

"You'd be a great cheerleader for Valley Oak," Cal commented after catching his breath. "No kidding. I had no idea you could do some of those stunts."

"I'm a dancer, remember? There's really a lot of overlap of movements."

"Sure, sure. But can you run?" Cal was suddenly off the ground. "How 'bout a run back to my house, and then I'll get you a ride home?"

"Serious?" Lilli complained. "Aren't you beat?"

"You better believe it!" Cal nodded. "But now I need some food! Up, up, up! Let's go!" Reluctantly, Lilli began a slow jog behind Cal, who attempted to rap a cheer of his own:

> Lilli with an "i"
> She jump and shout
> Uh … but a run with Cal
> Will wear her out!

"Thank you!" Lilli said to Cal with a mocking smile.

"For what?" Cal asked, jogging backwards, facing Lilli.

"For showing me something you are *not* good at!"

# 11

"You're kidding, right?" Levi asked in disbelief, as he watched Derek unpack what looked like an ancient radio. Two more remained in the box on his worktable in the Price's garage.

"What is it?" Lilli asked next, reaching for one.

"It's a walkie-talkie." Cal called it from where he sat on the arm of Derek's worn loveseat. "Just a guess."

"Cal is the only one here who would make a half-decent spy, and he won't even be on the job tomorrow," remarked Derek.

"'Sears and Roebuck and Company?'" Levi read off the back of the clumsy device that had a black bottom half and a silver top half that included a circular speaker at its center. "How old are these?"

"Came out in 1965." Derek spoke matter of factly. "Hey, they work!" Then he began his demonstration. "Each one of these has new batteries and has been set to the same channel, which happens to be the only one it picks up. So all you have to do is turn it on here." He flipped a button on the top, and the box crackled to life with static. Lilli and Levi did likewise. "Then pull up the antennae, like this.

Now, just hold down the black button on the side to talk."

"Breaker, breaker," Levi's voice sounded tinny through the walkie-talkie speaker. "Come in, Cheer Girl."

"I prefer Dance Queen," Lilli responded. Through Levi's speaker Lilli's voice sounded helium infused. Cal laughed, falling off the arm of the loveseat and landing on the cushion with a bounce.

"Were these Dad's or something?" Levi asked.

"Nope." Derek took the devices back and carefully packed them away. "Got them through The Groundhog."

"What'd you trade for these?" Levi asked with some suspicion, knowing his brother had already traded most of his worldly goods for computer parts.

"None of your business," Derek answered, still feeling the sting of dipping into funds set aside for his senior year, now on hold. "What's important is that I have a plan for closing in on Cal's stalker dude tomorrow—unless someone here has an idea they want to share." The room was silent. "Didn't think so," he continued. "So here's how it's going down."

Stopping occasionally to sip his iced coffee, Derek went on to detail his plan to intercept the man, posing as Cal's father, should he show at soccer tryouts. Derek had drawn out the entire school campus, map-like, on four sheets of paper. Each sheet was labeled either A, B, C, or D. Levi was assigned section A, which included the front of the school and staff parking at the entrance. Lilli would watch Section B, the area between the school building and the descent to the soccer field on the left. Derek took the two remaining areas: C, being the main parking lot in front of the field, as well as D, which began at the steps from the lot down to the field, and continued to the bleachers.

Armed with their walkie-talkies, the team would scout out their assigned areas for signs of the "suspect." If one of the team got a visual of the man, he—or she—would alert the others, so they could quickly close in on him. The goal was to keep the mystery man on campus long enough to question him. Derek assured his team that he had the head of school security, Mr. Biggers, on speed dial in case something unexpected—or dangerous—happened.

"What can I do to help?" Cal asked, feeling useless.

Derek could relate. It was the same way he felt most of the time these days, hanging around at home. "Your job is to tear it up on the field," Derek instructed Cal.

"What?" Cal stood up in protest. "That'll completely ruin my nerd rep!"

"This guy already knows you can play, Cal," Lilli reminded him. "He saw you playing soccer at the park."

"Yeah, he might turn out to be a college scout," Levi posed. "You need to give your best show!"

"Besides," Lilli added, flashing Cal a sly smile, "I refuse to cheer for a loser."

"Alright," Cal agreed to the scheme. "I get to wear my sports goggles though."

...

By the day of soccer tryouts, Cal, Levi, and Lilli were a wreck. Tension over the anticipated meet-up ran high all day as they moved distractedly through their classes. Lilli was afraid of somebody getting hurt; Levi worried they'd never catch up to the suspect, if he showed at all; and Cal was singularly focused on getting through tryouts without a show of temper and without holding back. It helped Cal to know he didn't have to take a spot on the team if it was offered. His top-siders were safe. For now.

At last, it was time. The final bell rang. Tryouts would begin in twenty minutes. Derek met Lilli and Levi at the side of the school overlooking the soccer field. There, they tested the walkie-talkies then moved to their assigned positions. Derek, who also brought along his camera, took up a spot on the far end of the main parking lot. From there he could easily monitor cars going in and out.

The three watched as about thirty anemic seventh and eighth graders assembled on the field. Clipboard in hand, the Wildcats' soccer trainer, Coach Lombard, began checking off the names of those present. The coach's distinctive Jamaican accent carried clearly across the field and beyond. By the time the name "Vandiver" was called, there still had been no sighting of the mystery man

It was then that it happened. Derek watched as a black Mercedes with tinted windows pulled into the lot by the field. Using his walkie-talkie, Derek alerted his team.

"Possible suspect in black car, parking in section C!"

"What?" Lilli responded in a sudden panic. "He's really here?"

Derek watched as an Asian man wearing black sunglasses stepped out of his car and walked casually toward the steps that led down to the field.

"Suspect confirmed and moving toward the field." Derek grabbed his camera and got off a photo of the figure.

At the steps, the man looked down at the field then headed toward the bleachers on the left. He didn't appear nervous or even out of place. Dressed in a gray running suit, the man was slim, athletic. The scene looked every bit like a jock-father coming out to support his son.

"What're we going to do?" Levi demanded an answer. "We can't call school security if he's not acting suspicious!"

"Stay cool, gang. Calling security is not an option. We have to work the plan." Derek issued his instructions: "Lilli, walk to the far end of the field to the trees. Cross to the other side then walk behind the bleachers and toward me. It looks like he's going to sit down and watch from over here."

"What do you expect me to *do*?" There was terror in Lilli's voice. "I'm not going down there alone!"

"Lilli! You are our best chance of talking to this dude. He's Asian, you're Asian—strike up a conversation! Levi, you and I need to move that direction. As soon as Lilli makes contact with this guy, we'll join her. Got it?"

"Got it," Levi responded. There was only petrified silence from Lilli.

Derek pleaded through the speaker. "Lilli, I promise we'll be right there!" Still nothing. "Do it for Cal!" At this, Derek and Levi were relieved to see Lilli begin to move down to the field. With the plan in motion, Derek began a slow descent from the lot to the bleachers. Meanwhile, Levi emerged from his post at the school entrance, following a few paces behind his older brother.

The man seated himself on the second row of bleachers and was immediately engrossed in the activity on the field where the boys were warming up. A few minutes later, Lilli arrived at her destination. She tucked her walkie-talkie in her backpack then stepped out from behind the bleachers. Though he sat alone in the stands, the man was seemingly oblivious to her as she moved toward him.

At her first step onto the bleacher, the man glanced over at her briefly then turned his attention back to the field. Lilli knew it was impossible for him to be unaware of her continued approach, yet he registered no surprise or curiosity at her presence.

Once she stood at the man's side, Lilli stuck out her hand and addressed him boldly. "Hello, Mr. Vandiver!" The man refused to engage. Lilli tried again. "In case you're interested, I'm Lilli, and I've been Cal's friend for—oh, about ten years."

While his eyes stayed on the field, the man responded in a deep voice and unmistakable Asian accent: "Then you also know that I am not Mr. Vandiver."

Just then Levi and Derek stepped up on the metal bleachers with a clatter. "Hi, Lilli!" Derek moved in beside her, followed closely by Levi. "Come out to see Cal play?" Derek asked.

Now Levi jumped in. "Say, who's your friend?"

Lilli looked from the man's face—still watching the field—and back to her companions. "Don't know that just yet. What we *do* know—all of us—is that this is *not* Mr. Vandiver, even though he enjoys practicing his signature on official school forms."

"He needs to play on a team." The man's reply was matter of fact.

Derek spoke up, not hiding his outrage, "That might have been a conversation to have with your son, instead of stalking him and manipulating him into coming to tryouts."

Now the man looked squarely at Derek. "You know nothing about why I am here. I will talk to the boy soon enough." Then he turned away once more.

It was Levi's turn. "Then you won't mind if we hang here until you do."

"Stay if you must—just be silent," the man said irritably, adding, "I do not wish to be distracted." Derek shrugged at Lilli and Levi and the three took their seat on the bleacher, alongside the silent stranger.

"Three laps around the field!" Coach Lombard could be heard yelling to the boys after they finished their stretches.

The players started a slow jog around the track that circled the field. It took everything Cal had in him to keep from breaking into a hard run. But he held back, keeping pace with the rest of the group. By the time they'd completed the laps and returned to their water bottles, it was clear to Cal, to Coach Lombard, and to those watching from the bleachers, that the majority of the boys were already winded. And the drills had yet to begin. Cal felt a creeping—and familiar—irritation about the players' lack of fitness.

At last the drills got underway. Positioned in front of the goal, Coach Lombard organized the players into two lines twenty yards out from the net.

"Zimmerman, the ball's coming to your line first," Coach Lombard shouted. "Kick it into the goal then circle around to the back of the other line. I want to see power and accuracy! Got it?"

From where he stood halfway back in his line, Cal watched those in front of him send the ball into the goal at a slow roll or miss it altogether. "Are you here to play soccer or to bowl?" Coach yelled. After chasing down the first seven balls that went awry of the goal, Coach assigned a player to take over the job.

Two players were still ahead of Cal when he heard a low "Messi, Messi" from behind him. He turned and searched the line until he saw a familiar Latino face smiling back at him. It was Miguel from Spanish class—and the park. Cal could hardly contain his excitement and reached past the skinny kid sandwiched between them to give Miguel a fist bump.

"¡Traelo!" Miguel looked Cal squarely in the eye and smiled cockily.

"Uh oh," the skinny kid whimpered.

Then Cal elbowed him. "What'd he say?"

"He said, 'Bring it!'"

Cal laughed out loud and leaned around again to give Miguel a second fist bump. The scrawny kid between them looked relieved and Cal began to think tryouts might be fun after all.

Next Coach divided the players into four teams. Cal was sent with the first two teams to practice area one, set up along the short side of the field. The remaining two teams, one of which included Miguel, were assigned to practice area two. With the practice fields set up side-by-side, Cal and Miguel could watch each other's teams—and each other.

A few minutes into the games, Cal began grumbling that he wasn't able to play either with or against Miguel. Just then a soccer ball from practice area two rushed toward him. Cal sent the ball screaming back in the direction of the other field. When it returned again, Cal realized Miguel had started a passing game with him using a second ball, even as both players continued their scrimmages.

"¡Traelo!" Cal laughed and called to Miguel across the field. With only one exception, Cal's fan section on the bleachers was standing and cheering, awed as they watched the two players pass the ball back and forth while leading their respective teams to victory.

"It's like a freaking game within a game!" Derek likened

what he was witnessing to watching a grand chess master play multiple games simultaneously. Though the expression on the stranger's face never changed, he raised his head and gave a slight nod each time Cal made a long, powerful kick that landed exactly where he had intended: at Miguel's still running feet.

"Who is *that* guy?" Levi couldn't remember seeing Miguel's face in the halls at school.

"He plays soccer at the park," Lilli said.

Though Coach Lombard caught on to the passing game, he didn't interfere. In fact, as tryouts progressed, the coach grew increasingly enthusiastic; he was going to score the Wildcats soccer team of his dreams.

Nearly two hours later, after Coach had dismissed the players, Cal and Miguel were still on the field, attempting to best each other in juggling the ball.

Mid-juggle, Cal caught a glimpse of his friends sitting in the bleachers. Someone was with them. Was it his watcher?

Cal gave his friend a fist bump good-bye and began a slow jog toward the bleachers. As he neared his fans, Cal slowed, finally stopping centerfield. It was then that the Asian man stood and began to approach Cal. The two stood just out of earshot of their audience. When, at last, black shades met tinted sport goggles, the two stood at about the same height, and both were determined to have their say.

"Why are you here?" Cal demanded.

"Here to watch you play soccer," the man responded evenly. "Impressive."

Cal drew a deep breath. "Are you my father?"

Now the man reached up and slowly pulled off his sunglasses, revealing clever, though traditional dark-colored eyes. "No, I am sorry." Sliding his glasses back on, the man announced, "My Chinese name is Bai Zhao Man. You can call me Jack."

"Why would I call you anything? What are you to me?" Cal asked with angry disappointment.

"I am a coach, of sorts; I was sent here by the U.S. Center

for Adoption. You know of it?"

"My parents told me about it. It's been tracking me."

"That is correct," Jack confirmed. "But in your case, it was not your academics that drew the attention of your reviewers."

Cal felt a stab of embarrassment. His grades had never met anyone's expectations.

"Concern has been expressed by the reviewers that you have exceptional abilities—athletic abilities—that are not being appropriately developed."

"What does that mean?" Cal suddenly felt cornered. "Whose business is it what I do?"

After giving Cal a moment to cool down, Jack responded calmly. "I would expect that attitude from an American."

Cal pulled off his goggles and spoke unapologetically. "I am an American."

"So you are. But you are also Chinese. And as a USCA participant, you have duel citizenship with your country of origin."

Cal was speechless. He was also a citizen of China? Did his parents know that?

"It is the position of the center that as a child of China—wherever you live—you must not neglect your abilities. It is a matter of national pride."

"What do you want from me?"

"The USCA wants me to make sure you are growing as an athlete." Then his tone turned sarcastic. "I must be able to tell them you are doing more than running in the streets and swimming at the YMCA."

"What does it matter?" Cal felt exposed by the man who knew the habits of his private life.

"Learning with others, having a coach to push you ..." Jack gestured toward the field, "... it will move you toward greatness. Then you will honor your gift."

"And if I refuse?"

"It will likely to be harder for other Chinese children who

have no families to be adopted into the States."

"So my playing soccer will make these people happy? That's all you want?" Cal was incredulous that he was a pawn in a game between two powerful countries.

"Perhaps for now. But I have learned much in my study of your abilities and have taken a personal interest in your future."

"Tell me." Cal was growing impatient. "What do *you* want from me?"

"It is the same thing you secretly want for yourself when you push the limits of your body."

Cal held his breath, feeling as though the man was seeing inside of him.

"You have been preparing for this moment." Jack looked out over the field then turned to face Cal. "Now I ask you to permit me to make you an Olympic champion."

# 12

By the time Derek pulled into the Vandiver's driveway, Cal was trembling. He hadn't spoken a word since he left the field with his friends. Levi and Derek quickly piled out of the car into the warm evening air to offer support to Cal as they made their way up the sidewalk. Lilli jogged ahead to open the door and was the first to meet the surprised and immediately concerned faces of Cal's parents.

"Son, are you sick?" Cal's mother put her hand to his face, checking for fever.

"What happened?" His father took over the support of Cal, seating him on the couch. His mother grabbed the decorative throw from the couch and wrapped it around her son.

Being the oldest, Derek felt an obligation to explain. "He's not hurt," Derek assured them, though he didn't sound too convincing. "He's had a bit of a shock though. We just came from tryouts."

"What tryouts?" Cal's dad looked from face to face for an answer.

"It was for Wildcats soccer, sir," Lilli answered weakly.

"Are you kidding?" Mr. Vandiver asked, confused.

"I didn't want you to get your hopes up," Cal spoke at last.

"Do you want to talk about it?" his father gently prodded.

"No, I just need to chill awhile, if that's all right."

Out of habit, his mother asked, "Do you need something to eat?"

"We should head out," Derek said, nodding at Levi to follow him.

Cal's mother stood up. "Thank you, boys, for everything."

Lilli sat on the floor next to the couch. "May I stay, please? Just for a little while?"

"Of course," Cal's mother answered. "Just give your folks a call."

As the brothers headed out the door, Levi spoke to Lilli: "Let us know how it's going, okay?"

"You got it."

Once Derek and Levi left, Cal's dad turned off some of the lights in the living room. His mom brought him a pillow from his bed. Lilli helplessly watched Cal who was awake, but quiet and still.

Just as Lilli began to doze there was movement on the couch. Cal wriggled himself upright, and his father stepped into the room. "Cal, are you ready to talk about what happened today?"

Cal didn't know where to start and was nowhere near processing the conversation he'd had with Jack on the field. He did, however, feel like he owed his family and his best friend some sort of explanation.

"I thought I might be meeting my father today—my birth father." Cal's admission was punctuated by a gasp from his mother. "Dad, this dude signed your name to a permission slip for me to tryout, saying I was going to play soccer. Then he showed up to watch me."

Lilli spoke up, "We made a plan to corner the guy and try and find out what he was up to."

"But he's not my father."

Digging in his pocket for his cell phone, Cal's father said,

"We should call the police."

"Not necessary," Cal assured him. "He's from the center you told me about, here to check on me." The room was silent as everyone tried to make sense of what Cal was saying. "Turns out he wants to see more than a jump in my GPA."

"How dare he contact you without our consent!" his father fumed.

"What is it he wants?" His mother asked, frightened.

"Don't know exactly." Cal shrugged. "You can ask him yourself. He'll be calling you guys." Cal stood and tossed the blanket across the arm of the couch. "I'm sorry. I think I need to sleep on whatever just happened. Everyone's been great."

"Of course, get a good night's rest, son." His father stood. "Lilli, how 'bout I get you home."

"See you tomorrow?" Lilli asked her friend.

"Oh, yeah. Got to keep up my grades, so I can be a Wildcat, right?"

"Rah, rah." Lilli gave her imaginary pom-poms a shake.

...

In the darkness of his room, wrapped tightly his bed covers, Cal hoped that when morning came his meeting with Jack wasn't just a bizarre dream—that he really had come face to face with someone who saw something in him. Something great.

When his mind finally faded to black, a dream began in which he was running, hard. Unlike his dreams in past weeks, Cal sensed that he was running toward something he really wanted rather than away from something threatening. It was a dream during which, for the first time, Cal dampened his pillow with tears of relief rather than the sweat of anxiety.

...

For the next hour or more, as Cal lay sleeping, Kimberly Vandiver watched over her son. Pulling around the director's chair that usually sat at Cal's computer desk, she relaxed into the sound of his strong, regular breathing, admiring how the evening light made Cal's skin glow bronze and marveling at the angles of his body—shoulders, elbows and knees—that never stopped moving, even in sleep.

At twenty-eight, Kimberly had earned her fine arts degree from the University of Arizona, where she met and later married education student Bruce Vandiver. After five years, her husband worried that if they waited much longer to start a family he'd be too old to coach his son's Little League or referee his daughter's volleyball matches.

The idea of adoption had always appealed to Kimberly. The artist in her loved the idea of working with existing material, honoring its natural attributes, adding her own touches, and watching what emerged. Why not make a home for a child that needed one?

When her husband began teaching his middle school social studies class about the crisis of abandoned baby girls in China, the direction of their family seemed clear. Both husband and wife embraced the idea of being part of the solution through adoption.

Their years raising Cal had been full of surprises—some good, some not so good, from a parent's perspective. While their son possessed astounding athleticism, he was frustrated by team sports; even with the fine education his parents provided for him at VA, Cal was uninterested in becoming a scholar; and though both mother and father longed to leave the Vandiver stamp on their son, he resisted, instead living a life quite separate from his parents.

Tonight though, as she watched her son tossing in his sleep, the artist-mother wondered, with an unexplained excitement, what surprises now lay ahead.

...

A week passed. Coach B's voice boomed from the doorway

of healthy living class as students headed out for lunch: "Don't forget to check the announcement board by the cafeteria." Cal's stomach flip-flopped in anticipation. "Congratulations to those of you who'll be playing for the Wildcats this fall."

Minutes later, Cal was engulfed in the crowd of students vying for a spot close to the gigantic bulletin board that hung in the common area. This was the place where students were judged by their peers to be worthy or unworthy, where friends were made or lost. Drawing the biggest and blondest crowd was a poster at the far left corner of the board with sparkly purple lettering announcing the names of the Wildcats cheer squad. Taking a close second in interest was the list of those named to play football for the Wildcats. The postings that followed became less and less glamorous, from the perspective of the onlookers: soccer team, volleyball team, fencing team, and lastly, the chess team.

Miguel was already at the board by the time Cal got there. He was pumping his arm in the air in victory when he turned to look for Cal. Catching sight of him, at last, Miguel smiled broadly and let out a loud "¡muy bien!" then reached over bodies to give Cal a high-five. Very good. Cal knew that much Spanish. What Miguel was really saying was that both their names appeared on the list. What now? He didn't want to play soccer, but he *really* didn't want to tell that to Miguel.

...

True to his word, Bai Zhao Man wasted no time in contacting Cal's parents. On the Thursday after tryouts, the elder Vandivers met Jack for lunch. Afterward the headmaster called the school receptionist to declare he would be out the office for the remainder of the day as well as the next. It was unprecedented for Headmaster Vandiver to take a day off, especially on such short notice. The news was, therefore, worthy of office gossip. It was rumored that the headmaster's only son, the one with anger issues, was struggling at his new school.

That afternoon, and on through the weekend, Cal's parents spent hours at home in the study. Sometimes Cal heard his mother typing at the keyboard; many times he heard his father using his headmaster voice on the phone. By Sunday night, the couple emerged at last. While the family was sitting together at the dinner table, Cal's father cleared his throat, signaling an announcement of import.

"Four hours a day?" Cal protested the news that his personal autonomy had, essentially, been handed off to a complete stranger—and without even asking him. "How do you know this guy's for real?"

"Cal, can you trust us?" his dad asked him, sounding very much like a headmaster addressing an anxious new student.

"You're not asking me to trust *you*," Cal pointed out. "You're asking me to trust *him*—with everything."

"This man knows what he's doing, Cal. He's coached two Asian Games, as well as the 2004 Olympics in Athens and again in 2008 in Beijing. He's even been a trainer for the Chinese military."

"So that's it? Done deal? I don't have any say in this?"

Mr. Vandiver took a deep breath before continuing. He hadn't warned Jack about how stubborn his son could be, how devoted he was to his daily routine, to his friends, to the familiar. "Son," he remained unruffled, "are you going to tell me that you are not willing to rearrange your schedule for a chance to compete with the greatest athletes in the world?"

It was a ridiculous question, of course. Cal spent most of his days competing in some way—taking first place in pretend swim meets; besting himself again and again in running speed and distance. Most recently, of course, it was soccer tryouts. Playing with Miguel, the only real soccer talent he'd ever encountered, reminded him that competing—and winning—was the fuel that drove him.

"I'm not saying that." Cal answered without looking up.

A fight against training with Jack was a fight against everything he had ever really wanted, even if it meant his world would be turned upside down. Cal's parents knew it. Cal knew it.

"It seems to me that you just had your say in this matter then. Am I right?"

"Yes, sir."

As his father went on to explain, their agreement to let Cal train with Jack included stipulations on both sides.

The coach insisted that he be able to train with Cal seven days a week for up to four hours. The rigorous workout schedule would require some dietary changes. Among them was the addition of a specially formulated supplement drink to be added to Cal's existing high-carb, four-meal-a-day regimen. And as Jack had made particularly clear, a poor effort or bad attitude on Cal's part would result in additional training time.

The Vandivers brought their own non-negotiables to the table. Cal's schoolwork would take priority over his training. They reserved the right to call a practice if they thought Cal was too ill. Also, their son was not to be transported anywhere by anyone without their permission.

To the Vandivers' relief, Jack announced that he would be taking full responsibility for financing the training he provided, including necessary apparel, equipment, and travel. It was further agreed that Cal's training would take place at the Y, since it was close, and would begin the very next week.

# 13

For days, the lunchroom at Valley Oak Middle was abuzz with news of who would be playing what sport for the Wildcats.

"The invitation to sit with us is still open," Kaitlyn Bens had reaffirmed her earlier offer to Cal. "I like an athlete with a brain." The answer was still no.

At the hot meal bar, Nick took a verbal jab at Cal. "Soccer, really? So now you're an athlete wannabe? You're just going to embarrass yourself, man."

"Relax," Cal shot back at the kid he learned ran track, like Kaitlyn. "Just because I made the team doesn't mean I'm going to play. I'm a busy guy."

"Oh, yeah. It would be fascinating to see how you spend your time."

"Fascinating—that's a big word, Nick. Good for you!" Cal returned the insult.

Cal had neither accepted nor rejected his spot on the team. He still had a week before that had to happen. Mostly Cal was thinking about how to break the news to his friends that his life was about to change. He was already inhaling his lunch when his friends joined him at their usual table.

"Whoa," Levi said as he took his seat across from Cal. "Have you forgotten your last cafeteria taco fiasco?" Levi reached into his backpack and pulled out a mangled pimento cheese sandwich.

"Serious," Lilli joined in the teasing. "Are you going to put that—whatever that is—into your soccer playing machine?"

"Give me a break," Cal said through his over-stuffed mouth. "I'm really hungry!"

"You sure it's not just nerves? You've got a big decision to make!" Lilli taunted.

Cal paused a moment then replied, "Okay, you got me—I'm hungry *and* I'm nervous. Happy?"

Lilli laughed. "Actually I am happy 'cause if you join the team I get to be head of the soccer cheer squad."

"What?" Levi stared at Lilli. "That's awesome, Lilli. Why wasn't it posted? I didn't even know there was a soccer cheer squad!"

Cal and Lilli stopped and watched Levi chow down on his pimento cheese sandwich and waited until he noticed their silence. Halfway through his sandwich, Levi realized that he'd missed the joke. Now he blushed slightly. "Ha. No such thing as a soccer cheer squad, right? I get it," he said and continued eating, undeterred.

Cal pulled a beverage can labeled "GameOn" from his backpack and took a couple gulps. He could only hope that the calorie booster that Jack gave him would also bolster his courage to tell his friends what was going down—starting that day.

"What are you drinking?" Lilli asked, mirroring Cal's sour expression.

"Something Jack gave me," Cal said with a slight shudder, setting the can down on his lunch tray. His assessment: filling—yes, great-tasting—no, especially at room temperature.

"Jack?" Levi asked.

"The Asian dude, Levi. I think you know the guy."

"You're the one who didn't want to talk about *him*. Now you're talking about *him*?"

"I told you I wasn't *allowed* to talk about *him* until there was something to tell.

"So now there is?" Lilli asked.

"Now there is," Cal answered, suddenly feeling queasy. "Listen, I've got something important to tell you guys." At these words, Levi's eyes widened, and Lilli's heart began to pound.

Cal began arranging and rearranging the items on his tray before he took a breath and began his tale. "Like we thought, Jack was here with the center. He was told that all the surveys they'd gotten from my parents over the years showed the same thing: basically, I was brainless but into sports. So after this last survey, they sent Jack to check on me."

"So are they going to get you a tutor or what?" asked Levi, who was suddenly struck with an idea. "Hey! Derek can tutor you! Please—give him a job!"

"They're not going to send you to a different school are they?" Lilli asked, anxiety in her voice.

"Listen, they've given up on my brain. Jack didn't offer to find me a tutor," Cal hesitated before continuing. "He's asked to be my trainer."

"I thought all the center cared about was that you went to college," Levi protested.

"This is something Jack wants to do on his own. He's even going to pay for it."

Levi was leaning forward now, "What's in it for him?"

Cal gave the only answer he could think of, "I guess he wants to coach an Olympian." Cal gave a sheepish smile.

"The Olympics? Are you kidding? You mean, like, for next year?" Levi stared, astounded.

"Yep. Starting today I train four hours a day—every day." He looked from one friend to the other trying to decipher how they were taking the news. Both sat stunned.

"That drink Jack gave you—is that part of your training? Lilli asked.

"Yeah. It sure wasn't my idea. It's extra calories for whatever it is he's going to do to me later."

"What about hanging out after school?" Levi asked, afraid of the answer.

"It's on hold for now, dude," Cal answered apologetically. "Stinks, I know. I'm going to go to school, eat, train, and sleep. Oh, and do homework—sometime." He threw up his hands in exasperation. "Then it starts all over again."

The bell rang, and students around them began the scramble to find backpacks, return lunch trays, and beat the late bell to their next class. Cal hurried to pre-algebra, all too aware that at the end of the day he'd be in Spanish class; there, Miguel would be waiting for him, waiting to hear if they would be playing soccer together as Wildcats.

# 14

Derek felt jittery, but not with caffeine—with excitement. He spent what little savings he had left on dry cleaning: a suit, three pairs of slacks, and three dress shirts. They were lying gently folded on the passenger seat next to him in their protective plastic, evidence that it was all coming together, that he wasn't a good-for-nothing-mooching college drop out, after all. He was, in fact, a working man. Well, he was about to be.

Life had taken an unexpected turn for the resident genius in August, just as classes were scheduled to begin at California State University, Fresno. Derek was prepared to show his professors that he was still the top student in the School of Information Technology. It was to be his fourth and final year of school and, presumably, his last year of living in the crowded Price home. Then he received a student-delivered invitation to meet with the head of the School of Social Sciences, Dr. Tan.

"I'm prepared to offer you the opportunity of a lifetime," Dr. Tan had prefaced their conversation. Then came the twist. Dr. Tan, Korean by birth, peered over his heavy black-framed glasses at Derek and told him that he'd have to be open to "a deviation in his timeline for graduation." That's when Derek began to sweat. There was no way he could shoulder a fifth year of college loans.

"I've been handed a grant that will require the full-time services of an IT professional," Dr. Tan announced. Tan went on to describe, in general terms, the "Asian Community Data Collection Project," or DCP for short. His department would oversee the project. Tan did not offer the name of the underwriter of the grant, nor did he attempt to explain how the information would be used. But Tan did tell him that the project was considered "high profile" and a "media magnet." Derek could also tell from Tan's animated delivery that the department head had high hopes that the project might be his personal ticket to a spot on the speaking circuit, maybe even a bestseller.

There was a lot in it for Derek too, as Dr. Tan pointed out. In exchange for his willingness to put off his graduation for as much as a year, Tan promised Derek one tuition-free year at CSU upon project completion. And during the months Derek was working, he would receive a stipend to help cover some of his work-related expenses. Tan was also quick to predict that the project would be "killer" on his resume.

Typically, Derek wasn't one to act on faith, but the deal seemed so sweet he couldn't find a compelling reason to turn it down. The one particularly painful drawback was that he'd have to withdraw from classes before they began, and until further notice, he wouldn't be able to tell his parents why. The project was under wraps.

In a short, painful call to his father, Derek broke the news that he would be leaving school, pulling out just days before forfeiting his tuition. Yes, he'd be moving home. No, he wasn't ill. Maybe he'd return to finish up sometime in the future. Even the university registrar hesitated before finalizing his withdrawal papers. Derek's reputation preceded him.

And there had been doubts since. Plenty. Then it happened. Derek got the call just as he was about to replace the torn window screen in Victor's room that had been shot out by an airsoft gun at close range. It was Dr. Tan. He got right to the point.

"Can you start on Thursday?" Dr. Tan asked.

"This Thursday?"

"Yes, this Thursday morning at 9:00 a.m."

"I'll be there," Derek replied, without hesitation. Afterwards, Derek went to his near-empty closet, pulled out the few neglected items that hung there, and headed to the Sunny Days Dry Cleaners.

...

The school day ended, and Cal, Lilli, and Levi burst out into the sunlight and stood together waiting for their rides. Each felt awkward about saying goodbye. When would they find time to get together outside of school?

First in the line of cars at pick up was Lilli's mom who sat waiting in her SUV to take her daughter to dance. Levi's mom, driving their dingy four-door, idled behind her. "Need a ride?" Levi asked Cal.

"Thanks, but, unfortunately, my carriage awaits me," he nodded in the direction of his mom's equally unimpressive sedan a few cars back. It was a humiliation they shared.

"Catch me up on email, guys!" Lilli called back as she hurried to her ride. Her cheery wave failed to match her not-so-cheery face. It hit Cal then that he'd forgotten to ask Lilli how things were at home, with the baby coming.

"Feels weird not running or doing the pool thing together," Levi dared to show a glimpse of his lostness.

"I couldn't have done this without you, you know. 'Keep pushing! Just one more lap!'" Cal mimicked Levi's poolside coaching. "I really don't know how I'm going to get through this training stuff without you hanging with me."

"How 'bout I come out for soccer practice next week? I'll run while you practice, and then we'll catch a ride home together. Maybe even jog—if you're able," Levi joked.

"Yeah, well, we'll see how the whole soccer thing shakes out. I'm not superman. I don't really know if soccer's going to make the cut in my new schedule."

The horn from the Vandiver car sounded, and Cal jumped. "Well, here I go! Later!" Cal weaved quickly through the line of cars before his mother was tempted to hit the horn again.

When he arrived, Cal was taken aback. It was his father at the wheel.

"Surprise!" came his father's jovial greeting. Cal hurried into the passenger side of the car, tossed his backpack in the backseat, and then climbed in next to his father.

"I thought I'd treat you to a carb frenzy at The Noodle House before your first workout with Jack." Cal relaxed at the thought of a steamy bowl of pasta.

"A seriously great idea, Dad."

"I packed up some running gear for you in the back."

"Cool."

On the way, Cal wondered what he and his dad could possibly find to talk about over their hot noodles. There had been a time when Cal and his dad made regular visits to The Noodle House. But that had stopped some time ago.

Cal's dad pulled into the familiar shopping strip comprised of The Noodle House, TopKid Karate School, and the Better Buy grocery store. Inside the dated restaurant, Mr. Vandiver slid into one of the red vinyl booths that looked out on the busy parking lot and the growing assortment of teens loitering there. Cal took a seat across from his dad and began browsing the menu that doubled as a placemat.

"I'll just have a small Caesar salad," Cal's dad told the teenage waitress who arrived at their table with chewed black fingernails and eyes that never looked up from her pen and pad. Cal, who was used to a third meal in the afternoon, asked for a Number 4, his all-time favorite. He hoped the large bowl of buttery noodles would hold him over through four hours with Jack.

"So you didn't have meetings and stuff today?" Cal asked in an attempt to discover why his father had—uncharacteristically—taken time away from the academy to surprise Cal with his favorite meal and to accompany him to the Y.

"It's a big day," Cal's father tried his best to catch his son's eyes behind the ever-present shades. "I wanted to be here." Cal looked down and attempted to find the hidden picture of the noodle shaped like a lasso on his placemat. "I feel as though I've been the last one to know what's been going on in your life lately," his dad continued. "I'd like it if that could change."

Without looking up, Cal asked, "You'd have come for soccer tryouts?"

"Of course!"

"I wasn't even trying to get on the team," Cal shrugged off his dad's response and looked out the window at a mother dragging her resistant toddler across the parking lot and into the Better Buy. He felt like that toddler pulling away, but from his father.

"You forget that I don't ever get to see you play—anything." Cal's dad spoke from the heart. "It makes me happy to watch you do what you do so well."

Just then the waitress arrived with a tray. She quickly unloaded their dishes and left a dressing smeared check under Mr. Vandiver's salad plate. "Enjoy," the girl mumbled dutifully and squinted a smile that dropped even before she turned to leave.

"Tell me, Cal," his dad picked up the conversation. "Did you *want* me at tryouts?"

Cal dropped his head. "No, not really."

"Exactly," came his father's reply. Cal began digging into

his noodles as his father continued. "You lead a very private life, son. On purpose."

"I embarrass you," Cal blurted out, surprised by his own confession.

His father cracked a smile. "I guess there have been a couple times when that might have happened." His son was well known for the insults he hurled at comparatively inept players on the Visalia community soccer team. Then there were the after-hours meetings his father spent with teachers to address Cal's inattentiveness to his studies.

A smile broke on Cal's face too. "Remember in fourth grade when Mrs. Kiser had a substitute, and I started juggling a pencil eraser with my foot, one of those big pink ones?" Cal grew animated. "By the time I got to two hundred, there were three classes in the room cheering!"

The man stabbed at his salad and drew a deep breath. He peered at Cal as a father rather than a headmaster. Amused. Even proud. "You know, I don't remember that one."

"Oh." Cal's eyes dropped.

"The point here is," his father attempted a summary, "I'm okay with the fact that you and I don't share a lot of interests—though we did have baseball for a little while," he chuckled. "But if I've failed to communicate to you that I love you for the person you are, I'm sorry." Cal wriggled in his seat.

"And while I have you captive here, I want you to know something else." Cal's father leaned toward his son. "Your mother may fight me on this one," he confided, "but I'm telling you that I am—and always have been—your biggest fan, and I couldn't be more proud that today you begin a journey of, well, working your butt off." It was Cal's turn to laugh. How long had it been since he and his dad laughed together?

"Not so sure I like the 'working your butt off' part," Cal remarked, "but it's great to know you support me."

The apprehension Cal had about the afternoon before him

began to feel more like excitement. He wasn't going it alone. Even if his friends would need some time to get used to the idea, he knew now that his family—even his dad—was along for the ride.

# 15

Levi got a shock at carpool that day too. To his dismay, Derek was in the driver's seat of the Price car. He was in no mood to get grief from his older, loser brother.

Levi opened the car door. "Wait, wait!" Derek stopped Levi from plopping down in the front seat.

"Why?" Levi asked impatiently, then watched, astonished, as Derek gingerly lifted his dry cleaning by the hangers and laid it neatly across the back seats.

"Sorry, meant to move that before you got here."

"What's with the clothes?" Levi probed irritably once he was seated. Dry cleaning was a rarity at the Price house.

"What's with the bad attitude?"

"Like you never had a bad day."

"Well," started Derek, his voice sounding surprisingly upbeat, "it just so happens I'm having a very good day, finally, and I'm wondering what stunk yours up so bad."

"Ever been dumped?" Levi asked Derek, looking out the window with a sour expression.

"You mean, like, by a girl?"

"Heck no!"

"Okay, you're really confusing me now."

At this point Levi thought it was probably a good thing Derek was the one to pick him up after all. He needed to vent. "I've kinda been dumped, by a friend," Levi grumbled.

"You only have one friend, dude."

"Too true. And today I find out we're not going to be able to hang out anymore."

"Why? What happened?" Derek pressed.

After a pause, Levi spilled it. "You remember the Asian dude from Cal's soccer tryouts?"

"Yeah," Derek answered, sensing that bad news—really bad news—was forthcoming.

"Well, he's still here."

"What for?"

"Get this: He wants to train Cal for the Olympics."

The announcement hung in the air for a moment while Derek struggled to process it. It wasn't exactly bad news. Just really, really big news. "Whoa," Derek finally drew a breath. "Didn't see that one coming."

"No kidding. Cal starts training today, and he'll train every day—no, really, *every* day—for four hours!" Levi felt hot angry tears behind his eyes. "He'll never be around."

Derek had a choice to make. He could rag on Levi for being selfish when his best friend struck it big. He could even point out Levi's lack of foresight in keeping his world so small, as if nothing was ever going to change. But Derek held his tongue. Those discussions could wait—as could the news about his new job.

Meanwhile, Lilli had slipped into the SUV next to her mother who was chatting into her Bluetooth. In spite of the shock of Cal's news, Lilli flashed her mother a smile that said everything was okay, pulled her dance bag from the floor of the vehicle onto her lap, and stared out the window. Her fingers felt for the decorative rhinestones on the outside zippered pocket of her bag. She needed to focus on something—anything—to keep the tears from coming.

Deep down Lilli had known that Cal would leave her behind someday. That someday was today. She would just have to concentrate even more on her grades, on dancing, maybe on her poetry. Even as Lilli made attempts to be optimistic, she could feel her arms and legs grow heavy. How could she dance today?

"I couldn't believe it!" Mrs. Cohen was still very much involved in her phone conversation when she stopped at the studio to drop off Lilli. "But I'm telling you, my clothes are already feeling snug!" Stepping out the vehicle it occurred to Lilli that she could, if she dared, get away with most anything for the next few months until the baby came. Neither of her parents was likely to notice.

Lilli willed her legs to carry her into the striking structure that was her second home, with its carefully maintained soft yellow stucco exterior and impressive ten-foot double-door glass entrance. On the left door was etched "Visalia Ballet Academy" in flowing script. On the right was etched a single, perfectly poised ballerina, head turned to the side, chin up, lost in her art. For the nine years since Lilli's mom first escorted her into the pristine building, Lilli had walked its halls pleased and proud, dance bag over her arm, dressed in the trendiest dancewear that never failed to draw compliments. But lately, Lilli thought her lessons felt stale and forced. And now she'd be doing it without the occasional outing with Cal to look forward to.

The studio was noisier than usual as Lilli stepped onto the gleaming hardwood floors of the practice room. A few girls were stretching on the floor or at the bar; others chatted in groups or traded lip colors, admiring themselves in the mirror-lined walls. Clearly, Mrs. Russ, who would have had the girls quietly moving through their warm-ups to soft classical music, was nowhere within earshot.

Just as Lilli and the others thought they might enjoy unsupervised time catching up on middle school gossip, a young, commanding voice silenced the chatter.

"Let's get started!"

Making her way to the front of the room was a twenty-something woman with a muscular, medium build, and a bob cut long in the front and short in the back. The top of her hair was colored black; the underneath was bright blue. She wore simple gray warm-up pants and a black t-shirt that matched her hair and the polish on her fingers and toes. She gave them all a moment to stare and get used to the idea that this would not be an ordinary day at the Visalia Ballet Academy.

"My name is Carissa Russ, and yes, Sandra Russ is my mother," she began by answering the question on everyone's mind. "I'm between gigs with my dance troupe, so I'm filling in for a few days to get the feel of teaching. It's good to try something new every once in a while, don't you think?" Lilli definitely thought so.

"Speaking of trying something different," Carissa continued. "Everybody take off your ballet shoes. Just put them by the wall. Good. Today we're going to learn a little about modern dance, which is the style of dance that I do with my troupe." Again, Carissa waited out the inevitable twitter among the students before she moved on, undeterred.

"Most dance students don't get a true introduction to modern dance until later," Carissa explained. "But, hey, let's see what we can do. Everybody with me?" It was more of a command than a statement. Carissa, it seemed, was about to take the class somewhere entirely new. Lilli found the idea intriguing. In fact, it was exactly what she needed.

# 16

It had been four hours. As the sun was setting, Cal saw his father's waiting car in the parking lot of the YMCA. From where he stood on the running track, where he had endured a grueling first training session with Jack, he thought the distance to the car looked like a day's journey off. Cal picked up his duffle, checked his pockets for the shades he'd pulled off when he was soaked with sweat, then picked up the unopened boxes Jack told him to take home. While Jack finished the day with his own jog around the track, Cal made the slow climb to the lot. Watching on, the boy's father stepped from his car and opened the car trunk for the easy deposit of whatever his son was balancing.

...

Having pushed his body to a new level, Cal felt soreness setting in. Before that day, everything about his relationship with the track, the field, or the pool was private. Admitting he was in pain, whether to his coach or to his own parents, would be still another new and humbling experience.

"We made it through day one," Mr. Vandiver tested the waters with some light conversation.

"We?" Cal let out a dramatic moan, as he dropped the boxes he'd carried into the trunk.

"Sure," his father added jokingly, "we did this together, remember? I was *thinking* about you all evening!"

"Yeah, well, I have trouble believing you felt my pain when I had a cramp in mile four or when I nearly bonked on mile ten. Next time you might want to actually be there with an ice pack and a double Big Burger with fries."

"Speaking of food, need some?"

After taking stock of his body, Cal responded, "No, believe it or not, I'm too tired to eat. Just show me to the bathtub."

Mr. Vandiver had to smile. Cal hadn't been in a bathtub since his mother gave him oatmeal soaks to soothe his bug-bitten skin after a day of play outside. "Maybe some still-warm-from-the-oven chocolate cake would be a good follow-up to a cool bath."

"Most definitely!" Cal answered with a sudden and markedly improved disposition.

"See? I'm going to be a great training partner!"

At home, father and son made their way into their living room and piled Cal's load on and around the coffee table. There, in the light, they could see the boxes were black with a neon green logo. Sore as he was, Cal couldn't restrain his enthusiasm. This wasn't second-hand sports crap. This was the good stuff.

The light was on in the studio, so Cal called to his mother. "Come in here, Mom. You gotta see what I brought home!"

Mrs. Vandiver entered the living room wearing her favorite "serene green" painting smock, which hung around her neck and tied in the back. It had a multitude of different sized pockets across the front to hold rags and brushes handy. Her hands were speckled with paint. Mostly gray. At the sight of her son, she emerged from her faraway place of thought and emotion and wonder. In a rare moment she wished she could capture in paint, she stared at Cal, sitting on the floor by his dad, smiling.

"What's all this?" she asked with all the anticipation of watching her child on Christmas morning.

"Jack got stuff for me," Cal explained. "Training stuff." Cal opened the first of the black boxes bearing the bright green logo. "Look! Zulegen gear!"

"What's Zulegen?" asked his mom, surprised to learn there was an athletic brand to which she had never been introduced.

Everything Call pulled out carried the Zulegen label. For the pool there was swimwear, including a towel and a pair of goggles. For cycling and running there were jerseys, shorts, socks, shoes, and water bottles. Like the boxes they arrived in, each Zulegen item was marked by the company logo, which looked like the letter "Z" tilted slightly to its left, the bottom stroke becoming an arrow pointing northeast.

"It's a German brand," Cal's dad explained to his wife, holding a running jersey up to his chest. "The only place I've ever seen Zulegen—or Zulee, for short—has been at the Olympics. A lot of the American teams wear it." Tossing the jersey back to Cal, his father asked in all seriousness, "Do we have a load of great gear, or do we have a sponsor?"

Cal stopped suddenly. The question hadn't occurred to him. Surely Jack had just gotten his hands on some overstocked sportswear. There was no way he could have found him a sponsor, especially when he'd never even competed beyond the local level.

"I think sponsors come later—way later, like when the athlete can actually make it through a workout without feeling, well, like I do now." Cal was aching along every inch of his body. In a moment of panic he wondered if he could really pull it off.

"Son, have you *ever* been sore before?" his father asked.

"Don't think so," Cal shook his head.

"Another first," his dad chuckled. "Welcome to the human

race! You're finding your limits, which no one has ever asked you to do before." Cal breathed deeply, and his panic subsided. It was time for a cool bath and chocolate.

Later, resting on his bed, Cal imagined how he'd look in his new gear. Having it—Zulegen stuff—somehow made a shift for him from just talking about the Games to really believing they were in his future. Jack believed in him. But how could his new coach be sure Cal was worth his investment?

For the first time, it occurred to Cal that Jack might know way more about him than he knew about himself. After all, he'd had access to Cal's records kept by the center over the years. Is it possible that he might even know something about his birth parents? In a strange way, Cal wished that he could be sharing this experience with them too, whoever or wherever they were. The thought brought Lilli to mind. With his last ounce of strength, Cal shot off a quick email to her:

> What's up? Let me know what I'm missing. Everything okay with your mom? I'm sore all over. Guess you know what that's like from dance. See you at school. Cal

The light from the computer went out, followed by the lamp on the bedside table. Cal easily drifted into a deep sleep dreaming in neon green.

...

Thankfully, Jack gave Cal some say-so about how they would structure Saturday workouts. Rather than 8:00 a.m., Cal successfully argued that a 10:00 a.m. start would give him some much needed recovery sleep plus time for a mega carb-fest before his four-hour training session. Though he didn't mention it, Cal also thought he just might have time to hang with Levi before he had to go to the Y.

An hour before he was to meet Jack, Cal was on the phone

to Levi, waking him, of course. A groggy Levi agreed to walk down to his buddy's house, making no promises about his level of alertness or his attention to personal hygiene. When Levi arrived, Cal was just getting ready to dig into a bowl of angel hair pasta with a mound of Parmesan cheese on top. Cal's mom opened the door for Levi who stood in wrinkled jeans and a t-shirt with pillow hair that made him look a little lopsided. Levi shuffled his way to the dining room table, pulled out a chair, and sat down next to Cal.

"Dude, you are awesome!" Cal was genuinely grateful to his friend for giving up his much-anticipated Saturday sleep in.

Levi thought his annoyingly exuberant buddy must have already downed his high-calorie GameOn drink. "You got that right," Levi complained. "I'm missing my beauty sleep."

"Pasta?" Cal offered.

Levi's stomach lurched at the thought of eating, and he was desperately trying to ignore the strong smell of the cheese. "No, thanks, really." Despite the food smells, Levi was glad to have a few minutes with his best friend. "So when you headed out?"

"In about an hour," Cal answered. "What're you up to this weekend?"

The question took Levi by surprise. He wasn't used to thinking about the weekend without Cal. "Nothing much," Levi answered and then remembered he hadn't told Cal about the news his brother shared at dinner the night before.

"Hey! Derek got a job!" Levi blurted with excited relief.

"Very cool," Cal responded. "Bet your dad's loving that. What is it?"

"He, like, dropped out of Cal State, right?"

"Right."

"Now he's working for the school on a project."

"You kidding?"

"For real. He gets some money every month for working, and then they give him a year of school for free when it's done."

"No way," Cal responded. The unexpected news served

as another reminder to Cal that life didn't move along predictable lines. Not anymore.

"And get this," Levi attempted to share the details he could recall, "he'll be using computers to do a study or something about Asians in the U.S. It's for the College of Social Sciences, I think."

"Tell him congrats for me," Cal said, then shared his own plan in the making. "I'm thinking about doing a little research myself."

"What do you mean?"

"Like, what if Jack knows a lot of stuff about me? Maybe about my birth parents or where I got these freaky blue eyes?"

"That'd be cool," Levi answered, even as he wondered where Cal's sudden interest in his birth parents had come from. As far as Levi could remember, the topic had never even come up between them.

Cal cleaned his plate and leaned back in his chair. "Hey, we got a few minutes. Care to join me for some running stretches?"

"Is that all you do—run?"

"Next week I start swimming and cycling too. Right now I think Jack's just trying to figure out how long I can run before I die on the track." Cal stopped suddenly and broke into a wide smile. "Hey, you know what? I'm gonna give you a little reward for dragging yourself out of bed this morning!"

From Cal's room, Levi suddenly sounded very loud and very much awake. "Zulegen! Really? Thanks, dude!"

# 17

"You move beautifully," Carissa complimented Lilli after her Saturday class. "So what do you think?"

Lilli wasn't sure if she was being asked to comment on Carissa as a teacher or about her introduction to modern dance, so she decided to cover both. "I thought you were great, really. I love the music and the way you showed us how to express our emotions in movement."

"Wow," Carissa was clearly pleased that at that least one student enjoyed her impromptu class.

"Will you be teaching us next week?" Lilli asked hopefully.

"On Monday for sure," Carissa answered, reaching up to re-tuck a loose black strand of hair into her wide red knit hairband. Today her nail polish was red too. "If there's enough interest, maybe we can hold some mini-sessions next week when my mom gets back." Then she qualified her statement, adding, "If she'll agree to it."

Lilli was hesitant but couldn't resist asking, "Do you think I might be able to learn enough to do a modern dance piece for my recital?" The recital, just two months away in November, was one of the two major presentations for the dance school each year. Already Mrs. Cohen had been asking Lilli about her recital plans, though Lilli suspected it was because her mother would have a "baby bump" to display.

Carissa shrugged and smiled, "We can ask, right? I think you have the talent, but you'd have to be willing to work really hard and put in some overtime with me."

"I'd love that!" The words spilled out of Lilli more quickly than she'd wanted. She didn't want Carissa to think she was silly.

"Practice some of the moves we did today, and we'll chat again during class on Monday. Maybe you can stay after?"

Lilli nodded enthusiastically. For Lilli, it was a moment bigger and more exciting than her very first dance lesson when her mother called Lilli "her little ballerina." The buoying effect of parental gushing had long since lost its ability to motivate Lilli; she was ready to decide what made her feel happy.

Later that night, in her bedroom, Lilli decided to do just as Carissa had suggested: practice. All of her CDs were of classical music, the kind she'd danced to since she was four, so she opened her computer and picked a pop radio station to stream. Then she sat on the hardwood floor, closed her eyes, and listened closely—for the first time—to the music that most of her friends knew word for word.

It was an upbeat song that played, and yet, Lilli was moved to tears. The emotion expressed in the music and the lyrics overwhelmed her. Love. Disappointment. Freedom. Following Carissa's instructions, Lilli began to visualize how she might express these emotions in the movements she'd learned. Soon she was dancing and feeling fresh joy in expressing herself in a new way. While her training had been excellent, Lilli realized she didn't want to be choreographed anymore. Dread over the upcoming fall recital was replaced by an excitement about the presentation she would create in a few short weeks.

# 18

The cramp in Cal's left calf started in mile four, just as it had on his first day of training. Dropping down into the grass, the runner wondered if he'd made any progress at all.

"Cramp!" Cal called out to his coach who watched from the sidelines. Jack jogged over to a grimacing Cal, a cold gel pack in hand. Jack patiently took charge, first massaging Cal's left calf muscle and then applying the cold compress.

"More stretching and longer warm-up," Jack commanded. Such clipped instructions had made up most of the dialogue between coach and athlete to this point. It seemed to Cal that everything he did was wrong.

"I did what you told me," Cal answered in his own defense.

Jack looked up at Cal suddenly. "Then you do more," he responded, launching into a mini-lecture. "Your body! You have to know what it needs, how much it needs, and how often. That's your job."

The pain subsided and Cal was more than a little amazed at how quickly Jack had eased his suffering. He also felt some embarrassment that this man, a professional trainer, humbly sat next to him in the grass, expertly moving his hands over Cal's calf muscle until it relaxed. Cal knew Jack didn't have to be in Smallsville, California, looking after an unknown, unproven thirteen-year-old kid. What he didn't know was why Jack had chosen to be there.

"Why do you care?" Cal asked with hesitation. The sincerity in the question gave Jack pause. Without looking up he removed the cold pack from Cal's calf and put it back into the black zippered bag of supplies he always carried with him. Then he raised his eyes to Cal's.

"Because I am a coach." It was the truest answer Jack could offer. "You train to be an athlete; I am trained to be a coach."

"But why are you doing it here—with me?"

To his experienced ear, the trainer understood that the young athlete was communicating his fear of letting him down. Jack too had wrestled with the question in the beginning. This was not the place, nor the job he would have anticipated for himself. The center called and offered him an exorbitant fee to observe and report back on Cal. In part, it was a favor for a friend.

For weeks he watched the boy as he swam, ran, shot hoops, and kicked the soccer ball. Jack had never seen such a talent. To be part of ushering such an athlete to greatness was every coach's dream. He had requested to become Cal's trainer, and the center had offered to compensate him and provide any and every possible resource he might need: Zulegen gear, for example.

"Your mother is an artist?" Jack asked Cal at last.

"Yes, she paints."

"Who is her favorite painter?"

It had been a long time since Cal had talked to his mother about her art, he realized with some embarrassment. When he was younger though, his mother often sat with him, leafing through the pages of *Great Paintings of the World*.

"She loves Monet." Cal answered Jack with relative certainty.

"Can she paint like Monet?"

"No."

"Ah, but she understands what makes a great masterpiece." Cal sat silently. It was the most he'd heard Jack ever speak at one time. "I was once an athlete at the university in Beijing. Not bad. But my gift was seeing what it took to make a great athlete." Now Jack smiled, "I told my friends, 'Lengthen your stride!' or 'Do these stretches before you swim!' In time they learned to listen because I was right."

"Don't you ever worry that you might be wasting your time with me?"

Jack's response was confident. "Then I would not be here."

"You know a lot about me, don't you?" Cal he looked intently at Jack. "Do you know about my past?"

"Ask me how to massage a cramp—I can help you. But I don't have the information you seek."

"But you've seen my records that go back to when I came to California."

Jack rubbed his chin in thought. "I know little of your past." Then he looked into the darkening sky as if to consult the clouds. "But if I had a guess, I'd say that a newborn would not survive a trip here from China without his mother. And if she came, it would likely mean that she planned to stay."

"How did you know I was here as a newborn?"

"This I learned from the center."

"What else?"

"Judging from your physical abilities," Jack continued, "I would guess that your mother was a Chinese athlete, or maybe in love with one. If so, she was hoping to start a new life after shaming her Chinese family with a pregnancy and no marriage." Jack stopped suddenly, wondering if he had said too much. "But I am not a detective, and I don't read tea leaves. Now run!"

Cal pulled himself up, drained his water bottle, and stepped back on to the track. Even though his calf muscle no longer hurt, he was off his game. Distracted. What if his birth mother *was* in the U.S.? The question brought Derek to his mind. Maybe his new job would give him access to such information.

...

It was beyond obvious at dinner that the artist-mother was anxious to get back to her studio. She never even took off her painting smock. When Cal offered to clean up the dinner dishes, she was immediately up and off to her studio with a wave. Tonight Cal welcomed the task, hoping it would interrupt the mental cycle of playing and replaying Jack's speculations about his parentage. His stomach had been knotted since their discussion earlier, and there was a slight but steady throb in his head.

To his frustration, he felt no better when the job was done. He had to know more. Peeking through the doorway into the studio, Cal saw his mom, seated on her stool, very still, again studying the three-canvas series that sat on easels. Quietly he entered until he stood next to her.

The canvases were no longer colorless. The initial layers of paint had been applied. A story was emerging.

"What do you see?" his mother asked, sensing her son's presence.

Cal knew better than to throw out a simple, "I like it," to his mom. She would demand a creative response to a creative process. "You don't tell a chef that his fine meal was 'tasty'!" she'd lectured him on countless occasions. "Describe it! Was the dish mildly sweet or jalapeño hot?" And so Cal made an effort to be descriptive of the unfinished work before him.

"Blues and grays touch all three pieces," he began. "The second has the darkest shades and the heaviest paint, like a storm." He continued, "Something different is happening by the third canvas though. The darker shades begin to swirl together with lighter ones until they fade to a calm."

"Well done!" remarked the artist. Fully aware that Cal was not in her studio simply to admire her work, she turned to him. "Now, what can I do for you?"

"I'm back on the adoption thing."

"Okay."

"Jack has a theory."

"Oh, really?"

"He guesses that my mother—my birth mother—was probably an athlete and brought me to the U.S. to give *both* of us a new life." Cal gave his mom a minute to change mental gears. "What do you think?"

"This is a new interest," she commented after a moment. "I'd have thought you had quite enough to think about these days."

"I don't know how it started exactly." Cal suddenly felt awkward. "It's just that if either of my birth parents were athletes, wouldn't they think it was cool that I was training for the Olympics? I would want them to know."

"Of course you would," the artist-mother turned on her stool toward him. "And there have been about a billion things *I've* wanted to share with them through the years—school artwork, soccer photos," now she smiled, "the bills for your shoes."

"Hope you're not mad, you know, about me wanting to know more."

"Don't blame you a bit. We didn't ask a lot of questions when you came home." She brushed hair from her forehead, marking her skin with gray paint as she did. "It was such a miracle. I guess we were caught up in the excitement of everything."

"Is there any reason why we couldn't ask those questions now?"

"I guess not. I think we'd all like some answers. There was a lawyer that contacted us on behalf of the center. I'll ask Bruce to give him a call."

"Here, let me clean you up with my permanently pruned finger." Cal removed the paint smudge above her brow with his thumb.

"A lot of good it does to clean up the dishes," remarked his mother. "You'll be eating again in—what—" she held up her watch and squinted to read it, "about ten minutes?"

"Too true," Cal nodded and turned toward the kitchen.

...

As it turned out, the friends made a way to spend time together. Cal and Levi kept their Saturday morning routine, and on Sunday evenings, Lilli was usually available too. They used the time to catch up.

"Dude, you gotta help me!" Levi complained to Cal as they sat with Lilli in the Price's garage. "My parents can't stand me hanging around here every day, instead of with you. They want me to join some clubs after school to stay busy. Like I want to spend even more time at school, right?"

Thanks to Derek, the garage had been recently upgraded with the addition of a secondhand couch placed next to the sagging loveseat; a plastic crate full of books served as a footstool.

Cal stretched out, working his sore calf muscles as he listened to his buddy describe his dilemma. "You have a serious decision before you, bro. May I suggest the Young Chefs Club or perhaps the Tweens Book Circle?"

"Not funny! This is your fault, you know."

"You can come learn modern dance with me," Lilli suggested, adding salt to the wound.

Ignoring Lilli, Levi continued his rant. "Now that Derek has reclaimed the title of Boy Wonder, my parents are all over me: I'm lazy; my grades aren't good enough; I'm not playing sports."

"You can run track in the spring," Cal suggested in all seriousness.

"Maybe," Levi responded grudgingly, "but what until then? How am I going to survive?"

"Maybe Derek can find something for you to do at his work," Lilli offered.

Levi suddenly looked as if he'd had an epiphany.

"What?" Lilli asked warily.

"That's it!" Levi exclaimed. Cal and Lilli exchanged a look of alarm. "Don't you see? Now that Derek is working, he'll have to pay *me* to do the chores that got dumped on him when he left school. Plus, he picked up some odd jobs—like walking Oscar, Mr. Ludlum's schnauzer, in the afternoons, and trimming the Hornsby's hedges on the weekends."

"Glad to know someone's got a little spare time," Cal remarked, already thinking about his run with Jack the next day.

"Serious," agreed Lilli. "I need to double the hours in my days to be ready for my dance recital."

"I'm so going to be in the money," Levi continued, his exuberance growing. "Take a back seat, big brother! I'm actually going to have something to do—and make money doing it!"

# 19

On the way to the Y Monday afternoon, Mr. Vandiver promised Cal he'd try to contact the law firm that handled his adoption thirteen years before. "We want to explore this with you," he assured Cal.

But it was something else his father, ever the educator, said in the car that stuck with Cal. "Remember—the greatest explorers of all time met challenges and disappointments along the way." After a brief pause he finished his thought: "The point is that their findings were, in the end, most significant for those who came behind."

Cal immediately thought of Lilli, how she'd talked about needing to find what she felt she'd lost when she traveled across the Pacific to her new home. He had dismissed her questions about her past as irrelevant, even selfish. As he saw it now though, a search for family was anything but selfish. Any answers he or Lilli could uncover just might change someone else's world forever.

"Later, Dad." Cal grabbed his Zulee bag as they pulled into the parking lot of the Y.

"No way I'm leaving just yet." Mr. Vandiver pulled up

alongside a truck bearing the name TriTech and hauling an impressive-sized trailer.

"That's not for me, Dad."

"I think it just might be."

His dad was right. Jack emerged from behind the trailer along with a slender, thirty-something man, wearing a polo shirt embroidered with the TriTech logo. The two men approached the Vandiver car, and Cal's father lowered his window.

"What's going on?" Cal called across his father to Jack, determined to find out exactly what it was he was getting himself into.

"What did I tell you we were going to do this week?"

"Swim and cycle."

"So what did you think you were going to ride—that clunker I saw you on, the one that fit you about a foot ago?"

Cal's dad reached for a box on the floor of the back seat. "Good thing we kept your new cycling shoes back here."

"Great," Cal remarked.

"Bruce, we're going to fit your boy on a tri-bike today and let him get a feel for it."

"Thanks for the warning. My guess is he's is about to discover some muscles he never knew he had."

"Oh, and I have a present for you, Bruce." Jack jogged to the trailer and picked up a black metal something with straps that was leaning against the trailer tire. He carried it to the car. "It's a bike rack that attaches to your trunk."

"Splendid," Mr. Vandiver said, considering the potential for additional scratches on his car. "Let's just put it inside the trunk, and I'll have it on when I come back later." When the bike rack was loaded up, Cal's father was off with a wave.

"Cal, meet Mr. Dixon," Jack introduced the man at his side, blonde with a receding hairline. He smiled and shook Cal's hand.

"Good to meet you, Cal," Dixon said, adding, "Jack here seems to be expecting big things from you!"

The three walked to the back of the trailer where Dixon opened the double rear doors and let down some steps. "Come on inside, and we'll do what we call a 'bike fit.' It's the single most important part of preparing for a triathlon." Dixon was quick to add, "—other than having a great coach!"

For Cal, riding a bike had always been a necessary evil to get from point A to point B. But he always preferred foot power. There was nothing he liked about the idea of giving over control of his body to a contraption with handlebars, pedals, and wheels. Was this something he could refuse to do?

The inside of the trailer was admittedly impressive. It was, essentially, a bike shop in a box. Along the walls hung rows of neatly arranged tools and bike parts. On the right side was a workbench that ran the length of the trailer; on the left was a fold out work stand that held a built-up blue and white bike frame with a TriTech decal. Two more frames hung on hooks from the top of the trailer.

"One of these frames will fit you, and each one has been customized according to specs required for the Games," Dixon promised Cal. "I have three sizes here. I'm betting on this one." Dixon slid his hand along the frame hanging on the work stand. "It has the best features of both the tri-bike and the road bike. You're going to love it."

"Cool." Cal rubbed at the muscles tightening in his neck.

"Let's get started." Dixon pulled out his measuring tape. "I bet you're anxious to get on the road."

Take all the time you want, Cal thought to himself.

An hour later, Dixon had checked and rechecked Cal's measurements and helped him select a seat, handlebars, pedals, and helmet. As Dixon worked, Jack talked about TriTech, which Cal learned was one of the premiere names in the industry. Dixon was known for customizing each bike to its rider. Most weekends, the truck and trailer were parked at the biggest triathlon and bike races in the nation, offering quick repairs and technical assistance as needed.

"Do me a favor?" Dixon asked Cal, as he finished buffing

out fingerprints left on the gleaming bike frame.

"What's that?"

Dixon reached into the cabinet under the workbench and pulled out a pair of cycling shorts and matching jersey. He tossed them to Cal. "Wear these sometimes when you're out." Dixon smiled at Cal. The gray and black cyclewear bore the TriTech name.

"Can I wear them now?"

"Sure, we're done here." Dixon climbed out of the trailer and started to close the trailer doors. "And when you're geared up, we'll take some test rides and make sure everything suits you."

A few minutes later, Jack was staring proudly at Cal who at least looked the part of a cycling veteran. "You're almost ready," he commented.

"Almost?" Cal was out of patience. It has been nearly two hours. Jack reached into his bag and pulled out some cycling sunglasses. They had black frames and blue lens that extended around the side of his face to block the sun at every angle. They were jaw-dropping cool.

"I think he likes those better than the tri-bike!" Dixon laughed.

Cal took the glasses from Jack and slid them up snug on his face. "These are definitely the finishing touch on a completely awesome package."

"Let's see how the 'package' can move." Jack gestured for Cal to begin cycling around the running track. After a couple laps and some final tweaks to the bike, Dixon packed up the trailer and pulled out of the Y, leaving Cal with an awesome new tri-bike and outfitted with the best possible gear. Expectations would be high. In truth, Cal wanted to ride well for Jack; he just wished he actually wanted to ride.

# 20

The next day, Cal learned Jack had mapped out a twelve-mile loop for him that began in the quiet neighborhood behind the Y, alongside roads Cal never knew existed. Jack gave him a listening device and followed the cyclist by car to keep him on course and to offer pointers along the way. The goal: work up to a fast twenty-five-miler required for an Olympic triathlon. Cal hit the road, quickly building speed.

"Cal, you're working too hard too soon," Jack's warning sounded in his ear. "You've got to pace yourself!"

"I'm okay, Jack!"

The tri-bike felt foreign to Cal. The seating position was steeper than he was used to, placing him closer to the handlebars, or what Dixon called the aerobars, which were padded and extended out to support his entire forearm. As it was explained to him, these features made bike and rider more aerodynamic and provided greater control.

"Slow down!" Jack's voice hit his eardrum again. But Cal couldn't resist pushing himself, hoping to impress his coach.

Traffic was picking up, and Cal was separated from Jack when a black spray-painted car suddenly pulled out of a driveway, forcing its way between them. The same car then pulled around Cal by mere inches. The car windows were up, but Cal could tell the bearded man was shouting expletives at him. After that, Jack turned on his emergency blinkers to draw attention to the cyclist.

The incident left Cal feeling shaky with images of lying in a hospital room in a full body cast. At last, Cal and Jack arrived back at the Y where Cal noticed the same black car parked at the Wok2China. The driver would eat a quick meal of chicken and fried rice and never know that he had nearly ended the career of an Olympian.

By this time, Cal also began feeling nauseous; whether from exhaustion, dehydration, or just nerves, he couldn't be sure. Jack walked over to where Cal was lying in the grass next to his bike, moaning softly.

"Two lessons for you, one for me," Jack began.
"Number one?"
"Drink, drink, and drink some more."
"Number two?"
"Save your push for the end of the ride."
"And what about you?"
"Never take you out on the road with maniacs again."
"I like that one."

...

At home, Cal gratefully dug into a heaping plate of his mother's chili-macaroni. By the time he'd finished, he was beginning to feel the weight of exhaustion overtake him. It was only days into his training, and Cal was already feeling weary, not to mention sore—again. True to his dad's prediction, Cal was feeling the pain of muscles he rarely worked. The tops of his thighs burned from pedaling hard and fast; his forearms ached from holding the new position on the tri-bike; and his back was tight where he bent low for the ride.

On his bed, Cal attempted to sort through the worries of the day. Did he have homework to knock out? Where was his backpack anyway? Did he even have anything clean to wear? Then Cal remembered the black box with the green neon logo Jack handed him earlier, just before his father swept him away to recover for the night.

"I hope this is a box of candy bars," Cal had said as his coach stood at the car window, passenger side, waiting for the boy to open his latest gift.

"You would like that, I know." Jack nodded at Cal to open the box. "Ah—something much better for you!"

As he lifted off the top, Cal wished hard for the smell of chocolate, only to be met with the irrefutable scent of leather. Inside were sleek black, cleated shoes and shin guards.

"Soccer cleats?" Cal's voice clearly communicated his incredulity.

Jack resorted to the stern tone of trainer. "You will need them this week for your team practice."

"Soccer practice is two days a week!" Cal's arguments came tumbling out. "Why would I be on the school team? What about training? What about homework?"

Jack was prepared for Cal's resistance. "One hour of soccer practice equals one half hour of training," he laid out the plan. "On Sundays we will cut outdoor training by one hour, so you can watch soccer on TV."

Cal hung his head in defeat. "And what about homework?"

"You will rise earlier in the morning to finish homework and ask your friend to make sure you know your studies. I will pay him for this job."

More change. Cal felt his panic building. "Who's going to pay for my trip to the loony bin?"

"Cal—" His father reminded him to mind his manners.

"I am asking you to trust me," Jack spoke with surprising empathy.

"I'll try," Cal answered but did not look up.

"Trust is a muscle that must also be trained."

Remembering the scene, Cal felt ashamed. He had disrespected Jack. Still Cal knew the truth of the matter: He was, in fact, untrusting. He doubted his parents' decisions on his behalf, his trainer's ability to take him to the Games, his ability to be a good teammate, and even questioned whether he would pass the eighth grade.

Though weariness swept over him like a wave, Cal slipped off his bed and sat at his desk with his computer. He missed his friends like crazy. Opening his email, Cal smiled when he saw he had messages from both Lilli and Levi. He opened Levi's first. It read:

> Guess what? You know the idea about taking over Derek's jobs at home for money? It worked! I walked Oscar, Mr. Ludlum's schnauzer, today. He isn't nearly as friendly as he looks though. The mutt bit me! I forgot to give him a treat before the walk. FYI, you might want to pack your lunch tomorrow. Hot lunch is salmon patties. See you.
> Levi

Cal smiled at the thought of Levi trying to get a leash on a disappointed and angry Oscar. He wondered if Levi would keep all his fingers when he started work on the Hornsby's hedges. He wrote a quick reply:

> Some people will do anything for a little cash! Ha! Better luck with Oscar tomorrow! Hey, want to stay after school while I go to soccer practice this week? Jack says I have to go. Thanks for the tip on the salmon patties. I like salmon. That's one thing I have to look forward to. See ya. Cal from California

Next he opened Lilli's email:

> Greetings from Babytown. After dinner tonight I

> helped my mom paint like eight different squares of colors on the wall of the nursery, so she can see what she likes (even though we don't know if I have a brother or sister). She's also picking out baby names. For a girl, she wants a name that has something to do with light—like Shine or Shimmer or Summer. Great, huh? For a boy she wants to go earthy—like Canyon or River. Go figure. Hey, I think I have a song picked out for my recital. I'll play it for you even though you are tone deaf (Ha!). Lilli

Cal laughed out loud and quickly typed a reply:

> Congrats on picking out a song! Tell me about it at SOCCER cheerleading practice on Thursday. Yep—can you believe it? I could really use a little Lilli boost from the sidelines. See you at lunch for sure. Good news! Salmon patties tomorrow! Do you like salmon? Cal

Closing up his computer, Cal thought that hearing from his friends was the best possible end to his overwhelming day. In bed he reached over to his side table, turned on his alarm, and then turned off the lamp. He loved the feeling of the darkness, of shutting down. Nobody could expect anything from him for the next seven hours.

# 21

As soon as the bell rang Thursday afternoon, Cal hurried out of the school entrance, finding a sunny spot to sit at the side of the school building that looked out over the fields. With only fifteen minutes before soccer practice, Cal reached inside his backpack and pulled out two peanut butter and jelly sandwiches and some pretzels, all of which had clearly taken a beating over the course of the day. He dove back in for a can of GameOn and a bottle of water.

Once he was finished with his meal-sized snack, Cal reached into the very back and biggest zippered pocket of his backpack and pulled out his cleats, socks, and shin guards. Hauling around his gear in his book bag all day had been grueling. He made a mental note to bring a separate sport duffel on practice days.

"Dude! Those are some awesome cleats!" Levi plopped down beside Cal, nodding with approval at the new gear and taking a whiff of the fine leather. "Yes! The good stuff!"

"Thanks for coming, Levi. You know, if you have stuff to do ..." Cal felt a little embarrassed by how much he needed Levi.

"I volunteered to get in a run and catch a ride home with you."

"Hey, speaking of riding together—you want another paying gig?" Cal baited his best friend.

"You know it!"

"So Jack has a plan he thinks will make it remotely possible for me to train *and* play soccer."

"Yeah?"

"He's suggested that we ride together to school, so you can make sure I have my act together for my classes. Said he'd pay you for your trouble."

"Piece of cake!" Levi was already considering a reasonable—or least an acceptable—amount he could extort from Jack. In addition, Levi received ten dollars from his grandmother for every A he earned, which he'd have more of simply by helping out his friend.

Looking out at the field, Cal saw something that made his heart jump. "Oh, man!" he exclaimed, interrupting Levi's fiscal calculations.

"What?"

"On the field! Jack is with Coach Lombard!" Cal pointed to the right side of the field where Jack was helping the coach pull the soccer goals into position.

Levi hadn't seen Jack since they cornered him on the bleachers at Cal's soccer tryouts. "What's *he* doing here?"

"I don't know. He didn't say anything about coming today." Cal shook his head warily. "But I bet it means I'm going to be icing or soaking some part of my body tonight."

"It's just middle school soccer," Levi remarked, trying to offer a little perspective.

"Not a chance," Cal said with resignation. "If Jack is here—it's training."

As Cal and Levi headed toward the field, they caught sight of Lilli walking down to the bleachers. She waived her mini purple and white pom-poms at them. Cal recognized them from years before—preschool maybe—when for months Lilli refused to come to class at the Chinese Cultural Center without them.

Cal broke out into a big smile. "Hey! My soccer

cheerleader's here!" The three met up at the same spot where Cal's friends had their first conversation with Jack.

"I can't believe you made it! I so need a cheerleader!" Cal's surprise was genuine. "Now all I need is a medic on standby!"

"Well, it is a big day," she commented. "Oh, and when I have *my* big day—also coming up—I'll be *very* excited to see both of you there."

"We will definitely be at your recital," Cal said, nudging Levi.

"You bet. The recital. We will be there," Levi promised, "though probably not with pom-poms."

Looking across the field, Lilli's expression turned sour. "Is that Jack?" she asked.

"The one and only," Cal responded. "I better get down there or I'll have both my coaches yelling at me."

Levi and Lilli watched as Cal jogged to the group of boys assembling on the field. "Want a running partner?" Lilli asked. Together they started a slow jog around the track.

Meanwhile, Miguel fell in alongside Cal in the group warm up run from one end of the field to the other.

"¡Hola!" Miguel greeted Cal with his usual big smile.

"Dude!" Cal responded, reaching over to meet Miguel's fist bump. Just as Cal found a relaxed cadence with his teammate, Miguel picked up the pace.

"It's not a race Miguel—just a warm up."

Miguel turned to throw Cal a sly smile, as if daring him to try to keep up. Cal took the bait. He accelerated enough to catch Miguel. But each time Cal caught up to him, Miguel would run harder until both boys were sprinting across the field. At that point most of the team stopped to watch the competition. Cal managed to pull ahead of Miguel, but not without some effort. It was a good sensation—being challenged, Cal thought. He couldn't remember a time when he had really needed to pull out all the stops with a peer.

Jack cracked a knowing smile.

"Save it for the field," Coach Lombard yelled out onto the field.

While the race was over, the competition was not. Miguel approached the day's scrimmages as if he was playing for the World Cup. Coach kept them on opposing teams, and both players kept the ball coming, surprising the goalies again and again with smart ball position and powerful kicks. Coach Lombard noted that the other players, most of whom were inexperienced, stepped up their game to support their "stars."

"A little intense out there," Cal remarked to Miguel later as they walked from the field. "What, you don't believe in playing for fun anymore?"

Miguel shrugged. "I love to play for fun." He nodded his head toward the two coaches standing together. "I was just doing what I was told." Ah, there it was. Only one person could have forced Cal to dig deep at a practice he typically would have blown through with minimal effort: Jack.

# 22

The air in Guangdong was dirty. All along the province on the southern coast of China, black smoke billowed out of the factories, eventually reaching the nostrils of Chan Ming Ming. Along with most of their neighbors, her parents worked long hours in a black monster that tried unceasingly to block the blue of the sky. What was made there Ming Ming did not know. Yet even her young eyes could see that the factory produced excellent slaves, giving its workers just enough income to survive, while stealing any joy to be found in family time, in rest, in dreams. Chan Ming Ming, without parents and without siblings, felt very much alone in the world.

At an early age Chan Ming Ming showed remarkable academic promise, particularly in math and sciences. Her parents could barely pay for her books and uniform, and not a day passed that they didn't remind her that she must pass the National Higher Education Entrance Exam, or Gaokao. If she passed, she would be allowed to enter a university; if she did not, she would be nothing.

Driven by her necessity to succeed, Ming Ming finished her mandatory nine years of school—plus three years of high school—at the top of her class, easily passing the Gaokao. Approached by many schools, she was especially excited to receive an invitation to apply to the University of Hong Kong. Ming Ming's emotions fluctuated between joy and terror. Just the thought that she might escape the pollution and poverty of Guangdong made her giddy with anticipation, which quickly dissolved into a panic about the truth of her circumstances: she had no means of paying her university expenses and no one to turn to for help.

It was her father who first suggested that Ming Ming join the Chinese Communist Party, the CCP. He, like many others of his generation, saw membership in the nation's sole political party, corrupt as it was, as key to a better future. The subject arose once again when Ming Ming met with the HKU admissions director who spoke of the opportunities afforded students who join the CCP as a show of devotion and gratitude to the motherland.

Ming Ming listened closely to the stern-faced man who gave a well-rehearsed spiel. But she couldn't help noting the layers of dust that covered much of the man's desk, his books, even the back of the chair in which he sat. Is this everything that the man had wanted? Perhaps it was, Ming Ming reasoned. Maybe working there in the world of academia had been his dream. It was certainly better than working in the rice patties as her grandparents had done, or laboring endlessly in the factories of Guangdong. Before the end of her interview, Ming Ming agreed to pursue membership in the party and, in turn, received her acceptance letter to the university.

Making money to go to the university became Ming Ming's obsession. She turned her attention to the busy tourist trade in Hong Kong. Already she had easy access to materials in and around Guangdong where factories supplied the world with electronics and cheap goods. She began to brainstorm.

The result of months of tedious night work with her father was a product Ming Ming called the Glo-Me charm bracelet.

The fashion accessory consisted of eight flat interchangeable "charms"—colored plastic tabs—that lighted at the touch of a finger. The idea was that the wearer could complement their clothing by lighting as many or as few charms as they liked, changing the colors or patterns on the Glo-Me again and again. To further its appeal to the internationals, each charm bore a Chinese character that represented a sentiment, such as love.

The entrepreneurial effort had been a dangerous one. Ming Ming's father traded herbs with those having access to materials, primarily discarded items from the factories. But it wasn't long before the product was showing up in retail outlets, from boutiques to high-end tech stores at airports. Sales were brisk, but Ming Ming was taken entirely by surprise when she was asked for an interview and photo session with the country's most popular fashion magazine, *ELLE Hong Kong*.

Ming Ming arrived for the interview dressed in her school uniform, the most presentable outfit she owned. A stylist was immediately called in to transform her unremarkable appearance, giving attention first to wardrobe, then to hair and make-up. It was at the close of her interview that the editor of the magazine politely suggested that Ming Ming consider a more "cosmopolitan name" to match her updated look. An English name. In that issue, Ming Ming debuted as Jewell Chan.

It was not the new name, however, that drew the interest of Chinese officials and the nation's manufacturers; it was the power source for the product. To light the charms, Jewell had perfected a chip-sized battery, which was powered by energy from the human body. The Glo-Me would never need a battery replacement as long as a human was wearing it. The thermoelectric technology that Jewell had harnessed over her summer break had eluded Chinese manufacturers who had, for years, put such technology on the back burner in response to pressure to produce more products, cheaper and faster.

Shortly before her university classes got underway, Jewell was called to a second meeting with the HKU admissions director, whom she thought was markedly more pleasant the second time around. By the end of their meeting together, the man, whose face cracked into a wax-like smile, was pleased to offer Jewell a generous sum that would certainly cover the cost of her education and living expenses while at the university. In addition, she learned that she had been selected for a position with the country's prestigious Ministry of Science and Technology in Beijing upon graduation. In exchange, Jewell had only to sign over all rights to the technology used in the Glo-Me to the Chinese Communist Party.

For Jewell, it was a moment of triumph. Her burden had been lifted. She had finally found a way to escape the dinge that had been her childhood.

...

The conversation ended with a faint click on the other end of Jewell Chan's headset. It was official. After two grueling years, Jewell had brought to completion the sole project she had been assigned since joining China's Ministry of Science and Technology.

"You have served your country well," Wong Bao, her boss, told to her by phone from his office three doors away.

Within the ministry there was no celebrity—only duty. Even so, twenty-three-year-old Jewell Chan indulged a congratulatory smile. In the beginning, Bao had assured her that this project would accomplish truly great things for China, unlike the Glo-Me, which he had told her repeatedly was "frivolous." From her cramped technology lab on the outskirts of Beijing where she'd put in long days for little money, Jewell felt she had earned her parents' pride.

Upon her arrival at the ministry, little had been said of the project that was assigned to her. As Wong Bao explained it, a critical "asset" to China had been "kidnapped" thirteen years before. Years had been spent searching in China to recover the unidentified asset without success. Now the team had been directed by the CCP to expand the search to the United States.

Toward that end, a plan was conceived in which the Chinese government would "partner" with a U.S. entity to conduct a study of the Asian population in America. An enormous grant came with the offer. Further, China officials graciously offered to supply the complicated computer program that would be used to collect, track, and report on results.

Developing that program was Jewell's job. Per Wong's instructions, the program was built to include specific search criteria designed to identify the asset, as well as fugitives of China, even as it accomplished the larger task of collecting information on the Asian population as a whole. As she was warned, any information discovered as a result of the "sub-search" for the asset was not to be shared with her American partners.

Unquestioningly Jewell dove into her work, with a strong sense that some of her country's most powerful leaders watched her progress.

At last it was completed.

In the phone conversation with her superior, Jewell learned she would continue on as the lead on the project. This would require a temporary relocation. Looking around, it was hard for her to imagine a place beyond the tiny office that had been her world for two years. But as she was told, she would oversee the study—and the asset search—in California.

It was decided that the study would be accomplished at CSU, Fresno and ownership was assigned to the College of Social Sciences. With no budgetary obstacles to slow the process, plans to implement the project got underway. Supervision of the project fell to College Head Dr. Tan, who was tasked with pulling together the best possible team for the job. That team, of course, would have to include computer wiz Derek Price.

# 23

The sign for the Law Office of Trey Foster looked as though it could use some updating. The less than impressive ground signage leaned a bit to the right, and there was a crack in the lower right corner of the acrylic cover. Though the house-turned-office sat on a small lot, the landscaping had been neglected. Cal's stomach did a flip-flop as his dad parked the car on the street in front of the building. This was the place where he had become a Vandiver?

As promised, Mr. Vandiver had, after numerous attempts, managed to make contact with Trey Foster, the young attorney who had contacted them on behalf of the center thirteen years before. At the time, Mr. Vandiver noted that Foster, who had just opened his law office in fast-growing Hanford, not far from Visalia, was bright and ambitious—ambitious enough to be selected to take part in an extraordinary venture involving the Chinese government and the U.S. Center for Adoption.

The two climbed the steps from the street onto the brick walkway that led to the front door of the office.

"Not exactly what I was expecting." Cal observed the weathered door marked by an outline of a missing kick plate.

Mr. Vandiver pushed the doorbell and smiled a bit self-consciously at his son. "Ah, humble beginnings. It'll make a great story for the sports channel someday."

A rumpled Trey Foster opened the door. The three exchanged hellos. If Mr. Foster had been expecting the Vandivers, he hadn't gone to much trouble to spruce up either himself or his workspace. Together they took turns stepping over piles of papers and the occasional book that made the parquet floor look a bit like an ongoing game of checkers.

"My assistant is out of town this week." Foster attempted to explain the disarray, as he made his way toward the large mahogany desk situated between two windows in what was once the living room. Directly behind the desk was an unkempt floor-to-ceiling bookshelf that reminded Cal of Levi's overstuffed backpack. For a moment he thought he smelled pimento cheese.

Cal and Mr. Vandiver seated themselves in the only other remaining furniture in the room—two burgundy leather wing back chairs that faced Foster's desk. They were the same furnishings Cal's dad remembered from his last visit when it seemed Foster's practice was a sure bet for success. Now it appeared as though he'd met a few obstacles along the way.

"It means a lot that you made time to meet with us on a Friday afternoon," Cal's father said, adding politely, "I hope your family is well."

Mr. Foster fiddled nervously with items on his desk. "Fine, fine. The practice keeps me busy, you know." Cal looked around for a picture of a family or the artwork of a child on the desk or bookshelf but found none. Even if Foster *did* have the brains to earn a law degree, Cal couldn't help feeling a little bit sad for the still-young man with old eyes.

"You look quite the athlete, Jamison!" Foster said to Cal as if just noticing his presence.

"I play soccer," said Cal, throwing his dad a look of complaint. "Oh, and I go by the name Cal these days."

"I see," Foster responded with disinterest.

"So," Cal's father made an attempt at small talk. "Has the center kept you busy over the years?"

There was a pause and Mr. Foster bit his lip thoughtfully before answering. "I am not currently pursuing adoption-related cases," the man answered, at last, intimating that the arrangement with the center had not been as lucrative as he had hoped. "Fortunately, I've been kept on retainer with the USCA for any follow-up work that might be necessary."

"Follow-up work?" Cal's dad inquired. Once the adoption papers were signed, Foster had never attempted to contact the Vandivers.

"Well, like you coming here today," the man offered by way of example. "You have questions, I'm sure. I hope I can assist you." Now he looked at Cal.

"I'm interested in finding out what I can about my birth parents," Cal blurted out what Foster already knew was coming.

"Understandably." Foster attempted to hide his rising panic, leaning back and forth in his squeaky chair. Foster had long worried about the day the Vandivers would again darken the door of his law office. His apprehension of this very moment had taken a toll on him, his family, and his practice.

"Can you help us?" The boy's father broke the silence.

"Certainly you remember, Mr. Vandiver, that the center has strict privacy rules, and I believe you understood those rules at the time of the adoption. This was not an open adoption."

Cal felt his anxiety climbing.

"I do remember the terms of our agreement," the boy's father answered, the irritation his voice was not lost on his listeners. "However, it has been nearly thirteen years, and I'm certain the center is aware of the importance of addressing questions of adoption and heritage, particularly at adolescence." Cal thought his dad looked and sounded more like the attorney at the moment. He continued, "And it may be that the birth mother may now be agreeable to exchanging information or meeting with her son."

"That might be the case," Foster responded. "It will take a little time for me to research the matter and to approach the center on your behalf. I'm sure you understand."

"Surely someone has approached you with a similar request over the years," the boy's father probed.

After first clearing his throat and rearranging the pens on his desk absentmindedly, the attorney responded: "I am not at liberty to discuss whether or not there have been other such requests or how they might have been received by the center." Looking up from his desk, he glanced from father to son. "I will, however, give you my word that I will do my best to assist you—both of you."

"When?" Cal jumped into the exchange.

"When?" The attorney returned the question, adjusting the lopsided knot of his tie.

"I think Cal is asking when we might expect to hear back from you."

The attorney sighed with resignation. "I think three weeks would be a reasonable estimation."

Cal and his dad stepped out onto the brick walkway in front of Foster's less than distinguished office with the man's business card and a vague commitment to look into the matter. Three weeks seemed an excessive amount of time to Bruce Vandiver, considering Foster admitted to being "on retainer" with the center. To Cal, it sounded like eternity.

Cal's mother stood at the door when her husband and son pulled in the driveway. "How'd it go?" she asked, reading dejection on their faces.

"Hard to tell," came her husband's less than enthusiastic reply.

"But that man was always so helpful before."

Inside Cal dropped onto the couch. "Yeah, well I think we

must have met Mr. Foster's totally disinterested evil twin."

"Bruce, is he going to help?"

"He says he'll get back to us in a few weeks." The sigh that followed conveyed his doubts. "I don't think it's a good idea to get our hopes up though. There's no money in it for Foster, at this point, and he doesn't seem to be in the mood to help anyone—not even himself. Seems he's hit on hard times."

"If it doesn't work out, it's cool," Cal said, surprising both his parents.

"But you want this, and we want it for you."

"Why?"

"Because your past is yours," his mother said with conviction. "And it's a story that shouldn't be lost. There may come a time when you need it."

# 24

It was a full hour after the Vandivers left the law office of Trey Foster before the man raised his head up from his desk. The culmination of years of anxiety around this day, together with the realization that he now had to contact the center with the news, left him exhausted. He had fallen into a sleep of escape and awakened with a jolt. It was time.

He wished that he hadn't tried to mentally avoid this moment for so long; it had been years. Maybe then he'd know where his procedure notes had been filed—or piled—away. It was too late now. While Liz could help him, she probably wouldn't. His wife and sometimes office assistant had taken the kids to her parents' home where they were spending more and more time.

Picking up a pen, the attorney attempted to get down to business, jotting down the exact time of the Vandivers' visit and making notes as to what questions had been posed and what answers given. He spent hours unearthing the agreement they had signed with the center thirteen years before and reviewed it over a microwave meal and a cup of strong coffee. At midnight he took a deep breath and dialed the center; in Hong Kong it was nine o'clock in the morning, and the business day was just ramping up.

"U.S. Center for Adoption." A woman with the high voice and thick Chinese accent answered the phone. "This is Waiyin."

He'd recognize that voice anywhere. Not much personnel turnover at the center. Waiyin couldn't walk away from the center any easier than he could. Everyone knew too much.

"Good morning, Waiyin." Foster attempted to sound cheery. "How are you? This is Trey Foster calling from Hanford, California."

"Ah, Mr. Foster. Either you are up very late or very early," she quipped.

"Let's say I'm getting a jump on a busy day."

"Ah," she began. "That means you need to talk to the Professor. Am I right?" She knew the answer full well.

"I'm afraid you are exactly right." At this Waiyin laughed.

"I will have to leave him a message, of course. He will be in touch with you in a short time."

"Thank you, Waiyin." When he got off the phone, the attorney pulled the two leather wing backs close into a makeshift couch and waited, caffeine and adrenaline coursing through his body.

An hour later, Foster's cell phone sounded. The call came from a number he hadn't seen for years.

"Professor," Foster answered respectfully.

"Mr. Foster," the man returned. "You have news this morning?"

Foster hesitated. Yes, he had news. Whether it was good or bad news for the Professor he did not know.

"I hope you will be pleased."

"So?"

"Mr. Vandiver and his son—Jamison—came to my office yesterday," reported Foster.

"You refer to Cal."

"Yes, Cal, as he prefers to be called," Foster replied, embarrassed to have the Professor point out his error.

"And their request?" The Professor asked what he already knew.

"The boy would like information on his birth mother and to meet her if possible."

The Professor's voice turned all business. "And what did you tell them, *exactly*?"

Though his heart pounded, Foster attempted to keep his voice calm. "I advised my clients that I would contact the center with their request and would be in touch with them in two to three weeks with a response."

"Today you begin to follow the procedures given to you regarding this matter, without the slightest deviation," the Professor commanded. "You understand the importance of our success on your career, Mr. Foster?"

"That was made quite clear to me, Professor." Foster wondered if the man was aware of the lackluster state of his law career. When the center contacted him initially, he envisioned years of lucrative work, but in the end, only one referral was made to his practice by the center: the Vandiver adoption. He had struggled to find a niche for his practice ever since.

After a brief pause Foster dared to ask, "Professor, is this good news?"

"It is *inevitable* news, Mr. Foster. And as long as we follow the plan, it will be good—very good, indeed. Should we fail on any detail, however, the loss would be devastating. Failure, therefore, is not an option."

Hanging up the phone, Professor Si Zhen—known simply as the Professor to his many contacts around the world—turned in his chair to gaze out his second story window. He took in the gray-blue of the sky, the impressive modern facilities, and the students scurrying to morning classes. Checking his watch and taking a final gulp from his coffee mug, the man grabbed his briefcase and headed out to teach his first class of the day.

# 25

Minutes into the performance of her recital piece for her long-time dance instructor, Mrs. Russ, Lilli let go of her self-consciousness; she became lost in the movements she and Carissa had choreographed for her contemporary song. No longer was she continually analyzing her every movement as she danced, from her pointed toes to the position of her hands; but after seven weeks of studying with Mrs. Russ' somewhat avant-garde daughter Carissa, Lilli was, once again, experiencing the shear joy of dancing.

When Lilli first heard the song "Undercurrent" on the radio, she knew it would be perfect for her recital. Carissa had agreed. Recorded by the pop artist Tiffany Grace, the song was upbeat with varying rhythms and powerful lyrics that inspired their dramatic choreography. And while the song was clearly about a past love interfering with a present one, Lilli felt it also described her own struggle living an all-American life that was often unsettled by the reality of an Asian heritage.

But a simple shake of the head from Mrs. Russ would put an end to seven weeks of arduous practice, and the three and a half minute performance Lilli dreamed of dancing would never make it to stage.

When the music faded, Lilli glanced first at Carissa, who was looking tentatively at her mother who sat watching from a folding chair. Was Carissa holding her breath?

Just as the silence of the studio grew awkward, Mrs. Russ spoke. "Do you two know how many years it has taken to build the reputation of this school?" Silence. She answered her own question: "Twenty-four years!"

Lilli's heart skipped a beat as she listened to the woman she'd worked so hard to please through the years. With sleek gray hair pulled back severely into a bun, the woman had retained her strong, slender figure and regal manner. "And do you have any idea *how* this school gained the reputation for being the finest ballet school in the region?" Mrs. Russ continued her monologue.

Now Carissa spoke up with more than a hint of sarcasm: "Because it hasn't changed in twenty-four years?"

Mrs. Russ snapped her head at Carissa. "Because we teach ballet exclusively—not Broadway, not jazz, not modern."

"And yet I, your daughter, dance and teach modern," Carissa dared to add. "It was my strong ballet background that led me here." Now it was Lilli who held her breath.

With a sigh of surrender, Mrs. Russ settled the matter. "We will make this dance a 'special presentation' of our visiting instructor Carissa Russ at the fall recital. That way we will avoid any rumors that modern dance will formally be taught at this school." Before leaving, the woman gave Carissa a nod, which her daughter knew to mean "job well done." Then Mrs. Russ turned to Lilli and looked her up and down, taking in the young woman she'd become. "I've never seen you dance more beautifully. Congratulations, Lilli."

# 26

Even though he was about to begin an actual job, Derek was painfully aware that he would still be making less money than his younger brother Levi, who was now tutoring Cal and drawing income from the odd jobs that he'd been forced to give up. The monthly stipend Derek would receive working in the CSU College of Social Sciences wouldn't cover much more than his day-to-day expenses. And he still had to live at home with four annoying siblings. Daily he reminded himself that when the project was over, CSU would cover the cost of his senior year, and he could live on campus. It would all be worth it.

And today was the day it all began.

The team would be complete with the mid-morning arrival of the Chinese representative—Ms. Chan—and the project would officially get underway. In preparation for the day, Derek grudgingly had his hair trimmed to just above his shoulders with the result that he was continually tucking stray strands behind his ears. He did, however, like the look of his clean khakis and pressed button down shirt, which he thought announced his new station in life.

Just before 10:00 a.m. Dr. Tan announced Ms. Chan's arrival. Derek looked out the window to the street to see a black limousine parked at the main entrance of the building. A limo? Really? Suddenly the fact that he was the CSU team lead didn't seem so impressive. He was about to meet the real brains behind—well, whatever it was he was getting paid to do. His stomach churned with nerves and caffeine.

...

Jewell Chan arrived in San Francisco the night before after a twelve-hour flight from Beijing. Her assigned driver whisked her to a five-star hotel where she enjoyed a late but delicious in-room dinner. As she ate, she sat in awe of the elegant room, which was more spacious than her apartment in Beijing. It was clean, completely clutter-free, and everything her eyes fell on was refreshingly unfamiliar. Then there was the king-sized bed, complete with a chocolate mint on the pillow. She wouldn't miss her musty futon.

Thankfully, Jewell had arranged for a wake-up call from the hotel the next morning, or she might have slept the day away wrapped in the plush terrycloth robe that she found in the bathroom, compliments of the hotel. Once she was finally dressed in the pale green linen business suit the ministry had provided for her, Jewell was taken by limousine to the doors of the CSU College of Social Sciences in Fresno.

Once there, the Latino chauffeur opened her door. "Have a nice day, Ms. Chan," he said, bowing slightly. "I will pick you up here this evening at five." He handed her a business card. "If necessary, do not hesitate to call me to make other arrangements." Jewell nodded, took the handle of her locked briefcase, and attempted to gracefully exit the vehicle and steady herself on her pumps. As the limo pulled away, she stood by the large glass doors of the building waiting for the arrival of Dr. Tan as she had been instructed. As she waited, she worked to smooth out the wrinkles in her linen skirt.

Moments later she faced her new coworkers.

"Lady and gentlemen, I'd like you to meet my counterpart on this project, direct from Beijing—Ms. Jewell Chan." Dr. Tan nodded respectfully to Jewell. The team responded with polite applause. While looking every bit the savvy businesswoman, with her dark hair pulled up into a twist and only a hint of color on her lips, Jewell was clearly embarrassed by the attention. To make matters worse, the typically chatty team was at a loss for words. They knew nothing of their new partner and even less about the project before them. Dr. Tan jumped in with introductions.

"Ms. Chan—" Dr. Tan started.

"Please call me Jewell," she interrupted softly.

"Certainly." Tan gestured in Derek's direction. "Our team lead on this project is Derek Price who is with us full-time." Derek smiled and nodded, a strand of hair breaking loose as he did. "Most of your time will be spent training Derek, so if you are not familiar with the Star Wars movie series—you soon will be!" Dr. Tan drew a laugh from the team and a smile from its newest addition. At least she has a sense of humor, Derek thought to himself and wondered just how close they were in age.

"And when you've had quite enough of Derek, you have a devoted worker in Stephen Le, who is a student here." The two Chinese members of the team exchanged hellos. "Do not, however, ever trust Stephen around doughnuts," Dr. Tan added with a chuckle. "They may not be a favorite in China, but around here they go fast!"

Jewell played along. "I know doughnuts. Doughnuts were served with my breakfast today!"

"Oh—at your hotel?" asked Stephen. Jewell answered with an enthusiastic nod. "Where are you staying?"

Jewell took a moment to recall the name, "I stay in San Francisco at the—Pinnacle?"

There were oohs and ahs all around, and Stephen released a low whistle. Everyone but Jewell knew that the Pinnacle was among the finest—and most expensive—hotels in the city.

Dr. Tan hurried on, turning to the final member of the team. "Finally, I'd like you to meet Suzanne Hemp who comes to us as a transfer student from the University of Minnesota. We made sure Suzanne stayed on with us by telling her this was a summer job. So she's been waiting for winter to come to California!" Again, there was laughter all around. The ice had been broken, and everyone was beginning to relax a little. Dr. Tan turned to Derek.

"Anything you'd like to add at this point?"

If Derek had a few bucks to spare, he would have liked to ask his new, attractive co-worker to dinner. "I'd just say that we have been anxiously awaiting your arrival, Jewell." Derek hoped he looked smarter than he sounded. "We hope that you and the ministry will be pleased with what we accomplish here."

"Thank you very much," Jewell responded. "I believe that this will be a most memorable experience." At this Dr. Tan invited Jewell and Derek to join him in his office. Jewell picked up her briefcase and followed.

In his glass office with a view to the campus, Dr. Tan apologized to Jewell and Derek that he would have to excuse himself to teach a class, but invited them to sit at the small round worktable in his office. "I'm sure you both have questions. If it's okay with you, Jewell, perhaps you and Derek could take this time to talk about 'next steps,' if you will."

"Of course," came her reply. Dr. Tan left, an extra bounce in his step; by all appearances, his plan for fame and fortune was on track.

Derek and Jewell looked at each other. "You have a very nice boss man," Jewell commented.

"He is a bright man and a hard worker." Derek nodded in agreement.

"I mean, he seems to be more like a member of the team." Jewell tried to describe what she had just witnessed—for the first time. "He seems like he cares about all of you."

Sensing her surprise, Derek realized Jewell could not have worked in many—if any—American settings before. "It's how we do things; at least that's the goal, to work together."

"I like it."

"Have you been to California before?" Derek probed.

Jewell looked a little embarrassed at the question. "No, this is my first trip out of the country." It dawned on Derek that the hotel, the limo—it had all been part of a show put on not by the esteemed guest, but by the government that sent her.

"Well, this is absolutely the best place in the U.S. to visit," Derek assured her. "So, boss lady, what can you tell me about what we're here to accomplish?"

When Dr. Tan did not reappear, Derek and Jewell continued meeting, gradually covering the small conference table with project notes. Through the course of the day, Derek and Jewell took only two breaks: one to grab a sandwich at the student cafeteria, commonly called the Café, and another at the Starbucks across the street where Derek ordered espresso for himself and hot tea for Jewell.

"I remember when they opened the first Starbucks by my work," Jewell reminisced as they sat at a window-side table for two, watching students pass. "It was my first year at the university."

"So you are a fan?"

"I never went inside the Starbucks—until now!" Jewell shook her head, suddenly amazed and embarrassed at her own lack of curiosity.

"You didn't try it out?" Derek searched the face of his new friend, a highly intelligent woman who seemed disconnected even from her own fast-changing culture.

"I had money for books and some food. That is all I needed," she shrugged. Now, sitting in the fashionable shop that catered mostly to college students, sipping her first chai tea latte with her new workmate, the young woman wondered if that would ever be enough again.

Every minute Derek and Jewell spent discussing the

program she developed to collect information on Asians living in the U.S., Derek was exponentially awed by Jewell's intellect—and her humility. It was as though no one had ever told her she was off the chart bright. The program would detect and link with databases, extracting requested information on Asian residents, details regarding everything from education and income history to shopping preferences and medical records.

By 5:00 p.m., the two had succeeded in drafting a timeline for completion of the project. It was left sealed in an envelope on Dr. Tan's desk.

Catching a view of the limo outside the building, Derek turned to Jewell somewhat reluctantly. "Uh, I think that's your ride."

"You are sure?"

"Very big, very black limo. Hmm, is that yours—or mine?" Derek laughed. Though she smiled at Derek's joke, Jewell felt annoyed to be told when her workday was over. She was not used to stopping simply because the clock told her it was time. After a moment, she hesitantly reached under the conference table and grabbed her briefcase.

"What time do you get here in the morning?" Already Jewell was anticipating her next workday.

"I'm here at eight, coffee in hand."

"Starbucks?"

"Nah. That's a bit expensive every day. I drive through the Coffee Cup. I'll bring you coffee tomorrow, if you like—or would you prefer tea?"

Jewell thought a moment. "Coffee, please." She smiled as if taking her first dare.

Offering a quick wave, Jewell headed for the door, nodding good-byes to Stephen and Suzanne as she went.

Derek watched as she disappeared into the black limo and wondered what she would do all alone in San Francisco. Dreading his evening at home, Derek stayed until Stephen and Suzanne left for the day. Then he stepped out of Dr.

Tan's office, the door locked behind him. It was then that it occurred to him how he might make his evening in the Price house of horrors more interesting. In the privacy of the garage, on his resurrected computer, Derek decided he would poke around the Internet to see what more he could learn about his Chinese co-worker.

# 27

It was three weeks to the day when the Vandivers heard from Trey Foster, attorney at law. When the call came in, Mr. Vandiver was still at the school, and Mrs. Vandiver was in her studio, lost in her work. It was later, when she stepped into the kitchen to prepare dinner, that she noticed the flashing light on the answering machine. Her heart jumped, as it had again and again over the past week. She started the message.

"This is Trey Foster calling," the message began. Surprised—and alarmed—Mrs. Vandiver reached to stop the message. It was a phone call that could change their lives; she would not listen to it without her family. Instead she went about her activities in the kitchen as if it were any other night, setting the table, layering the lasagna—one of Cal's favorites. Her husband arrived first; still she said nothing. A little later, she heard the front door open again.

"I smell lasagna!" Cal's announced upon entering. After weeks of tri-bike training, Cal had been given the green light to travel to and from the Y on his own, parking the bike securely in the garage each evening.

"Maybe it's spaghetti," his mother tested her son.

"Not a chance," Cal continued with certainty. "There is cheese, lots of cheese!" The delight in Cal's voice made her smile. Cal's dad emerged from his study.

"Hey, Pop—" Cal addressed his dad playfully. "So you think you're going to get some of this lasagna too?"

"Hey, I worked hard today," his dad returned good-naturedly. "What did you do? Ride your shiny new bike around the Y? What a goof off!"

Mrs. Vandiver was glad everyone was in a good mood; she thought that might make hearing the news—whatever it was—a little easier. "Okay, okay, have a seat. Your day isn't over," she reminded Cal, referring to the homework that still awaited him.

"Hear that? *My* day isn't over," Cal repeated. "Sounds like I deserve at least seconds or thirds of lasagna, Dad. So don't hog it all."

When all three Vandivers were seated for their much-anticipated meal and the end-of-day catch up session, Mrs. Vandiver dared to break the news.

"We had a phone call—" she started. All eating and chatter halted.

"Foster?" Mr. Vandiver ventured. He had stopped asking after two weeks of no contact from the attorney. His wife nodded.

"What'd he say?" Cal asked anxiously.

"I thought we'd listen together. He left a message earlier." She walked into the kitchen, reached over to the answering machine on the counter and hit PLAY.

"This is Trey Foster calling," the message began, and each braced themselves for the news. "I hope everyone there is well. I wanted to let you know that it would seem all parties are agreeable to a meeting between Jamison—uh, Cal, excuse me—and his birth mother. This meeting will take place in three weeks, and I will be available to accompany Cal on behalf of the center. We can discuss details going forward. Just give me a call at my office. I look forward to assisting you."

After a moment in which no one could speak, the family looked at each other wide-eyed. Finally Mr. Vandiver spoke, "Three weeks?" A second later the boy's father was on his feet, pacing and thinking loud. "Do they expect us to get Cal a passport, pull him out of school, and fly him to China in *three* weeks?"

Mrs. Vandiver sat, her hand over her mouth, in shock. Suddenly Cal slapped his hands on the table and stood with his father, a look of revelation on his face.

"Jack was right!" His parents looked at him, bewildered. "She's in the States—not in China!"

"You don't know that," his father dismissed the theory.

"Call the man, Bruce!"

"He's not going to be at the office now."

"Could you try, Dad?"

At his family's dogged insistence, Mr. Vandiver took his cell phone from its case on his belt, pulled up the number, and dialed. When it began to ring he put the call on speaker, so his family could hear that, in fact, they weren't going to get their answers so late in the evening. Surprisingly, after the fourth ring, a female voice answered.

"Trey Foster's office."

Cal's father didn't know which surprised him more—that someone answered so late or that Trey Foster did, in fact, have an office assistant.

"Good evening," came Mr. Vandiver's startled voice. After taking a few seconds to recover, he asked, "Would it be possible to reach Mr. Foster, please?"

"Your name?"

"Bruce Vandiver."

"Of course, Mr. Vandiver. He is expecting your call. One moment." The line went silent, and the Vandivers exchanged glances.

"Trey Foster," the attorney's familiar voice came on the line, sounding upbeat and confident.

"Mr. Foster—Bruce Vandiver—thank you for being available to take our call."

"I certainly didn't want to leave you all hanging over the weekend," Foster answered. Mr. Vandiver thought the attorney's tone suggested that he was, in fact, doing them a favor, rather than providing a service.

"Thank you. That was very considerate," Mr. Vandiver demonstrated the phone etiquette of a seasoned headmaster. "I have my family listening in, if that's alright."

"Of course," Foster replied.

"What can you tell us at this point?"

"Well," Foster started, "the news was better than we could have hoped for, to be honest. The center agreed to let me attempt to contact the birth mother, and she was agreeable to meeting with your son."

Cal felt a little dizzy.

"Further, she is right here in California—in Mendocino, in fact—so there won't even be the complication of overseas travel. What do you think about that?" Foster sounded proud of himself.

It took few seconds for Mr. Vandiver to find his words. "That's—that's incredible. She's right here in California?"

"I so called it!" Cal whispered excitedly to his mother who sat motionless, hanging on every word of the conversation.

"So what do you say, Cal? Ready to make the trip up to wine country to meet your birth mother?" Foster asked.

"Yes, sir!" Cal answered. "Anytime!"

"Well, it won't be for another three weeks as I understand it. But that doesn't seem to be too much to ask, does it? Tell you what—in a couple days I'll have a few dates and times to choose from, and we'll set it up."

"We'll be waiting for your call then," Mr. Vandiver echoed his son's readiness to make the meeting happen.

"Good evening, everyone," Foster ended the call.

For Cal, the moment was surreal, almost as though he had stepped into a suspense film.

Later in his room Cal worked out his adrenaline rush by doing some floor exercises. The pain in his abs helped him manage his panic but did nothing to stop the questions that bombarded him. Did he do the right thing? Did he really want to make room in his already crazy existence for another mother? Had she known he was in California? Was it possible she'd been following his life?

Before attempting sleep, Cal crafted an email addressed to both Lilli and Levi. Levi would be excited, for sure. But for Lilli, he knew the news would be a painful reminder that she also had a birth mother—somewhere. His fingers hesitated over the keys, and then he typed:

> Hi guys—Guess what? Got news that my birth mother lives in CA. I'm going to meet her in a few weeks. Now we'll find out where I got my striking good looks! Ha! Gonna try to sleep. Jack in the AM! Cal

Sleep. Cal knew he better find a way to rest. Jack would demand that his young Olympian-to-be bring 100 percent to training in the morning. Even if his whole world had been rocked the night before.

When sleep finally came, it was fitful. In one dream, Cal rode a tri-bike, and no matter how hard he pedaled, he couldn't increase his speed; he was failing. In another one he met his birth mother. In the dream she was looking at him for the first time; her expression was one of disappointment. This was the dream that frightened him the most.

Cal was up the next morning, but Levi didn't show. After dressing for his scheduled swim with Jack that morning, Cal headed to the Y. He was taking warm up laps when Levi strolled in, dressed in his tropical trunks with a towel around his neck.

"Dude!" Cal called to his buddy. "You set off any alarms with those trunks on the way in?"

"Hey," his friend responded with a laugh, "I'm the red cape, and you're the bull. Bet you get your best time ever, thanks to me!"

When Jack arrived to see Levi on the scene, he moaned. "Sit down," Jack ordered Levi. "Make yourself useful." Jack pushed a black bag across the floor to him. "You run the video camera while I take time."

"Deal." Levi agreed to his assignment with the hope that he just might score a tip for his contribution.

"No talking," Jack warned Levi, as they watched Cal move through the water. "I'll tell you when he's ready."

Talking wasn't a temptation for Levi. From behind the lens of the camera, he was speechless. For years he'd watched Cal take laps but never with the strength and intensity that he now saw.

...

The workout at the pool had, in fact, been brutal. By the time Cal arrived home, every muscle in his body screamed. Cal heard his dad moving down the hallway toward his study. Commanding his body to move, Cal dragged himself and his duffle that direction. As soon as his dad caught sight of him, Cal stopped, flashed his dad a pained smile, and waited for the anticipated exchange.

"Break any Olympic records today, son?" Mr. Vandiver asked just as he was about to step into his study. When Cal didn't answer right away, his dad stopped and looked questioningly at his son.

Cal ruffled his still wet hair, as if giving deep thought to the question. Then he met his father's gaze and nodded in response.

"As a matter of fact I did," Cal spoke at last. "Just the four-hundred meter freestyle," Cal pretended to shrug off the news. "No big deal."

"You beat the current record for your age bracket?" Mr. Vandiver asked, his eyes wide and intent.

"Actually, it was the Olympic record," he answered with nonchalance. "Not bad, huh?"

"The record for the Olympic Games?"

"Ah—" Cal continued the game, "—that's only if you go by what Jack says. You know how he exaggerates stuff."

Cal's father rushed to give his son a congratulatory pound on the chest. "Good thing I gave you such awesome genes!"

# 28

After Cal crashed for the night, his parents conspired together to pull off a surprise celebration brunch for Sunday morning. It was the only morning Cal had "off," that is to say he slept until 8:00 a.m., ate leftovers from dinner the night before, then watched recordings of the "best soccer games ever played," according to Jack.

Mr. Vandiver started on the phone, rounding up guests, apologizing for the late hour, while his wife brainstormed about Cal's favorite breakfast foods. Most of what Cal ate in the mornings would turn the stomachs of even the hungriest teenager—lasagna, spinach macaroni casserole, meatloaf. Instead she decided on deli items, fruit, and an early run to the Sugar and Spice bakery.

The next morning, Cal pulled on his red Wildcats t-shirt and gray sweat pants. After doing some stretches, he settled into the chair in his father's study to watch his assigned soccer matches on the big screen. By the time his mother began welcoming guests at the front door, Cal was absorbed in Liverpool's come-from-behind win against AC Milan in the 2005 Champions League Final, Jack's personal favorite. Cal hadn't even stopped to eat.

"Come get some breakfast, Cal!" his mother called to him. Cal paused the game, wondering why his mother wasn't at work in her studio. "I have something special for you," she called a second time. Cal's stomach growled in response, and he went in search of hearty leftovers. But the smells that met him as he moved toward the dining room were altogether different from those he expected. Stepping into the dining room, Cal was surprised to discover a roomful of people—his family, trainer, and best friends—gathered around a table loaded up for brunch. "Congratulations!" they shouted in unison.

"No way!" Cal responded, looking around the room, his eyes stopping on Lilli just long enough to let her know he was especially surprised and glad she was there. "Food and all you guys—this is awesome!" Then he asked jokingly, "So if every time I do something like halfway okay, I get a seriously amazing party?"

"I guess you'll just have to break another record to find out!" answered his father proudly.

After polishing off a bowl of fresh fruit, Jack excused himself, but not before warning his Olympian-in-training to stay away from the chocolate-frosted doughnuts he'd seen the boy eyeing. "Though you have come far," he said to Cal in a half-serious growl, "there is a great distance still to go."

Cal was in no mood for Jack's relentless nagging. He had every intention of indulging himself with a chocolate-frosted doughnut. Later he also invited his friends to stay and watch the soccer game with him, which would also have peeved his trainer. But Cal reasoned that if he was going to make it through everything that was coming his way—meeting his birth mother, surviving Jack, and passing the eighth grade—he was going to need downtime with his friends.

"Glad I don't have to tutor you in soccer, dude," laughed Levi who sat next to Cal on the floor of the study, his legs crossed and a plate of doughnuts at his feet. Derek helped himself to Mr. Vandiver's super-snug computer chair, and Cal insisted that Lilli enjoy the roomy leather one.

"You'd pretend to be a soccer ball if you thought you could make a buck," remarked Derek. Levi dismissed his brother's comment as he happily cleaned his plate.

As Jack would have predicted, the game became background noise for the friends' conversation.

"So the school team's closing in on a district win?" Lilli asked Cal.

"And another team bites the dust," Levi jumped in with his TV announcer's voice. "Valley Oak Wildcats demolish the Maiden Middle Stallions 6-1 and advance to the finals with an astounding 9-0 record for the season!"

"You know what I think," Lilli offered thoughtfully. "Not to brag—but I think we're on a winning streak because it's the first year—ever—that the Wildcats soccer team had its own cheer squad."

"That's it!" Cal agreed.

"Okay, there is that." Levi rolled his eyes. "Then there's the small matter that Cal and Miguel are the dynamic duo!"

"Miguel *is* amazing," Cal threw out the compliment to his teammate who had more drive and more natural talent than any other young athlete he'd met. On the field, it was like they could read each other's mind. Coach Lombard had pretty much given the two boys full control of team practices, including brainstorming game strategy and assigning player positions. Halfway through the twelve-game season, only one team had even given them the slightest challenge—the Hanford Middle Trojans.

There had been other benefits to his new friendship with Miguel. More times than Cal could count, his Latino buddy had come to his rescue in sixth period Spanish class. In fact, Miguel was the reason Cal was passing the class; though Levi fully intended on cashing in on the small miracle.

Derek's phone chimed, signaling a text and interrupted the chatter.

"Sorry," he apologized to all the faces that turned to stare at him. Clearly everyone wondered who might be contacting him on a Sunday morning. Outside of his new job at CSU, Derek was a loner.

"Who is it?" Levi pried.

"Work." Derek threw his brother a look that said it's-none-of-your-business.

"Not buying it," insisted Levi. "You're the only geek at CSU who would be working on Sunday morning."

"It's someone *from* work—not at work," Derek replied. "And that someone wants to meet for coffee."

"Is this the girl genius from China?" Levi sounded slightly impressed.

"There you go stereotyping Asians," Cal quipped and turned to share the joke with Lilli.

"Not a stereotype, bro," Lilli responded. "Chinese *girls* are, in fact, all geniuses." Both laughed.

"For sure this one is," Levi commented. "She came to the U.S. just for this project at Cal State." Levi showed more excitement about his brother's recent employment than he meant to.

Derek had been dying to tell someone what he had learned in his personal research of Ms. Chan. Now he couldn't resist. "This won't mean much to a bunch of uninformed middle-schoolers, but my co-worker is Jewell Chan—the creator of the Glo-Me."

"Shut up!" Lilli exclaimed. "That is so cool!"

"What's that?" Cal turned from the game to stare at Derek.

"It's a fashion bracelet—thing—that lights up using the electrical charge of the human body. In the scientific world, it was the first working thermoelectric battery, and she developed it when she was only fifteen."

"So it's a big deal, why?" requested Levi.

"It's a big deal because it opened an entire industry. The battery's already being used for medical purposes. There's even a beta version of a cell phone that charges itself off the user."

"And she's working on this study—with *you*?" Levi asked. "Sounds like a waste of talent."

"While she is the brains behind the study, she can't do it all herself. It's a massive project. We'll be able to track every Asian in the States and find out just about anything about them." Then Derek stopped himself, "But I didn't tell you that."

"Track them, why?" Lilli asked.

"Classified." Derek knew Jewell alone could answer that question.

Cal sat up. "Will it track me?"

"It could, I guess, if we were to target California," Derek answered. "But for now, I think we're starting in the areas around Ivy League schools—Harvard, Yale, Columbia, you know."

"But if California *was* a target, then it could pick up information on both me and my birth mother, right?" Cal theorized.

"Probably so."

"Hey, maybe you could test this data thing on Cal's birth mother," suggested Levi. "And he could find out stuff about her. That would be awesome!"

"That's a not-so-dumb idea, actually." Derek spoke the words to himself, as if already working on the idea.

Suddenly Derek was on his feet. "Well, I better get going. I have an irresistible urge for some Starbucks coffee." Before leaving, Derek addressed the man of the hour. "Congrats, Cal, and keep up the hard work, man. Later guys—Dance Queen." At the door he turned and spoke to Lilli, "Maybe I can introduce you to Jewell sometime, if you wanted." Lilli nodded enthusiastically.

It was nearly noon by the time the surprise celebration broke up. Cal took over Lilli's still-warm spot in his father's chair. He couldn't stop thinking about the "classified" tracking system Derek described. Would it really be possible to find out about his birth mother? Had she been an athlete? Did she speak English? Then there were the questions no amount of data could answer: Was she agreeing just to meet him, or was she hoping to build a relationship?

Cal's dad stuck his head in his study. "Have a good time?" Cal noticed his father held the new Wildcats mug Coach Lombard gave him. His once-favorite Visalia Academy mug now collected dust in the cabinet.

"For sure!"

Cal's dad was about to find another location to enjoy his morning coffee, when his son called to him. "Hey, Dad?"

"Hmm?"

"I've changed, right?" Cal asked hesitantly. "I'm not the same as I was when I played community rec."

"You're about two feet taller," his dad joked. "And you haven't been asked to leave the soccer team for being a jerk."

"How will she know I've changed?"

His father knew Cal was referring to his birth mother. The mother he now knew lived a few hours away but who likely didn't know the first thing about her blue-eyed son.

"She'll only know what you tell her, so talk about what you think is important."

"There's too much," Cal responded in frustration. "What's the use?"

"If someone told you today that you couldn't meet your birth mother, that the deal was off—what would you do?"

Cal knew exactly what he'd do. "I'd try to find her myself."

"Yes, you would. So when the time comes, learn what you can and share what you can with the time you have. And remember," now his dad smiled at him, "your mother and I have seen the whole shebang—the good the bad and the ugly."

"I know that's right," Cal had to laugh. "Speaking of ugly," Cal looked his father up and down. "Maybe I can score you some Zulee wear."

"That would be appreciated considering what we put out for groceries around here. Otherwise, you're stuck with this."

"It could be worse."

The remark was the closest Cal had ever come to

complimenting his dad, and the boy's father savored the moment. Yes, Cal had most certainly changed, he thought. All of them had changed after years of navigating their journey together. Finally, they were feeling like a family.

# 29

The cool of the Starbucks and its respite from the glare of the California sun made Jewell feel especially glad to be there. The location was familiar to her now. Since her arrival, she had returned to the coffeehouse alone only a few times without Derek, perusing the brightly colored tea sets, coffee mugs, and music CDs on display. She discovered, however, that such outings left her feeling guilty for spending money or time unproductively. But today she had something to celebrate, and Derek was the only one she could think to call. Besides, being with Derek never felt to her like wasted time.

When Derek stepped into the coffeehouse, Jewell smiled and gave a timid wave to catch his attention. She sat at a table for two with steaming coffee cups waiting. Derek had never seen Jewell outside work hours. Today she wore her hair down, softly falling around her shoulders, and looked relaxed in a white polo style shirt tucked into blue jeans.

"Congratulations!" he said sitting down across from Jewell.

Her smile turned to astonishment. "You know?"

Derek laughed, and Jewell looked confused. "I don't know anything!" he confessed. "You just have that I've-got-a-secret look on your face."

"Really?" Jewell suddenly felt self-conscious. She wasn't used to anyone reading her face. "I don't really have a secret," she continued, "but guess what?"

"What?"

"I moved!"

"Serious?"

"I moved from San Francisco—to here!" she announced. "I have a new place to stay, and I can come to have coffee anytime!"

"You got an apartment?"

"Oh, no, but I have a room at the Lunar Eclipse hotel. It is very nice." Derek knew the Lunar, as the locals called it, was moderately priced and a short drive to the university. And while Derek could see how Jewell would be pleased to be closer to her work, he suspected the decision of when and where to move was made for her.

"It is good to live here," she said.

"You know, if you ever decided to get an apartment by the school, you could meet a bunch of students. That would be cool. Or maybe you could find a house at some point—something with a pool would be nice!"

There was an awkward pause.

"Is the American government going to buy *you* a house?" Clearly Derek had unknowingly struck a nerve.

"Uh, not a chance!"

"Why then would you think that my country would buy me a big house?"

"I wasn't thinking anyone would buy you a house. I was just thinking maybe you could buy one on your own, you know, if you thought you might be here for awhile." Derek paused before continuing, "I'd love to think that California agreed with you."

"I do not have any money," Jewell looked away from his gaze. "The ministry gives me a small salary. In Beijing, I pay for my own small apartment. Here, they pay for my room until the project is done. That is all."

Derek was trying to make sense of what she was saying and all he had recently learned about Jewell Chan the inventor. Was she just being modest as might be expected of an Asian woman?

"But you developed the technology for the Glo-Me—which is, by the way, completely awesome."

"That technology does not belong to me," she announced, her jaw clenched with emotion.

"But I thought you would have made your fortune—" Derek attempted again.

"I was fifteen," Jewell stared down into her mug of coffee now. "The only thing I wanted was to go to a university." Derek sat quietly, watching Jewell attempt to hide the tears gathering at the corners of her soft, almond-shaped eyes. "They gave me tuition and board at Hong Kong University and promised me a job with the ministry when I completed my studies."

"In exchange for what?" Derek felt his sense of justice rising.

"For the Glo-Me—and the battery. I thought it was my duty." Lilli dropped her head in her hands. She couldn't bear to see Derek disappointed in her. "You think of me as a fool."

"Never," Derek answered her gently. The honesty in his voice gave her courage to meet his eyes through her fingers. "When we are young, we have no power. And we do not ask questions." He gently reached up to pull her hands from her face. Then he seized the opportunity to lighten the moment. "I promise to do my duty, as a Westerner, to corrupt you, beginning now.

"How?"

"Lesson one is how to ignore the impulse to always do what's best."

Jewell had to smile.

"We begin by spending our hard-earned cash on some decadent dessert to go with our now lukewarm beverages."

"Do they have chocolate here?"

"I have no doubt that there are a numerous chocolate selections."

"And probably they are too big for only one person. In my country that would be considered wasteful," Jewell laughed at her own joke. "Would you share with me?"

Together they settled on chocolate silk pie.

...

Lilli woke up Monday morning, smiling. The song she would dance to in her upcoming recital had been the musical score for her dreams, and she was already looking forward to another week of rehearsals. While she purposely hadn't mentioned it at Cal's surprise celebration, the dance was progressing well—very well. Carissa even let Lilli make suggestions for the choreography and actually liked them.

Lilli's improved mood made for a happier Cohen household. Consumed by pre-and-post-pregnancy planning, Lilli's mother felt free to delete her daughter from her list of concerns. The new mother-to-be spent hours online shopping for the little boy they learned was on the way. Lilli's brother, it was decided, would be named Canyon. The nursery was coming along too, as Lilli's father was, at last, released to paint it a color called "eco-green."

What Lilli's parents didn't know was that their daughter had also taken on a new look, at least the one she would present on stage at her recital. Neither noticed the pink duffle Lilli packed for practice was considerably less bulky these days. No tights. No ballet shoes. In fact, that "exposed" feeling Lilli felt dancing barelegged and barefooted had taken some getting used to. On the big night, Lilli would wear only a sleeveless leotard that graduated in color from a deep ocean blue at the shoulders to a sandy color, not unlike her own skin, at the bottom; A sheer skirt with a touch of glitter would be tied at her waist and flow down past her knees. The dancer was fully aware that response to the first-ever modern dance presentation at the Visalia Ballet Academy could go either way.

She looked forward to Mondays and Thursdays when Carissa picked her up from school in her bumper sticker covered "jimmy," as she called it, with the top down. With a wave, Lilli threw her friends, waiting in carpool, a you-wish-you-were-me look as Carissa zipped through the parking lot.

"I have a surprise for you today, girl!" Carissa told Lilli as she swooped up her protégé after school, her voice barely audible over the radio and the air that rushed by them.

"Yeah?"

"You know how we've been talking about how to strengthen the end of the dance?" The wind wrapped both their faces in jet-black hair and in Carissa's case some blue as well.

"Got an idea?" Lilli yelled back.

"I think I have just what you need," she said with finality and a smile that made Lilli a little nervous.

A motorcycle was parked at the studio when they arrived. Inside the front door they heard Lilli's song selection, "Undercurrent," blaring from the large practice room at the back of the building. Carissa stepped into the room followed by a hesitant Lilli. Inside, Lilli's eyes fell on a dark, handsome, and muscular teenage boy who was putting hip-hop dance steps to her song. The dancer flashed the girls a smile but didn't stop. So Carissa and Lilli sat down cross-legged on the floor and watched. It took a minute for Lilli to make the jump from her own interpretation of the song to the hip-hop version. But she had to admit that the fast, strong movements punctuated the song with emotion in a surprising way. She watched wide-eyed, unaware that her jaw had dropped open slightly.

"Like it?" Carissa leaned over to speak directly in Lilli's ear.

"This is crazy good!"

Lilli was equally shocked by the dancer's hip-hop look, which included baggy black sweat pants that sagged just enough to show the top of his plaid boxers. His gray t-shirt with cut-off sleeves and cropped bottom succeeded in revealing the dancer's broad shoulders and lean, muscular midsection. Black high-top shoes with yellow laces, untied, matched his yellow braided wristband.

When song ended, the girls clapped, and the dancer took a low bow. Then he moved toward Lilli and extended his hand.

"Hi, you must be Lilli. I'm Ben." The boy—man—was at least sixteen, and his voice was low, his handshake firm. Lilli smiled shyly.

"So do you like hip-hop?" he asked Lilli, his brown eyes searching hers for a genuine reaction.

"I do now," Lilli laughed. "That was great."

"Very cool," he responded.

"Ben is a guest dancer with our troupe," explained Carissa. "When a song needs a little extra 'oomph,' he's the guy we call."

"Sometimes hip-hop can force an audience out of observation mode to actually experience the emotion of a piece," Ben explained. "And when it shows up in a dance that is primarily in a different style, it can make it even more meaningful and definitely more memorable."

"How's that gonna happen?" Lilli worried aloud. "I don't dance hip-hop."

"Maybe I could step into the dance with you at a couple points," Ben answered, looking over at Carissa.

At that moment, Lilli started feeling panicky, aware of how little time was left to get the routine performance ready.

"I think we need to introduce hip-hop at the song's most powerful point, which in this case is at the chorus," Ben suggested. "And since the chorus closes out this song, it'll give the routine a really powerful ending."

"What will Mrs. Russ say?" Lilli asked anxiously.

"It's all good," Carissa reassured her. Now she stood and motioned for Lilli to join her on the dance floor. "Let's do this thing!"

Feeling self-conscious, Lilli stood, wondering if any of her skills would translate to the new dance style. At the same time she wondered what kind of mess the windy ride to the academy had made of her hair.

# 30

Mr. Cohen was waiting for Lilli in the SUV after practice. She slowly eased her body into the front seat, her muscles already complaining about the demands of the new hip-hop moves. Lilli was glad her dad had come. It was reassuring to know he remembered she existed.

"Hey there!" He greeted her.

Lilli arranged her dance bag and backpack at her feet, making a pained grunt as she did so, then settled back gently into her seat.

"Wow, you must have had a tough work out," he commented, taking the speed bumps in the parking lot extra slowly. "You okay?"

"You might want to ask me again tomorrow," she attempted a smile.

"Thought you already had that recital piece down," he remarked, knowing that it was unlike Lilli to be anything short of perfectly prepared this close to the big night.

"So did I," Lilli answered with a weak laugh. "But we added a few new moves, some contemporary stuff. Pretty cool."

"That's great," he commented distractedly.

"The recital's next weekend, you know."

"I know!" he nodded and transitioned to the next order of business. "Hey, we've got some other cool stuff going on at home too." Lilli could tell her father was pumped about something, which made her a little nervous. "Guess what's happening at our house right now?"

"Uh, let's see, Mom's working with a team of designers on a new line of clothing for babies?"

"Not a bad idea, dumpling!" Lilli's father seemed to make a mental note. "But not today! Today mom is video blogging from home!" Pause.

"Why?" Lilli hadn't given much attention to the video recording, or vlog, her mom did every week that aired on the Internet. She did know it was usually shot from upscale or historical locations, shops, or celebrity hot spots.

"We've hit the big time! Things were feeling a little stale, so we phased out your mom's column and made a shift in the format and content of the vlog. It's crazy, but the media is loving the switch up, and it seems to really hit home with a lot of new viewers."

"So she's dropped the whole 'finding your beautiful you' thing?"

"You bet! Right now audiences want to talk about healthy living, you know, living 'green,' and they *love* following your mom's pregnancy. It's a killer combination!

"She's talking about being pregnant?"

"Think bigger, Lil! The new name for the show is—get this—*Growing Up Green with Linda Cohen*!"

"For real? And people like it?"

"The vlog has exploded! Everyone is watching! This morning your mom was referred to as the 'Green Mom' on *Good Morning, San Francisco*!"

"How long's this been going on?"

"Well, when your mom got pregnant, we started testing the idea—and voila—it worked!"

To get to their driveway Mr. Cohen had to pull around

two vans parked at the curb. Both trucks bore the name Techtronix, under which the motto appeared, "Making Your World Bigger Than Life." For the second time that day, Lilli's stomach was doing flip-flops.

"So—" she turned to her dad, "what are we supposed to do?"

"Well, they're in the living room recording now. Your mother said she'd *really* like to introduce you to her viewers—" Lilli folded her arms in defiance and turned her face to the window. Anticipating her resistance, her father quickly added, "—just briefly. In and out. Promise." Lilli was not consoled.

"It's not fair!" Lilli felt her face grow hot. "I don't ask her to come up when I'm on stage!"

Mr. Cohen gave her an empathetic look. "You can't blame her for wanting to show off her beautiful dancer."

"I'm not her beautiful dancer." Lilli felt cornered by her mother. "I'm a recycled daughter—how's that for 'green?'"

"Hey, hey," her dad reached over and gently touched Lilli's arm. "You're an original, our only daughter." He gave Lilli a look of unmistakable gratitude. "You saved your mother."

"Fine, I'll do it!" she gave in, knowing full well that Linda Cohen always gets her way. "Ow!" she cried as she made the enormous step down from the SUV to the brick paver drive, landing on stiff, sore legs.

Her dad hurried around to help her, throwing his daughter's dance bag on one shoulder and her backpack on the other. In an attempt to improve his daughter's mood, he nudged her with affection and said, "Smile, my ballerina! You are about to be seen around the world!"

Quietly they entered the house from the garage, stepping into the Cohen's gleaming kitchen. A smiley twenty-something guy with short-cropped blonde hair intercepted them. "Hi, I'm Nick." Lilli dubbed him Neat Nick on the spot. Dressed in a navy embroidered Techtronix golf shirt, Neat Nick also wore headgear that included earphones with a microphone attachment. The effect was that of a teen's orthodontic nightmare.

"This way," he whispered to father and daughter, stopping at the kitchen island. Beyond the dining room, Lilli and her dad could see their transformed living area and hear Linda Cohen's enthusiastic voice.

Even with its lofty ceiling and continuous wall of windows, the massive living room seemed crowded. The space now included two cameras with operators; an audio technician sitting at a soundboard; and a shoulder height display shelf on wheels that held CDs and DVDs—the recordings that were the vlog topic at the moment. And then, of course, there was the hostess herself in a full-length tie-dyed designer dress that wrapped around her body and tied at her waist.

"They're here!" Neat Nick spoke softly into his mic. At this, the soundboard guy glanced first at the waiting guests then nodded to the hostess. Even Lilli was impressed with her mother's seamless transition from the must-have music CDs for boosting the IQs of "green" babies to the introduction of her daughter.

"And speaking of brilliant children," her mother motioned for Lilli to join her on camera. Lilli took her place, smiling, next to her mother. As she did, she could feel the shelf being moved out the shot. "Everyone should have one of these! Oh, but you can't have this one, she's mine!" her mother joked to the camera. "This is my beautiful daughter, Lilli, and she will be bringing untold joy to Richard and myself this Sunday—"

"Saturday—" Lilli politely corrected her mother.

"Just teasing! We've been looking forward to Lilli's fall dance recital for months. We'll put up some clips for you all on our website. Then you can be right there with us!" Mrs. Cohen charmed her audience. "But that's all the time we have today. Thanks for joining me for *Growing up Green with Linda Cohen*. See you here next week—bring a friend! Bye now!" Lilli felt her mother's elbow jab her side, her cue to join her mother in waving at the camera.

"And we're clear!" declared the audio dude, who Lilli later learned was Techtronix owner Kevin Bower.

. . .

It was still early; the alarm had not yet sounded. The sun was just beginning to filter in through the partially opened curtains at the window behind Cal's bed. Still exhausted, the boy sat up but held his head in his hands.

He'd awakened from another crazy dream. This one involved a soccer field, a soccer ball lost in woods near the field, and a helicopter chase that threatened to keep him from finding the ball he needed to finish the game. Cal's face and body were drenched with sweat. What day was it? Saturday. He had a game. Feeling shaky, Cal slid from his bed, his bare feet hitting the cool wood floor.

Cal tried to push aside the truth that he had been sleeping poorly for at least a week. Anxiety gnawed at his appetite, and his stamina waned. The pending meeting with his birth mother unnerved him and seemed to occupy his entire mental bandwidth. Jack had been all over his case during training. Even Levi noticed his friend's lack of focus as he tried to drill Cal in his studies on the morning ride to school. Now just two weeks away from the meeting with his Chinese mother, Cal was increasingly afraid of going somewhere new to meet someone new, accompanied by someone he didn't know.

In the hall bathroom, Cal stepped up on the scales. Down three pounds. He heard his mother in the kitchen attempting to rustle up a meal that would appeal to him. As recently as the day before, Cal had been more than a little surprised to find a frosted doughnut on his breakfast plate as part of her scheme to increase his calorie intake.

"You don't look good," his mother observed aloud as Cal plopped down in the dining room in front of a plate of quiche.

"Not possible. I'm handsome as always."

"I think you should skip the game today," she continued.

"Maybe you need to see the doctor."

"I don't need a doctor," Cal insisted. "Besides, Jack would never let me miss a game."

"Why not?" her voice rose with frustration. "You haven't missed a single training day or soccer practice."

Three humongous bites later Cal rose, stuffing the last of the crust crumbs in his mouth. "I gotta shower, Mom," he announced. "I'll grab one of Jack's protein shakes and be good as new, I promise."

Later in her studio, Mrs. Vandiver stared at her paintings, which were once again on easels when Cal appeared at her side. She thought he looked somewhat revived, now dressed for the game, hair still wet, and sipping from an open can of GameOn. Cal scanned her work for recent revisions.

Firstly, he noticed the addition—or rather the extraction—of paint in the form of a single scrape into the heaviest part of the paint, like a tangle appearing at the height of the storm.

"That's new," Cal said, pointing at the second canvas. "What does it mean?"

The artist-mother took a moment, as if listening to the work before answering. "It's the story within the story, I think."

Secondly, Cal's eye was drawn to the new color on the third panel, where the sky brightened. "I like this," he referenced the third canvas. "It feels like a happy ending."

"To be determined."

"By what? How do you get to the happy ending?"

"It's a choice, I suppose."

"But what if a decision is risky, and you have limited information? How do you choose then?"

"I guess you keep doing what you *know* to do until you decide what you *must* do."

Worries about his approaching storm would have to wait. Cal determined to focus on the happy ending he felt confident would come at the end of the Wildcats soccer game.

...

Stepping onto the Wildcats soccer field, Cal was never so glad to see Miguel or Lilli with her pom-poms or to be part of a team. He had learned to work with his peers, and it had made him a better person—even happier. While he'd never admit it aloud, Cal knew Jack had been right all along.

Ninety minutes later, Cal was enjoying a congratulatory hug from Lilli. The Wildcats celebrated a shut out game, 6-0. That put them only two wins away from the district championship.

"You did it again!" Cal credited his soccer cheerleader with the win.

"Don't I know it!" she agreed, laughing. "That was close!"

"Hey, you got some hang time?" Cal asked Lilli hopefully.

"Sorry," Lilli apologized. "This *was* my hang time for the day. Now I have to go work on my recital."

"What—some more?"

"Oh, yeah," Lilli assured him, turning toward the parking lot. "See that guy up there on the motorcycle?"

"Uh, huh," Cal could make out a red bike and a body with a helmet.

"That's my new partner, and he thinks I'm going to be a hip-hop dancer by next Saturday night!"

"What? Hip-hop? You're kidding, right?"

"Not even a little. If you thought there were changes going on in the Cohen house before …"

"There might be such a thing as too much change." Cal looked toward the motorcycle with suspicion.

"I'll let you tell that to Carissa!" she laughed and threw Cal a wave. "You saved the date, right?"

"I'll be there to cheer you on!" Cal assured Lilli as he watched her jog to the lot to meet—whoever this guy was. But already Cal was not a fan.

# 31

It was early Monday morning when Derek arrived at the university juggling two coffees. Arriving on the third floor, he was pleased and surprised to find the door already open. Derek knew to look for Jewell at the worktable inside Dr. Tan's office.

Jewell did not look up until Derek was standing next to her.

"Hard at work before your coffee?"

"You are very kind," Jewell said, taking a steaming cup from her teammate who sat down beside her.

"And you are in way early," Derek returned, smiling. "So how are you feeling?" Derek asked now, looking for signs of anxiety in Jewell, who had spent two years preparing for the project that would officially begin that day.

"I believe we are ready, don't you?" she asked.

"Absolutely," he answered with confidence. "Speaking of getting this party started," Derek began then stopped when Jewell looked confused. "What I mean to say is—before we officially get started—would you consider a test run of the program?"

"Explain, please."

"It's kind of an interesting story," Derek began. "I have a friend—well, he's more like my little brother's friend—who was adopted from Hong Kong."

"Oh, yes!" Jewell responded with interest.

"Well," Derek continued, "he is supposed to meet his birth mother in a couple weeks. Apparently she lives in Mendocino, California—north of here in wine country."

"That is very good!"

"Pretty amazing, really." Derek agreed then proceeded to make his case for a program test. "But the attorney who is handling the arrangements for the meeting is being a bit secretive about the mother."

"What do you mean?"

"Well, for example, her name is being withheld and the exact location of her residence. No details have been offered, really."

"Oh!"

"As you can imagine, a kid about to meet his mother is interested in learning about her. There are a number of questions that he might have about how long she's been here and, perhaps, a bit about her history—medical history, for example."

"It is classified information, perhaps," Jewell commented.

"But if she agreed to the meeting, why the secrecy?" Derek countered.

"Surely the boy will ask the woman what he wishes to know," Jewell suggested. Just then Jewell and Derek heard Stephen enter. He held up a colorful box Derek recognized from the doughnut shop.

"Doughnut holes to share!" Stephen announced, setting the box down next to his computer.

"Don't be fooled," Derek whispered. "He shares about as well as a piranha!" Jewell laughed which made for the best possible start to her coworker's day.

"Okay," Derek picked up the conversation, "so this kid has tons of questions to ask his birth mother, but he's wondering if someone is controlling what she's allowed to share? That would explain the secrecy."

"You think we can help?"

"The idea is fairly simple, I think, unless you see a problem. What if we tested the DCP by searching the Mendocino area for an Asian woman, in the thirty-five to forty-five age range, born outside the U.S., and see what shows up?"

Jewell leaned over her coffee cup deep in thought. When Suzanne arrived, Jewell looked up. "I know—let's take it to the team," she suggested.

"Great idea." Derek agreed. Even as he spoke, Derek wondered how Jewell's boss at the ministry would react to a decision to do a test run of the program. Her work—like her life—was closely monitored.

...

It had been a quiet morning. Late fall was always that way. Most of the work in the vineyard was done. The few workers who remained were there to scrub down the winery crush equipment. Only the irrigation sprayers in the fields broke the silence of post-harvest. Between April and October there were scads of people—workers mostly—in and out of the house and fields, giving the woman endless occasions to entertain on the wide wraparound porch with tall glasses of flavored teas and, of course, excellent wine.

The woman truly believed she lived in the most beautiful place in the world. She never tired of the view of the lush vines of summer followed by the breath-taking beauty of the barren fields in winter. The sunroom offered a glimpse of the blue Pacific that sometimes beckoned to her. But this was her home, and it had been for thirteen years. She had grown used to the rhythms of life here, the regularity and beauty of each change of season and the quiet mornings and evenings when she indulged memories of the past, her years of glory.

In the living area, the woman kept photo albums filled

with memories of sports events featuring a younger version of herself, beginning with long distance running when she was about ten. The pictures progressed to her years playing volleyball, including the Olympic Games in 2000 and again in 2004. There was one album she had kept in a drawer, virtually untouched until a month ago. That was when she received a call from Trey Foster, the American attorney. Since then, the silence of the season had grown noisy with the memories of all that had been. And Trey Foster was back to remind her of them at least once a week.

The doorbell rang, and the woman turned slowly. That would be Foster. It would be another evening of drills and another night of dreams of all that had been hidden coming to light.

...

As Derek had anticipated, the team was on board with what they called Project Muquin—translated "mother" in Chinese. Jewell meticulously input the criteria for the test according to what little information Derek had available. The project would begin with a simple search of residents in and around Mendocino. If necessary, the search would be followed by a more in-depth exploration of potential matches by tapping the databases of Mendocino area businesses, physicians, hospitals, banks, credit card companies—any conceivable location where consumer or personal information might be stored.

It was Suzanne's idea to increase the number of test subjects to four, running additional searches using the profiles of three Asian students she knew that lived near the university. It was a brilliant idea actually. Running more than one search would make it easier for Jewell to explain the test runs to her boss, if necessary.

By the time Stephen had polished off the last doughnut hole and Suzanne left the department to catch the first of her evening classes, three of the four searches had finished successfully. The names of the three test students were discovered, resulting in pages of personal, medical, financial, and professional information on each. At 8:00 p.m., Jewell sent Derek home, promising to call him when Project Muquin was complete. Just before midnight, Derek's phone sounded at last.

"The news isn't good," Jewell started in an anxious voice.

"What is it?" Derek pressed, his mind racing. Had the program crashed?

"The system can't find Muquin."

That was the last news Derek expected. "How can that be?"

"There are only two explanations that I can think of right now," Jewell answered with a weary sigh. "Either there is a flaw in the program—something I missed ..."

"Or—" Derek prodded, hoping for a second, more hopeful scenario.

"Or something is wrong with the information your friend has given to you. According to the program, there is no such woman in the Mendocino area. She does not exist."

Derek couldn't speak. He had considered the possibility that the program would find too many matches to positively identify Cal's birth mother. The idea that they would come up completely empty-handed never entered his mind.

"Let it go." Derek attempted to ease Jewell's mind, knowing how unanswered questions haunted her. He regretted putting her through the agony of uncertainty. "It's not the program," he assured her. "You proved that with the other tests." Derek heard Jewell exhale in relief on the other end of the line. "There has to be something more that we don't know—or can't know—about this woman."

"I'll go with that." Jewell wished the reassurance came with a hug.

"Go get some sleep."

"It isn't as nice at the Lunar as where I was before," Jewell confessed in her exhaustion.

Derek had to laugh. "No terry cloth robe?"

"No robe."

"How 'bout I bring you coffee with a shot of mocha in the morning? Sound good?"

"Better."

"Good night, Genius Girl."

"I'll be sure to tell her if I see her."

# 32

When Lilli joined her friends at the lunch table, she avoided their glances and determinedly plopped down a green-tinted bowl in front of her. The bowl had three-compartments—each with its own an airtight flip top. Then she waited for the inevitable questions.

Cal, who had already downed three-quarters of his crunchy corndog by this time, looked over at Lilli quizzically. "Hi, Lilli." He considered how to safely broach the mystery of the green bowl. "Interested in the rest of my corn dog?" He asked, knowing full well that hot dogs were on the "no-no" list in the Cohen household.

"I have my lunch, thank you," she answered shortly. Most of the time, Lilli brought a normal-looking sandwich from home, always on whole wheat, along with fruit. And what she didn't finish usually ended up on Cal's plate. Scoring extra food from Lilli today was out of the question though. Cal was afraid of whatever it was that was in the green bowl.

Miguel sat with an unappetizing school lunch choice of over-fried chicken bites and wilted broccoli. Levi was well into his smelly deviled ham sandwich. Even a kid seated the next table over made a face and moved still further away.

"What's in *that*?" Levi peered over Lilli's shoulder as she opened each compartment of her lunch bowl in turn, revealing unsalted crackers, sliced apples, then an orange dip-like glob.

Lilli glared at Levi. "Well, I know this looks different from the mangled white bread and processed meat you are accustomed to, but this is real food." She pointed at the orange blob. "Is this what's bothering you?"

"Mostly," answered Levi. Cal and Miguel nodded in agreement.

"It's hummus," she said coolly. "It's good for me—protein and stuff."

It was Cal's turn. "This looks like the work of the Green Mom. Am I right?"

Lilli jumped at the remark. "Where did you hear that?"

"That's my mother's favorite show," Miguel mumbled as he crunched on his chicken. "She watches it with Spanish subtitles."

"Lilli, are you for real?" Cal was surprised that Lilli was clueless regarding the skyrocketing celebrity of her own mother. "Everyone knows about it!" Now he gave her a friendly shoulder bump. "It's okay! You know we'll be your friends no matter what color you grow up to be!" At this Cal and Miguel laughed together. Levi just looked confused.

"This is ridiculous. You guys shouldn't know this! Look, Levi doesn't know!"

In spite of the fact that Levi was, at that very moment, chewing half of his sandwich at once, he managed a muffled response: "Yeah, well, I have no means of communication with the outside world because my brain dead little brother is addicted to video games and the other one—with the over-sized brain—hogs the computer. Now he directed his remarks at Cal, "On the bright side that leaves me more time to be ready for stuff like quizzes in physical science."

"Yes, let's talk about Cal's academics, shall we?" Lilli dipped her cracker into the hummus, thankful for the change of topic.

"Plate tectonics—I got it covered."

"Hey, you actually got that stuff?"

"I was listening in the car, really. Jack's going to be happy and, most importantly, you'll pull an A and collect your reward money. All's right with the world."

"No!" Lilli blurted out suddenly. "All is not right with the world." Her friends' eyes turned on her.

"You don't really like the hummus, do you?" Levi asked innocently.

"No, actually, I do not. I don't even like green—I'm more of a purple person. But that's not the problem here."

"Then what is the problem?" It dawned on Cal too late that he had just invited himself into whatever drama was going on in the Cohen household.

"On Thursday my mother is going on the *Lucy Linn Show* in L.A. and will, no doubt, spout off about me and my unborn brother, about how we're going to be the perfect little family!"

"You have to admit, Canyon has been pretty darn perfect so far," Levi remarked, setting off a round of snickers.

"Know what's going to happen then?" Lilli raged on.

"What?" Miguel was hanging on Lilli's every word like he was watching a soap opera.

"There'll be cameras everywhere at my dance recital. If I blow it, the whole world's going to see!"

"My mother, she likes that Lucy Linn too," said Miguel.

Now Cal interjected, "And then there's that little matter of dancing with a hip-hop guy. That's gonna take some people by surprise, right?"

Lilli stared at Cal, suddenly aware that her best friend wasn't particularly excited about the addition of Ben to her recital.

Packing up her container of half-eaten hummus, Lilli stuffed it in her backpack and rose to leave. "If you'll excuse me, I have places to—hide."

"Can you get a Linda-wrap for my mother?" Miguel asked Lilli in all seriousness.

Lilli walked away with a huff.

"A what?" Levi asked.

"It's a cloth thing, like a scarf, made out of some plant. It goes around your neck, I think. You get one free with any purchase over $75 dollars."

With Lilli gone, Miguel leaned over to Cal who was scanning the table for leftovers. "Some advice?"

"On the quiz?"

"No, dude. I only can help you in Spanish. It's about the *guy*."

"The *guy*?"

"The dancer dude. You better find out if he's Latino."

"Why?"

"Are you kidding? If he is a hot Latino dancer *you* have trouble. Those guys can't be trusted with tu novia."

"Lilli's not—my girlfriend."

"Uh-huh. Don't say I didn't warn you."

A second later Cal was remembering the moment he saw Lilli's partner on the motorcycle. "So," Cal tested the waters with his soccer buddy, "you're good if I skip a day of practice to go to Lilli's rehearsal?"

"Dr. Phil and I would recommend it, amigo."

...

On Thursday, after dismissal from homeroom, Cal bolted outside in hopes of catching up with Lilli. "¡Buena suerte!" Cal heard Miguel's voice calling from behind him. Good luck. He'd need it. Would they even let him come along to the rehearsal?

Finally Cal spotted Carissa's Jeep. Lilli was not yet on board. He took a breath and attempted to pour on his thirteen-year-old charm for Lilli's multi-colored new friend.

"Hey, Carissa!" Cal jogged to her vehicle.

"Do I know you?" she asked with disinterest.

"I'm Lilli's friend, Cal."

"Oh, yeah," she seemed to look at him more closely—

the way one looks at an unusual insect. "The one with the sunglasses."

Really? That's all Lilli told Carissa about him—that he wore sunglasses? "Hey, I know it's a big week and all—really big. I thought it might help Lilli if I hung out and watched you guys rehearse today."

Carissa saw right through the request and smiled wryly: Cal's worry wasn't so much about Lilli as it was Ben.

"Did you ask Lilli?"

Cal felt heat in his cheeks. "I was hoping to surprise her. I'm usually at soccer practice today."

"Alright with me if it's alright with her—and you have your own ride home." Carissa suddenly sounded her horn, making Cal jump. He turned to see Lilli making her way across the now busy parking lot.

"Whatcha doing?" Lilli asked warily, when she arrived. "Does your mom want a Linda-wrap too?"

"Uh, no—but, thanks." He laughed off the remark. Clearly Lilli was still smarting from the lunchroom debacle earlier in the week.

"Actually, I'm playing hooky from soccer today. I was hoping I could watch you rehearse." Cal braced himself for a brush off. When Lilli looked as though she was weighing the idea, Cal continued: "It might be cool to have someone else in on the big surprise besides Carissa—and your dance partner, of course." At this Lilli cracked a knowing smile.

"Okay, it's not a bad idea." Lilli agreed. "But no lunchtime discussion about this, agreed?"

"Agreed." Cal hopped up into the tiny back seat behind Carissa, feeling like he was boarding a ride at the fair. He slipped off his sunglasses and tucked them in his backpack for safekeeping.

The ride was everything Cal feared it would be, like taking a spin in a tornado. Fortunately, the dance studio was a short drive from the school, and he recovered quickly with enough wits about him to notice how Lilli worked to smooth her hair from the Jeep to the practice room.

Inside the room stretching over his legs was the *guy*. His hair was black and wavy, and his skin was a warm brown. Miguel called it, Cal thought. Latino. The dancer wore black warm up pants and a white t-shirt that fit tightly around his muscular arms and shoulders.

"Hey, guys!" he greeted them as they entered, his eyes stopping on Cal. Pulling himself up from the floor, the dancer walked over to greet Lilli's guest. "I'm Ben," he smiled. And as much as he wanted to, Cal couldn't find a trace of malice in his eyes.

Cal took his hand and gave it a firm shake. "Cal," he returned. "Mind if I hang with you guys today? I'm hearing some pretty great stuff about the routine."

"It'll be the highlight of the night." Ben leaned down and pulled his body toward his calves. "They'll either love it or hate it." Ben and Carissa shared a laugh. Cal glanced at Lilli who wasn't laughing. Instead, she looked intense as she shed her school clothes to reveal her blue leotard and then tied the full, sheer skirt around her waist.

"Let's get started!" Carissa cued the dancers to their places.

Cal sat down against the back wall. The music started. He recognized the song. Lilli had played it for him weeks before, surprising him with the edgy, chart-topping music of Tiffany Grace instead of Tchaikovsky.

As Lilli began, she was immediately lost in the dance, in the story which had become her own. She moved across the floor, light and carefree, mimicking the rise and fall of waves. Innocence and freedom radiated from her face, her expressions as much a part of the dance as her body movements.

Cal knew some of the lyrics, though now he saw them:

Never saw you waiting there
The wind just took me where
I wanted to go

I so wanted to go

Riding high-solo
How was I to know
I'd be pulled in to this place
And we'd meet face to face.

At the chorus, the dance style turned hip-hop, with all the forcefulness—even the anger—that made the genre so popular with youth. Ben joined Lilli, leaping, flipping, as if roughing the waters around her, playing the part of the undercurrent that emerged from the deep. Cal witnessed Lilli's transformation before his eyes. The outrage she felt at the disruption of the "undercurrent" shown on her face as well as in the power and strength in her movements. With outstretched arms she attempted to hold back the force that was Ben, until exhaustion overtook her.

Undercurrent
Took me by surprise
Unleashed my world
Opened my eyes
To the pain that swelled in me
And how strong I'd have to be

The dance geared down again for the verses, only to jolt the audience again at the chorus as Ben stepped on the scene to confront Lilli and to throw her "waters" back into chaos.

In the final bars of the song, the two dancers moved in synch, a show of harmony. The anger in Lilli's face was replaced with joyful surrender. Then came the powerful finish: Lilli ran into Ben's arms that lifted her body over him as they continued to move together—like a single wave—in the direction of her outstretched arms.

Undercurrent

You took me by surprise
Lifted me up so I could see
The strength I had in me
And that I'd never be
Alone

When the music stopped, there were whoops from Carissa. "You guys killed it!" Ben threw his arms around Lilli in a congratulatory hug.

When the music ended, Cal realized he had pressed himself against the wall as if to put more distance between him and the explosion of story and emotion that had played out before him. Lilli looked over at him with a timid what-do-you-think question on her face. How should he respond? The dance had been unexpected and overwhelming. After a moment he mouthed back to her the one word that best summed up his reaction—"Wow!"

After a few more run-throughs, everyone seemed pleased that all the parts of the dance had come together at last. There were congratulations all around. Ben pulled off his sweaty tee, pulled on a baby blue polo, and made his way over to Cal. "What'd you think?" he asked Cal, who was unhappily noticing Ben's broad chest and impressive biceps.

"Amazing," Cal answered honestly. "How long have you been dancing?"

"Long as I can remember."

"I bet you tear it up at school dances! Where do you go?" Cal pried a bit further.

Here Ben hesitated.

"I'm not presently in school," Ben started. "It wasn't so cool at home, so I started dancing for people—like Carissa. Last year I tried out for *Dance Club*, you know, the dance contest on TV? Made it into the top twenty-five before I got cut. Flashing a dazzling smile, he added, "but that won't happen again."

"Why's that?" Cal asked, hoping to hear that Ben was

giving up dance and moving to Alaska.

Instead Ben threw a glace toward Carissa, as if the two dance veterans had shared a similar discussion. "Cause I'm gonna *own* the *Club* after tryouts next summer!"

Carissa laughed and mimicked Ben as she headed out the door: "Yeah, you gonna *own* the *Club*!"

A second later Ben leaned down and spoke to Cal in a low voice. "Oh—and in case you're wondering—Lilli is an awesome dancer, but too young for me." Before Cal could explain that he and Lilli were just friends, Ben headed for the door, pointing at Lilli as he went. "Later, partner!"

Cal and Lilli stepped from the building into the bright afternoon sun, where Lilli's dad was waiting for her. Standing next to the Cohen's SUV with arms folded was Jack. Cal's heart skipped a beat.

"Blame me!" Lilli whispered to Cal.

"I got this," Cal said, trying sound to calm.

Hoping to avoid an unhappy exchange between the coach and his AWOL player, Lilli hurried to the SUV and climbed in beside her dad and waited.

"You were not at soccer today," Jack said to Cal gruffly.

"I made sure Miguel was good with it. Sorry, I—Lilli needed me."

"Ask my permission next time."

"Yes, sir," Cal responded, wondering what physical punishment his coach had planned for him at the Y.

"No practice today."

"No practice? Why?"

"I must meet with the Olympic Selection Committee. Tomorrow we train *five* hours," Jack ordered, holding up five fingers. "Bring your bike." Cal dropped his head and Jack turned to leave. The excitement of a free afternoon was gone as quickly as it had come. An extra long day on the tri-bike awaited him.

"Cal!" Lilli called to him from her car window. "Got some time?" Unexpectedly he did. Minutes later Cal was in the vehicle with Lilli and Mr. Cohen, headed toward the Cohen estate.

"Glad you could come along," Mr. Cohen spoke to Cal in the back seat. "It's kind of a big day."

"I'm glad too," Cal said. "So Mrs. Cohen was on the *Lucy Linn Show* this morning?"

Lilli sighed loudly.

"Yup! But wait 'til you see who else is watching Linda Cohen!"

"Now who is Lucy Linn exactly?" Cal hesitated to ask. Even Miguel knew.

Mr. Cohen jumped at the invitation to provide a little history on the well-known talk show host. "Back about five years ago Lucy Linn was a contestant on a country music show. She did very well, but not so much for her singing. She was just really likable and funny. So they gave her a talk show. Now she has one of the top-rated daytime shows in the country."

# 33

In the Cohen's grand living room, the three sat down on the giant caramel-colored sectional. Mr. Cohen picked up the remote. "Everybody buckled in?" he joked.

"Just play it, Dad."

Together they watched the open of the *Lucy Linn Show* where the hostess teased her upcoming interview with Linda "Green Mom" Cohen, assuring her near riotous studio audience that they had indeed come on a very special day. Mr. Cohen fast-forwarded through the commercials to Lucy Linn's introduction of Linda Cohen, who stepped onto the set looking a bit like a mermaid. Her full-length sleeveless dress featured layers in differing shades of green that tapered at the calves with a small train following behind.

"*What* is she wearing?" Lilli said, her mouth agape.

"Isn't she stunning?" Her father smiled widely.

The Green Mom sat down in the chair next to Lucy Linn, waving to the audience.

"I'll have to get my mom a dress like that."

"Don't worry about it. I'll have one for her as soon as my mom gets home." Lilli rolled her eyes.

"Shhhh, here it comes." Lilli's father watched with rapt attention, even though it was obvious he'd played and replayed the segment.

"I know we have more than a few fans today of the *Growing Up Green with Linda Cohen* video blog!" Lucy Linn paused to let her audience respond with wild applause. "But—" she said pointing to her in-studio audience, "—you guys have some competition." Now the talk show host turned to her smiling guest. "Linda, you haven't even seen this footage!" Lucy Linn announced with a southern drawl. "Coming to you from Beijing, China, meet our international Green Mom fans! They're just crazy about this movement you've started! Roll the tape, Ron."

The video showed a large hotel conference room full of Chinese women seated around tables, excitedly watching *Growing Up Green with Linda Cohen* on a big screen mounted on the wall. Most wore green Linda-wrap scarves and chatted as the translation of the lively hostess rolled across the bottom of the screen.

"Now *that* is a Growing Up Green PAR-TY," Lucy Linn yelled over the din of her audience. "And they are happening all over China!" The host smiled and turned to her guest. "We are just so lucky to have Linda Cohen right here in L.A.—and we're going to PAR-TY right here, right now!"

The interview portion of the show was actually shorter than the introduction. Linda Cohen touched on a few of her favorite topics, including Lilli and her upcoming dance recital, as well as Canyon, Canyon's nursery, Canyon's onesies made from actual bamboo, and then finished up with an invitation to check out the show's website. By the time Mr. Cohen stopped the recording, Lilli hid her face in a decorative couch pillow and moaned something about her recital going international. Cal felt pinned to his spot, unable to shake the irony of watching Chinese fans of Linda Cohen on TV, just days before he would visit his own birth mother.

...

"Wish you had time to help out Coach Matthews with the soccer team, son. These kids are struggling," the headmaster lamented at the dinner table.

"You've always got basketball," remarked Cal, going in for seconds of pot roast and veggies. It was true. Historically, VA fared slightly better in basketball.

"It's not enough," his father shook his head in defeat. "These days everyone's looking for student scholarships anywhere they can find them. Not a day goes by that I don't get an email from a parent who thinks we need to be more competitive in one sport or another. Unfortunately, they always forget to send along a check to cover the expenses to make it happen."

"You could ask Jack to help out," Cal offered.

Cal's father chuckled at the thought of VA students being drilled by Coach Jack. "They'd never get to their homework."

"They might not be able to get out of bed," Cal added.

"Yeah, I don't think my email account could handle the volume."

"Do you know anything about this meeting Jack had today?" Cal asked.

"Didn't Jack mention something about that when he was here for the party?" Cal's dad asked his wife.

Kimberly Vandiver tried to recall the conversation she'd had with Jack. "As I understood it," she began, "he's hoping to enter you into some of the Olympic trial events using video recordings. That way you don't have to take time away to travel."

"Which gives me more time to train," Cal summed up Jack's plan.

"Sounds like Jack," his father agreed.

"Some pound cake, Cal?" his mother asked.

"Better wait," Cal responded. "I promise myself dessert

once homework is done. Clever, huh?"

A knock sounded at the front door.

Cal immediately thought of Jack. "Uh, oh."

Cal's dad stepped to the front door and leaned into the peephole. "Have no fear, son. It's just Derek."

"Derek?" Cal felt a rush of excitement. "Maybe he has news about my birth mother." The door opened to a sheepish looking Derek.

"What a nice surprise!" Cal's father greeted the bright young man he knew had been recently employed at CSU and offered to use the computer technology there to find information on his son's birth mother. "Come on in!"

"Thanks," Derek responded. He shook Mr. Vandiver's hand. "Good evening, everybody." With his hands deep in the pockets of his jeans, Derek explained how the DCP team had set up four test searches, one of those being a search based on what information they had on Cal's birth mother. As he described the details of the trial, an anxious Cal studied Derek's face for any clue as to the outcome of the search.

"So?" Cal asked at last, unable to wait any longer.

"I'm sorry. Truth is," Derek admitted, "the search for your birth mother was not successful."

The shocking report hung in the air. "What does that mean?" The boy's father broke the silence.

"I'm not sure," Derek shrugged. "It would seem that there isn't a single match for this woman in either the city of Mendocino or anywhere within a fifteen-mile radius."

"Not a single hit?" Cal asked, incredulous. "What about the other searches? Did they work?"

"Yes, each of the other tests was successful."

"So she's not there?" Cal felt panic rising up in him. "Who am I meeting then?"

"I can only guess that there was either an error in the limited information we had to input," Derek offered, "or that your birth mother lives somewhere other than Mendocino."

Mrs. Vandiver sat Derek down in front of a slice of pound

cake. "Well, there's an explanation. We just won't be able to figure it out today." Then she handed him a fork. "Have some dessert. I insist."

A clean, quiet home and the lure of sugar won him over. Derek took the fork gratefully. A moment later he pulled a folded piece of paper from the back pocket of his war-torn jeans. "This is for you, Cal," he said. "It's from Levi."

It turned out to be an extra credit worksheet for Cal's physical science class. On it, Levi stuck a neon orange Post-It note that read: "Points toward your quiz grade if you turn this in by tomorrow!" Shifting mental gears to homework just then would be a monumental task for Cal. Fortunately, it would leave him no time to think about all he didn't—and couldn't know—about his birth mother.

...

That weekend, the Wildcat's overtook the Alexander Middle Blue Devils in an epic win: 12-0. In the last minutes, Coach Lombard ordered his players to simply pass the soccer ball until time ran out. No more goals. Cal and Miguel sat out the entire game, giving their teammates the opportunity to pull off the win on their own. Witnessing how much each member of the team had grown made the celebration twice as sweet. The next game, the last of the season, would determine the district champs.

# 34

It was a spectacular day at the winery. The woman who looked a decade younger than her nearly forty years sat in the expansive sunroom that overlooked the grounds, cross-legged in her favorite wicker chair, wishing she could escape her present company. She was sick of everything about him. Trey Foster wore his hair gelled stiff, and even in khakis and a sports jacket he still looked disheveled. His voice grated on her nerves.

"Let's go over it again," he ordered the woman for the ninth time since his arrival that morning. She had been counting.

"What exactly is it that you are still concerned about?" the woman's voice revealed contempt for the man.

"My concern—and what should be your concern—is that this kid leaves here with all of his questions answered. It's your job to give him a sense of closure, got it? It ends here."

"This kid?" She took offense at his flippant reference to the child she had carried, even though she was not his biological mother. Just the paid surrogate turned kidnapper. But Foster had no concern for her deceit. His paycheck came from ensuring the truth never came out. He continued to pace, taking his reading glasses on and off. The woman reached back to touch her ponytail and remarked, "Nothing ends here. It only begins, doesn't it?"

The comment rattled Foster, as she knew it would. His face grew sterner. "Tell me the story again!"

Now the woman's temper flared. "I know this story!"

"What will you say when he asks to see you *again*?" Foster drilled the woman on the part of her script she most dreaded. The boy would be hurt. It was the last thing she wanted to do, and yet it was the very reason she had spent years hiding out at the winery. Painful as it was, now was the time for her to play out her small part in changing the world.

# 35

The first arrivals to what was considered one of Visalia's biggest events of the year were met with small explosions of glitter released by exuberant greeters. The fourth and fifth grade dancers, decked out in their sequined dancewear, welcomed parents, siblings, even grandparents who shielded their eyes, clearly wishing for a little less hullabaloo. The music of Prokofiev's *Romeo and Juliet* filled the lobby as attendees made their way into the hall. There was, however, a bottleneck just outside the glass entrance of the Visalia Ballet Academy.

"I love your show!" a twenty-something woman called out to the city's only celebrity of note.

"Oh, thank you, thank you for watching! But this is Lilli's night!" Linda Cohen arrived with her husband and an entourage of videographers in Techtronix shirts. The local media followed close behind.

"Was all this really necessary?" whispered the celebrity's sister Valerie who always drove in from San Francisco to see her niece perform.

"What could I do?" The Green Mom responded helplessly.

"You know I promised to post the performance on the vlog. I had no choice but to bring them!"

Miguel made it into the front lobby just before the Cohens arrived. He had come with his family to see his cousin Maddy dance. Catching a glimpse of Cal and Levi standing at the back by the water fountain, Miguel pushed his way past the growing crowd to join them.

"Hi, guys," Miguel greeted his friends, shaking glitter out of his thick hair. Just then the volume in the lobby jumped as the Cohens made their entrance. Cal recognized Lilli's Aunt Valerie from past birthday parties and recitals.

Crowded rooms made Cal feel a little panicky. It reminded him of riding his tri-bike: anything could happen at any time. He was grateful Lilli only had two recitals a year—fall and spring. But he always made it there and was always astounded by Lilli's talent.

"Looks like the show's already begun, huh?" commented Cal. The three boys agreed they were thankful that Lilli was backstage, unable to witness the scene.

Over the years, Lilli had become the centerpiece of the programs presented at the academy, a distinction she had earned without the assistance or influence of her well-known mother. At every previous recital, Lilli danced ballet, as did all of the students. Tonight, Cal knew, would be a break with tradition. According to the recital program, which was stuffed into his hand by a super-smiley little girl wearing too much make-up, Lilli would perform her modern dance as the evening finale.

The three boys found seats together in the center of a row near the back, so people wouldn't be asking to move past them again and again. Touching strangers ranked second behind crowded rooms on Cal's list of things to avoid.

Cal's stomach flip-flopped when at last the lights went down and the music started. He envied his friends, who were blissfully unaware of the potential calamities of performance night, many he had witnessed firsthand: a flaky sound system; the stage tech who missed his lighting cues or lights that simply failed to work at all; the dancer with stage fright. Tonight needed to be perfect for Lilli.

The program always began with the youngest dancers, the idea being that they could get home and in bed early. In reality, the younger kids all wanted to stay to watch the more experienced dancers and, of course, Lilli.

With Miguel's eight-year-old cousin Maddy in the program, Cal didn't have to worry about him nodding off during the seemingly endless stream of tiny, sparkly dancers. Levi, on the other hand, required repeated elbows to the ribcage from Cal to stay upright in his seat. After Maddy performed with her age group, Miguel released an ear-piercing finger whistle that startled everyone seated around them.

"Dude—just clap!" Cal complained.

"That's how she knows it's me!"

At intermission, Miguel disappeared and was gone until the lights blinked, signaling the start of the second half of the program. To get back to his seat, Miguel worked his husky frame around knees and baby carriers, smashing some toes along the way, until he finally dropped down next to Cal.

"We thought you were out of here!" Levi said.

"Family pictures with Maddy. It's a big deal."

"Look, they're setting up for the finale." Cal nodded toward the front where cameras had moved into place on each side of the stage. "Don't rush out before the fireworks."

"Fireworks—*inside*?" Levi asked, alarmed.

"Cool! Maddy didn't say anything about that."

"That's because nobody in this audience—including Lilli's parents—knows much about her finale dance. No telling what might explode afterwards."

"I don't get it," admitted Levi.

"You will," Cal promised.

As the eighth grade dancers—with the exception of Lilli—performed on stage, Cal was barely aware of them. Instead he was caught up in the preparations being made down front between the camera operators and sound techs. He caught a glimpse of Mr. and Mrs. Cohen who were seated near the front, center stage. After what seemed an interminable amount of time, the dance ended. The applause turned riotous on the left of the auditorium as the Wilmer triplets took their bows. Apparently every member of the Wilmers' immediate and extended family was present for the big night.

Once the stage was clear, the voice of Mrs. Russ came over the sound system.

"Ladies and gentlemen," she began, "my name is Suzanne Russ. On behalf of the Visalia Ballet Academy, I would like to thank you for coming out tonight to support our very talented, very dedicated group of dancers." It was time. Cal elbowed Levi.

"To close the evening we asked guest artist Carissa Russ of the LightPlace Dance Troupe based in Seattle to choreograph a unique piece for us. Performing this evening is long-time student at Visalia Ballet Academy and one of our most accomplished performers, Lilli Cohen. Enjoy the presentation and thank you for joining us this evening."

As the audience applauded, dancers could be seen filing out from the stage door to the right side of the auditorium and flanking the back wall to watch Lilli, their sequins twinkling like Christmas lights.

The music started. At first, Cal thought it seemed louder than other tracks played that evening. Then it occurred to him that it was probably just the surprise of the pop music at the close of an evening of orchestral pieces. Seconds later the spotlight fell on Lilli. Cal was struck by how grown-up, how professional Lilli appeared this year as compared to last. Squeals and applause went up from the dancers in the back thrilled to see Lilli in her blue leotard and sheer, flowing skirt and excited by the upbeat song most knew by heart.

As Lilli began her smooth wavelike moves to the music, the sheer skirt swirling around her, the auditorium fell silent.

From the serene look on her face, Cal could tell Lilli was oblivious to everything and everyone else. In spite of all her worrying in the weeks leading up to the recital, there were no nerves tonight. She was ready to say what was on her mind—through her dance.

At the chorus, when Ben stepped onto the stage, there was an audible, unified gasp from the audience. There had been no mention of a second dancer or the unexpected style of dance Ben brought to the stage. Cal thought he felt the people around him lean back in their seats, just as he had done at the rehearsal.

Cal felt Levi tap his shoulder. When he turned, Levi nodded in the direction of the Cohens. From where Cal sat he could see Mrs. Cohen, her hand held up to mouth, aghast. Mr. Cohen's arm was wrapped tightly around his wife's shoulder. The fuse had been lit and the sparks were beginning to fly.

Along the side and the back of the auditorium, the young performers were dancing along with the music. And each time Ben took the stage with Lilli, cheers and clapping erupted from among them. Ben was clearly a hit with the female contingency.

As far as Cal could tell, only two people in the building had to work to appear pleased with the presentation: Mrs. Russ and Mrs. Cohen.

"Dang, you weren't kidding about the fireworks," Miguel remarked to his friends.

"Yeah, well, I think we're just getting started," Cal answered. The music ended and the audience stood to their feet in stunned appreciation.

Afterward, in the lobby, an excited Maddy reached up to give Miguel a big hug.

"Lilli Cohen is your friend?" she asked. Miguel nodded. Now she asked shyly, "And do you know that *guy* too?"

"No, Maddy—sorry." Despite her disappointment, she quickly recovered, skipping over to join a small group of her fellow dancers who were whispering together excitedly.

The camera crews made their way to the lobby too, recording rave reviews of the dance finale. Moments later the lights flickered and Mrs. Russ' voice came over the speakers: "Thanks again to choreographer Carissa Russ for our finale and to our finale dancers Lilli Cohen and Ben Holtcamp." On cue, the two dancers entered the lobby, greeted with enthusiastic applause and the flash of cameras.

After the crowd thinned out, Carissa made her entrance and gave a brief interview to the camera crew. The focus, however, was on the beautiful couple and the Techtronix crew wanted interviews with Lilli and Ben together and individually.

"She has been a wonderful dance partner, and yes, I would welcome the opportunity to dance with Lilli again!" Ben's voice could be heard across the lobby where Lilli stood with Cal, Levi, and Miguel. No one there could deny that Ben, even as a newcomer, had come off like a shining star that evening. He was a natural for *Dance Club*.

While Lilli thought the program and the reception couldn't have gone better, she was beginning to feel a bit nervous. Her parents had not yet arrived on the scene. What did they think of the performance?

Miguel turned to Lilli, "My cousin, she says you are her new hero!"

Levi even attempted a compliment. "I never thought I'd actually enjoy a dance recital and I didn't, really, until you danced! Wow!"

"Thanks," Lilli answered, uncomfortable taking compliments from her school friends.

Just then both cameras finished up with Ben and were quickly moving in Lilli's direction. "A moment, please?" The first cameraperson approached Lilli, a young woman Lilli recognized from the vlog taping at her home. A second camera manned by Neat Nick quickly moved in for side shots.

"Can my friends stay?" Lilli asked.

"Certainly," the interviewer responded.

Lilli pulled her friends close, reaching her arms around Cal on her right and Levi on her left. Miguel pushed in close to Levi to ensure he made the shot.

"We're talking to Lilli Cohen, everybody. Lilli, we know you're growing up green, but you sure were brilliant in blue onstage tonight!"

"Thanks. It's been really fun doing something a little different."

"Lilli, who do you have supporting you here tonight?"

"These are my best buddies, and I'm really proud of them because dance isn't really their thing, you know, but they were here, and I'm so glad!"

"Any of you gentlemen a little jealous of Ben after that performance?" It was the kind of question that sold tabloids and sparked reality shows.

Cal spoke up. "Of course we're jealous!" He laughed at Lilli's surprised expression. He continued, "Lilli has to practice a lot, and we miss hanging with her." In the spotlight, Cal instinctively reached for his sunglasses that hung at the open collar of his button-down and slipped them on.

Miguel jumped into the conversation, determined not to miss his fifteen seconds of fame. "Ben and Lilli are both fantastic dancers, and together they were the dynamic duo!" Now the group of friends laughed at the reference usually reserved for Cal and Miguel on the soccer field.

"Final thoughts on the evening, Lilli?" the interviewer asked, looking for a strong closing clip.

"I just want to say how grateful I am to the Visalia Ballet Academy for letting me do a modern dance piece. It was so much fun. And I definitely want to say 'Love you!' to my mom and dad who always support me and made all this possible."

After her friends headed home, Lilli went looking for her parents. The camera crew was gone, as were Carissa and Ben. One door to the auditorium remained propped open.

Stepping in, Lilli caught the faint outline of her parents still seated there.

"Hey, you guys," Lilli started timidly. "Where've you been?" As she sat down in a seat behind her parents, Lilli felt their eyes on her like they were looking at her for the first time. Her mother was uncharacteristically quiet, and her dad held his wife's hand protectively.

"Honey, that was truly a wonderful performance." Lilli's dad broke the ice.

"Mom?" Lilli felt a wave a panic, suddenly caring very much about her mother's reaction—something she hadn't given much thought to in all her weeks of preparation.

"Lilli," her mother was choking back emotion, "are you angry?"

Taken aback by the question, Lilli paused and searched for courage to be truthful without being hurtful. "Of course I'm angry," she began. "First of all, I'm thirteen—almost fourteen. Comes with the territory, doesn't it?"

"But are you angry—at me?" her mother looked stricken, as if faced with the realization that she may have pushed or bruised or even broken her only daughter without even realizing it.

"Mom, it's annoying to be the daughter of a celebrity—or whatever—but I get it. It's important to you. It's just that I'm finally learning what's important to me."

"Ballet isn't important to you anymore?"

"Ballet brought me to this place. Yes, it's important." Lilli touched her skirt that had come to represent her need to grow beyond the walls of the academy. "But I couldn't say what I needed to say doing the same movements to the same music just like always."

"What do you need to say?"

Mr. Cohen spoke gently now. "Tell us, Lilli. Anything you say is okay. We love you."

"I'm Chinese." It was the last statement her parents expected to hear, she could tell. "For a long time it didn't matter. I just thought I was supposed to be like you." Lilli met her mother's eyes. "And you're great. It's just that I'm not like you.

I don't have beautiful blonde hair or freckles. I'll never be a Miss—anything. There's like another part of me that's pushing its way out. A part of me I don't know anything about."

"Can we help?" her mother asked. Lilli felt her mother's full, open-minded attention lovingly touch the place inside her that always feared disappointing Linda Cohen. It gave her courage.

"I need to dance like this. Expressively. At least for now. Can that be okay?"

Her mother nodded, and her dad reached across the back of the auditorium seat to give his daughter's arm a reassuring squeeze.

"You don't even have to show the dance on your vlog, Mom."

"Are you kidding? I can't wait to see what our Green Party Girls across the Pacific think of this!"

# 36

The very next week, Lilli's Aunt Valerie dropped her overnight bag in the guest room at the Cohens' home. The twenty-nine-year-old was a freelance marketing consultant, single, and knew Linda Bakker Cohen better than anyone. And right now her sister needed her. Unlike Linda, Valerie stayed clear of the public eye. Rather, she took pleasure in stepping in as her sister's marketing consultant and, as needed, her life coach.

The sisters were on their third cup of coffee when the Techtronix truck arrived. The Cohen living room was again transformed into a studio while Valerie helped the hostess dress and touch up her make-up. The masses were waiting for the next installment of *Growing Up Green with Linda Cohen*.

At the savvy advice of Valerie, the Techtronix crew had prepared two versions of Lilli's dance for broadcast. The first was a one-minute clip Linda Cohen debuted, as promised, on the vlog the day before. And a second full-length version, including interviews, was made available to visitors of the Growing Up Green website. Getting viewers to the site was, after all, the way to sell merchandise.

Response to the short clip that aired the day before was immediate and overwhelming. The "Tell It to Linda" comment section on the website was hit with thousands of rave reviews of the performance. And, according to Techtronix owner Kevin Bower who was monitoring the site, scores of viewers viewed the full presentation of the dance within minutes of the close of the show. Further, the enthusiastic response was happening on both sides of the Pacific. Lilli and Ben were officially an international hit.

"Not a single mention of my interview with Dr. J. D. Warren!" an incensed Linda Cohen studied her face in the lighted mirror on the coffee table. "His book is a bestseller! How can people not care about giving their pre-born babies a head start in their education?"

"Come on! Aren't you thrilled for Lilli?" Valerie asked as she sat on the couch with her laptop scrolling through the flood of posts. "I mean you didn't get near this response to the bamboo baby onesies—even with the buy-one-get-one-half-price offer!"

"I'm excited, okay?" came the celebrity mom's unconvincing reply. "It's just—what happens from here? This is my daughter, you know? I don't really feel comfortable broadcasting her all over the universe."

"You mean you don't feel comfortable broadcasting Lilli in China." Valerie said what her sister would not.

Linda Cohen sighed. "It's a little like letting someone else have part of her."

"Yeah, well, the fact that she feels a very natural connection—at least a curiosity—toward the country where she was born is only news to you."

"And her father," Linda added defensively. "I mean, Lilli doesn't even remember China!"

At this, Valerie was silent. She really had no idea how difficult this was for her sister. She wasn't a mother.

"Just tell me it's going to be all right," the older sister pleaded.

"Everything's going to be amazing," Valerie assured her.

# 37

It was lunchtime, and while Li Daiya seldom let her staff leave the office, even to eat, today she acquiesced. For weeks she had heard her young office assistants Mei and Lien talking together with other young women in the building about the upcoming Green Party, featuring the wide screen image of the American celebrity Linda Cohen. The event was to be held at Beijing's Capital Hotel, a short walk from their workplace—the offices of the Beijing Committee of the Communist Party.

According to the China News Service, the Green Parties were held each week in hotel conference rooms across the country. The hotels were only more than willing to open a conference room to partygoers and the media that inevitably followed. The arrangements were simple. All that was required for a party was an oversized TV and access to the Internet.

Across China it would be standing room only at today's group viewing of *Growing Up Green with Linda Cohen*. As Li Daiya understood the bits and pieces of news coverage and office conversation, this was the day the American video blog would carry a portion of a dance performance that was being hailed as an "international phenomenon." It featured Cohen's daughter, Lilli, adopted from China.

In Li Daiya's opinion—which she openly shared with her office subordinates—the program drew lazy, ignorant women who embarrass themselves by following American celebrities and mimicking Western culture. On a deeper level, Li Daiya understood that the show appealed to Chinese women who lost daughters to adoption as a result of government policies. Watching the celebrity woman helped viewers believe that all was well with their own daughters, born in China and raised in the U.S.

Year after year, Li Daiya's objection to the party's decision to release tens of thousands of its children—mostly its daughters—for adoption to American families had been dismissed.

"You are speaking as a woman without a child," accused her male counterparts in the party, many who stood to benefit financially by the continued flow of American dollars into China.

"You misunderstand my concern," Li Daiya had respectfully responded. "There will come a day when our factories will lack workers, when our young men search for wives that have been moved abroad, when we discover that our children—the best and brightest in the world—shine from America." She pleaded her case to no avail.

The national crisis she had predicted was now upon them, Li Daiya knew. Families were needed to fill the universities with students who could preserve Chinese thought. And, just as she had warned, the Americans held up the best and brightest, such as Cohen's daughter, as if they were trophies of their own making. The party itself was in need of such strong, young leaders. This was to be the time of her son. But the thirteen-year long search for him had turned up nothing.

After Mei and Lien left the office, Li Daiya decided to step out herself and grab some lunch to bring back to the office.

In the business district, there were many small restaurants to choose from, but Li Daiya hated lines and noise and headed straight for her preferred street vendor.

The man at the stand saw her coming and nodded a greeting. "Noodle soup with pork today?" the man asked in Mandarin. It was the lunch she most often requested. The aged vendor wished the business lady would bring a friend to his stand sometimes, but she was always alone. Li Daiya nodded, and the man carefully prepared her lunch to go, double-checking the seal on the lid of the soup container, so it would not leak on his important customer. It occurred to Li Daiya that the man who stood on this corner knew her better than almost anyone she could think of, that he witnessed her loneliness.

While the man worked, Li Daiya reached into her pocketbook for money enough to pay for her lunch and a little extra for the man who always showed her respect. With gratitude, the man reached down and opened a drawer of fortune cookies, which he kept on hand for tourists, mostly Americans. She smiled and slipped the sealed cookie in the pocket of her suit jacket. It was a joke between them. The sugary cookie folded around a fortune was, in fact, an American creation.

Back in her office, Li Daiya's computer sat before her, beckoning. She couldn't deny her curiosity about the gathering of women just up the street. Shouldn't she know what was going on there? First she went online to the China News Service site. There it was—the big story of the day. The news reporter was "live" at the Capitol Hotel in a conference room filled with round tables and seating for as many as 100. As he spoke to the camera, women filed in around him, hurrying to claim seats for themselves and family and friends still on their way. The young, well-groomed reporter spoke with one matronly attendee about the purple tie-dyed style tablecloth she'd used to "claim" her table at the event.

"I dyed it with pokeberry," the woman explained in

Mandarin. "All natural!" She went on to tell the reporter that it was a tip she'd picked up on a recent edition of the popular vlog. The reporter quipped that perhaps a plant that yielded a dye in a shade of "green" might have been more appropriate.

Five minutes before the broadcast, the noise in the room rose to such a level that the reporter simply gave up his efforts to interview attendees, deciding instead to step out into the lobby in an effort to solicit comments from hotel employees and passersby.

Li Daiya pulled out the fortune cookie from her pocket. She tore open the cellophane wrap around the cheap, factory-made treat, broke it in half, and pulled out the slip of white paper with red lettering. On one side of the paper was printed the holder's "lucky" number for the day. On the other was a brief message, or fortune, believed to offer a clue to the reader's future and a happier life. Li Daiya's fortune was printed in English and read: "What was lost will be found."

Perhaps one day, Li Daiya thought to herself bitterly. It had been thirteen years. She stuffed the fortune back into her pocket.

Opening a second tab on her browser, Li Daiya keyed in the Growing Up Green vlog address provided by the news service. There, for the first time, she came face to monitor with the Green Mom. The show was just beginning. Music started and the show's hostess appeared. Cohen's delivery was expressive and Li Daiya thought she observed a glow about her. She looked like an American movie star.

The woman was telling her audience about an interview coming up later on the show with a doctor who says children can be taught before they are born. "I'm going to go ahead and get my little one's name on the list for Harvard—and you should too!" That explains the glow, thought Li Daiya, feeling the long-familiar pain of loss. The woman was pregnant.

"And now what we all have been waiting not so patiently for—it's Lilli time!" The hostess nodded to someone off camera, and the short-version of the dance filled Li Daiya's computer screen. Together with countless Green Party goers across her country—and probably many more around the world—Li Daiya held her breath.

The performance was radically different from what Li Daiya had anticipated. More like a story than a dance, she thought. The girl, Lilli, was very beautiful and talented; her partner, mesmerizing in every way. Equally striking was the contrast of dance styles performed, which was unlike anything she'd ever seen. With a touch of the computer mouse she returned to the China News Service page to see how the local Green Party goers were reacting to the clip.

The scene had changed in the conference room as the camera caught partygoers arguing with hotel personnel. According the reporter who was narrating the hubbub, viewers were demanding that the hotel extend the time allotted for the Green Party so that those without Internet access at home could view the complete, unedited dance available only on the website. Faced with an insistent and unpredictable crowd of women, hotel officials were adamant about concluding the Green Party on schedule.

Click. Li Daiya was back on the Growing Up Green site, scrolling down until she stopped on the link entitled, LILLI'S RECITAL DANCE: FULL LENGTH WITH INTERVIEWS. Ah. This was what the partygoers were demanding to see. She opened the link—in the interest of keeping up with news, of course.

After watching the dance from start to finish, Li Daiya was impatient for the interviews that would follow. First came Ben, who she noted was adept at addressing the camera, even when hounded by young admirers. Next up was Lilli, who the camera caught in a group hug with three of her friends—all young men. Here, Li Daiya paused the recording to study the group. One was an Asian boy—athletic-looking—standing next to Lilli with his arm around her shoulder. The other boys, on her left were also Lilli's age, Caucasian and Latino. When she hit play again the Asian boy spoke to the camera, in flawless English: "Of course we're jealous! Lilli has to practice a lot, and we miss hanging with her."

    Li Daiya watched as the Asian boy, seemingly bothered by the glare of the light mounted on the camera, pulled on sunglasses. But it was too late. She had seen it for herself. The boy's eyes were blue. After taking a moment to catch her breath, Li Daiya reached with trembling hands for her cell phone, remembering the promise of the paper fortune she'd carelessly stuffed in her pocket only moments before.

# 38

For nearly thirteen years, Gao Cheng had been in Li Daiya's list of phone contacts. In the beginning they had talked frequently about how to recover her kidnapped son.

"We'll find him," he assured her at the time. The young, connected businessman took the reigns of the search. How hard could it be to find a male Asian infant with blue eyes? Over time though, they had spoken less and less. Together they had used every resource available to the Chinese Communist Party to find the boy. Much to Gao Cheng's embarrassment and Li Daiya's frustration, they had turned up no trace of the boy and were out of leads. Until now.

Director Li Daiya. The name appeared on Gao Cheng's cell phone that sat on the bed next to his open but still-packed luggage. He swore quietly under his breath. After three rings he decided to answer.

"Director Li," Gao answered. "How good of you to call."

"I am delighted that you are available."

Gao Cheng knew her words were a jab at the fact that he had, for many months, routed Director Li's calls to his assistants. Calls he rarely returned.

"I only arrived in Beijing by plane this morning." The man's answered a bit defensively.

"We must meet. There has been a development."

These were the last words Gao expected to hear. His pride was bruised, and he paused to compose himself. "I have not been contacted," he replied evenly.

"The lead is irrefutable."

"An informant?"

"We cannot talk now. Meet me at my office."

"In one hour?"

"In one hour," Li Daiya confirmed. She would send her staff at the Department of Propaganda out on an errand, so she and Gao could speak privately.

When Li Daiya hired Gao Cheng, she believed he represented the future of China. The son of the country's most renowned geneticist, Gao was rapidly building his own reputation with a prosperous business empire. His commitment to the Chinese Communist Party had worked to his advantage.

A decade passed, and Li Daiya's confidence in Gao's efforts on behalf of the asset waned. It was then that Gao came to her with a plan to expand the search to the United States. It would require new, sophisticated technology. With renewed hope, Li Daiya ordered the development of a search program for the purpose. It was Gao who approached the California State University, Fresno, offering a sizeable grant for a "study" of the Asian population in the States. The strategy was to begin the "study" with searches in areas near prestigious universities. Gao Cheng reasoned that whoever took the boy would most certainly give him the best possible education.

Now it would seem that a chance glimpse of video on the Internet would narrow their search to a single region of a single state.

...

# THE BLU PHENOMENON

Before leaving the Price home for work, Derek received a text from Jewell. The message simply read:

> No coffee for me.

That was the first hint of trouble. Stopping in to grab coffee for the two of them had become a ritual in the weeks since the Data Collection Project got underway. By the time Derek arrived in the office, Jewell was seated at her computer, her focus so intense he couldn't tell if she knew he was there.

"What's up?" he asked, looking over Jewell's shoulder. Beside her was a large coffee cup, half-empty and stone cold.

"The ministry has made a change in our instructions." She broke the news as if it should come as no surprise, as if their time spent in meticulous preparation for the DCP start-up was of little consequence. But Derek's logical mind required an explanation.

"What kind of change?"

Derek could feel Jewell trying her best to avoid another uncomfortable discussion about the objective of the project, which Derek openly questioned. While Jewell had been taught to do what she was told for the honor of her country, without asking questions, Derek had not.

"Not a big setback." Jewell sounded composed. "We've been instructed to alter the data collection search points."

Derek sat down at Stephen's desk, resting his elbow next to the computer keyboard that was decorated with multicolored doughnut sprinkles. Weeks before, he had questioned the reasoning behind setting up search points around prominent universities. The methodology seemed illogical, and he and Jewell had argued the point.

"Why not start at one end of the country and move across to the other?" Derek had posed the question then. "Or begin with areas highly populated with Asians so that a significant amount of data can be immediately accessed and analyzed?"

"There is a reason." Jewell had responded weakly. Truthfully she had not given much thought to where the initial search points were to be set. Why did it have to make sense to her? That was what she was told to do. So she did it.

"So—what's changing?" Derek asked now, with renewed suspicion.

The change in direction came from Wong Bao in a phone call that interrupted Jewell's sleep just after midnight. She had been unable to sleep afterward in anticipation of this very conversation. Jewell sighed. "The search points have been moved to the West Coast—here."

"Here?"

"California, specifically, starting with the southern region and moving north."

"Any reason given?"

Jewell gave a slight shrug without looking up from her work. "Maybe you were right. Maybe they decided to move to areas with the highest Asian populations." She continued to avoid his gaze. "Is that logical enough for you?"

"It definitely makes more sense," admitted Derek. "But why now?

"This is research. A shift in strategy is to be expected."

"Not without a compelling reason," Derek reasoned. "Not this far along."

Jewell pursed her lips nervously.

"Has the criteria changed?" Derek continued his probe.

"It has not."

While everything in him wanted to avoid what would follow, Derek knew he had to state what seemed obvious to him. "So there is only one reasonable answer as to why the search points have changed—suddenly."

Jewell held her breath, hating every moment that she did not tell him everything.

"They are looking for someone in particular."

The asset. When Wong Bao told Jewell there was someone that must be located for the good of China, she had felt proud to be part of the solution. It had driven her night and day for months. Now she just felt ashamed for keeping this information from her partner and not daring to consider whether it was, in fact, in the best interest of the "asset" to actually be found.

# 39

When Cal climbed off his tri-bike, he was sweating profusely. He was overheated, dehydrated, exhausted, and nervous. While he had succeeded in pushing himself two miles beyond the nearly twenty-five miles required for an Olympic triathlon, Cal still had no sense of his time and, therefore, no idea whether his trainer would be pleased or not.

The feeling of not knowing how to judge his own performance was new to Cal. He rarely gave a thought to it when he pulled himself from the pool or finished a run. For these he'd developed an internal timer of sorts that checked in with his limbs and reported back the results to his brain. But not with cycling. The sound of spinning wheels and the pain in new parts of his body—knees, calves, shoulders—didn't provide the information he needed to calculate his time and distance accurately. Then there was the panic. On the tri-bike, there was always the unforeseen: potholes, loose gravel, the car that passes so near to him that, as he told his father, he can make out the flavor of the driver's gum.

"It was a good time." Jack offered his brief assessment.

"Not great. Good."

"What does 'good' mean?" Could he pull off an Olympic triathlon or not?

"Good means you keep working at it. When you are great, I will tell you."

"I need more—information!" Cal insisted. "Please, help me. How much do I need to take off my time?"

"It isn't that simple," Jack replied. "Even if all your times are good, in a triathlon, there are the transitions to consider."

"You mean when you switch from one sport to the next?"

"Yes."

"How's that a big deal?"

"Transitions are like the fourth sport in the event," Jack explained. "If you cannot move quickly and seamlessly from one sport to the next, you fall behind.

"How do I train for that?"

"This we will do on Sundays."

"What about my soccer games and my video 'studies' on Sunday?"

"Soccer's almost done. You have learned to be a teammate, to cooperate. We must move on."

It was true. For the first time ever, Cal had gone a whole season without kicking a soccer ball at a lazy teammate, walking out on a game in a huff, or even uttering a verbal insult at a player or referee.

"How long before I can be done with cycling?" Cal knew he would not get the answer he hoped for.

"When you no longer fear what you cannot control."

"Good luck with that one." Cal took a long drink from his water bottle, squirting some on his head to cool down.

"You have a crash course in this area coming up. True?" It was a reference to the Cal's upcoming meeting with his birth mother. "What day is the meeting?"

"This Sunday."

"Then we begin next Sunday."

For Cal it had been three very long weeks in coming.

"You'll have no control over what you learn that day, how it makes you feel, or what happens after that."

"At least I won't be on two wheels, risking life and limb."

"Different circumstances, same lesson."

Cal returned home that evening from training ravenous as usual. The smell of chicken potpie met him at the door, and he made a beeline to the dining room.

"A day on the bike, huh?" His father asked as he watched Cal inhale his meal.

"Yep, an afternoon of sheer joy," came Cal's sarcastic reply.

"Have you heard about Lilli?" his mom asked.

Cal stopped mid-bite. He looked from his dad to his mom to determine if the news was good or bad. "I saw her at lunch. She seemed okay."

"She was on the news tonight." His mother smiled broadly.

"Really?"

"Seems she and that fellow she danced with the other night were a big hit overseas."

"What do you mean 'overseas'?"

"Well, they only really talked about China. Apparently her dance was broadcast on her mother's program—the *Green Show* or whatever it is."

"Yeah, I know about that," Cal tried to hurry the story along.

"So according to the news, there's a big following for the show there, and response to Lilli's recital was crazy. Apparently the dance school was getting calls all day from people who want the two of them to do a live tour in China!"

Cal sat back, taking in the news. "That's pretty cool." Cal wondered if Lilli and Ben planned to celebrate. Together.

Just then the phone rang from the kitchen. Though no one had mentioned it all week, everyone at the table was anticipating a call from the Vandiver's adoption attorney, Trey Foster, with the final arrangements for Cal's meeting with his birth mother. Glances were shared around the table. The boy's father picked up the phone.

"Bruce Vandiver," he answered in his commanding

headmaster voice.

"Mr. Vandiver—Trey Foster." Mr. Vandiver nodded a confirmation to his family that it was indeed the call they had been waiting for. He put the phone on speaker and set it on the table.

"Good to hear from you, Mr. Foster. We have certainly been anticipating your call." Cal's father resisted the urge to inform the attorney that his return call was, in fact, late to the point of being unprofessional.

"Well, we do have a few details to discuss, don't we? Is this a good time to talk?"

"It is," Mr. Vandiver assured him. "So our meeting date is still on—"

"Definitely," Foster returned. "It is a long drive for one day, about six hours. An early start would be advisable."

"I understand. We can leave here as early as you'd like. We will need directions, of course. Will you also be making the trip to Mendocino?" Cal's father asked.

"Mr. Vandiver," Foster began again, somewhat hesitantly, "it is customary for us to follow the lead of the birth mother as far as the details of such meetings. In this case, it has been requested that I accompany your son to the home of the birth mother in Mendocino—without you or your wife.

"You mean we're expected to send our son across the state to meet someone we don't know—without us being present?"

"You make it sound unusual, Mr. Vandiver, when in fact, it is quite common." Foster continued in a condescending tone. "Often the birth mother is overwhelmed by the thought of meeting both her child and the adoptive family in the same visit. What we want is to ensure a positive, non-threatening experience."

"Is this something that can be discussed further with the birth mother?" Cal's father verged on pleading.

"Let me assure you that your son will be completely safe. He will be provided a car and driver, and I will be his escort. A phone is available in the car, so Cal can contact you at anytime during the trip. Also, it may also be helpful for you to know that I have met with the birth mother on a number of occasions. Cal will find her to be pleasant and welcoming. You have my word on that."

"It just seems unusual—" the boy's father tried again.

The attorney attempted to end any further discussion of the matter with a warning of sorts: "Mr. Vandiver, I know you won't want this opportunity to slip away for Jami—excuse me—Cal."

"He cannot be kept overnight." Cal's father was insistent, knowing full well he was being strong-armed to agree to whatever arrangements Foster made. "And you will accompany him at all times."

"Of course," Foster was relieved the boy's father was cooperating. "We'll be there Sunday morning at 7:00 a.m., okay?" The attorney was anxious to finish the conversation and report the good news back to the Professor.

Left without a choice in the matter, Cal's father agreed. "He'll be ready."

"It's all right," Cal said to his dad when he hung up. "If this is what she wants …"

"We don't know for sure that it is," Cal's mother spoke, looking anxiously at her husband. "We don't really know anything, do we? Derek couldn't even verify that this woman lives in Mendocino. They could be taking our son anywhere!"

The truth of this statement caused Cal's stomach to flip-flop. Who might want to steal him away? It was the unanswered question of the dream he'd carried for years.

"The phone …" Mr. Vandiver was thinking out loud.

"There's a phone in the car. That helps, I guess," commented Cal.

"But you won't always be in the car," his mother countered.

"He can take his own cell phone though," Cal's dad continued his thought. "It has GPS tracking on it—"

"You've been tracking me?"

"No," Mr. Vandiver assured his son, "but it does have that capability. If we activate it, you can carry it with you, and we can track you by computer."

"But if he needed us, we still couldn't get to him," Cal's mother argued. "I'm not feeling good about this."

Cal jumped in with an idea. "What if you guys just followed us?"

His father shook his head, defeated. "We don't know that we aren't being watched ourselves. If we break the agreement, they could call off the whole thing."

"Ah, but I have *friends* who can follow us!"

"I don't want to put anyone else's family at risk," Cal's father rejected the suggestion, though without much conviction.

"Derek's twenty-one—and a brain!"

"They *are* young adults, Bruce. And I would feel better knowing they were close by if Cal needed them."

Mr. Vandiver's silence was his reply.

"I'll see who can go," Cal said with finality. It was a good plan, and Cal felt his whole body relax.

That night, Cal sent an email to Levi, Lilli, and Derek. He knew Miguel would be on the soccer field on Sunday. It was the district championship, and Cal would miss it. He'd be there to take the state championship though. But at the moment, Cal was just anticipating the visit with his birth mother. It would be worth it all: the missed game; the long drive; the pre-visit nerves; the possibility of disappointment. In the late-night email to his friends, Cal wrote:

> Hey Guys—Road trip! Who's up for a six-hour ride to Mendocino on Sunday morning? (Gas and food provided.) Only the best spies in Visalia need apply. Meet up at the Price place tomorrow night at 8. Respond if you can make it, so I can bring enough of my mom's cookies!

# 40

Whether it was loyalty or Mrs. Vandiver's cookies that brought them, each of Cal's invitees showed Tuesday evening at the Price's garage. Derek was alone tinkering at the computer when Cal arrived. The two were the first to the tin of still-warm M&M cookies. Lilli was next to appear, followed by Levi.

"Better be some left for us." Levi gave a look of warning to his older brother.

"Not my problem you can't tell time."

"You knew I was studying!"

To avoid a brawl, Cal handed the cookie tin to Levi. "Plenty here, dude," Cal assured him. "By the way, I think I passed my literature quiz today."

"Passed?" Levi worried aloud. "As in, *just* passed?" He knew Jack would blame the tutor if Cal's grades fell off.

"Eat a cookie, you'll feel better," Lilli suggested to Levi from her spot on the floor where she was massaging first one foot then the other. Soon all eyes were on her.

"Now that's *pretty*," Levi managed the snide remark, even with a mouth stuffed with cookie. "Not!"

"Sorry! My feet have been cramping all day. But they don't smell!"

"Yeah, well, if you want a cookie," Levi scrunched his nose, "I'll hand it to you."

"I don't do white sugar, thank you."

Derek was the one to get the meeting on track. "So tell us about this meeting with your birth mom."

"I'm not sure I believe it's real yet," Cal said. "I mean, you guys didn't even find her on the computer. And it kind of freaks me out that my parents can't even go with me."

"What?" Lilli erupted. "They can't go, but *we* can?"

"Well, technically, you guys can't go either. Hence the reference to 'spies' in my email. I'm told my birth mother requested I come alone—or the deal's off."

"Something's not right about that," Derek said, rubbing his stubble of facial hair.

"What do you need us to do?" Lilli now sat at attention, her legs tucked under her.

"My dad plans to use the GPS tracking on my phone to keep up with me, but I need you guys to be there, at least in the area, in case something weird happens and I don't ever get to Mendocino."

"I'll gas up the car," Derek said. "Who's coming with me?"

"You know I'll be there," volunteered Levi.

"No way I'm not going," Lilli stated, completing the list. "Any chance we'll get to see her?"

"I wish." Cal answered. "You'll be close enough to see that everything is okay, but far enough away that no one gets the idea that I've been followed."

"So you get a car and a driver, and we get Derek?" Levi complained.

"Yeah, well, I'm stuck in the car with a lawyer dude born with no personality—for real," Cal grumbled.

"Can we even agree on food or music?" Lilli asked half joking. "It's a long drive."

"I could ask Jewell to come—if Cal doesn't mind." Derek

looked at Cal. "She's cool."

"Ooh! Yes!" Lilli squealed.

"Who's that again?" Cal asked, embarrassed.

"She's Derek's smart girlfriend," Levi offered, hoping to get a rise from his brother.

"She's not my girlfriend," Derek clarified. "But I did promise to introduce her to Lilli."

Cal shrugged. "Good idea. Then there'll be *two* famous ladies in the car."

"I'm not famous." Lilli tightened her ponytail. "Maybe Ben is famous. He's the one with all the girls crashing my mother's site."

"They crashed the site?" Derek's mind shifted into fix-it mode.

"Nearly. Techtronix is, like, working 24/7 to manage all the posts coming in. My aunt's been at our house for days helping keep track of stuff."

"From cheerleader to international celebrity!" Cal joked.

"Yeah, well, I'd trade my so called 'celebrity' to get the chance you're getting on Sunday. I'm really excited."

"I wish you guys could be right there with me," Cal confessed, looking apologetic. "Finally we all get a day to be together, and we're not even—together. Instead we're connected by satellite!"

"It's all good," Levi said. "We wouldn't want to be anywhere else."

"Even if it means leaving at seven in the morning?" The three spies groaned in unison.

...

At 7:00 a.m. on the dot, a silver Town Car with tinted windows arrived at the Vandiver driveway, where the family stood waiting. The driver stepped out of the car, and Foster emerged from the back seat dressed in suit and tie. Cal suddenly felt a little embarrassed by his jeans and white button down shirt. He also carried his backpack, in which he tucked his cell, earphones, and his physical science textbook—as strongly suggested by Levi.

After exchanging hellos, Foster introduced the uniformed Latino man who would be their driver for the day. "This is Sergio."

Cal's parents nodded at the man. "Sergio," the boy's father made eye contact with the driver, "I am entrusting you with the safety of my son."

"I understand, sir," the man answered politely.

"Shall we?" Foster gestured for Cal to load into the back seat, anxious to avoid unexpected or uncomfortable questions.

"It's going to be okay," the boy's father said to his son.

His mother forced a smile and resisted the urge to give him a hug. "Hurry home," she said. Cal thought this must be what it felt like to leave for war.

Cal took a seat behind Sergio and next to Foster. Three blocks away, the compact car, loaded with Derek and Levi in the front and Lilli and Jewell in the back, prepared for their mission.

Levi let out a low whistle when the impressive silver vehicle passed their street.

"That's our cue," said Derek.

"Geez, Louise," Levi said admiringly, his mouth ajar.

"Quit gawking and make sure we're tracking Cal on the laptop."

"I told you I've got it covered," Levi snapped.

"I wish we could track where the mother is coming from this morning," Jewell said, still frustrated that the DCP failed to locate the woman. "She has to be coming into Mendocino from somewhere else. What other explanation is there?"

"If anyone can figure it out, you and Derek can," Lilli remarked. She still couldn't believe she'd be spending the day with Jewell Chan, Derek's famous inventor friend. There was so much she wanted to learn about the person, her career, and about their shared country of birth.

"I appreciate your confidence," Jewell responded with modesty.

"Would you mind," Lilli began shyly, "telling me the story behind the Glo-Me? I think it's so cool!" Levi interrupted their chat when he turned and began searching around the floor of the backseat.

"Can I help you?" Lilli asked, clearly annoyed.

"I want to take a peek at the munchies Cal's mother packed us."

"Really?" Derek's tone was meant to warn his brother not to embarrass him in front of Jewell.

"What? It's going to be a long ride!"

...

The Town Car had all the bells and whistles: light gray leather interior, a stereo system and TV with headphones, and a compartment loaded with snack items complete with a cooler for drinks. But what Cal really wanted was to have his friends with him. He didn't like long trips, especially when he didn't know where he was going. And he most certainly didn't like strangers. To keep his mind from playing out potential disaster scenarios, Cal slipped on the headphones and played with the stereo system until he found a station he liked. Then he concentrated on breathing deeply and slowly.

After half an hour, Cal decided to attempt conversation with his backseat companion.

"You're pretty dressed up," Cal remarked to Foster.

"I'm on the job; I wear a suit."

"Can you tell me her name *now*?"

"Sorry."

"You told my parents that you met with her lots of times."

"A few. It's not unusual."

Cal didn't bother hiding his irritation. "I bet it's unusual for a kid to be escorted without his parents to meet his birth mother and not even have her name, no photo—nothing."

Foster squirmed in his seat. "Her situation is unique."

"Yeah, well, my situation is unique too, isn't it?"

The lawyer stared out the window as he spoke, "It could be a lot worse, kid."

Cal knew it was true. He had a family. Great friends. Everything he needed and more. But knowing where he landed didn't erase the questions about how he got there. How had he escaped an orphanage? Where did his blue eyes come from? How did Coach Jack end up in his life? Why did he have dreams of being taken from his family? What was the big secret around his birth mother that he couldn't even learn her name?

The boy laid his head back against the cool leather and hoped answers awaited him at his destination. To kill time, he allowed himself to drift into a state of half-sleep.

By the time Sergio pulled the car into a gas station, two hours had passed. In the restroom, Cal checked his phone for texts. No news. It would appear that he was on his way to Mendocino after all.

# 41

The woman kept to her routine, walking the post-harvest vineyard, watching the break of a clear autumn day in northern California. Inside, she brewed her coffee and seated herself on the brightly colored couch in the sunroom that overlooked the estate. The workmen who had spent the past weeks irrigating and fertilizing the empty, browning vines were told to stay home today. The faith she had that the vines would again hang heavy with sweet grapes come summer was the same faith she needed now: faith to believe everything she'd done in the past fourteen years mattered.

The ring of the phone broke the silence. She smiled knowing the sound signaled the start of the most anticipated day of her life.

"Good morning!" the woman answered.

"Good morning!" came an enthusiastic greeting from the Professor. "You are well, I hope," came his deep voice again, "and ready for your visitor?"

"Yes!" she answered, genuinely happy. "Tia and I are ready for a little excitement."

"I am envious." The Professor's words carried deep, pained honesty.

"But you are patient," she replied. It was a trait the woman admired. As she had come to observe, Professor Si Zhen used careful timing to accomplish great things. Knowing when to wait and when to move was his gift.

"May we enjoy a result as sweet as your harvest."

"I only ask that you spare me from crossing paths with Foster ever again." Si Zhen laughed at the request. When he had recovered, he spoke of the future.

"Foster will be out of your life soon. You will come, and the work will continue. We will watch the world change before our eyes."

"It will be worth it all," she answered, her hopeful sigh audible across the ocean. "I must excuse myself now."

"Today, you take the gold."

After the woman hung up she walked the living spaces of the house, checking her desktop, the fireplace mantle, the pictures on the coffee table. Everything was in place. It was time to dress for the day.

...

Cal woke again when he felt Sergio exit the highway. At 3:00 p.m., the driver announced, for Cal's benefit, they had arrived in Mendocino. It was an especially bright day, and Cal could feel the nearness of the ocean. Farther down the road, brightly painted homes and meticulous landscaping gave way to long stretches of land where homes appeared like small islands in oceans plowed into neat rows: vineyards.

Sergio slowed and turned right at a huge iron gate that stood open, as if awaiting their arrival. Once through the gate, the car began a trek down a tree-lined road that hid all but the short stretch of road to the next curve and continued until Cal could no longer hold his silence.

"Does she own all this land?" Foster made no reply.

When they emerged rather suddenly from the trees, Cal looked out across acres of vineyard, hilly and barren, marked out by rows and rows of vine stakes as tall as himself. It was an impressive view made even more so by the large home that appeared on the horizon, in the midst of the fields.

The sprawling Spanish-style ranch with ivory stucco exterior and striking orange roof tiles was unlike any home Cal had ever seen. Sergio pulled the car around the side of the house to a shady double carport. A wide brick paver walkway offered visitors the option of entering by the side door or continuing around to the front porch and the huge, gleaming wood door. A sunroom jutted off the back of the house. The bark of a dog sounded their arrival. Cal stepped out of the car and was greeted by a brown and white collie that happily sniffed at his jeans, ignoring Foster.

"Away, Tia!" Foster ordered the dog.

"She's nice," Cal said in the dog's defense, leaning over to pet Tia's thick, unkempt coat. Even Sergio opened his door to reach out and give the dog a pat on the head. Cal looked up again and thought he saw movement in the sunroom. He pushed his shades up on his head; it would be rude to have them on when he met his mother.

# 42

Foster made his way to the side door nearest to the driveway. Ivy-covered lattices framed the entrance. Cal wondered if it would be more appropriate to make their appearance at the front door, but Foster didn't hesitate. Despite a bark of protest from the dog, the man stepped up and rapped on the door.

To Cal's surprise, a youngish soccer-mom type answered the door. A blonde ponytail poked out the back of her sports cap.

"Well, hello!" the woman greeted them.

"Candace, this is Cal Vandiver," Foster started. "Cal, meet Candace Latham." The boy shook her outstretched hand. The woman wore no make-up, and Cal noticed she was slender, accustomed to physical work. She showed no formality with Foster, as if they were well acquainted, though not necessarily happy to be so. But for Cal she had an intentional, welcoming smile.

"Call me Candace."

Foster offered no further details about the woman's identity, leaving Cal to wonder. It appeared as though she worked at the winery. Did she also live there?

"Come on in." The woman opened the door wide. Cal entered first, followed by Foster, Candace, and Tia. Inside, Cal stifled a "wow!" Though very different in style, the home rivaled the Cohens'. The space had two-story beamed ceilings, huge arched doorways, and warm-colored hardwood floors. The furniture in the main room was also wood, rustic but with big cushions and bright colors. And there was a certain smell in the room, a light sweetness. Was this how his mother smelled?

Candace opened the glass doors that led to the sunroom. Tia joined them, pressing up against Cal's legs like an old friend. The view out the back, across the grounds, nearly took Cal's breath. It was a few moments before he became aware of the cushioned wicker furnishings arranged for conversation. A glass pitcher filled with a rose colored beverage and drinking glasses beckoned from a side table.

"This is my favorite place to sit and talk." Candace reached down to pat Tia and gestured for Cal and Foster to take a seat.

"Thank you, Candace." Foster straightened his suit jacket.

"Please, help yourself to a glass of sparkling punch—a local specialty. It'll give you some idea of the flavor of the grapes we grow here—not now, of course, but in the summer."

Where was his mother? Was she on the grounds? Had she gotten cold feet—or was she bedridden? Cal thought he would burst before the adults got around to the reason they sat there, waiting.

"Excuse me, Candace—" Cal started but was interrupted by Foster.

"Cal, let me tell you a little about Ms. Latham," he began his well-rehearsed dialogue. "I know the name is probably unfamiliar to you—being so young, of course—but many around the world know Candace Latham as a former Olympian."

"Probably wouldn't guess it now, but I did play volleyball at the Games in 2000, and again in 2004," the woman explained. "But that's been a long time ago. Really, I've had at least one much greater accomplishment since then."

"Awesome," Cal responded distractedly. Why were they talking about the Olympics?

The cap came off, and the woman smoothed the top of her hair.

Foster continued, "The greater accomplishment to which Ms. Latham refers—is you."

Blue eyes. He hadn't seen it under the shadow of the cap; the woman had blue eyes with the hue and intensity he'd only seen once before. In the mirror.

"Cal—I'm your mother," the woman's said, her eyes filling with tears.

The boy was unable to speak. He just stared, trying to process the unexpected announcement. Besides the color of her eyes and maybe her propensity for athletics, he could not find himself in this woman. She was Caucasian. Blonde no less.

"I don't believe you!" Cal was on his feet, aware that he had nowhere to go. The thought of his friends and a dramatic rescue flashed through his mind.

Foster lunged toward the boy, as if to keep him from running, but Candace held up her arm to stop the man.

"I know all this is hard—" she started.

"It's impossible!" Cal interrupted.

"Cal, your father is Asian," Candace answered softly, convincingly. "But look, you did get something of me," she lied, pointing to her eyes. He would learn the truth another time, she reminded herself. In another place.

"Your eyes were blue when you were born, but I never dreamed—" She stopped and looked at Cal intently.

"Yeah, I'm a freak!" came his pained response. Cal knew his words stung, but he was unrepentant. Was he supposed to pretend that his eye color didn't matter? If she was his mother, why hadn't they been able to go through life blue-eyed together? At least something would have made sense.

"I have pictures," she offered gently. "Can I show you?"

Without answering, Cal dropped down heavily on the couch.

This was the moment. If there was any truth to this woman's claim, he had to know. It could be the key to unlocking his mysterious past and releasing him to a future without fear dogging his every step.

"Show me," Cal insisted. "But I don't need a babysitter." He looked out across the grounds and away from the attorney.

Foster was quick to respond. "While he is in my charge, I feel it only appropriate that I stay—"

"This is *my* time!" The words erupted from Cal. "My parents would want you to honor this simple request!"

"Fine," Foster reluctantly agreed. "I'll be just outside the door." He stood to leave. "As you know, our time is limited." The statement sounded like a warning. "We'll be returning late as it is." Candace and the boy sat in silence until they heard the side door click shut.

Candace reached under the couch and pulled out a photo album and set it in Cal's lap. He opened the heavy, leather-covered album to pictures he recognized of himself. Many of the pictures were identical to those he'd seen again and again in the Vandiver home. But there were others.

"Here we are in the hospital, showing off our matching identification wrist bands," she pointed out. "Yours reads, 'Baby Latham.'"

In another picture, Candace pulled a piece of rolling luggage while wearing a loaded floral baby sling across her chest.

"That was in the airport in Hong Kong," she explained. "You were on your way home."

"Who took the pictures?"

The question brought a smile to her face. "We had an escort from the center. You know about that, right?"

"Yeah."

Now Candace sat up, looked at the door and spoke to Cal in a whisper. "Would you like to walk the fields? Just us?"

"Sure."

From where he stood at the side of the house, Foster

cursed as he watched Cal and the woman leave the porch for the fields. He had only wired the house for sound, and Candace knew it.

"I love coming out here," Candace admitted. "I never thought I'd live here this long."

"How did it happen?"

"In 2004, at the Games in Athens, a diver friend of mine named Sarah introduced me to her very handsome brother. Thomas was a diver too.

"Is he my father?"

"Yes." She pulled at her ponytail. "He and Sarah were good friends to me. After a shoulder injury put me out of competition, Thomas asked me to return to China with him, and I did. I taught students to speak English at the University of Hong Kong."

"Did he leave you because of me?"

"Actually, his parents were the ones to end things. They thought I was a distraction to their son's training and, basically, told me I was on my own. Sarah stayed by my side though. She introduced me to a professor who kept China-born infants out of orphanages by matching them with American educators. After you were born, he escorted me here."

Rather than looking at the perplexed face of her listener, Candace pretended to examine the vines as they walked.

"What aren't you telling me?" Cal stopped and waited for the woman to meet his eyes. It was a question for which she was unprepared.

After first glancing up the hill at Foster, she continued in a low voice. "The man who brought me here is known simply as 'the Professor.' You will meet him one day soon, and he can tell you much more." Candace turned abruptly toward the house. "Time is running out. Let's go inside, I want to learn about you."

In the open living area, the two sat together on the huge couch. There, Cal shared—or rather spilled—the details of his life as a Vandiver. He described his parents, his friends, and confessed his own dream of Olympic gold. News of his Olympic training didn't seem to surprise Candace. She simply remarked, "It's in your genes."

A framed Olympic medal dated 2000 sat on Candace's desk. "The U.S. team made the podium—bronze—in Sydney," she explained. "But in Athens, four years later, my shoulder went out on me in the semi-finals, and we came in fourth. That was tough."

"So you stopped playing?"

"Had to," she answered. "It was a career-ending injury, and I'm reminded of it every morning." She winced as she rotated her right shoulder.

"Who's that?" Cal asked, pointing to the picture of an Asian couple on the fireplace mantle.

"That's Sarah," she answered with fondness, "and Thomas."

"Could you come to Visalia sometime?" Cal asked on impulse. A second later he wished he could take it back. The small Vandiver home couldn't compare to the life of Candace Latham. Would she pity him?

Candace busied her hands, arranging the copies of the photos she had made for Cal to take home. "This is the hard part," she said without looking up. "I won't be able to see you here again."

"What do you mean?" Cal's heart pounded. Why wouldn't she want to see him?

"Please—it has nothing to do with you." She reached over and touched Cal on the knee. A tear escaped down her cheek. "I'm leaving."

"You're moving? From this house?" Cal was stunned. Already he had envisioned visiting Candace at the winery for years to come.

"I'm going back to China," she explained, attempting a smile. "I still have a lot of life ahead of me. I've been asked to come and do some coaching there." Now she hesitated. "Maybe I'll even catch up with Thomas and tell him all about you."

"You hardly know anything about me."

"It's true," Candace continued. "But you also know we're not going to see each other much here, not with your training and the distance between us." She gave him a moment to recover before speaking again. "You could come to me though."

Cal looked up, confused. "How am I supposed to visit you in China?"

"Maybe not right now, but you will be an Olympian. Your world is going to grow very big. You may very well find yourself near to me, and we can see each other again."

"What about your own family?"

"There is no one left for me in Michigan, where I'm from. There was a parting of the ways when I went to China with Thomas. And when you came along," she bit her lip and chose her words carefully, "life changed." With a sincerity Cal tucked away like a present, Candace told him, "Then as now, you are a gift to my life, and I don't regret anything that's happened. I *do* want to stay in touch, but I wanted you to know that I won't be six hours away."

"Maybe we can video chat?"

"That would be great," she brightened. "I don't know exactly where I'll be yet, but I know how to get in touch with you." There was a knock at the side door. "Uh oh," Candace made a sour face. "There's the warden."

"Guess I have to go." Cal gathered the photos he'd been given. What a story he had for everybody at home.

"Just one minute," Candace called to Foster. Mother and son stood, and Tia pushed by them towards the door.

"That wasn't much time," Cal remarked, working to etch his mother's face into his memory.

"There's a Chinese proverb," Candace said. "It goes, 'From a good beginning cometh a good end.' This is our beginning."

Using her cell phone, Candace took some photos, including shots of Tia, the view from the sunroom where they'd met, and one of her Olympic medal.

"You believe we will see each other again," Cal said, searching her eyes and finding honesty behind them.

"I do," she assured him. Then she leaned in and gave him a kiss on the cheek. It seemed to Cal that she wasn't just hopeful that their paths would cross again—but certain of it.

At the door, Cal reached down to give a consolatory pat to the dog that pressed affectionately against his leg. "Hey, I forgot to ask, how did Tia get her name?"

"Tia is short for Tiananmen. As in Tiananmen Square," Candace answered. Now a serious expression crossed her face. "If you don't know that story, I highly recommend that you learn about it."

Outside, the sun was low but still bright and warm. Foster and Sergio waited in the car.

"Let's take a selfie!" Candace insisted.

Cal slipped off his shades for the parting picture, so his mother would remember what they shared.

"Put your number in my phone, and I'll send these to you," Candace suggested.

"Great idea."

"When will you leave?" Cal asked, as he keyed in his number.

"Soon."

Reluctantly, Cal slid into the waiting vehicle and waved. Sadness had settled on him even before Sergio had backed them down the driveway. Already this place felt familiar to him. Now Candace was disappearing into the most populous country in the world. How did she think he would ever be able to find her there?

# 43

A mile past the gated entrance, the band of spies sat parked at an ancient gas station. With no working gas pumps, what remained was a small convenience store that catered to tourists. By this time, the elder Price was at the end of his patience with his younger brother. Had Jewell not been there, Derek would have pounded his brother hours before, either for the endless trips into the tiny store for junk food, for snoring, or for telling lame jokes that Jewell either didn't understand or politely pretended not to.

"There's movement on the GPS!" Jewell was the first to notice. Everyone in the car was immediately at attention.

"Yes!" Derek exclaimed. Even with six hours of driving ahead of him, he was relieved to be on the move again. "They are definitely taking off. Let's see if they leave the way they came." Now Derek's phone sounded. It was Cal's father.

"Yes, sir," Derek confirmed that they were seeing the same movement. "They are definitely headed back to the highway. We're pulling out now, and hopefully, we'll all be home with Cal soon."

"I think the snack man will be sad," Lilli pretended to pout as they pulled out of the gravel lot of the lonely store. "He almost made enough off Levi to plant his own winery."

"Just doing my part to stimulate the economy," Levi defended himself. "You should be thanking me."

At last, the Town Car deposited Cal and left the Windswept neighborhood. Derek pulled into the Vandiver driveway and onto a scene that indeed resembled a soldier's return. Friends and family gathered in the yard and on the small lighted front porch to welcome Cal and to celebrate the safe return of the carload of tired spies.

With everyone together at last, Cal was bustled into the house and released to the best seat in the house—his dad's lounger. In spite of the hubbub, the first thing Cal noticed was an expertly-prepared chocolate frosted cake that sat on the dining room table. A gift from the Cohens, no doubt, and the work of Juan. Cal's stomach rumbled at the sight of it.

When everyone was settled in and around the living room, Cal did his best to give his audience a dramatic telling of what was, in actuality, a pretty uneventful tale. There had been no attempted kidnapping. He did, however, have a few bombs to drop on his audience.

"Jack, here's one for you," Cal started. "Guess what my birth mother was doing during the years before I was born?"

Jack played along, taking a stab in the dark. "Coaching girls' soccer?"

"Nope! She was training and competing in the Olympic Games!" While Jack's prediction had been spot on, now he looked at Cal with skepticism.

"No, really! She medaled a bronze in volleyball. I saw it myself! But before I go on, I have another million-dollar question—for Derek and Jewell." Everyone's eyes fell on the couple sitting shoulder to shoulder on the floor.

"Guys! There's a crazy mind-blowing reason why you couldn't find my birth mother using your high-tech, fancy-schmancy search program. Care to take a guess?"

"No clue," Derek responded.

"Please, what is it?" asked Jewell who had lost many hours of sleep trying to answer that very question.

After a dramatic pause that had everyone in the room listening with rapt attention, Cal blurted the unimaginable news. "My birth mother—Candace Latham—is not Asian. She is Caucasian with beau-ti-ful blue eyes!"

"This is good news—and so exciting!" came Jewell's relieved response. "Will you see her again?"

Cal shrugged. He had no answer to that question. Only a picture of the two of them on his phone.

...

The next morning, Derek and Jewell, coffees in hand, got an early start in an attempt to catch up on work missed while in Mendocino. In the time that they were away, thousands of names had been picked up by the search program, which then gathered and stored confidential information on each entry. From spending habits to political preferences, it was all there. And the Asian subjects would never know their privacy had ever been breached. With each passing day, Derek grew more concerned about how easily such information could be abused in the wrong hands. Could the Chinese government be trusted? Could Jewell's boss Wong Bao?

Derek heard a gasp from across the room where Jewell sat at her computer.

"What's up?" Derek asked, alarmed. "You okay?"

"I should have come in last night." Jewell's voice trembled. "I was foolish to take a day away."

"I know there's a lot of catch up, but we'll get it done." Derek looked again and saw that Jewell was not checking the program results at all. She was reading her work email.

"It's not that." Jewell stared at her monitor. "I missed something."

"Was there a malfunction?"

"No, no!" Jewell shook her head. "It was information—a

record of interest—that came in, and I wasn't here to find it before—"

"Before what?"

"Before the record was automatically sent on to Beijing."

"But you have the information now, right?"

"It doesn't matter now. It's too late. The program flagged an entry—for some reason—and sent an alert to me. When I didn't respond within thirty minutes, it was sent on to Beijing without my review."

"You can't work 24/7!"

"They will see that I failed."

Derek pulled a chair up next to her. "Jewell, you're looking at this all wrong." Even though she refused to look at him, he continued. "The DCP did its job, flawlessly—which is really quite genius. You had permission to leave, for Pete's sake. It's all good!"

Jewell was in no mood to be consoled. The information she should have been the first to receive was routed to her boss. Now he knew something that she did not. She thought of the asset.

"What determines a 'record of interest' anyway?" Derek asked now, as if reading her mind.

"Any number of things." Jewell answered, choosing her words carefully. "Beyond the primary goal of analyzing the U.S. Asian population, the DCP has a secondary search function with specific criteria built in to help identify known fugitives from China, that kind of thing." Derek noted that Jewell busied herself at the computer and didn't look at him as she spoke.

"But until now, this has been the only record flagged, right? That means the criteria must be very, very specific. First we're told—rather suddenly and without explanation—to redirect the search to California. Now, a particular record has been identified. And my guess is that I would *not* be allowed to access that record. Am I right?"

"That is protocol." Jewell spoke matter of factly. "Access to a flagged record is restricted."

"But *you* can access that record, correct?" Derek felt his temper rising.

"The reason it was flagged is only of interest to my country—not yours."

"Let's review," Derek began. "You have information about someone—perhaps even a U.S. citizen—that was obtained in partnership but are now withholding that shared information?"

"The data is shared, not records of interest. These are confidential," Jewell returned, hoping to quell the discussion. "Please don't make this an issue."

"I have a better idea," Derek shot back. "You share that record with me, and I don't have to explain to Dr. Tan that the study he thought was a gift from the universe to ensure his cozy retirement is no more than a gross intrusion on the private information of our citizenry for the purpose of tracking persons—or a person—of interest to the Chinese government."

"You're being paranoid," Jewell responded. "I will just finish the work here myself. You are free to go."

"Yes, I am always free to go," Derek pointed out. "But I choose not to. I think I'll finish what I started here. I like my coworkers to know they can count on me." The two finished the day in silence. Derek left at dinnertime without offering Jewell a ride back to the Lunar. She would have to call for a car.

Even in the noisy Price house it was evident to all that Derek was out of sorts. Even the cat stayed clear of him. Skipping dinner in an effort to avoid questions, Derek disappeared to his room. He worried that he had overreacted to news of the blocked record. As Jewell pointed out, the record was flagged for reasons that had nothing to do with the study results. In the end Derek decided that the disagreement wasn't important enough to him to affect his friendship with Jewell. He would apologize and hope she would accept. Eventually he fell asleep, his stomach churning with worry and hunger.

Sometime in the wee hours of the morning, Derek's cell phone sounded. After some scrambling he retrieved it from his bedcovers. It was Jewell. Derek braced himself for whatever was coming. At the last second he decided to try a bit of humor.

"Obi-Wan Kenobi," Derek answered. There was a pause at the other end of the line. "Oh, yeah," he jumped in, "I keep forgetting you haven't seen the Star Wars movies. I think we should do that."

"Should we make up first?" Jewell asked timidly.

"Absolutely," he answered. "I was wrong."

"I wish you were wrong. But you weren't."

"Okay, I was right, in principle, but I do understand the sensitive position you're in, and I'm willing to let it go to keep my coffee partner. The deal is, though, that you cannot tell anyone that I caved in an argument."

"Derek, listen to me," Jewell continued, insistent. "Something is not right, and I'm scared."

"Tell me."

"I accessed the record, the flagged one. I was hoping I was wrong and that it would be insignificant." Here Jewell paused. If she continued there would be no going back. "But it's not."

"Don't say anything more."

"But I need to tell you—"

"Not now. Not on your phone. I'll pick you up half an hour early. Don't be afraid, okay?"

"I'll try," she said weakly.

"There is no try—only do," he paraphrased the words of the Master Jedi Yoda before he could stop himself.

"What?"

"Sorry—it's dialogue from a movie. I'm an idiot. See you in a little while."

Jewell felt only minutely better when she hung up. At least she was on speaking terms again with her partner. But worry gnawed at her, and she was still very much awake when her cell phone rang an hour later. It was Wong Bao.

"Good morning, Wong Bao," Jewell said respectfully to her boss.

"Your day of sightseeing wine country was good, I hope?"

"I enjoyed it very much. Thank you for permitting me time away."

"It has been my experience that something always happens when I leave the office. It is the same for you, am I right?" he asked without malice.

Jewell forced a little laugh. "I am sorry that you did not receive the news directly from me."

Wong Bao spoke as a man who had come into good fortune. "It is no worry. You have served your country well in this important matter." Jewell did not feel the happiness she once did when Wong offered her a compliment.

"Thank you. Do you have further instructions for me?"

"Only to continue your work on the project, which will be of great benefit. The other matter is already being addressed, thanks to you. Please, forgive me for disturbing your rest."

"It is always an honor to speak with you," Jewell said before hanging up. It was some time before she fell into a restless sleep.

When Derek pulled up in front of the Lunar a few hours later, Jewell was already waiting for him at the curbside. The two exchanged a smile as Jewell settled into the seat beside him, eyeing the two cups of coffee that sat in the center console.

"Sleep okay?" Derek broke the ice.

"Let's just say I waited for it to be morning—all night."

"Sorry about that," he commented. "But I have something for you!" Derek tossed a pink fuzzy something into her lap, and Jewell let out a small squeal.

"What is it?" She refused to touch it without further information.

"It's my sister's cell phone," he answered, chuckling. "Can you believe it?"

With two fingers, Jewell pickup up what looked like a hot pink mouse, examining all sides then flipping it open. "Why do you have it?"

"I don't have it—*you* do," he answered. "It's our 'hot line'—meaning I think it's a good idea if we have some of our conversations on a phone that we know for sure hasn't been tampered with. Don't you agree?"

"You think someone might be listening to us?"

"If you have sensitive information, it's possible."

"Your sister—she will miss her phone!"

"True, but nobody in our family will miss my sister having her phone. It's okay, really."

Jewell opened her briefcase and attempted to stuff the phone and all its protruding pink into it. "Thank you, I think."

"So what's the scoop on the mysterious record?"

Jewell wondered now, as she had all night, where to begin. "I'll start by saying you were right to be suspicious about the flagged record."

"So what you found—it's important?"

Jewell nodded, picking up the coffee cup from the console. "Please don't be angry with me. I have always done what I was told, without question. But it's different now."

The car stopped at a red light. "I know that." Derek touched her arm gently. "It's okay."

"When I was given this assignment, I was told that an asset to China had been kidnapped. Years of searching in China brought no results. It was decided to expand the search in this country. So I was directed to design a search program that would include very specific criteria that would allow us to identify this person." Here Jewell took a deep breath. "And it worked."

The light turned green, but it took the blast of a horn behind him to get Derek moving.

"Derek, I am betraying the trust of the ministry and my country by telling you about the record."

"How could it possibly be important for me to know?

Maybe you shouldn't—"

"It has to do with your friend."

"My friend?" Derek asked, suddenly feeling queasy.

"The criteria specified an Asian male, born in Hong Kong, now thirteen years old." Jewell stopped to collect herself. "And the asset has blue eyes."

# 44

A small television sat on a shelf on the far wall of the Professor's office. A male reporter with the China News Service was delivering the midday news.

"A record-breaking number of flights into the country have been recorded at each of China's eight major airports in recent weeks," the reporter stated in Mandarin. "The majority of those flights are arriving from the United States, but as of yet, there is no explanation for the jump. Officials say an investigation is underway to ensure the influx in no way poses a safety threat to the people of China."

Si Zhen broke the quiet of his quarters with laughter. "Waiyin—" he called to his long-time assistant, who took calls and made appointments for the Professor from a tiny adjoining room. When she appeared at the doorway, the Professor nodded toward the television but couldn't resist delivering the news himself.

"They can't figure out why there's been an increase in the number of flights from the U.S. to China!" Now they listened together. The reporter continued: "Airport security has indicated that a large number of the travelers are Asian women adopted out of Chinese orphanages." The Professor beamed.

"You have opened the door of healing," Waiyin congratulated the Professor.

"Ah, but we hope for so much more, don't we?" he asked rhetorically.

"Professor," Waiyin started timidly. "He is coming?"

"Soon," came his thoughtful reply. "Next Thursday is the American Thanksgiving. With your assistance, I will be giving thanks in California."

"You wish to arrive on the Tuesday before?"

"Tuesday, yes. That would give me time."

"Shall I arrange the meeting with Bai Zhao Man?"

"I will contact him myself." It was the Professor's intention to wait until late in the evening to call, when the esteemed trainer would be taking his morning tea.

He would also make time to meet with Kevin Bower at Techtronix to thank him for his fine work. Bower had been most accommodating when the Professor contacted him with a plan to expand *Growing Up Green with Linda Cohen* into China. The Professor himself paid the company to provide Chinese translation for the vlog. The super fan page had also been his idea.

As Bower had explained to Linda Cohen, the super fan page gave viewers the opportunity to submit their email addresses in order to receive the Growing Up Green blog and product promotions. The hostess was unaware, however, of the second opportunity afforded to super fans. Even Valerie missed its significance.

Super fan participants received an automated request to complete a personal "profile." Among other questions posed, super fans were asked to indicate their ethnicity. Those identifying themselves as Chinese were asked to indicate if they were either a Chinese birth mother or an adoptee. A checked box routed respondents to a highly protected chat room, where they could search the names of other super fans, in hopes of connecting with their birth family.

Super fans in China quickly caught on to the secret nature of the chat room, and news of the tool spread by word of mouth. Quite suddenly, children given up as a result of China's "one-child rule" or stolen and sold on the black market were exchanging notes with a lost parent or sibling. And in America, adoptees weren't just settling for contact via the chat room; they were flying into China—in droves.

# 45

The headmaster's executive secretary, Tami, stuck her head into her boss's office. He had been on the phone for the better part of an hour, and she couldn't wait any longer. It was after five, and rush hour was already underway.

At Mr. Vandiver's desk, Tami set down a pink message slip, making eye contact with her boss to communicate its importance. Then she hurried on her way.

The message was from Levi and Derek's father, Franklin Price, the local pharmacist, and read: "Pick up the prescription for your son ASAP."

Prescription? Pulling at his tie, the headmaster searched his brain for any possible reason Cal might have a prescription waiting. He couldn't even remember a time when his son had been sick. Not even a cold. He determined to put a quick end to his interminable phone conversation.

"It's time to raise the bar and hire some real coaches," insisted Ted Leyman, father of Hudson, star of Visalia Academy's boys' tennis team.

It was that time of year, the halfway mark, which meant parents were on the phone to the headmaster about any number of concerns. Some, like Mr. Leyman, wanted assurances regarding the spring sports program. Others hoped to strike a deal with the headmaster to transform earned F's into passing D's. Then there were those searching for creative solutions as to how to pay tuition for a second semester.

"It's a priority of this school to give talented kids, like Hudson, every opportunity to grow and get in front of the universities," the headmaster assured the long-winded caller.

At last the headmaster successfully ended the conversation without making any promises he couldn't keep. Briefcase in hand, he left his office and the pile of unreturned messages still on his desk. While he wanted more than anything just to head home, he drove to the drugstore where Franklin Price worked.

Inside the fluorescent-lit store, it was Christmas even though it was still days before Thanksgiving. Near the entrance, silver Christmas trees inspired the spirit of holiday shopping, and a huge, waving Santa whirred next to the candy aisle.

Mr. Vandiver made his way to the back of the store to the pharmacy. "I need to see Mr. Price, please," he informed the employee at the pick up counter. A moment later the head pharmacist emerged from the back in his white lab coat.

"Giving away any candy samples today?" Mr. Vandiver joked. "I could use a sugar boost."

"Too bad you missed the post-Halloween sales," Mr. Price chuckled. "We unloaded a ton of candy corn that could have done the trick."

"It's going to take a lot more than candy corn to get me through to New Year's," the headmaster let down a bit, exposing a bit of weariness to his friend who he knew worked long hours, particularly through the holiday seasons.

"Listen," Mr. Price spoke softly as he handed his friend and neighbor an empty prescription bag. "I don't know what this means exactly, but Derek told me to pass something along to you."

Mr. Vandiver experienced an immediate non-candy induced rush of adrenaline. "Go ahead."

"You remember the Data Collection Project Derek's on?" Mr. Price started. Mr. Vandiver nodded. "Turns out the program was designed to track down individuals meeting very specific criteria."

"What criteria?"

"Asian. Age thirteen. Blue eyes."

"What? Someone is looking for my son?"

"Bruce, how much do you know about that adoption agency? Is it possible Cal was kidnapped and brought to the U.S.?"

"Anything is possible," Mr. Vandiver answered, looking up at his friend helplessly.

"No one is saying that there is reason for concern," Mr. Price hurried to add, "but in the remote chance that something is not right, it could be that someone—"

"May want him back," Bruce Vandiver completed the thought. He hung his head, overwhelmed, terrified.

"I'm just repeating what Derek was told." The man in the lab coat was used to doling out advice, but this was information he did not want to pass along. "You might want to think about taking some precautions, you know, for his safety."

"I'll call Cal's coach. They're at the running track now. And I'll sure as hell call that rat of an attorney, Foster." Mr. Vandiver drew himself up with the strength that comes to a parent whose family has been threatened. "Thanks, Franklin."

The text message the boy's father sent to Coach Jack read:

> Cal may be in danger. Keep an eye out.

In his return text, Jack wrote:

> Bring Cal's swim gear, and we'll go inside to the pool.

Just as he sent the text, Jack looked up and saw someone. A man holding something black in his hands was standing partially behind a tree at the edge of the Y property. Had he not been forewarned, Jack could have easily missed the figure in the falling darkness.

Jack looked back at Cal who was making his way to the end of the track nearest the man. Jack took off like a shot toward the intruder. When the man saw Jack's hulk-like form coming at him, he ran, attempting to get to the parking lot hidden behind the trees.

But it was no contest. Jack tackled the man before he reached the lot, put his knee in the man's back, and pinned his arms to the ground.

"What are you doing?" Jack roared at the man who he could see now was young, twenty-something, and Asian, carrying a high-end camera. Jack knew Cal wasn't far behind him. Jack yelled to him, "Cal!"

"What's wrong?" asked a frightened and winded Cal.

"My phone—in my pocket—call 911," he ordered.

By the time the boy's father arrived, Cal stood with Jack outside, and a policeman was escorting an Asian man in handcuffs into the Y. After questioning the man, the officer spoke to Jack and to Cal's dad. "Nothing I can do here, sorry," he said.

"What do you mean?" Jack argued. "He was on private property taking pictures of me and my runner—this man's son—without permission."

"I understand that," the officer stated. "But his story checks out. He's with the *Seattle Asian Times*, following up a lead that your son is some kind of star athlete. His press credentials identify him as James Wo."

"Look, you don't understand—" Cal's father tried to appeal to the policeman who was clearly not concerned about what appeared to be a harmless run-in with the media.

"No, you look," the officer interrupted, holding up his hand. "The Y isn't pressing charges for trespassing, the man is unarmed, and—at your request—the guy has deleted the pictures he took. We're done here."

At this, Wo walked past them and smiled cockily. "Pleasure to meet you all, really." Wo looked back at Cal and said, "Good luck, dude. You really are good. And I hear Bai Zhao Man is one of the best coaches—like, anywhere." Then he spoke to Jack, "Did I get that name right?" Jack remained silent. "Oh, yeah. I got it right."

"Out of here." The policeman took a warning step toward Wo.

The trio of onlookers knew the photographer would be back. Someone sent him for first-hand information about Cal, and he discovered Coach Jack in the process. James Wo would surely be rewarded for striking gold twice in one night.

...

"Trey Foster," the unshaven man answered on the fourth ring. It was nine o'clock in the morning, and the attorney lacked coffee and motivation.

"Foster—Bruce Vandiver here."

"Yes?" The attorney finally asked irritably. In a word he made it clear he wanted nothing more to do with the elder Vandiver or his son, ever again.

But the distressed father wasn't about to be intimidated by the attorney—if he was really an attorney. The headmaster's door was closed, and Tami was holding his calls. "I need some answers—now," he demanded.

"Really, Mr. Vandiver, you know as much about your son, his adoption, and his mother as I do. I can't see what you think I might possibly—"

"Excuse me," Cal's father interrupted, "but if you can't answer my questions then you are the only one who can get me answers. And I expect you to do just that, immediately." Foster held his breath as his former client continued, "I have been advised that my son may have been kidnapped as an infant. Kidnapped! As in, not lawfully matched with our family!"

"That's an absurd and baseless rumor," Foster sputtered.

"Baseless is it? Then how is it that a highly reliable source tells me that my son has been the subject of an international search and that, just last night, a man claiming to be a journalist was caught taking pictures of Cal and his trainer? Tell me why someone would be looking for him?"

"I am an adoption attorney, not a private investigator. What do you expect me to do?"

"I expect you to contact the center and get me some assurances that my son is not going to be taken away from me and isn't in any danger. And if you don't, I will make that call myself, after which I will be talking with the Hanford Police Department."

With great effort Foster maintained his calm. A negative story in the *Hanford Tribune* would, undoubtedly, shut off his small trickle of business for good. "As a favor to you, I will make contact with the center," Foster offered. "However, since we no longer have remaining business together, contractually, I can't promise your concerns will be a priority."

"I expect to hear from you—or the person who made the mistake of hiring you—within twenty-four hours." With this Mr. Vandiver ended the call, angry and with little hope that Foster would call back at all.

...

When Professor Si Zhen arrived at the university in the morning, a steaming mug of coffee sat at his desk as did a memo with information left on the answering machine fifteen hours before. The call came from Foster, and it was both unexpected and unwelcome.

He called to his assistant who he could hear in the next room. "Good morning, Waiyin. Thank you for preparing my coffee."

"You're welcome," came her preoccupied response.

"News of my flight?"

"All taken care of. You leave Tuesday morning. Your hotel

and transportation have been arranged."

"Excellent." Now he seated himself at his desk and let out a weary sigh before reading the waiting message.

Caller: Trey Foster
Request: A return phone call from Professor Si Zhen
Urgency: High

The Professor swore under his breath.

Foster was up late, awaiting the Professor's call. He'd had his coffee and his heartburn medication and picked up on the first ring.

"Trey Foster," he answered, dreading the conversation that would follow.

"I had hoped, Mr. Foster, that you and I would be on to other pursuits by now."

"There is another request from my—our—client," Foster answered, feeling his heartburn kick in.

"What is it now, Foster?"

The Professor listened as the attorney recounted his conversation with Bruce Vandiver: the suspicion that his son may have been obtained illegally by the center; the "reliable source" that suggested the boy was the subject of an international search; and news that an Asian photographer was following Cal.

"He's demanding answers." Foster's said. "He wants assurance that someone's not trying to take back his son."

"But someone is," the Professor stated matter of factly.

"I wasn't prepared to deal with this," Foster answered weakly.

"Use your head, man!" the Professor barked. "Have you even looked in the Vandiver file? It's all there—the record of Candace Latham's admittance to a Hong Kong hospital and the birth of the child, along with her relinquishment papers! Foster furiously took down notes as the professor ranted.

"As for the photographer, Coach Bai has submitted videos of the boy to the Olympic Selection Committee. That's public information now and very much of interest to the Asian community. Am I wrong?"

"No, sir."

"Unfortunately, news of a 'search' for the boy is troublesome," the professor mused. "They have his location now. Took them long enough. Give Vandiver the proof you have and dismiss the 'search' as error or rumor. Deal with it! I'll be there in a couple days."

"Thank you for your time, Professor," Foster said meekly. "I'm glad there was some information of interest to you."

"In the future, you may converse with my assistant. I don't want to hear your voice again."

Then the line went dead.

# 46

Cal wished he could fast forward to Thanksgiving Day. Already he was thankful for a holiday that would bring him a few hours of rest and food, lots of food. Jack was pushing Cal harder and longer lately. Was he stepping up training because all of China would soon know of Jack's work with him, thanks to James Wo?

After a few days passed and Wo had not reappeared, Jack had Cal back out on the track. He brought a young man along with him who he introduced as Kyle, a track star at Auburn University home for the holiday break. Jack knew that the third-year runner had more than a handful of advantages over Cal that included years of actual racing, and he was anxious to learn how his Olympian-in-training measured up.

"Where'd you get this guy?" Cal asked Jack while Kyle stretched on the track, waiting for his opponent.

"He was named in the 'Athletes to Watch' feature of *Runner* magazine."

"Well, *they* sure are watching," Cal commented, nodding toward the girls in workout spandex making their way to the track to cheer on the tall blonde runner. By the time Cal joined Kyle at the start line, there were six shapely reasons for the Auburn runner to leave him in the dust.

Cal and Kyle ran for thirteen miles, twice the distance required for an Olympic triathlon. In the beginning the two ran side by side. But by mile six, it was clear that Kyle, unlike Cal, actually spent some of his time studying and socializing. Cal outran the Auburn standout by a quarter mile.

Jack looked both pleased and surprised. Cal, however, found it difficult to savor the win. Post-race, Cal squirted down his hot body with his water bottle, while Kyle was wrapped in cool towels and treated to a tall cup of shaved ice—watermelon-flavored, compliments of his admirers. Winning was a rush, but Cal couldn't help thinking how nice it would be to spend a day in Kyle's humongous and totally uncool shoes.

...

The day before Thanksgiving, school let out at noon. Jack and Cal agreed to meet up at the Y pool afterwards. It seemed everyone was gone for the holidays, and Cal swam alone, just the way he liked it. When Jack stepped out to take a call, Cal took advantage of the opportunity to rest his waterlogged limbs. That's when he heard it: a faint "click" from the other side of the pool.

"Not exactly an action shot, Wo." Cal spoke to the stalker he couldn't yet see. He listened for the sound of Wo making a quick getaway. Instead the young photographer stepped out from the locker room entrance.

"Then give me something good," Wo suggested and readied his camera.

"Fine," Cal agreed. After securing his goggles, Cal slid back in the water and swam one pool length of freestyle and another of butterfly. Then he pulled himself back up on the pool edge.

"Seriously, dude. I don't get why you don't want press," Wo commented while keeping an eye out for Jack. "You don't want to see your face on a cereal box?"

"Yeah, well, there's a rumor that someone other than the Wheaties people are looking for me."

"From what I hear, you're the next big celeb. Everybody's gonna want in on that."

"So you're getting big bucks from a newspaper for photos of me training?"

"Big bucks, yes. From the paper, no."

"So you're moonlighting as a stalker?"

"Whatever pays the bills."

"Any chance I'm in danger?"

"Hey, man, it's just photos. That's it." Wo let his camera down. "What's your story anyway?"

"I don't have a story," Cal answered with a shrug. "I just swim."

"That's not all you do. Remember—I've seen you in action before today," Wo said, referring to his near-arrest at the Y track.

"Throw me that towel," Cal said, nodding at the thick black towel hanging on a hook.

Wo grabbed the oversized towel and tossed it to the swimmer. Cal draped it around his shoulders, turned the Zulegen logo toward Wo, and flashed the photographer a charming smile.

"Zulegen? For real?" Wo hurried to get off some shots. "Impressive."

There were footsteps on the tile, and the door to the pool opened. In an instant, Wo was gone.

"Good, you're drying off." Jack's voice echoed against the tile. "Get dressed, please. We have an appointment."

"Where?" Cal asked, wondering if Wo was within earshot.

"Soccer field at your school."

Cal's stomach became an immediate knot. "Is this another 'Kyle' kind of thing?" he asked, prepared to launch into a first-class tirade.

"Not this time," Jack answered. Then he added, "This is a change-your-life kind of thing."

...

All Jack told him about the man they would be meeting was that he was "invested" in Cal's career. When Jack and Cal arrived at the soccer field, there was a solitary figure seated down on the bleachers, home side. The man stood as they approached. This man, too, was Asian. He wore a shirt, rolled up at the sleeves with a sweater vest. His hands were pushed into the pockets of his khaki-colored dress pants.

"Good afternoon, Professor," Jack greeted the man, cracking a rare smile.

Professor? Cal's heart began to race. Was this the man Candace said would be able to fill in the missing pieces of his life?

"And to you, Jack." The men shook hands. "Thank you for meeting me on such short notice."

"It is my honor, of course. Professor, I would like to introduce you to Cal Vandiver."

An elbow from Jack reminded Cal that he was still wearing his sunglasses. Reluctantly, Cal pulled off his shades. But the man showed no surprise when he met Cal's blue eyes. "You are a very handsome young man." The Professor gave Cal a good-natured slap on the arm. "That is why I asked Coach Jack here to keep you very busy—and away from the girls. Come, let's sit." Jack and Cal followed the Professor's lead and sat with him on the bleachers.

"How do you know me—and Jack?" Cal asked.

"Bai Zhao Man was training great athletes in China when we met. He was well known for his successes. At the time I was still a student at the University of Hong Kong, doing all I could to make an impression on this great man."

"Did you reach the Games?"

"I did not," the Professor answered. "But I enjoyed sports through my university years. In time, I turned to talent development. By that I mean selecting the most promising talent and matching them with the right coaches. That's how I was introduced to you."

Now Jack picked up the story. "The center felt your talent needed to be assessed, as you know. They asked the Professor to find someone to do that, and I got the job."

"The center—" Cal was working to put the pieces together, "that's how you know my mother."

"So she mentioned me to you?" the Professor smiled. "Candace Latham. We met when she was offering instruction in English at the university. A marvelous athlete. Her injury was a great loss for the Americans."

"She's going back to China, I think," Cal said, studying the man's reaction.

"I heard that, as well," the Professor smiled knowingly. "She is unafraid of hard things."

"She seemed to think I might see her there."

"Did she? Can I tell you how that might happen?"

"Yes, sir."

"Okay, let's get down to business then." The Professor and Jack exchanged glances. Both knew it was a moment that had been years in the planning.

"Jack has made me aware of your extraordinary abilities, Cal. The goal, as you know, is Olympic gold, and I'm ready to take you all the way."

"Is this, like, a sponsorship?"

"Even better," the Professor answered. "I'm pulling together a dream team of athletes for the Games. The best of the best. And I want you on it."

"What does this have to do with my birth mother?"

"Some of your training will take place in China."

"China?" Cal repeated in disbelief.

"Think of it! This is an opportunity for elite training, as well as a chance to explore your heritage. It is, after all, part of who you are."

"How long would we be there?"

"Three weeks at the end of the year and again this summer for the month before the Games."

"Three weeks? I have first semester exams coming up!" Already Cal had started cramming for exams with Levi. Clearly the Professor didn't understand about school schedules in the States.

"It would be over your winter break," the Professor replied calmly. "You wouldn't have to miss a single day of school."

Cal looked over at Jack, trying to read his face. "You'd be there?" he asked.

"If that's what you wanted."

"Could we miss maybe just a couple extra days of school?"

At this the Professor laughed aloud. "Don't forget I am a teacher!"

"Can I ask my parents?"

"Of course, and we'll discuss it again when we meet for Thanksgiving dinner," the Professor remarked.

"You'll be there—at the Cohens'?"

"The Professor will be coming as my guest," Jack explained.

"Cool!" Cal was on his feet.

"Does that mean you like the sound of the idea?" the man asked.

"Two thumbs up as far as I'm concerned. I don't know what my mom's going to say about it though. She's pretty protective."

"You think your mom won't jump at the chance to not have to feed you for a few weeks?" Jack chuckled. "What a Christmas present!" The three stood and were walking toward the parking lot when the Professor stopped and looked back at the bleachers.

"Excuse me. I believe we need to have a brief press conference." Sure enough, Cal saw the slight figure of James Wo squatted behind the spot where they had been talking.

"Let me at him!" Jack was ready to charge.

"Wait," the Professor said to Jack. "I have an idea." Back at the bleachers, the Professor summoned Wo out into the open grass. He emerged, at last, from his hiding place holding his camera. The two spoke in tones so low that neither Jack nor Cal could hear the discussion, though Cal thought it looked as though they were in negotiations.

"New Year's then," the Professor said as he left Wo.

The Professor offered no explanation of his conversation with the reporter. And neither Jack nor Cal dared ask.

# 47

Hours before her alarm was set to go off Thanksgiving morning, Jewell received a call from Beijing. She was still trying to make sense of it as she dabbed cover-up under her tired eyes. Unlike last time, she hadn't called Derek right after hearing from Wong Bao. She'd waited, knowing they'd have time to talk on the way to the Cohens' home.

In the meantime, Jewell was unclear about what was expected of her on Thanksgiving Day. Everyone assumed she understood all about American holidays and traditions, and she didn't like to ask questions. Derek had mentioned something about the color green being important, so she decided to pull a green sweater across her shoulders, collegiate-style, for the occasion. Grabbing up the tin of Chinese almond cookies she bought at the Asian food mart, Jewell headed for the lobby of the Lunar to wait for him.

. . .

With Derek already out the door, the elder Prices had only four unruly offspring to make presentable and squeeze into their compact vehicle.

"It's Thanksgiving!" Celeste whined as everyone pulled on seatbelts. "I have to have my phone!"

"I wanted to wear my tights," complained four-year-old Jana, who was scrunched between her mother and father in the front. "Lilli will be there."

"Believe me," Levi addressed Celeste, "nobody is upset that you can't yak our ears off today."

"Like you know anything—friendless in Visalia!" Celeste shot back. "I actually have friends, and they do want to talk to me on Thanksgiving Day because they have dork families too!"

"You know what you are—besides really annoying?" Levi determined to have the last insult. "A nomophobic!"

"Cool word," remarked Victor seated between the feuding siblings. "What's it mean?"

"Don't know. Don't care," Celeste said. "Nobody wants to hear from a talking dictionary, Derek Junior."

"Fear of being without a mobile phone," Levi answered his brother.

"Nomophobic! Nomophobic!" Victor began singing at his big sister.

"Enough!" Mr. Price wielded his voice like a weapon in the small space. "Use the drive to think about something you can be *thankful* for today. And if I catch any one of you moping, you can forget second helpings of your mother's sweet potato pie!" All in the car fell silent, and Mr. and Mrs. Price smiled the rest of the way.

. . .

The Professor insisted on picking up Jack in his luxury rental car, and they were the first to arrive at the Cohens', parking along the front curb.

A minute later, a Techtronix truck pulled into the driveway. "Not good," remarked the Professor.

"I guess the show must go on," Jack said. "People around the world want to know what the Cohens eat for Thanksgiving."

"Anyone else I should be warned about before we make our entrance?" the Professor asked warily. Clearly this was going to be more than a casual gathering of friends.

"There's the Price family. Five kids, though one is an adult, Derek, and he'll probably bring his girlfriend, Jewell Chan. She's never been to a Thanksgiving before either."

"Jewell Chan?" the Professor asked, staring wide-eyed at Jack. "You can't possibly be referring to Jewell Chan, inventor of the Glo-Me?"

Jack gave a little laugh, "Uh, don't know anything about a Glo-Me—hope it's working for you though."

The Professor wasn't laughing. "Tell me what you know."

"She's a smart one, like Derek Price. Works with him at Cal State on a computer project of some kind. They flew her in from Beijing."

"Beijing? Are you kidding?" The Professor exploded. "There's our leak!"

"What leak?"

"The leak that helped them find Cal." The Professor bristled just thinking about sitting at a Thanksgiving feast with the enemy.

"Whoa," Jack responded. "As I understand it, Jewell was the one who discovered that someone was searching for Cal. It came out while she and Derek were working together."

"It is possible that she doesn't know she's being used," the Professor theorized.

"Why would someone be looking for the boy?"

"There are those in the party who would take advantage of all our work and use him for their own purposes," the Professor answered. "You of all people should understand that."

"All *our* work? Do you mean all *my* work in preparing him for the Games?"

Now the professor looked hard at Jack. "Surely you don't think I've only just discovered our future Olympian?"

The idea that the Professor had been following Cal's life for some time had not entered Jack's mind. It made sense though. The Professor was an extraordinary man, a man of business, capable, calculating. At last he had an opportunity to develop an athlete who was not under the thumb of the Chinese Communist Party.

"You believe the party is involved?"

"They see a future for him there, and they are used to getting what they want."

Jack knew this statement to be true. The party had been behind the deepest losses of his life.

The Vandivers were now filing into the house behind Derek and Jewell. The Prices pulled up behind the Professor. The conversation would have to wait.

"Ready?" Jack asked, as he unbuckled.

"I suppose I better be," the Professor said. "Much rests on the success of the day."

...

A gasp escaped Kimberly Vandiver upon stepping into the Cohen living room. Leaning in close to her ear, her husband teased, "Nice little place, huh?"

"I might cry," the artist-mother replied weakly. Linda Cohen had transformed her home for the season. Everything was perfect—from the couch pillows to the artwork on the wall to the place settings on the banquet table that ran the length of the back windows with a floor-to-ceiling view of the backyard. And as only the Green Mom could, Linda Cohen had even managed to find a coordinating maternity dress.

"Oh, Kimberly—" gushed the celebrity mom, reaching for the platter she'd carried in. "You brought veggie pinwheels! How very green of you! I'll just take these and put them over with the salads."

Cal's mother wondered how long it would take for her son to realize this would not be a comfort foods affair.

"You are so welcome, Linda! Everything is simply *beautiful*!"

Just then the Price family made their entrance. Cal's mother waived at Barbara Price, grateful to see another family in their income bracket. The busy mother of five looked as though she'd already endured quite a morning and now took on a still weightier task of keeping the younger ones away from the "breakables."

Soon the guests were mingling and enjoying appetizers served by Juan, dressed for the occasion in a gold cummerbund and bowtie. "Who wants a sneak peek at Canyon's room?" Linda Cohen spoke over the chatter.

"Who would miss an opportunity to see your world-famous *nursery*?" Kimberly Vandiver responded immediately, certain she was the only guest who knew Canyon was the name of the coming prince.

With the ladies gone, the men discussed how they might, at some point, retire to the home theatre to catch some Thanksgiving Day football. Outside, the Price children, supposedly under Derek's watch, explored the back patio, pool, and outdoor entertaining space. Cal, Lilli, and Levi met up at the appetizers.

"Why is it I always find you guys around the food?" Lilli teased.

"That is because we are growing into big strong men," remarked Levi, as he reached for the plate of meatballs on toothpicks.

"Ugh," he complained after taking a bite. "What is this?"

"I believe those are the honey and ginger glazed turkey rounds," Lilli announced.

"What?" Levi hurried to chew and swallow.

"They're healthier than hamburger," she continued. "Everything that's on a green platter will be included in the soon to be released *Growing Up Green Cookbook*."

"Oh," Levi's responded with disappointment. "I get it."

"But there is *real* dessert—sweetened with natural cane sugar, of course—so don't have a panic attack. It's good, I promise."

"You look nice, by the way," Cal said to Lilli who was fashionably dressed in a short flared skirt and flats, her hair pulled back into a neat French braid.

"My mom entertains a lot. I actually do wear something other than dancewear sometimes." Lilli decided to enjoy the compliment and to put off telling Cal her big news. "And you're not wearing your shades," she said approvingly. "This *is* a special occasion."

"Not much use," he shrugged a response. "Just family here."

"Then maybe you wouldn't mind taking a few extra with you on the way out," Levi suggested. Through the glass, they could see Derek on the patio, checking email on his phone. Next to him sat a pouting, phoneless Celeste. In the yard Victor tormented a squealing Jana with bugs from the grass.

"So you gonna get this guy through eighth grade at our fine educational institution?" Lilli asked Levi. Both boys moaned, knowing that reviews for end of semester finals would begin the following week.

"I've got my work cut out for me, honestly ..." Cal stopped listening to Levi when he noticed Jewell break from the nursery tour and approach his father. Jewell had been the one who warned his family that someone was looking for him. That news now threatened his chances of joining the Professor's dream team in China. The pair walked into the study. About the time Levi was boasting that Cal "had a good chance of passing," thanks to him, Cal saw them emerge again, smiling.

...

The conversation had gone well. Jewell was relieved to tell Mr. Vandiver about the call she'd received from Beijing that morning, the one that explained how Cal had wrongly been detected as a "record of interest" by the DCP. The criteria had been incomplete, as Wong Bao had explained to her, and she delivered the welcome news with her apologies to the Vandivers. The complete criteria list, which she'd received just that morning, included physical anomalies of all sorts and, once input into the DPC, would serve to provide vital information on the general health of the Asian populations in the U.S.

"So you no longer believe my son is the 'target' of a search of some kind?" Cal's dad had asked her pointedly.

"As it was explained to me, no one person was purposefully being singled out," she had answered apologetically.
"I should have never jumped to a conclusion without discussing it with my superior. Please forgive me for causing your family to fear for your son's safety."

"But the birth year—"

Jewell nodded, in understanding. As the developer of the program, Jewell knew that the DCP sorted its subjects by gender and age group. It was possible, as she explained, that any Asian male, with blue eyes, between the ages of thirteen and nineteen, would also have been flagged. It just so happened that Cal was the only one to be identified in that group. It was, in fact, fortuitous that Cal's file came to their attention so that the error could be quickly addressed.

"Your news came at just the right time," Mr. Vandiver told her, thinking of the Professor's offer for Cal to join his dream team and to travel to China for training. "Thank you."

Before Jewell could ask what "just at the right time" referred to, Cal's father took her by the arm and steered her in the direction of the esteemed professor.

The Professor who stood with the other men as they discussed football games of Thanksgivings past was only too glad to be introduced to the Asian woman about whom he was anxious to learn more.

"Jewell Chan, I'd like you to meet—" Mr. Vandiver began, but was interrupted.

"—Please, just call me Professor," the distinguished man insisted, smiling amiably.

"Professor, I think you will find Ms. Chan's company

engaging. If you will excuse me, however, I have some good news to share with my wife—thanks to Ms. Chan." And with a polite bow to Jewell, he turned, leaving Jewell alone with the Professor.

"Jewell Chan," the Professor began. "It is indeed an honor to meet you. While not particularly conversant on the world of high fashion," he made reference to her interview in *ELLE Hong Kong*, "I am an enormous fan of innovation for which you have earned my respect and admiration."

Jewell blushed, surprised that he knew of her early work, and nodded politely.

"And what brings you to the States?" he asked.

"I'm working with Derek Price at Cal State, Fresno," Jewell gestured toward Derek on the back patio. "The university is working with the Ministry of Science and Technology in Beijing on a comprehensive study of the Asian population here in the States."

"Fascinating," the Professor commented. "And so your focus has shifted from that of innovation to observation?" The question struck Jewell as rude.

"The focus is to make a thorough and timely record of history," Jewell answered defensively. "The Asian population has grown exponentially in the U.S., a result of the adoption of Asian children and the draw of the American universities. The work is innovative, and the result, I believe, will be enlightening as well."

"Interesting reading, I have no doubt. But to what end?" The Professor's tone turned hard. "Perhaps a mind such as yours might best be used to address the oppression of the Chinese people?" The intensity of the Professor's glare caused Jewell to look away. "It will require the talents of an innovator to end the tyranny of the Communist Party. What will be *your* role, Jewell Chan?"

Silenced by the man's attack on her country—or was it on her?—Jewell struggled to remain composed.

"Perhaps one day we will enjoy our own feast of thanks for

freedom in the land where you and I were born."

"I am compelled to ask," Jewell probed, whether out of offense or curiosity she was unsure, "what is *your* part in the transformation of China?"

The sound of silver tapping against glass caused the room to fall silent and put an end to the uncomfortable conversation between Jewell and the Professor. Lilli's father held high a wine glass and declared, "It is *time*!" The young people moved close to the buffet area as Lilli's mother gave precise instructions as to how to proceed: "Take a plate from the table then form a line for the buffet at the island by Juan." With profound relief Jewell excused herself from the Professor and joined Derek in line.

"Having a good time?" Derek tried to read Jewell's face. Pretending to study the array of foods, she kept her eyes from his.

"Everything is lovely," she responded unevenly, leaving Derek to wonder what he had missed.

When everyone was settled at the exquisitely set table, Techtronix owner Kevin Bower stepped on the scene equipped as cameraman for the day. It was then that Lilli's father rose from his seat at the head of the table and again raised his wine glass high.

"I'd like to make a Thanksgiving toast," he announced to his international audience. "I am thankful for family and long-time friends and for *new* friends. Hopefully, we've all had an opportunity to say hello to the lovely and talented Jewell Chan of Beijing," he nodded her direction before continuing, "as well as the distinguished Professor from Hong Kong."

There was applause followed by the clinking of glasses meeting.

"And now," Lilli's father continued, cuing the cameraman with a nod of the head, "I believe my lovely wife Linda has something further to add."

Linda Cohen donned her TV smile as she rose and addressed her captive audience. "It comes as no surprise," she looked from her guests to the camera, "that my lovely daughter Lilli has received a number of truly amazing offers to dance following her international debut on my video blog."

Seated next to Lilli, Cal leaned over and whispered, "You dance? Really?"

Even with butterflies battling inside her, Lilli teased back, "You didn't need a soccer cheerleader anymore. What was I supposed to do?"

Mrs. Cohen continued, "So you may or may not be surprised to learn that Lilli has been invited to spend her Christmas break on a dance tour with Ben—her partner—in China!" The hostess let everyone at the table take a gasp before she continued. "Zulegen Sports has offered to sponsor the tour, and well, Richard and I have—with much trepidation—agreed to let her go!"

The table erupted with clapping and congratulations.

When Lilli did not turn to meet his stare, Cal studied the back of her tidy black braid. They would be apart over their school break and she had not told him. More concerning still was Cal's fear that Lilli would cross the ocean and find whatever she believed she had lost and return home—different.

Before the buzz had even died down, Cal's father was on his feet. "On behalf of the Vandivers—congratulations, Lilli! You are an amazing talent, and we are so very proud of you." After a deep breath he continued. "I—we—have a bit of news ourselves." He cleared his throat and continued.

"First, I'd like to acknowledge Jack, Cal's trainer, for his hard work in preparing my son for the Olympics." Light applause followed as every eye looked expectantly from Jack to the boy's father. "And Cal has also been made an offer that we're excited about." It was Cal's turn in the hot seat. Had another decision been finalized without him knowing?

"The Professor, who has many years of experience in developing Olympic talent, has graciously offered Cal a spot on his dream team of athletes. These athletes will be the focus of his attention in the months leading up to the Games."

"Sweet!" Levi's voice could be heard above the animated conversation in the room.

Before the din grew any louder, Mr. Vandiver attempted to finish his announcement, "What that means is Cal—along with Jack—will also be spending the winter break in China with the Professor." The cameraman worked to capture the surprised reactions of guests, which included Cal, Jack, and the Professor who didn't see it coming. Now Lilli swung around in her chair and stared at Cal accusingly.

They had kept secrets from one another.

"I thought the deal was dead," Cal whispered to Lilli. What's *your* excuse?"

"Maybe we should all go!" Victor suggested loudly from two seats down, waving his fork until his mother caught his wrist mid-air and returned it to the table.

"I don't believe Canyon and I will make the trip this time," laughed Mrs. Cohen, giving her protruding belly a pat. Like a good hostess, she turned her attention back to her guests. "Juan, do I see some empty glasses here?"

# 48

The sound of a car horn out front meant Miguel made it over for the post-feast festivities. From the window, Cal and Levi saw Miguel's two younger siblings waving good-bye to him from the bed of their father's work truck, the one with a door that was a distinctly different shade of washed-out red than the rest of the vehicle. The friends took off for the front door as Miguel walked warily, mouth agape, up the driveway of the Cohen home.

"Dude, you made it!" Cal greeted him from the front porch. From behind Cal, Levi tossed a football at Miguel.

"Sorry I couldn't be here for the dinner," Miguel apologized to his buddies. "Family in town. You know how it is."

Miguel threw the football to Cal. "Hey, you pulled off the district championship without me. You're my hero. Besides, you didn't miss much, believe me." Cal then sent the ball spiraling back to Levi.

"No soccer today, huh?" Miguel looked around at the manicured lawn with flowering natural areas and perfectly placed miniature palms. "Too bad." He shook his head and rubbed his belly. "I need to run off all I ate today."

"How 'bout that, Cal! Now we know where the real Thanksgiving feast was this year—at Miguel's!" Levi threw the football to Miguel with the force of a hungry bull.

"You're kidding, right?" Miguel asked, sending the ball spiraling back to Levi. He had imagined his friends enjoying a gluttonous feast inside the doors of the biggest house he'd ever seen.

"Dinner was a little like the yard, dude, more to look at than enjoy," Cal summed it up.

"What? No brown, crunchy turkey?" Miguel held the ball now, looking from Cal to Levi trying to decide if they were joking.

"Thinly sliced, organic and skinless turkey breast only," Cal responded disappointedly.

"Rice and beans?"

"Not here," Cal answered.

"Any tamales?"

"Really, Miguel? Linda Cohen eating tamales?" Cal laughed.

"Not even any pernil?"

"What's pernil?" asked Levi, his stomach rumbling.

"Roasted pork! Sheesh. Now I really do feel thankful!"

"Yeah, well, Christmas should be even *more* interesting," Cal said soberly. He signaled for Miguel to send the ball his direction.

"What about it?" Miguel asked, suspicious that Lilli had talked Cal into going vegan over the holiday.

Cal spun the ball in his hands as he spoke. "I'm going to China over the winter break, Miguel. Some training stuff." He sent the ball back to Miguel.

Before Miguel could comment, Levi jumped in with the other breaking news of the day. "Get this—Lilli's going too, but for a dance tour in China sponsored by Zulegen!"

"Not Just Playing Games," Miguel said, passing to Levi.

"What's that?" Levi asked.

"It's the new slogan Zulegen's using to announce their line of dancewear."

Cal and Levi looked at him in stunned silence.

"I read stuff, okay?" Miguel said, insulted. "Is that *guy* going too?"

Cal knew where his friend was going with this question. "Yes, Miguel, and he's Latino—"

"¡Cuidado con los latinos!"

Throwing the ball to Cal, Levi asked, "What's that mean?"

"Serious, Levi? You are the worst at Spanish," Cal remarked, as he aimed and threw the ball to Miguel. "Good thing I had Miguel to help me out!"

"Beware of the Latinos!" Miguel translated for them. To Cal it sounded a lot like "I told you so."

Just then Lilli bounced through the front door and plopped down on the front steps. "Hi, Miguel!"

"Just got here," Miguel explained. "Family stuff, you know."

"There's still dessert if you want." The three boys exchanged a knowing smile.

"Thanks," he answered. "Only if these guys can make me work up an appetite again. So far, they look more like they need a *siesta*!"

"Maybe we should play soccer—what do you think?" Lilli asked with mischief in her voice. "It's not like she's going to make us quit! You're our guests!"

The front door slammed again. This time it was Derek who stepped out into the sunlight, looking a little lost without Jewell who agreed to a tour of the outdoor kitchen.

Suddenly Lilli jumped to her feet. "Who has a soccer ball?"

"That's funny. Like you don't have a soccer ball," Cal teased.

"I do," Lilli said, thinking. "But I'm pretty sure it's in the garage somewhere behind all of the Techtronix cameras and stuff."

"I have one in my trunk." Derek looked up from his phone. "Hang on." He took off down the driveway. The foursome watched as Derek pulled a ball from his trunk, tucked it under his arm, and then opened the door to the backseat. After a minute he emerged with a pink, fuzzy object. "Hey! Look what I found" Derek announced, "Celeste's phone!"

"You did *not* just find that!" Levi accused his brother. "You had it! For days we've been listening to her whine about that phone! Why did you have it?"

"I didn't have it," Derek answered, dropping the ball on the lawn. "Jewell did. I gave it to her in case her calls were being monitored after the you-know-what flagged you-know-who."

"Brilliant, double-o-seven! Like I needed that misery!" Levi complained.

As the friends scrambled for possession of the ball, Celeste could be heard inside, squealing in excitement. Derek, it seemed, had found her phone at last, tucked deep into a car cushion.

In the drama of the moment, the Professor took the opportunity to appear at the side of Kevin Bower of Techtronix as he reviewed the recordings he'd made earlier in the day.

"May I watch the video from our feast together?" the Professor asked politely.

A shrewd businessman himself, Bower understood what the deal he'd struck with the Professor had done for Techtronix. The man had funded enhancements to the Growing Up Green website that garnered an international audience. That success had brought his company more than a few mentions in business magazines as well as new clients.

"Help yourself." Bower replied and hit PLAY, starting the recording from the beginning. "Excuse me a moment. I'm just going to pull together some cables over here, so I can pack up for the day."

The Professor nodded his appreciation.

On a small screen, the Professor watched a replay of the day's festivities, beginning with Mr. Cohen's Thanksgiving toast, followed by Mrs. Cohen's announcement of Lilli's plans for a dance tour in China. At the close of the applause that followed her speech, the man unfolded his arms and reached down and hit STOP. Then he punched RECORD. The following footage of food and guests disappeared, as did the news of Cal's plans for the winter break.

By the time Bower returned with cable coiled around his shoulder and chest, the Professor was no longer in the room. He knew that leaving the Professor alone with his recording was a risk. And it only took a minute to confirm his suspicions. Bower had been left with the uncomfortable task of explaining the missing portions of video to Linda Cohen. But he would ask no questions of her guest. The Professor apparently had a job to do and did it. Bower had only to clean up behind him. Experience told him it would work out for both the men in the end.

...

For a second time, Jewell managed to slip away from a home tour; this time to find the Professor. They had a conversation to finish. She found him in the study alone, the other men having gravitated upstairs to watch football.

"You spoke rudely to me." Jewell descended on the man who perused the book-filled shelves.

The man looked up as if he'd been expecting her. "Did I?" he asked with nonchalance.

"Why?"

"It may have something to do with an apparent 'leak' to Beijing about my Olympian-in-training."

"A leak?" Jewell was stunned by a second accusation—the first being a disregard for her own people—from a man she didn't even know. "The leak to whom—about what?"

Now the man looked intently at Jewell. "If Beijing should 'somehow' learn of Cal's upcoming trip, I will know the source. I suspect you are also the one who revealed the identity of the boy to the CCP in your bogus work at the university."

"No one is looking for Cal! It was a mistake!" Jewell insisted. "And it was Beijing that pointed out the error!"

"And now—quite suddenly—it has all been explained away,"

the Professor said. "Am I right?"

Jewell sputtered, "I have no reason to question—"

"You have every reason to question the explanations of the Chinese government. They are *using* you."

Her heart pounded, and Jewell knew there was some truth to the man's ranting. "Why is someone after Cal then? Why?"

"Because there are those who intend to reclaim him," the man spoke through clenched teeth.

"Why?"

"For the purposes of the party."

At that moment Jewell gave up denying what she had begun to suspect. The Professor had said it. All she'd wanted was to accomplish something deemed important to her country. Wong Bao had lied to her.

"They told me an asset had been kidnapped," Jewell admitted, the words sounding foolish as they left her lips.

The Professor looked away from her out the window. "The boy was not kidnapped. He was rescued." He turned again to face Jewell and continued, his voice quivering with emotion, "and now he is threatened once more."

"I should tell his parents?"

"No," the Professor's voice was resolute. "In a few short weeks, he will be with Jack and me in Beijing—the last place on earth they would expect him to be." Now he paused. "Unless, of course, someone tells them."

In that moment Jewell knew she had been invited to be part of the second rescue of Cal Vandiver. She'd also been challenged to grow up and to begin by questioning all she'd been taught was true and honorable.

"What about when he returns to the States?"

"We won't have to stand guard around the boy for long. Soon, the eyes of the whole world will be watching him."

...

In the days that followed the "Growing Up Hungry"

Thanksgiving, as it came to be called, the whole world seemed to undergo a swift, sparkling pre-holiday transformation.

At the Cohen estate, Christmas trees were lighted and expertly decorated for the holiday. On one tree, dedicated to Canyon, hung ceramic blue bird eggs at different stages of opening; one for each month since his conception. There was a tree with a Lilli theme as well, which featured ornaments she'd received every year along with her earliest dance shoes, hair bows, and her beloved pom-poms. On the Growing Up Green tree hung decorations made from all-natural materials from around the world. There were even small "goo-filled" earths, as Lilli described them, that when shaken resulted in a "world" coated in a serene green.

In the days leading up to the break, Lilli spent most of her time in the rec room over the garage, practicing every spare minute that she wasn't eating, sleeping, studying, or working with Carissa and Ben.

For the most part, the Price children occupied their time making Christmas lists. Now nearly five, Jana compared her demands with those of her friends; Victor faced the excruciating task of choosing between umpteen new video games released just in time for the holidays; Celeste deliberated the latest available phone upgrades and accessories; Derek, meanwhile, hoped for a loaded Starbucks gift card and comics to replenish his now depleted collection; and Levi kept late hours in the pursuit of straight As on his first semester finals, which he'd exchange for cash from Grandma Price.

At the Vandiver house, the thankless job of packing for Cal's three-week trip fell to the boy's mother, even as she worked to put the final brush strokes on her son's Christmas gift. Unfortunately, this meant that the job of decorating the house and tree was delegated to amateurs: Cal and his father. As an artist, it pained Cal's mother every time she looked at the family's sad little Christmas tree that stood in the living room, leaning ever so slightly. To make matters worse, the lights sagged unevenly from the branches around hastily hung ornaments. Then there was the problem of the Christmas candle, which appeared at the center of the Vandiver dining room each year on the first day of December. It was missing altogether, and she had sent husband and son up into the attic again and again to look for it, to no avail.

...

In the busyness of the season and travel preparations, Cal and Lilli found it nearly impossible to find time together. When a meet-up time was determined at last, strict ground rules were set for the occasion. At Lilli's request, Cal would leave Levi at home. Also, Cal was not allowed any further discussion of the Wildcat's recent first-ever win of the State Middle School Championship in soccer or the resulting four-foot trophy on display by the school office. In turn, Cal asked that Lilli have a "real food" snack on hand and refrain from bringing up either his grades or Ben.

 The Cohen rec room was as big as the Vandiver living and dining rooms combined. If he looked up, Cal could see dusk falling through huge skylights on the vaulted ceiling. The media center with theatre screen covered an entire wall. Cal and Lilli sat side by side on an overstuffed chocolate-colored sofa. They shared chili nachos, compliments of Juan.

 "You know, you probably won't have anyone to fix your nachos or fluff your pillows over there," Cal teased.

 Lilli cocked her head at Cal. "Really? You're worried that I won't have Juan to get me through? Huh! And I don't think Jack will have any part of fixing you dinner for breakfast either!" Now she laughed. "We may be going different places tomorrow, but we're sitting in the same boat."

 "Okay," Cal tried again. "So what about this trip makes you nervous, for real?"

"Talking about it."

"But you always want to talk."

"Just not now," Lilli smiled playfully. "I think there's a better way to prepare for a long trip and lots of sitting!" Hopping up from her spot, Lilli bounded to the cabinet that housed the stereo system. Once the music was blaring she announced, "Tonight, you learn to hip-hop!"

Without Cal noticing, Lilli reached over and flipped on the video camera she used to record her routines. After moving the sofa to the side, Lilli dared her friend to join her on the open floor.

"What? Soccer players can't dance?" she taunted him.

Cal didn't know anything about hip-hop, but he had long been familiar with working out his nerves with physical activity. For him, being able to do that now with Lilli made for the perfect good-bye.

# 49

Cal still felt some soreness in his muscles after his attempts at hip-hop dancing—crumping, popping, and spinning—with Lilli the night before. He had returned home exhausted with only a few short hours to sleep. At 4:30 a.m. the alarm sounded, abruptly starting the day that would begin with an early drive into Fresno to catch a flight to Los Angeles and, from there, boarding a plane to Beijing. His traveling partner, Jack, had spent the night cramped on the Vandiver couch.

In L.A., Cal followed Jack closely, carrying his laptop and an oversized duffle bag, which was light compared to the guilt he felt for missing Lilli more than his parents. They boarded a Boeing 747-400, which according to Derek had the capacity to carry up to 383 passengers. And everyone seemed to be present. The duffle Cal's mother had packed with love was stuffed overhead and Cal held his laptop as he took his seat next to Jack.

There were three sections of seating, and Cal felt as if he'd made a late entrance to a movie theatre. Clearly this was not first-class, as Derek had also described in great detail.

It would seem his dream team status didn't count for much, Cal thought, worrying for the first time about the quality of his accommodations on the other side of the ocean.

Cal had to give the Professor some credit though. The coveted window seat had been reserved for him. He imagined a discussion between Jack and his parents about ways to help him endure hours and hours of close quarters. Cal was, in fact, pleased to be one window away from sky that went on forever.

"So what'd you do with your dog?" Cal asked his companion suddenly.

"My dog?"

"Yeah, your dog. The one Lilli and I saw you with."

"Ah," came Jack's response. "That is Chum." Cal wondered if Jack might have a sense of humor after all.

"Three weeks is a long time to be away."

"Chum is not my dog. It would be too difficult for me to keep a dog. I rent him."

"What? You rent a dog?"

"Chum is a shar-pei, a Chinese breed that needs lots of care and discipline. He will not go to anyone but me. He will be there on my return."

"Bet he'll miss you."

"Like I said, Chum is Chinese. We have an understanding."

Cal shook his head and decided to let it go. He had way too much to think about without worrying about Jack's rent-a-dog.

A row up, an Asian teen was attempting to stuff his duffle bag in the overhead compartment. "Need help with that?" asked a male flight attendant who looked to be in need of a few more hours of sleep and some sunshine.

"I think I have it," the young man answered politely in his Chinese accent, nodding slightly. Dressed in a blue oxford button down and pressed khakis, the young man squeezed his way into the seat between two adults, neither of whom seemed to know him. After a few minutes of eavesdropping, Cal learned that the boy was a high school exchange student returning home for the break. Cal felt his coach watching the student too. His presence seemed to unnerve Jack who shifted in his seat again and again in an attempt to get a clear look at him.

At last Jack gave up the effort. "Maybe we'll have an open seat here." He patted the still-empty seat to his left.

"Good! We can put a giant bag of popcorn there. I feel like I'm waiting for a movie to start, and it's making me hungry."

While travel plans had necessitated an early Christmas for Cal and Jack, there were still plenty of reminders among the passengers that the holiday was, in actuality, still a week away. Some carried on wrapped gifts that they stowed under their seats; one woman wore a bright red coat and dangling jingle-bell ornament earrings; and from time to time, holiday tunes escaped into the air via headphones, ringtones, and laptops.

Just as the pilot was instructing passengers to buckle up for take off, a woman, Asian, with an enormous purse, still breathing hard from her rush to board, plopped down into the seat next to Jack.

Jack's first glance at the late arriver was immediately followed by a second. Cal looked over to see his companion wide-eyed, stunned. Even his breathing had stopped. Was the woman a ghost from his past? Was the student? Cal began to be concerned that a return trip to China had come too soon for Jack. Whatever he had escaped by coming to the States now seemed to collapse on him in an avalanche of memories.

Though the woman didn't seem to recognize Jack at all, she smiled in a way that suggested she was pleased as punch to be seated next to the handsome man. "Hello," the woman greeted Jack with a polite nod and then wrestled her purse under her seat.

"Hello," Jack returned warily. With one hand, the woman did a quick inspection of the state of her hair and then attempted to purse her lipstick into place. Satisfied that she was sufficiently "put together," the woman, who looked to be close to Jack's age, relaxed into her seat.

"Did you have difficulty boarding?" Jack asked the woman. Since Jack never socialized, Cal concluded that he was, in fact, looking for a way to observe the woman more carefully.

"I decided—perhaps a little late—to catch an earlier flight out." She met his inquisitive eyes with a smile. "I think I have made a good decision." Cal wondered what it was that made the woman so interesting to Jack. She was attractive, he supposed, for a middle-aged woman—well dressed, her hair neatly pulled up on her head, a slight graying at the temples.

The plane began moving into position for take off. "And now comes the waiting," Jack said to Cal, his hands trembling slightly.

"You aren't afraid of flying, are you?" Cal quietly asked his coach. Jack's eyes darted between the dark head of the boy in front of him and the woman next to him, who was now leafing through a magazine offered her by the flight attendant.

"Not usually," he answered, swallowing hard and fixing his eyes out the window.

Once the plane leveled out and the seat belt warning light went out, Cal turned to his trainer, hoping for an in-flight game of chess on Jack's tablet. But the man had closed his eyes against the faces around him. Whether he was actually dozing or not was impossible to tell. So Cal reached under his seat and pulled his own laptop from its sleeve. With less than an hour in the air, he was already hoping for contact with the familiar via email.

Yes! Cal smiled broadly when he found five new messages waiting in his inbox.

The subject line of the first email simply read *Miguel*. There was also an attachment. Though Miguel had reminded Cal that he wasn't geeky "like Levi" and probably wouldn't send many emails, there it was. The first of many, he hoped. Cal knew Miguel's older brother was the only one in the family with a computer. They'd probably wrestled over it.

The "sleeping" Jack opened his eyes in curiosity. "Americans are addicted to their computers."

"It's email from Miguel!" Cal read it aloud for Jack:

> When you wonder if you've got what it takes, remember this! Buena suerte (good luck!)—Miguel

Then Cal clicked on the attachment, which revealed a photo of the gigantic trophy awarded the Wildcats at the state playoffs, when Cal and Miguel led the 14-2 slaughter of the Forsyth Falcons to take the championship. The fingerprints on the glass display case, Cal knew, belonged to his soccer pals who touched it as they passed, remembering an amazing season.

Cal swiveled the computer screen in Jack's direction.

"Ah!" Jack nodded his head. "My trophy!"

"Oh, yeah?" Cal snapped. "Remind me, how many goals did you make this season?"

"Your goals, my goals; your wins, my wins. Do not forget that."

"Yeah, yeah." Cal mocked his coach knowing full well that without Jack there would never have been a Dynamic Duo.

Cal clicked on his second email with the subject heading: *For my favorite son*. It was a joke he and his father enjoyed—repeatedly, to which Cal would reply, "Because I'm your *only* son!" Again there was an attachment. Cal thought about how much his relationship with his dad had changed in the past months. Different as they were from one another, his dad had emerged as Cal's unwavering supporter. And, over copious amounts of steaming noodles, they had begun to genuinely appreciate one another. The email read:

> Dear Cal, I'm already wondering what excuse I will give your mother for my frequent visits to The Noodle House while you are away. When you get home there will be a gift card to "our place" waiting for you. Consider it a belated Christmas present. We'll talk soon, I hope. In the headmaster's grade book, you get an A for Awesome. Dad

The next waiting email had the subject: *From Tia the Dog*. An email from Candace? Cal didn't even know where she was. Maybe he was about to find out. After drawing a deep breath, Cal clicked on the attachment and was met with an automated message that a book had been purchased for him. There was a link to start the download and, under that, a box for a personal message from the sender. It read:

> Happy traveling! Thought you might be interested in reading this when you had some down time. Love, Candace

She knew he was on his way to China! Was she already there? The email raised a barrage of unanswerable questions. The only part about the email that didn't surprise him was the book his mother had purchased: *Remembering Tiananmen Square*. Not exactly light reading, but clearly information his mother wanted to pass on to her son. A minute later the book was downloaded to his desktop. Even more than the book, Cal enjoyed the feeling that Candace was thinking of him.

Cal turned his attention to his next email that carried the subject line: "A Christmas Memory." This one was from the mom who had worked so hard to pack his bag for the trip, even tucking hard candies in his duffle, the mom who tried her best not to cry when he stepped away from her in the airport.

Her email was brief:

> By this time tomorrow the canvases will be hanging in my studio, so when I work I can feel you here with me. Be safe, Cal. Love, Mom

Also included in the email was a jpeg file Cal promptly opened. It was a photo of the three-part painting his mother gave him for Christmas. While it was impossible to see the detail of the work in the picture, Cal knew every part of it;

he had watched it come to be. Together he and his mother had named each panel. "Brewing" was the name of the first panel, which began with pale yellow that was nearly overtaken by brushes of gray then blue that darkened into a troubled horizon. Panel two took the viewer into the fray of the storm with overlapping brushes in different sizes and dark blues swirling dangerously together. A tangle scraped into the paint added to the confusion. This panel they named "Choices." The final panel seemed to depict hope with the gray-blue fading to a pinpoint where yellows began to emerge like sunshine. It was appropriately named "Breakthrough."

Cal nudged his coach with his elbow. "Look," he insisted, again turning the screen toward Jack. "My painting!"

The coach nodded in genuine appreciation. "It tells the many stories of your life. Most have not yet happened," commented Jack.

"Why do you always have to be so mysterious?"

"Chinese are supposed to be mysterious. I should give you lessons."

Pulling his seat to an upright position, Jack reached for the computer and placed it on his lap. "Where are you now in this story?"

The thought was entirely new to Cal. If he were to place himself on one of the three canvases, which would it be? Likely he was emerging from the deep blues and greys that were the mystery of his birth mother and the pain of training. "Here," he pointed to the third panel.

"If that is the end of the story, what is next?"

"How am I supposed to know?"

"Here," Jack pointed at the first panel, "Brewing," with its bright start and gathering clouds. "The story moves in a circle."

Now Cal saw it. If he were to move the third panel, "Breakthrough," in front of panel one, the piece as a whole would still have a unified look. The painting, he suddenly realized, wasn't about the challenges of getting into the

Games; it was about his whole life, made up of a series of beginnings, middles, and endings. And lots of gray areas.

"Where are *you*?" Cal asked his trainer.

Without hesitation, Jack pointed at the first panel. "There are many difficulties ahead," he predicted. As much as Cal wished he were not a part of the reason Jack stood before a fast-approaching storm, he knew it was true.

Two emails remained. The next subject line read: *Beijing or Bust*. After opening it, Cal scanned to the bottom to discover the sender. It was Lilli. She wrote:

> Cal—I made an oh-so-entertaining video of our dancing debut last night as part of a plot to blackmail you. Here's how it's going to go. I asked my parents to contact the big wigs of this tour and make sure we can meet up on Christmas Eve. Awesome, right? Of course, if you can't make it, I'll have to release the attached video. Get it? See you then! Lilli

Too cool! Cal dared to hope that Lilli's plan might actually work. The idea of the two friends being together in China at Christmas was surreal. If anybody could make it happen, it was the Cohens.

Muting the volume on his laptop and placing the screen where Jack couldn't watch, Cal double clicked on the video taken without his knowledge in the Cohen's rec room. In the video, Cal was trying his best to copy Lilli's hip-hop moves but came off looking completely ridiculous. She had him. He would do anything to keep that video from getting out, especially to Levi or Miguel.

"Ladies and gentlemen, we anticipate some turbulence in the next few minutes," came the pilot's warning over the speaker. "At this time, we would ask that all carry on items be stored safely and securely under your seat or in the overhead compartment."

Cal had a single email to check before closing his laptop. The nosey male flight attendant had begun his sweep of the aisles, insisting that passengers stow their items immediately. The plane jostled about, and Cal felt his stomach lurch.

The final email was addressed to: *All Members of the Dream Team*. Cal quickly opened it. The sender was the Professor. The email read:

> Effective immediately, the newest member of the dream team, Cal Vandiver, will assume a new name—Blu. Hereafter, all members of the team will refer to him exclusively by this name, to include trainers and those in contact with the media. I speak for all of us in welcoming Blu as he brings his unique talents to further the cause of the dream team. Professor Si Zhen

Blu? Could this man change his name? Why? And what was this "cause" the Professor mentioned? Was he referring to the Games—or something else?

"Young man, you'll have to close your computer now," the attendant said then lingered to ensure the Asian kid wearing shades did as he was told.

"Any more communications of interest?" Jack inquired.

"Something from the Professor," his companion answered, as he reluctantly tucked his computer away.

"Ah."

Now it was Cal who closed his eyes. During the next few minutes, as the plane and its passengers endured the promised turbulence, he felt as though his whole world was shaking loose. In his mind's eye he slipped from panel three, "Breakthrough," to panel one, "Brewing." Something was up.

"You could have left your sun glasses at home," Jack remarked. "Now you will be famous for your eyes, eh—Blu?"

"You knew?"

"Yes. I received an email about the name change last night.

I kind of like it. Going by one name is a *thing*, isn't it?"

"I guess so," the boy mused. "Like Shaq."

"Or Messi," Jack suggested.

The teen known as Blu relaxed. "This could be all right."

Hours later, as the flight neared its destination, Cal slept and the male attendant made his final round with refreshments. "Some carbonated beverage to settle your stomach?"

The woman in the row seat shook her head no.

"None for me either," said Jack.

Now the woman abruptly turned to him. Her friendly manner had vanished without notice. "Are you certain? It has already been an unsettling flight, has it not?"

Jack returned a look of confusion, yet said nothing.

Cal woke at the sound of the woman speaking.

"Just as well," she added, darkly. "The drink helps with nausea, but it cannot help you forget, eh, Coach Bai?"

Just then the exchange student turned in his seat and spoke directly to Jack in Mandarin. The seemingly polite collegiate had turned vicious. He continued his diatribe as Coach Jack sat stone-faced and silent. Cal felt eyes all around, watching the bizarre scene. The flight attendant stayed close, pressing his headset to his ear, as if receiving instructions, but never attempting to intervene.

Over the speaker, the pilot announced the beginning of the plane's descent into Beijing, instructing passengers to pull seats into an upright position and to fasten their seatbelts. The student turned at last. Tension had replaced oxygen in the cabin. Jack began scribbling notes and hammering out emails on his tablet as the plane dropped in the sky. To Blu, it seemed as though they had not only crossed the ocean, they had also, at some point, crossed into enemy territory. He gripped the armrests against the unexplained and wondered what awaited the two travelers when their plane finally touched down in China.

# PART II

# 50

At last, the wheels of the plane met the ground. Blu felt desperate for air—and space—and was poised to bolt. He felt sure that, if necessary, with his small stature he could slip past Jack, squeeze around the woman with her oversized purse, and shove aside the lean, pale flight attendant who lingered at the end of their row.

As the plane came to a halt, passengers were instructed—first in Mandarin then in English—to remain seated until further notice. Blu exchanged an anxious glance with his coach. Just then two men dressed in light blue shirts and navy slacks with police caps filed into the cabin. Reaching the attendant, the first officer turned and spoke to Jack in Mandarin.

"He says they are our escorts," Jack translated for Blu in a low tone. The flight attendant opened the overhead compartment from which the second officer pulled Jack's suitcase then Blu's duffle. As he did, the first officer ordered Jack and his companion to gather their carry-on items and disembark. Blu wasn't sure if they were in some sort of trouble or this was a rolling out of the red carpet—Chinese style. As they emerged from the plane, the answer became painfully clear.

Just outside the Jetway stood a second committee of grim-faced men in uniforms. Two men approached Jack, pulled his arms behind him, and handcuffed him. Before he was led away, Jack whispered to his terrified companion, "Your jacket—check the pocket."

"You can't take him!" Blu yelled over the other passengers and the din of the busy airport. Heads turned, but no one stopped. When Blu attempted to rush through the crowd, the other officers blocked him. A moment later, Jack was out of sight.

Determined arms bustled Blu to a nearby gate where a tiny-framed and expressionless Asian woman stood at a counter. A uniformed man handed the woman a plane ticket. Asking no questions, the woman scanned the ticket and nodded for Blu to move along to the Jetway.

"Where are you taking me? I need to go with my coach!" Blu insisted. "Isn't this Beijing? I'm supposed to stay in Beijing!"

At this the woman looked at the boy, unmoved. "To Kunming now," she said.

"What?"

With his laptop underarm, Blu was escorted by an officer on to still another plane and deposited at his assigned seat on an otherwise empty row. His duffle was stuffed into the overhead by the officer who then handed him a folded sheet of paper. Blu hurried to unfold it. The name Professor Si Zhen was typed at the bottom. It read:

> I have learned there has been a change in plans. You will be flying on to the Kunming Sports Training Center in southwest China. You will find the facilities and trainers there to be excellent. I will come to you. Be strong. An Olympian understands that every day is another opportunity to triumph.

Nausea overtook the boy suddenly, and he reached for the gag bag in the seat pocket in front of him. But he had nothing to expel beyond fear. Blu remembered Jack's instructions and reached into his jacket pocket, finding a handwritten note. He imagined Jack stuffing it there as they gathered their belongings at the order of the police. Jack wrote in hurried print:

> At the Beijing Games, I was arrested for the death of an athlete I trained, Qin Ji, who died suddenly after failing to qualify for competition. To punish me for this loss, the government publically accused me of his death. Though the charges were later dropped, I lost everything, and China no longer welcomes me. Only the Professor stood with me. He will keep you safe.

Blu wondered how his parents had missed this bit of information on Coach Bai Zhao Man. Opening his computer, Blu hurried to type an email to Levi before take off. It read:

> Levi—
> The police took Jack in Beijing. I was put on another flight to a place called Kunming. The Professor is supposed to meet me there. Tell James Wo at the Seattle Asian Times. Maybe he'll know more. By the way, I am now called Blu.

The email sent, Blu put his computer away. Now he addressed the female Asian flight attendant that stood ready to help boarding passengers. "How far to where we're going?" he asked, hoping the attendant understood English. He had nearly given up on a response when the woman spoke at last.

"Three hours," she answered curtly.

Blu closed his eyes, desperate for escape. It was nearly

an hour before he rested, finding the temporary relief he sought from his nausea, the pounding in his head, and the overwhelming reality that his future was completely unknown.

• • •

"They got separated!" Levi exclaimed to his brother Derek, who sat with him at the card table in their garage reading the worrisome email from their friend.

"Yeah, well, you have to wonder if maybe that's a good thing," Derek was thinking aloud. "There's obviously something about Jack we don't know."

"Wo will be able to explain it—or at least find out what's going on, right?"

"He certainly has more resources than we do," Derek answered.

"I'm going to Google this place." Levi started typing.

"You do that," Derek responded. "I'll call Wo."

• • •

The phone rang at James Wo's desk at the tiny satellite office of the *Seattle Asian Times*. The young journalist moved to the small cubicle in San Francisco after receiving a tip about an Asian athlete in Visalia training for the Olympics. His editor rightly judged the potential of the story; circulation was up. In addition, the anonymous source of the story offered the paper significant sums for information and photographs of the boy and those with whom he kept company.

"*Seattle Asian Times*, Wo speaking."

"James Wo, good morning, this is Derek Price."

"Do we know each other Mr. Price?"

"I'm calling on behalf of my friend Cal Vandiver." Pause. Wo grabbed pen and paper.

"I'm listening."

"Just a question."

"Vandiver can call me himself."

"He can't break away from training right now."

Wo knew two things off the bat. First, Cal wasn't even in the country. Wo had been present at the soccer field at Valley Oak Middle when Professor Si Zhen invited Jack and his trainee to go to China over the winter break. In a quick text, Wo had passed along the tip to Vandiver's generous "fan." Minutes later, the Professor found Wo hiding behind the bleachers and offered him an exclusive interview if he kept quiet about the trip. Secondly, Wo knew a call now from Derek signaled something was wrong, and it was his job to find out what.

"What can I help you with?"

"So it may be that Cal's coach had some trouble in Beijing in the past, something related to the Games? Cal was interested to know if you knew what happened, if anything."

"I think I know what you're referring to," Wo lied, kicking himself for failing to dig into the backstory of Coach Bai Zhao Man. Wo pulled up the paper's archives. "Hang on a minute, and I'll check for the details."

Wo knew very little uncensored news made it out of China before the underground bloggers found their way onto the Internet. But there it was. Actually his search pulled up two news briefs, dated three months apart. Wo scanned them quickly. "You're talking about the arrest?"

"Yeah," Derek attempted to sound calm. "I think that's it." Derek put the call on speakerphone at the insistence of his brother.

"Coach Bai was arrested following the death of a kid he was training. A cyclist."

"Did he go to prison?"

"Nah. Under house arrest for a few months."

"So he was cleared of any wrongdoing?"

The answer was in the second news brief. Wo answered, "Yeah, he was released after Professor Si Zhen accused the government of arresting Coach Bai to punish him for an Olympic loss. The actual cause of death was never released."

"Wow. So maybe that's when Jack moved to the U.S., huh?" Derek attempted a chuckle. "Sounds like he was invited to train elsewhere."

"I couldn't tell you that," Wo commented, even as he sent an email to one of his blogger contacts in China and started a second one to his boss at the *Times*.

"Well, thanks for the info."

"Sure thing," Wo ended the call, hit SEND, and waited. Moments later, a return email from the blogger confirmed that Jack and Cal had arrived in Beijing, where Jack had immediately been arrested.

The news came as a blow. Wo realized Cal and Jack's travel plans had been shared with the Chinese government, and likely, he had been the leak.

The second email Wo sent landed on his boss's computer in Seattle. In it he requested permission to follow his assignment to China, where the story was, apparently, taking a new twist. Travel expenses would be an issue, he knew. Since it was unlikely the leak could be traced to him, Wo thought of the Professor, who might be inclined to buy a plane ticket to have an American reporter—with an Asian following—close at hand.

# 51

The light that forced its way between the bars on the windows of Blu's tiny living space announced the new day. Memories from the night before were spotty. He remembered watching Jack taken away and a long car ride at the end of his second flight. It was late when he was escorted to a small, dorm-like room with a single bed, a side table with a lamp, a wooden chair that sat in a corner, and a dresser with a TV.

Once fully awake Blu sat up. His lungs hurt. His breathing was labored. As a result, his heart pounded, and his head ached. There was a knock at the door and a stocky young Asian let the Professor into the room. The man unbuttoned his heavy black coat.

"You *just* got here?" Blu complained.

"It was not my intent that you make the trip to Kunming alone," he said. "You were to make your debut—with your new name—in Beijing before joining the rest of the dream team."

"The dream team is here?"

"Yes, this facility—"

Blu interrupted with a cough. "I can't breathe."

The Professor nodded in understanding. "You are 1,900 meters above sea level. The air is thin, but you will adjust. Athletes come to this facility for high altitude training. This environment has proven advantageous to many athletes."

"How can not being able to breathe possibly be advantageous?"

"The reduction in air pressure sends more oxygen to your muscles. You can work longer and harder."

"Awesome."

Unruffled, the Professor continued. "The accommodations are not luxurious, but they are free of distractions, and the food is hot and plentiful. It is time for the midday meal. You will meet some of your fellow trainees shortly."

"What about Jack?"

"He was detained in Beijing. There is a matter to be dealt with there before he can come to you."

"Why did you let him come at all—either of us? You had to know that he wasn't safe here."

"It was his choice. He believed that the disagreement with the government of China was behind him."

"Not so much," Blu held his aching head.

"Jack will be returned to us. Until then you will continue your training."

The guard was at the door again. "Can I escort you to the cafeteria, sir?"

"Food. Yes, but just the boy. Blu, have you met Feng? He is the dorm attendant for the dream team."

"Hello."

"Don't eat too much or too fast," the Professor warned the athlete.

"I'm so hungry."

"Too much, too fast, and all will be lost."

Blu moaned in understanding.

Before leaving, the Professor gestured to the small TV. "You may wish to follow the news from time to time. We record news stories of interest for the team."

"Will you watch with me?"

"Come back for him in ten minutes, please," the Professor instructed Feng. The Professor used the remote on the bedside table to turn on the TV.

It didn't matter that the first news story was delivered in Chinese. He had seen the story himself. Blu watched video of Jack being handcuffed at the airport. Then a photograph appeared on the bottom right of the screen. It was Qin Ji, the athlete Jack had been accused of pushing beyond his physical limits, resulting in his death. Blu shivered. The boy was the spitting image of the exchange student aboard their plane to Beijing. Qin Ji, of course, would be much older now.

Next came news of Lilli. She stepped from her limousine, looking like Chinese royalty, fans pressing around her.

"She looks amazing," Blu spoke.

"Her first appearance is tonight. There will be another story later."

"I feel better knowing she's alright," Blu confessed. He relaxed a bit into the assurance that the Professor would see to Jack's release, that he could connect with his friends by email, and that he had a meet up with Lilli on Christmas Eve to look forward to. Now he was ready to eat.

...

The facility was cold and drafty. Everywhere. Even the cafeteria. Dressed in sweats, Blu stood alone in line to get food. The other athletes were already seated at tables in small groups. Each appeared to be all or part Asian.

Bodies shifted and eyes followed him with interest, as if there had been some anticipation of his arrival. What was he to them? Blu wondered. A large woman, Russian perhaps, slopped a mound of steaming and colorless—something—on his plate. He sat down at an empty table. It wasn't his mother's meatloaf, but he ate without complaint. He didn't even mind the cloudy water he was given with his meal. At least it was warm.

When a shadow fell over his meal, Blu looked up to see the face of the Professor accompanied by another man, also Asian, who looked as though he made a career of bossing people around. He was slightly taller than the Professor, muscular, pock-faced, and entirely without expression.

"This is For-Now," the Professor introduced the man. "He is your coach—for now."

"That's not your real name, right?" Blu debated whether the Professor was joking.

"You do not need to know my name," the man responded without humor. "I am your coach for now, and we begin working today. Meet me at the running track in one hour." The Professor nodded at Blu, as if to confirm that—yes—this was for real.

...

The running track, like the facility as a whole, was a disappointment to Blu. The windows in the concrete walls were high and small. He felt claustrophobic. And the track was old, just like his second string coach, For-Now.

Blu felt as though he had been away from his training for a long time. Both mind and body had been taken on an unexpected journey. Even after stretching, his muscles remained tight. The charity of his coach ran out quickly, and soon the man-turned-bulldog barked at him from the side of the track. This was not Jack's way.

"Why do you run?" For-Now hollered at Blu as the boy passed the coach on the track. It was a ridiculous question.

"I run to win!" Blu yelled back.

"You run to win?" the man sounded indignant. "That is all?" Blu felt the contents of his stomach rising in his throat. The man continued his rant.

"And so you win, what do you have then?"

"A gold medal!"

"To hell with the gold medal!"

Blu stopped at the large open barrel beside the track and expelled his lunch. What did this man want?

"Did you see them take Jack away?" Coach For-Now continued his verbal assault.

Blu nodded. The memory of that moment brought a second wave of nausea.

"Would you run for his freedom?"

Of course he would run to free Jack, but what did his training have to do with the politics of China?

"Would you run if they took your friend, the ballerina?"

At this Blu collapsed to the floor. Face down, he buried his face in his hands and yelled. "They wouldn't do that!"

"It happened already! Don't you understand?" For-Now refused to let up. "She was taken from the arms of her mother—like a million others. Only *one* child allowed then! Maybe the dancer came second! Or maybe a mother hoped for a life of *freedom* for her daughter. Or perhaps a trafficker found a *buyer* for such a beautiful child!"

Blu dropped to the floor and curled himself into a ball. "She is safe!" Blu insisted. "She is free!"

"No one here is either safe or free!" The man stepped forward and pulled Blu to his feet. "You rest now. Swim later. Tomorrow you cycle."

Pale and shaken, Blu followed Coach For-Now down a hallway past other dorm rooms toward his own at the very end.

As they walked, For-Now yelled, "Why must we run?" Athletes emerged from their rooms.

"To win the race!" one student yelled back, followed by a unified reply from all who stood watching: "It is a race for freedom! I will do my part!"

The moment transported Blu to his childhood dream and to the words spoken to him: "It is time for you to do your part."

Later, in the blue of the pool, Blu took his cleansing laps. Still, the united voice of the athletes echoed there. He wondered how it was that in Kunming, living like prisoners, members of the dream team spoke of freedom. It was ironic really. Each pursued a dream in a country that denied the same for its own. He was beginning to understand why Candace insisted he learn about the tragedy at Tiananmen; injustice yet prevailed; Jack had suffered in the past and again now. It could have been Lilli. It could have been him. This new thought overtook his body as he swam, and Blu knew, even without Levi, he'd clocked his best time ever.

...

Night fell, and Blu was again in search of carbs. Meat of some kind lay on the plate before him along with a mound of mashed potatoes and limp broccoli. Again, the other athletes gravitated to their own tables, but Blu was too tired and hungry to care. Halfway through his meal, a second body dropped down next to him. The lanky Asian boy put down his heaping plate and ick-colored water.

"You speak English?" Blu asked, cutting into the meat-like lump.

"Of course," the boy answered. "I'm from Indiana."

"Adopted?"

"We all are."

"Why are you talking to me? No one else does."

"They're just, like, in awe."

"They care what I think about *them*?"

"You're Blu, right? You got the blue eye thing going."

"So?"

"So now it starts."

"What starts?"

"The Blu Phenomenon." When Blu responded with a blank stare, his companion asked, "What, you don't know?"

"No idea." Blu took a long drink of water and made a face.

"Everyone here knows what a badass athlete you are." The boy talked while spearing his broccoli. "They also know your arrival means it's our time to make things right."

"I don't even know you. Any of you. What's your name anyway?"

"Dwain."

Blu laughed. Dwain from Indiana.

"You're here to be an Olympian like me, right?"

"That's the plan." The boy had crooked teeth and bangs. Blu wondered how long he'd been in Kunming.

"What's your sport?"

"Chess." At this Blu tried not to laugh but ended up sending his potatoes up through his nose.

"Problem with chess?"

"Sorry, dude." Blu blew his meal into his napkin. "Everything here is just so bizarre. So, like, when you say it's time to 'make things right,' what does that mean?"

"Talk about bizarre," Dwain said, staring at Blu.

"What? You don't think this place feels like a different planet? Or that it's a little odd that all the athletes here are Asian? Or that chess is really a sport?"

"We are all adoptees from China. Every one of us has a story that brought us here."

"What's your story?"

"My father was a professor. A year after I was born, another professor reported him for lectures that criticized the Chinese government for what happened at Tiananmen. After that he disappeared, and my mother was put in prison."

"He was a hero."

"More likely, he was trying to undo his past. As a kid he joined the Red Guards."

"I don't know about that."

"Serious? You don't know China's history?"

"I have a book," he started, "but I haven't read much of it yet. What are the Red Guards?"

"What *were* the Red Guards," Dwain corrected Blu. "They were groups of kids, mostly, whipped into a frenzy by Chairman Mao, you know, the father of Chinese communism. He challenged the Red Guards to destroy 'Old China.'

It became illegal to have books or artwork or anything considered a threat to Mao's vision."

"But they're gone now."

"Yeah, well, the madness didn't stop until after my father accused his own parents, my grandparents, of breaking the law when they hid some old books."

"What happened to them?"

"They died in prison after refusing 're-education.' My mother too." Dwain scraped his plate clean and dropped his fork down with a clink. "And now it's time to make things right; time for a second Tiananmen."

"Revolution—for real?"

"Not the kind with drone strikes and cyber attacks. It'll happen more like a wave." Dwain stood and looked at his clueless blue-eyed comrade. "Maybe you need to finish your book or whatever."

"Yeah, maybe."

...

Back in his darkened room, Blu felt soreness setting in and longed for sleep. But even more, he wanted to see the coverage of Lilli's first performance. Sprawled across his too small, rock hard bed, Blu started the TV recording. The story opened on the performance venue. The auditorium was large and packed. The report, delivered in Chinese, included shots of young girls cheering before the event, followed by clips of Lilli and Ben killing it. Blu liked Ben less and less.

The story closed with short interviews of excited attendees and a scan of the crowd. Blu didn't see it until he had watched the segment for the third time. There, at the end in a wide shot, Blu noticed older men milling together, looking somewhat out of place among the young fans. Attached to a column near where they stood was a sheet of paper with the image of a wave. There were no words that he could see on the page. It was random. It was blue.

The news clip that followed appeared to be an interview of Jack, though the story was reported over the scene. His coach was seated in what looked like a living room. The lighting in the room was low, but Blu thought he saw bruising on Jack's face. The now familiar face of Qin Ji also flashed on the screen. Who would have planted a Qin Ji lookalike on the plane? Why? The woman also must have been an attempt to inflict some kind of mental torture on his coach. Both represented the life Jack left behind in China twelve years before.

More than anything Blu wished that he could dive under the blue waterline of the pool, but he could not. He was confined to his tiny room with his deluge of questions. Moving to the floor, Blu stretched his aching body and attempted to prepare for the day to come. It would be his first time cycling in China—with For-Now.

Before turning off his light, Blu checked his computer for emails. Nothing. He had been unable to get an Internet connection since his arrival. To escape the panic of feeling cut off—caged—Blu opened the book he'd downloaded onto his computer from Candace. Less than an hour later, he bookmarked his page and closed down the computer. Reading the story of Tiananmen brought no relief. As far as he could see, little had changed in the country of his birth.

# 52

Blu woke to pounding. A moment later Feng, the dorm attendant, opened the door and tossed clothes at him. "Dress now. Coach For-Now will meet you in the cafeteria." Blu longed for the music alarm that gently woke him at home—so far away now, like another life altogether.

"But I brought my own cycling stuff," Blu argued.

"*Extra* clothes," Feng replied, as if to warn him.

A brief examination of the items forced a realization far worse than his rude wake-up call, worse than the nightmares that had plagued his sleep. He was going to cycle outside. In the cold.

"Where are we going?" he asked irritably.

"The Dianchi."

"What's that?" The door closed before he received an answer.

While there had rarely been an occasion when Blu was not agreeable to eating, he wished he could skip breakfast. Skip Coach For-Now. Skip cycling. Out of respect for Jack, Blu pulled on his cycle wear from home, layering it with the additional gear provided—an insulated vest with gloves stuffed in the pocket, knee warmers, and wool socks. Fortunately, he remembered to pack the super cool shades Jack gave him. Wearing them made him feel close to Jack and, at the same time, distanced from Coach For-Now.

In the cafeteria line, Blu was handed a steaming blob of grey in a bowl along with a tall glass of chocolate-colored slush. This was new.

"Protein," the server answered Blu's questioning gaze. Coach For-Now sat alone at a table and was also dressed for cold temperatures. The man grunted a hello. Blu knew the day would be all business. And lots of yelling. His shoulders and neck tightened.

"What is Dianchi?"

"It is the lake here," Coach For-Now answered shortly, as if Blu should know such things. "You have not seen it?"

"I haven't seen anything but a running track, a pool," he looked around him, at the eyes that watched his conversation, "and this place."

"To circle the Dianchi is 101 miles," the man offered matter of factly.

"The triathlon only requires twenty-five miles of cycling."

"Tell me something new," barked For-Now. "We will ride twenty-five miles at a time—until you've made it around the Dianchi."

"I'll ride better if you don't yell."

"Don't tell me how to coach. You are spoiled."

...

Both conditions and attitudes were cold from the start of the training day to its disastrous finish. Blu was ordered to cycle then run then cycle and run some more. All the while, Coach For-Now exercised his vocal cords. Four hours later, Blu returned to his room exhausted. Four water bottles sat at the bedside, and he downed them all then slept. When he woke his chest hurt, and he felt dizzy, whether from a lack of oxygen or an excess of For-Now.

Blu made his way to the door. "I need to see the Professor!" he called to Feng. "Hello?"

"He is in a meeting," Feng rounded the corner.

"Take me to him!"

Standing eye to eye with the newest addition to the dream team, the dorm attendant faced a dilemma. His job was to keep the athletes in place and on schedule. He was, however, alarmed by the distressed state of the athlete called Blu—a favorite of the Professor. With a nod of the head, Feng turned and Blu followed.

...

After a quick knock, Feng opened the door to the sunny conference room where the Professor stood at a long table. Four others sat with him, one woman and three men. Light streamed in through large windows behind the Professor, reminding Blu of the cafeteria at Valley Oak Middle, which reminded him of Lilli, Levi, and salmon patties.

"I'm sorry to interrupt." Blu felt his face go hot.

"Actually we were just speaking of you," the Professor said, the others nodding in agreement. "Come in." The Professor motioned Blu closer. "Meet my colleagues," he continued without offering any names, "supporters of the dream team effort." Blu shook hands with each at the table. He thought they looked at him as if they had seen him a thousand times. Yet he knew nothing of them.

"Please, sit," the woman offered. Blu chose a seat at the end of the table.

"Have you ever seen an Olympian on a TV commercial?" the Professor asked.

"Uh. I guess. Sure."

"How do you think that happens, that an athlete ends up selling toothpaste on television?"

Blu paused. "I guess the toothpaste company pays them a

lot of money to act like they use their product, right?"

"You are right. The arrangement is a win-win for everyone."

Blu imagined himself brushing his teeth in front of the world. "Do you have any idea how such opportunities are arranged?"

Blu felt ignorant. "No."

Olympians are kind of like movie stars, believe it or not. They even have public relations people to manage their affairs."

Blu wondered why they were talking about a future he'd certainly never have without Jack.

"This team is here to manage your PR needs."

"I have PR needs?"

With both hands on the table, the Professor leaned toward Blu and answered with confidence, "You will."

Blu raked his hair in frustration. "Can we talk about Jack?"

Looking around the table, the Professor replied, "Yes, let's do."

"I can't train with For-Now anymore. It's not working."

"As I said, it is a temporary—"

"I'm *worried*," Blu laid bare his inner anguish.

The Professor winced at the pain in the boy's voice. "The arrest of your coach was unfortunate, certainly. But as we see it," the man gestured to those seated at the table, "it does present an opportunity with the potential to benefit you both going forward."

"I have no idea what that means. I just want my coach back. Please."

"Understood." The Professor finally sat down at the opposite end of the table. "There are challenges in working with the Chinese government. You understand this, don't you?"

"I'm not in Kansas anymore. I get it."

"The Chinese government is corrupt," the Professor nearly spat the words. "If you want cooperation here, you must be prepared to buy it or to make a sort of—arrangement."

"Can you help me or not?"

"This team here has, in fact, made an arrangement. But you have a part to play."

"What? You said you'd 'manage' stuff for me!"

"This one thing we cannot do."

"Why not?"

"It requires that you meet directly with a high profile member of the Chinese government, from the Department of Propaganda."

Blu was on his feet. "That's crazy! I don't even know the language or the laws or what to say!"

The Professor stood and walked to the windows. The Asian woman with soft eyes interjected. "Language will not be a problem," she promised. "Your job is simple. Respectfully listen to what she has to say. When she is done, you may request the release of Coach Bai. If you listen to her, she will listen to you."

"Great. Whatever. When do I go?"

"In the morning," one of the other men answered. "It has been scheduled."

Hoping to further improve his circumstances, Blu dared to ask, "And why can't I get my email?"

It was the Professor who responded. "As it is now, I have no control over this. The government has interrupted all Internet service to American athletes." The door opened, and Feng reentered the room, a sign that the visit was over. The Professor offered a parting gift: "You may be encouraged to know that soon a familiar face will be joining the others here on the team."

"Who's that?" The only name Blu wanted to hear was *Jack*.

"I'm sure you remember the photographer from the *Seattle Asian Times*, James Wo?"

...

Something resembling shredded pork sat heavy in Blu's stomach that evening as he returned to his room, flanked by his friend Dwain.

"When did you come here?" Blu asked, sitting on a sweatshirt that marked the spot where he routinely watched the news at the end of the day. He reached for the remote, anxious to see Lilli.

"A month ago," answered Dwain, who sat cross-legged at the end of the bed.

"What about school?"

"I've always been home schooled, so I can spend more time training."

"Sounds dreamy."

"Not so bad. What about you?"

"No school now," Blu answered. "I'm just here on my winter break."

The TV flickered to life. The story began with music, the familiar song, "Undercurrent." Enter Lilli.

"Who's *that*?"

"My friend. She's on a dance tour here in China over the school break."

"Weird that you're both here."

"Yeah. More than weird."

"What do you mean?"

"She's, like, amazing," Blu answered. "The tour makes sense and all, it's just—"

"What?"

"It's just the timing. I'm here to meet up with the dream team for a few weeks. But Lilli—I mean, the tour could have waited until summer."

The camera scan of the scene revealed a larger more exuberant crowd than before. If Blu had not been looking for it, he would have missed it. Amidst the families and young girls, he spotted a piece of paper waving from a post; again he saw the image of a wave. A clip of Ben doing a solo hip-hop routine was followed by a closing shot of the two dancers, arms locked, taking their bows.

"Is she from here?" Dwain asked.

"Born here, but adopted like us."

"Is she, you know, *angry*?"

Blu looked at his geeky new friend, confused. "Angry about what?"

Dwain shrugged. "Angry about what she doesn't know, or what might have been?"

Blu thought of the dance Lilli now performed before an international audience; how she had worked with Carissa to choreograph it; how she had risked offending her teacher and her parents to express herself. "Yeah," Blu answered at last. "She's pretty angry."

The recording ended, and Blu went silent.

"So," Dwain decided his next best move was to change the topic, "interested in some chess?"

"Nah," Blu responded. "I think I'll take a short swim, just to clear my head. Tomorrow I have to meet some official with the Chinese government."

"Oh, yeah. It'll be a big day."

Once the door clicked shut behind Dwain, Blu dressed for a swim. In the pool he took his laps slowly in an effort to relax. But it was to no avail. His mind raced: there had been a second appearance of the mysterious wave image; he would be meeting with a Chinese official the next day; and everyone around him—even Dwain—seemed aware of something that he did not.

Upon returning to his room, Blu noticed that the single drawer of the small bedside table was partially open. Since his arrival in Kunming, he'd been living out of his duffle. Unpacking seemed way too permanent. He pulled at the wooden knob of the drawer. Inside was something he'd only seen a picture of. It was the bracelet that Jewell Chan invented, a Glo-Me.

He stretched it over his hand and onto his wrist. One at a time, he touched the tiles, each marked with a Chinese character, and watched them light up in their colored casing. He remembered being told how it ran on a thermoelectric battery, drawing power from his own body. The next to last tile, the purple one, failed to light. It also bulged slightly. When Blu attempted to press it into place, it came off on his fingertip. Inside was coiled a tightly rolled piece of paper.

Using the tile, he pried the paper from the tiny compartment.
His hands shaking, Blu carefully unrolled the thin paper. It read:

> A Christmas gift for Lilli. A message just for you. Tomorrow you meet Li Daiya, your biological mother. I carried you to safety in my body, but you do not carry my genes. I only hope you hear my heart. Listen to it as your mother speaks, and you will know what is true. Candace

Candace! Blu rolled the paper up and tucked it inside his zippered pillowcase. He secured the loose tile, checked that it lighted properly then returned the bracelet to the drawer. The news from Candace revised every part of the story he had come to believe about his life to date. And yet Blu felt at peace. It was as if he had somehow sensed what he could not have known. And he wondered what part his birth mother would contribute to his life that was yet to be.

# 53

Li Daiya stood alone in the ornate conference room of The Capital Hotel in the heart of Beijing. It was the same location where the crowded Green Party was held months before. As it happened, that event directed her to the Growing Up Green website and, ultimately, led to the fulfillment of her paper fortune: What was lost will be found. While perusing the post-performance footage of Lilli Cohen on the site, she saw him at last.

The decision to have a son was perhaps the most impulsive decision Li Daiya had ever made. Her station was enviable, as the only female member of the Chinese Communist Party's elite seven-member Politburo Standing Committee and head of China's Department of Propaganda. The position gave her the power she worked her whole life to possess. But she was not unaware of the threat. Every day she woke to a fear that an uprising pressed just outside her door, one with the strength to cripple the party and render her work obsolete. Li Daiya had begun to dream of a son who could breathe new life into the party, giving it a long-overdue infusion of sorts.

It was then that she enlisted the well-connected

businessman Gao Cheng to pull together a team to produce her very own "princeling," the title reserved for the male child of a party elite. Gao's father, a world-renowned geneticist, would oversee the procedure. It was a routine laboratory exercise turned groundbreaking when the doctor successfully altered the child's genes, resulting in a change of eye color. They would be blue. Blue eyes would, the mother concluded, help her son to win over his peers with Western-like panache. At the same time, the procedure would ensure the child could always be identified—or found—should the unimaginable happen. And it did.

While still in the womb of the American athlete, Candace Latham, hand-picked following her career-ending injury during the 2004 Games in Athens, the child was taken. Just days from the date the child was to be induced, the night nurse went to check Latham's vitals and found the patient gone. Security had been high. It was unfathomable.

In the beginning, Gao's team sought to accuse Li Daiya's carefully selected donor-father of the kidnapping. It was only logical. But just months into the pregnancy, the man had died in a car accident. Li Daiya had taken every precaution. She was not stupid.

It was Gao Cheng who eventually suggested the search for her son be moved to the U.S. The initiation of the Data Collection Project was a good idea. But a long shot. It might have been years before they found him had she not spotted her son on video. Coordinates for the search were changed to California. The DCP determined his exact location, and photographs provided by a hungry reporter kept her abreast of the life to which her son had been reassigned. As she had learned, that life included Olympic hopes, Coach Bai Zhao Man, and Professor Si Zhen.

The involvement of the prominent Chinese men in her son's life was troubling. So much so that Li Daiya had ordered DNA testing. Time would tell the rest of the story. Until then, all that mattered was that she was about to meet her blue-eyed princeling for the first time. And she could begin her work to guide him to his rightful position as her heir and a leader of the Chinese Communist Party.

...

Blu was made to feel like a VIP. At the airport in Beijing, a car awaited to carry him to the hotel to meet Li Daiya. As they passed the people on the busy streets, Blu looked for the face of his coach. He was likely still in the city—somewhere. The thought gave him the courage he needed to follow through with the arranged meeting. Maybe the woman was his mother, or maybe this was just another tale. Did it matter? The goal was to get his training back on track sans Coach For-Now.

Blu stood outside the meeting room long enough to take a deep breath. Then his well-dressed Chinese escort swung open the doors and announced the boy in Chinese. At the center of the sunlit room was a long table, and the woman stood alone at the far end. She turned from the window, leaving her face in the shadow. For certain, she did not resemble the Asian woman in the shampoo commercial Blu had long imagined. Her face was older, of course, and her expression more resolute than cordial. She smiled slightly and nodded but did not step toward him. The attendant gave Blu a gentle push at the elbow to indicate that he was the one expected to close the gap between them.

The woman spoke, and the man left the room. When, at last, they stood face to face, she held out her hand. "I am Li Daiya," she said in fluent English.

"They call me Blu," he responded, taking her hand. "I am pleased to meet you."

She allowed Blu time to study her face, which he did, even as she studied his. They stood at the same height, and he thought perhaps they shared the same shape of mouth, the same strong jawline and arch of eyebrow. But then, he thought, it may not be so. He had been tricked before.

For Li Daiya, there was no question that she looked into the eyes of her son. He carried the features of their ancestors. She thought it regrettable that she had altered the line with the change of eye color, but believed the alteration would best serve her country in the generations to come. There would always and forevermore be reverence for the lineage of blue-eyed Chinese leaders.

"You have just arrived, and already your face appears on every newspaper." The woman's smile revealed the polished teeth of a politician. "How does that feel?"

"I didn't know," the boy responded. "Why am I in the news?"

"Because my son the Olympian is home."

"I'm in training for the Olympics, not an Olympian," he returned. "And who knows if I am your son. I've heard a lot of stories."

"Oh, you are most certainly my son," she said smoothly. "It was I who arranged for your eyes to match the color of the sky."

Blu fought the urge to shake the woman. "Then tell me why you made me—different."

"You are the 'princeling' of Li Daiya. Who would not want to take you as their own?" Here she paused. "Foolishly, I never believed it *could* happen. Your conception was a well-guarded secret." Blu recognized the way the woman clenched her jaw and moved it slightly in her anger. It was the same reaction he had to the voice of Coach For-Now.

"What is a 'princeling'?"

"It is the heir of an elite member of the party. These, like you, move into positions of influence. It is in their blood to know what is best for the people and to guide them."

"I'm not even smart."

"Aren't you? Perhaps you are not deemed 'smart' in another culture. But you will, no doubt, be wise in discerning what is good for the Chinese people."

"I'm a swimmer. I swim."

Her voice turned sharp. "You do not know what you are. Have you lived in your own country? Do you know its people?"

"I have a home."

"A home is a place to rest your head. That is all. Your country, the place you were born, that is the place of your destiny."

"I'm sorry. I don't understand."

Li Daiya regained her composure. "It is not too late to learn. For the next days, you will see how you were meant to live—and why. You have a room here at the hotel that I believe will please you. The Professor explained this arrangement, did he not?" Blu felt her clear distrust for the man who'd brought him to China.

"He did."

"Then we will begin this long-overdue time together as mother and son." Li Daiya clapped her hands, and Blu's escort reentered and awaited instruction. She spoke again, and servers dressed in black began filling the table with food. "There will be a feast," she announced. "There are many who are anxious to meet the newly arrived princeling!"

# 54

As Li Daiya had begun to suspect, a DNA search of the database at the University of Hong Kong revealed the truth. Professor Si Zhen was, in fact, the father of her son.

She struggled to piece together the story. Clearly, her high-level security was breached long before Latham and the child were taken. The circle of those involved was small, made up of highly skilled staff loyal to the party. Together they worked in secrecy—from the selection of the donor to the delicate genetic engineering to the transfer of the embryo. At no point was there any indication that her plan had been compromised. Until they were gone.

The Professor. She barely knew the man. Yet there had been a single encounter. It happened fourteen years before at the time of the annual Lantern Festival, celebrated at the first full moon of the Chinese lunar year. A spectacular show of lighted lanterns against the night sky drew thousands to the city of Chengdu, the capital of the Sichuan province in Southwest China. Many from the country's elite were present—politicians, intellectuals, artists. Li Daiya remembered her brief exchange with the Professor, as if from a dream.

She accepted a glass of beer from the distinguished man, who introduced himself as Si Zhen, a university professor. As she observed, the man was quite well known and respected; many greeted him warmly by name.

"Perhaps you have a son at the university?" she inquired.

"I am not a family man," he answered. "No wife, no children. Only books."

"And I have my service to the people."

"To the success of our endeavors," he offered a toast. "These will be our legacy, yes?"

Whether it was the beer or the man's charisma or a sudden inkling of what she was not—a mother—she had hesitated. Seeing it, he had dared to suggest a solution to her hidden regret: "You are young, perhaps there will yet be a princeling."

It seemed to Li Daiya, in retrospect, that her dream of a son was birthed then. She had been transported by the idea that her work—and influence—might be extended in a way she could never accomplish in her lifetime. She believed now that the Professor had read her face and made note of it. And in the months that followed, as the dream unfolded, he managed to bypass her safeguards and to steal her growing child for his own purposes. In retrospect, she understood that a university professor, particularly one in rebellious Hong Kong, had no regard for her government work; he would have a very different dream for a son.

...

Blu shifted in his seat and fought the urge to yawn. The meeting of the Politburo Standing Committee was conducted entirely in Chinese. Li Daiya was the only female in attendance, and the only one—besides Blu—who looked to be under eighty years old. And yet, Blu, an invited guest for the day, didn't miss the intensity of those who spoke. There was a sense of urgency and passion in the exchanges.

Li Daiya's eyes were alert and quick, reading the faces of the other members, preparing her rebuttal. When she spoke, she did so with no hint of intimidation. And when spoken to, even harshly, she was unflinching.

Dressed in the suit and tie provided for him, Blu accepted and returned the respectful nods of officials as they filed in that morning and later when they were dismissed. He'd never been considered "college material" in California. Would that matter here? Would he study under Li Daiya and, in time, move into an enviable position and a lifestyle that didn't require working his way up from flipping burgers?

For the two days that followed, Blu awakened in plush surroundings, enjoyed food—lots of food—at his bidding, and submitted to Li Daiya's daily agenda for him. While she had detailed the events of his days, Li Daiya was not always available, and others accompanied Blu, taking him on tours that included luxury hotels, efficient factories, sleek office buildings, and bustling universities. Even in her absence, Blu felt the weight of his mother's unspoken expectations.

At last came Blu's final day with Li Daiya. Once again mother and son faced each other in the conference room of the hotel. It seemed odd to him that in the carefully planned time with Li Daiya he had learned little about her. Before his arrival, he had envisioned long talks in the night, during which she would ask him about himself and what he wanted for his future. In turn, he would ask her why she loved China and why she had wanted a son when her life seemed so full. As it happened, however, they had barely seen each other and had shared nothing personal. He wondered if his habit of keeping people at a distance was an inherited trait.

"I hope your morning meal was adequate?" asked Li Daiya who was already dressed smartly for the day with a navy dress and jacket, her hair in a roll along the hairline. She stood with impeccable posture by the long table.

"More than adequate," he answered truthfully. "Wonderful, really. I haven't missed the cold cafeteria or the gray stuff they serve there."

"Good health and comfort are the companions of the wise," Li Daiya remarked, her eyes scanned their surroundings before resting on her son's face. "You understand that now?" Blu understood her perfectly. The royal treatment he'd experienced as a "princeling" was reserved for those willing to bear the weighty matters of the largest country in the world.

"Come, let's have tea. Our time is short." She stepped toward the table, and a waiter rushed to pull out her chair. Blu seated himself across from her. In an instant, a clay teapot appeared along with small china teacups.

"You haven't asked me anything about myself," Blu started.

The woman busied herself spreading the white cloth napkin in her lap. Her jaw shifted slightly as she lifted her eyes to his. "What is it that I must know about you that I do not already know?"

"It might be simpler to ask what you *do* know."

Li Daiya responded with bitterness, "You were born to greatness but raised to believe you are, at best, mediocre. There is wisdom in your blood, but you have been given an abysmal education. You have the strength to rule, yet you express your feelings of loss and anxiety through sport."

It took everything in the boy not to throw his delicate cup across the room. In a single moment, she had reduced his life, his feelings, his one strength—his athleticism—to nothing.

Blu refused to answer her criticisms. Instead he changed the subject. "Tell me about my father."

"That is something else I have learned about you," she added, pouring tea into both cups. "You are often curious about the wrong things."

"You knew I would ask."

"Of course," she conceded, "but he is not here. I *am* here. Now is the time to learn about the work to be done and the magnitude of the opportunity before you."

"I don't know anything about China."

Color rose to Li Daiya's perfectly made up face. "Here is a fact that may be of interest then," she began tersely. "More people live in China than anywhere in the world—nearly three and a half *billion*. That's one in every five people on this planet!"

"It's run by only a few though, right?"

"If you are suggesting that China should be governed in the same way as the United States, you are spouting learned foolishness. We are an ancient people, not like the American melting pot. Our people have a respect for the past and are ruled according to what we know to be best for our own. Ours are the greatest people in the world."

"Jewell Chan seems pretty happy in America."

"Happy or content? Miss Chan is devoted to the future of China. She would tell you that success is not about 'happiness' but about accomplishing important work."

"Competing is my 'important work.'"

Li Daiya rearranged the napkin in her lap. "It is a worthy pursuit at this time," she seemed to be consoling herself. "But you have had no one to advise you regarding the future to which you were destined—the future that yet awaits you."

"My father is part of me too. Who is he?" Blu asked again.

The woman turned her cup in its place, reluctant. "I did not know him."

"I was made in a test tube—or something—and carried by Candace Latham." Blu followed the woman's troubled gaze to the window and the garden beyond. "I know that. Why don't you want me to know my father's name?"

"Your birth father is not the one I intended."

"What does that mean?"

Li Daiya dabbed her mouth with her napkin and laid it next to her cup.

"There was a man who was also interested in having a son. Like me." She swallowed hard. "He found a way."

"He became my father instead? How do you know?"

"DNA."

"Then you do know him!"

"I do know him, but not well. He is intelligent, to be sure.

And strong in his body, like you."

"What else?"

"Somehow he knew everything: he knew the surrogate; he knew about your eyes; he knew when you were to be born." The woman raised her cloth napkin to her tight lips. "He stole you, and then didn't bother to even raise you."

"Why would he do that?"

"He watched as others raised you in America, and when he saw opportunity to make use of his fatherhood, he stepped back into your life."

Now Blu was on his feet. "Is it Jack?"

She shook her head. "Not Jack, as you call him. He was busy with his wife, his career."

"Do I know him?"

"You know him—and then you do not." Her contempt was palpable. "He is a Chinese scholar turned traitor. He is called the Professor."

Blu froze at her announcement. While he could not be sure, the likeliness of the truth of it started a throbbing in his head. It was as if he floated without tether, and he was, in that moment, desperate to see or feel something familiar in order to return to himself.

"Please, can I continue my training with Jack?" There was agony in his plea.

"You care about Coach Bai Zhao Man."

"Yes."

"You have the power to change his life—and your own."

"We will do that at the Games," Blu responded, holding his aching head in his hands.

"That will change *your* life, certainly. But Coach Bai will remain an outcast in his own country, a presumed murderer."

Blu took his seat again. "It was an accident."

"Does it matter? He lost everything didn't he? And he is under arrest even now." Here the woman held up one finger. "He has but a single hope to regain all that he so unfortunately lost."

"What do you want?"

The woman smiled.

"I can see to it that Coach Bai is publicly declared innocent in the matter of Qin Ji."

"In exchange for what?"

"Simple. You compete in the Games for China."

Blu swallowed down the rising contents of his stomach. "I would have to discuss this with Jack."

"Certainly. He will meet you at the pool in Kunming this afternoon." Li Daiya stood, and Blu followed suit. Their eyes met with equal intensity. "Yours is the opportunity to fulfill both dream and destiny," she commented and followed with a prediction: "You will compete for China, later to serve this great land having won the respect of your people."

Li Daiya called to the attendant who appeared at Blu's side. Mother and son nodded their farewells. The woman knew Blu was already considering her offer. Her son was fiercely loyal to his coach; it was an attribute they shared. She could only hope that her offspring would reconsider his loyalty to country when he again laid his head on a hard bed in Kunming.

# 55

Lilli and Ben spent the entire morning in the studio with photographers, providing fodder for the tabloids—Chinese and American. According to the director of promotions for the tour, a demanding Chinese woman who never tired, it was advantageous from a business standpoint to fuel a public perception that the dance duo was, in fact, an "item." Ben appeared to enjoy brushing cheeks and holding his partner close. Lilli—not so much. While her partner had swept the entire female population off its feet, he would not have her heart.

Where was Cal—Blu—anyway? Lilli had yet to receive a single email from her BFF. After three weeks she had given up making excuses for him and was beginning to take it personally. The plan to meet up on Christmas Eve became more remote by the day.

"Hey, Lilli!" Ben called to her as she stood smiling for photos to be made into posters. "Your Olympic dude friend is in the paper!" He stood by the snack table and held up the folded paper. "And it looks like he found himself an older woman!" he joked.

In an instant Lilli jumped out from under the studio lights, despite the objections of the director-lady-general. On the front page of a Chinese newspaper, there was a photo of Blu—barely recognizable in suit and tie—together with an attractive, older Asian woman. Turning to the young male photographer who joked with Ben in English, Lilli demanded, "What does this say?"

The photographer obediently scanned the photo caption and first lines of the story. "Unreal!" he exclaimed. "You know this kid?"

"Of course I do! What does it say?"

"Do you know who *that* is?" he asked, pointing to the older woman.

"No, tell me!"

"That's Li Daiya," he declared. Lilli responded with a blank stare.

"So it says here that your friend is her son."

"His mother? But his mother isn't even Chinese!"

Now the photographer laughed. "Look again. That dude is full Chinese, and if the news service says he is her son, then he is her son."

"Well, who is she?"

"Li Daiya? She's on the Politburo Standing Committee of the Chinese Communist Party." Again he met her blank stare. "Like if the U.S. had extra vice-presidents, she would be one of them."

"What else?"

He scanned the next couple paragraphs. "It says he's training for the Olympics."

"They got that right. Go U.S.!"

"I don't know about that. Seems there's a rumor that he might be competing for China."

"No way!" Lilli stomped her foot and all eyes fell on her. "Where is Jack?"

"Who's that?"

"Jack—his coach. He has a Chinese name …"

"Coach Bai Zhao Man?" The photographer pointed at the name printed in the article.

"That's it!"

"Yeah, well, he's in Beijing too, but he's under house arrest." After scanning a few more lines of the story the photographer added, "Here it is, Coach Bai left China after being charged with murder!"

"No way! I don't believe *any* of this!" Lilli threw the paper down on the table and bolted for the door. "I need to take five!"

...

Blu arrived in Kunming by plane and was escorted back to the drab training center. After lunch and a hot shower, Blu slipped on his swim trunks. After just three days away it felt like his training had been derailed, physically and mentally. Even in the pool he struggled to keep his thoughts from Li Daiya's offer concerning Jack's freedom.

After a couple of laps, Blu became aware that he was no longer alone. He looked around to see Jack, arms folded, standing at the other end of the blue water. Blu pulled up onto the pool's edge. Neither spoke. As Jack approached him, Blu searched the man's face. He thought Jack's eye looked bruised. Once Jack stood beside him, Blu saw further evidence that his coach had been mistreated in Beijing: a bandage at his jawline; clothing that hung loose on his once robust frame.

In spite of himself, Blu broke down. His head dropped into his hands, and the tears came, tears of relief and of helplessness. It would be impossible, from that moment on, to ignore the reality that adults didn't hurt one other on purpose, for unjust reasons. Tiananmen.

"Breathe," Jack spoke softly. "I am fine. You are not to worry."

"Why did they do this?"

"I was made an example when I left China and, now again, as I return."

"What happened before?" Blu hadn't meant to ask.

"I lost a boy I trained, Qin Ji."

"He looked like the boy on the plane."

"Yes. Exactly like him."

"How did it happen?"

"There was no explanation. A weakness of the heart, it seems. But I was blamed because I voiced my opposition to the rigorous training demands on our athletes. I also complained of corruption in the Communist Party that tainted the Games. At that time, there were no bloggers to tell the truth, just the official news service controlled by the government. And they told the world I was a negligent coach and a traitor."

"What happened—when they took you in Beijing?"

Jack was moved that Blu had been so affected by his detainment. This was the boy whose world had been so very small—before. "I was put under 'house arrest' where I was confined to part of a heavily guarded building. They beat me for a confession of wrongdoing, so they could remove me as your trainer."

"What wrongdoing?"

"Murder and other crimes against the Chinese government, including the kidnapping of Li Daiya's son."

Blu looked up. "But they know you didn't do it!"

"So you know."

"Yes. At least I know what I was told."

"How did you find out?"

"They told me I could get you back if I would meet with her," Blu's words tumbled out. "She said the Professor is my father, and he took me—us."

"I knew she would find a way to see you."

"She told me you were happy here—before the accident."

Jack responded, "It was a long time ago."

"You loved someone. Someone who looked like the woman beside you on the plane that freaked you out."

"It was like a moment out of my past," Jack said slowly, remembering. "I knew then they were coming for me."

"Li Daiya says you could live here again, free, if—"

"What did she ask of you?"

"She said you could have your life back, if I compete for China." Jack shook his head, incensed.

Blu argued, "But you loved someone. You were—famous. It could be that way again."

"How can a man relive his youth?" Jack responded without hesitation. "The pain heals and you train again, smarter." He touched the wound on his jaw.

"I want to undo what was done," Blu confessed, looking away.

"And so you will," Jack responded. "Are you able to swim?"

Blu pulled on the goggles that hung around his neck. "I'm a little rusty."

"Rusty is temporary, but what is dead is dead." Jack gestured for Blu to resume his swim under the eye of his rightful coach.

# 56

Delivering a message to the Cohen girl had not been on Gao Cheng's itinerary for that morning. But there he was, approaching the studio where she and her dance partner were having their final shoot of the tour. Gao had put off his doctor's appointment to do Li Daiya's bidding, and a stab of pain in his lower abdomen accompanied every step. He hoped to complete his assignment quickly and return home to rest.

Steps away from the sleek studio reserved for the country's biggest celebrity shoots, Gao could hear angry voices—some American, some Chinese. He winced and held his hand to his side.

Inside the room, Gao called a greeting in Mandarin. The woman in charge fell silent just long enough to approach Gao and pick up her complaint: Lilli was holding up the shoot over some nonsense in the newspaper.

Even as the woman continued her rant, Gao held up his hand, as if to say, "I've got this." A few strides later, he stood beside the beautiful Asian dancer who had taken China by storm.

Lilli composed herself. "Do I know you?"

"You do now." He extended his hand. "I am Gao Cheng,

a consultant with Zulegen. We set up this tour, which you made amazing, by the way." He nodded at Ben who had taken a seat against the wall with a tabloid, his comb, and hair gel by his side. Turning his disarming smile on Lilli, Gao asked, "Is there a problem?"

"It's nothing to do with the tour," she answered, blushing.

"I'm glad to hear that," he grinned. "But you do seem concerned. Perhaps I can help."

Lilli picked up the newspaper and pointed to the picture. "Do you know these people?"

"Blu—yes—and Li Daiya."

"Is it true that this woman is his birth mother? I thought it was—someone else."

"Candace Latham was your friend's *surrogate*. She carried him, but yes, Li Daiya is his actual birth mother."

"Then she was the one who had Jewell Chan on the lookout for him—an Asian boy with blue eyes?"

"As I understand it, the project in California turned up the boy quite by surprise." Gao filed away the name Jewell Chan, certain he had heard the name before. But when?

"Now his 'mother' wants him to compete for China?"

"Very much so."

"Would he stay here then?"

"It is possible. Does that bother you?"

Lilli was desperate for answers. Even from a stranger. "He is my best friend. I haven't been able to talk to him since we arrived in China," she confided. "I don't like not knowing what's happening."

Such strong feelings, Gao observed. Young love, perhaps. And yet this was only the beginning of all that Li Daiya envisioned. The dance tour had only been a means of making Blu and his parents more receptive to training in China. Lilli was no longer useful to her.

"Perhaps I have news that will brighten your day," Gao hurried on to accomplish his ugly task.

"You've spoken to Cal—Blu?"

"Actually I have not, but I have spoken to his mother who is, by the way, a huge fan of yours." His delivery was smooth, his smile winsome. "Blu mentioned to her that you wish to locate your own birth mother."

Lilli stopped breathing. In that instant, the frustrations and questions that plagued her seemed of little consequence. Was such a thing possible? She hung on Gao's words. "I would like that very much."

"Li Daiya is a powerful woman with many resources." Gao paused for effect. "She sent me to tell you that she believes she has found your mother. A meeting has been arranged."

Lilli's heart began to pound. "For real?"

Gao nodded. "For real. She is able to meet you on Christmas Eve."

Lilli's face fell slightly. She had hoped to see Blu on that night.

She was, however, quickly consoled. This was Blu's gift to her, she concluded. After all, he was the only one who understood her search for something of her past.

"Yes, of course, I'll meet her. Please, could you let Blu know that I will not see him that night? We had plans, kind of."

"Absolutely. And I'll make all the necessary arrangements." Gao held her hands in his. "Best wishes, Lilli. I must go but will be in touch very soon."

Mission accomplished, Gao Cheng tucked away his disgust for himself and for Li Daiya, who had successfully used him to keep the friends apart. Her hope: to sever one more tie to the U.S. and her son's life there. Now she had only to convince him to compete—and stay—in China. Gao wondered if the corruptive nature of his work hastened the corruption of his body.

Lilli was jolted back to the present when the director threw up her hands screaming something in Chinese, and the crew began clearing out. Apparently, the woman had called it a day. In the quiet of the room, Ben stepped up behind Lilli and spoke softly.

"I couldn't help but hear," Ben confessed. "This is

something you really wanted, isn't it? I'm really glad for you." Touched by his sentiment, Lilli turned to meet Ben's eyes, to thank him, and there was an unexpected flash of a camera.

"Best shot of the day!" said the photographer who had been following the emotional exchanges. Like a pro, he had rightly anticipated Lilli's moment of vulnerability. The fans would love it.

...

Near the end of a three-hour long session in the pool, Blu looked up. Through his goggles he made out the outline of the man standing with Jack, the man Li Daiya said was, in fact, his father—the Professor.

"Enough for today!" Coach Jack announced.

Blu reached for his towel. He watched as the men spoke quietly. At last, they bowed to each other, and Jack left the pool area, a slight limp in his gate. Blu felt rage for the man who remained. Why hadn't the all-powerful Professor intervened when Jack was arrested and beaten? At a deeper level still, he wondered why the man had disappeared from his life at birth.

There was only the sound of flip-flops on tile as Blu made his way toward the man who stood waiting for him.

"Professor," Blu offered his unenthusiastic greeting. The boy self-consciously arranged the towel around his neck.

"We should talk," the Professor suggested.

"Pretty bushed," came the boy's disinterested response.

"Perhaps after you've rested. Before you have your evening meal."

"We should have talked a long time ago, don't you think?" Blu glared.

"I'll be back."

Blu showered, slipped on dry clothes, and returned to his room. It was an hour until the evening meal. His intention was to escape into sleep. But when his head hit the pillow, tears started. He wept hard from a place he didn't recognize, about events and people and hurts he couldn't even name.

Later, in the washroom, he splashed his tearstained face then stepped into the hall. There the Professor stood waiting at his door. *That's my father.* The boy turned the strange phrase around in his head several times before speaking.

"Come in." Blu reached past the man to open the door.

The Professor carried a black coat that was draped over one arm. From under the coat he revealed a paper bag. McDonald's! In spite of himself, Blu smiled at his father's peace offering.

"If Jack finds out …" Blu started.

"He won't find out unless you tell him."

Blu took a seat on his bunk and unloaded a Big Mac, fries, and milkshake onto his side table, considering where to start his unexpected feast.

"Candace was here," Blu said as the Professor pulled over the heavy wooden chair from the corner and sat down.

"Yes, I know." The man didn't invite further discussion, content to watch his son indulge the forbidden fast food. "I hope your body does not reject foods not on Jack's dietary regimen."

"It'd still be worth it," Blu confessed, his mouth full of french fries. "Are you the one who got Jack back for me?"

"No, no, you did that."

"Yeah, well, you made it happen. That's what you do, isn't it? You arrange things so that they happen the way you want them to."

"I am no magician. I am just old and understand those of my country. When I can, I correct what is incorrect."

"Li Daiya thought she was correct to build a Frankenstein son," Blu stopped his chewing to gaze at the man. "Is that why you stole me from her? Because you thought she was incorrect? Doesn't that make *me* incorrect?"

"While stealing is incorrect," the Professor's voice rose in passion, "to see a child in a burning building and to turn away is unconscionable. You run to save a child. You run with everything you have."

"You're saying you *had* to save me?"

"I had to—it was correct. And, to be truthful, I wanted you for my own—correct or not."

"But you chose not to be a father to me."

"If I raised you in China, they would have found you." The Professor spoke haltingly, revealing uncharacteristic emotion. "Such a tragedy would have set back China's dream for decades."

"So it was correct that I would be crippled by what I never knew rather than to grow into a man to make my own decisions?"

"Surely you see that she would have made you one of *them*!"

"What? A person of influence who lives in safety with lots of money?"

"She would train you up to lead the next generation of communists. No! You must be *free* in order to make correct decisions for yourself."

"Why do you care?"

"How does anyone *not* care?" the man stood and paced. "Who dares make a law that tells families how many children they can raise? Who shames their own people by forcing them to produce inferior—even dangerous—products for little money until they die at their work or take their own lives? Who jails their own people for speaking out or for their faith or for exposing corruption? Who tells young people the reason they live is to do the bidding of their government? Who tells people that dreams are for the foolish?"

"You had a dream."

"I still do."

"Why did you bring me here?"

"You are here to remind the people of China that they can dream, and this time the dream will not be taken from them."

"The second Tiananmen?"

"It is called the wave."

"I have a dream too, to be an Olympian! But they will take Jack—and you—and me—if they find out whatever your 'public relations' people are up to."

"That is why they must not know until it is too late."

"What do we do until then?"

"As far as Li Daiya's offer, we play along. I will arrange for you to finish the school year here, as an exchange student, while you continue to train."

"Why would I do that?"

"Li Daiya will believe you are being swayed to be her princeling."

"Lilli won't understand—or my parents."

"I will see to it that they understand. Meanwhile, you will train; Jack will regain his freedom; and China will have her dream."

# 57

The next morning, Dwain caught up with Blu before he headed out for a run with Coach Jack. He tossed a manila envelope on his friend's bed.

"What's that?" Blu asked distractedly.

"It's from the Professor. I found it under my door this morning with a note," he answered, unnerved.

"What'd the note say?"

"It says, 'You'll know what to do.'"

"So?"

"So I *don't* know what to do."

Dwain emptied the contents of the envelope on Blu's bunk, so they could study them together. Inside was a flier for the final performance of Lilli's dance tour, scheduled for the next day—the same day Dwain would be traveling to the area for a chess match. Also inside was a paper with the image of the wave, like the one Blu had seen in the news clips, along with a letter-sized envelope stuffed with Chinese yuan—cash—to which was clipped a handwritten note in Mandarin.

"Cool!" Blu exclaimed.

"Not cool!" Dwain returned. "This is my first assignment

from the Professor. I don't know what to do, and I don't want to screw it up!"

"Assignment?"

"You got an assignment with Li Daiya, right? We all have assignments."

"I wonder what the note says," Blu said.

Dwain looked at him questioningly. "It says, 'Request for entrance and escort to Lilli Cohen following the performance.'"

"You know Mandarin?" Blu stared, amazed.

"What, you *don't*?" Dwain responded, equally amazed.

"I think I get it," Blu said. "He told me he would help Lilli and my family understand why I have to stay."

"So this is for you."

"I guess."

"Should I be offended that he doesn't think I look the part of a spy guy?" Dwain wondered out loud.

"Oh!" Blu went to his side table and pulled open the drawer. "Take this too," he handed Dwain the Glo-Me bracelet. "It's a belated Christmas present for Lilli."

...

The next day, Dwain took down his chess opponent easily, in spite of his apprehensions about getting into a sold-out event to meet up with Lilli. His heart raced as he stepped up to the ticket counter in the packed lobby of the auditorium, where an agitated little man shouted in Mandarin: "No tickets! Sold out!"

First, Dwain slipped the man the note. When he nodded, Dwain showed a corner of the envelope stuffed with cash that he'd tucked up into his shirtsleeve. The man opened his register and pounded on the counter. As if by magic, an Asian escort, twice Dwain's size, appeared. Once the money had passed hands, the powerful body of Dwain's assigned companion plowed through the crowd in the lobby to the seating area inside. There he unfolded two seats in the nosebleed section and sat down with Dwain for the duration of the performance.

Afterwards, the man took Dwain's arm and moved toward the stage that fans had showered with brightly colored flowers. The people milling about there pleaded with guards to meet the dancers. Only Dwain, it seemed, had been given a backstage pass.

At a dressing room door, the man gave a hard knock.

"Who is it?" Lilli sounded surprised, or suspicious.

"Jun," he answered.

The door opened, and Dwain was face to face with Lilli, still in her dancewear and make-up. Her face fell in disappointment. It was not Blu.

"Who are you?" she asked not entirely politely.

"My name is Dwain. I am a messenger," the chess player stammered.

"Thanks, Jun," Lilli waved away the guard and let the delivery boy into the small space that was just barely big enough to accommodate the tiny vanity, the rolling hanger rod, and Lilli.

When the door was closed, she looked into the face of the geeky, unmistakably non-threatening Asian boy.

"Is Jun friend or foe?" Dwain tried to break the awkward moment between strangers.

"Jun goes everywhere with me. So did Blu send you?"

Dwain nodded. "We both train in Kunming."

"You don't look like an athlete."

"I play chess," he laughed nervously, finding the dancer to be far more beautiful in person than on TV.

Lilli relaxed. "Seriously?"

"It's a sport. What can I say?"

Lilli laughed. The easy-going delivery boy reminded Lilli of Levi.

Dwain reached into his coat jacket. "He asked me to give you something." When his hand opened, it held the Glo-Me bracelet. "It's a gift—from Blu."

A gasp followed, and Lilli lifted the bracelet carefully. "From Blu, really?"

"Yeah," Dwain answered, "it's a late Christmas gift." When she didn't immediately inspect the bracelet, Dwain grew impatient. But once she recovered from the surprise, she tried lighting each tile until she found the one with a corner popped out of place. She looked at Dwain, who nodded yes to her unspoken question. Finding the scrolled paper tucked underneath, she opened it gently. It read:

> Are we on for Christmas Eve? I will find a way. No Internet here. Meet Dwain from Indiana. Miss you.
> Blu

Lilli looked up and smiled. "Thank you, Dwain."

"You're welcome." The black eye makeup Lilli wore pooled at the corner of her eyes and released down her cheeks before she could catch them. "A bit more news," Dwain continued.

"What is it?"

"Blu met his real birth mother—and father."

"I know about Li Daiya. Their picture was in the paper. But his birth father too?"

"It is the Professor."

"What?" Like Blu, Lilli was incensed that this had been kept secret while the man played the role of talent developer—investor—whatever.

Dwain continued with the most unpleasant part of his task. "I also have to tell you that Blu will be staying in China with the Professor to train through the start of the Games. He'll finish the school year here as an exchange student."

Immediately her hands were at her hips. "He's not coming home? Does he have a new trainer here?"

"Jack is free," Dwain stated, hesitating before he continued. "But—there had to be some compromises."

"Don't tell me Blu is competing for China!"

Dwain reached into the pocket of his pants and pulled out the last page the Professor had included in his spy packet. He unfolded it to reveal the image she had noticed at each of her venues: the wave. Across the top of the page was written:

> Don't speak of this. The wave is coming, and there is work to be done.

Lilli reached for the flier, but Dwain shook his head and returned it to his pocket. Now she knew. The wave had something to do with the dream team, Blu and, most certainly, the Professor. Lilli looked up at Dwain and bit at her lip. It was her turn to share some difficult news.

"I'm so sorry to have to say this, especially since Blu won't be coming home anytime soon, but I can't make it on Christmas Eve. Li Daiya arranged for me to meet my own birth mother on that day. He'll understand what that means to me."

Dwain nodded and turned to go when he remembered the last thing he was asked to relay. "Oh, and Blu asked that you don't put up the dance video."

Lilli smiled, thinking of the joke they shared. "Tell him not to worry. I have my own reputation to protect."

...

After Dwain left, Lilli pulled on jeans and a hoodie. Typically she hurried to a waiting SUV with tinted windows. Ben did not travel with her, preferring a loud and low sports car to shuttle him to and from performances. Lilli stuck her covered head out of the door and called to Jun who stood watch just down the hallway. "I'm ready."

Lilli pulled her packed duffle onto her shoulder and followed Jun to the lobby. There she hesitated. "Give me a minute, okay?" Lilli asked Jun. She wanted to see for herself who—if anyone—lingered at the venue. From a bench in the lobby, Lilli observed some teenaged girls admiring each other's newly purchased tee-shirts featuring Ben. There were also some older men near a bulletin board used to announce upcoming events. There she saw it: the wave.

  Her face hidden by her hoodie, Lilli watched the men who stood in groups of two or three. They spoke in low voices and, every few minutes, rotated from one group to the next. Occasionally one would scan the area for—someone. The police? After a few minutes, Jun took her arm protectively and walked her to her ride.

  Before she had even stepped up into the vehicle, Lilli heard a familiar voice say "Congratulations, Lilli!" When her eyes adjusted, Lilli saw her recent acquaintance Gao Cheng, who she learned had arranged her tour. In his arms he held a dozen red roses. "The tour has been an outstanding success!" With this, Gao transferred the explosion of red into her arms. As beautiful as they were, for Lilli, they didn't compare with the Glo-Me she wore, a gift from Blu. Gao continued to gush enthusiasm: "Maybe we need to take all this love back to America!"

# 58

Li Daiya was furious, as Gao Cheng knew she would be. Though not telling her wasn't an option. Lilli's business was usually very much of interest to Director Li.

"Zulegen got nervous when they heard Blu was invited to compete for China at the Games," Gao explained. "So, understandably, they decided to take some precautions."

"And a U.S. dance tour for Lilli Cohen is a 'precaution' for what exactly?"

"America is Zulegen's biggest market. If Blu agrees to compete for China, Zulegen would be forced to pull his sponsorship. Zulegen could recoup its losses by piggybacking on the Cohen girl's recent success."

Li Daiya was visibly irritated. "My son has not yet accepted my offer."

"He will," Gao said with confidence. The woman who had made his life hell for years always got what she wanted. "Meanwhile, the Americans will follow Lilli on Twitter and travel in buses to see her on tour at the largest Chinatowns in the U.S."

"The plan is flawed, to say the least."

"In what way?"

"If Blu decides to take a spot on the U.S. Team, what happens?"

When Gao hesitated, Li Daiya began her lecture in marketing. "Come now, Geo, you are a businessman," she scolded. "If that happens, I will see to it that his coach is detained *indefinitely*. Without Jack, Blu will return to California in obscurity. In turn, Zulegen loses its poster boy and all that it has invested in him. No dance tour in the world could make up for that kind of a hit."

"That is a possibility."

"Let's consider the other possibility then," Director Li continued. "Blu decides to compete for China. As a result, my son, along with Zulegen, is propelled into the international spotlight. Who wouldn't respect a company for standing by its athlete rather than taking sides between superpowers?"

"It would require a tremendous amount of money to pull off such a marketing feat."

"I could see to that, couldn't I?"

"No doubt you could. But why?"

"It is in the best interest of China that my son continues to train with Coach Bai, to whom he is so very devoted, and to bring home gold. Then he will never leave China again."

"I see your point."

"I knew you would."

"The dance tour is in the works, however, and I have to catch a flight out to see to the details," Gao informed her.

"Go then," she said with a condescending wave of the hand. "By all means, see about the girl. I have important work to do."

Gao was only too happy to leave Li Daiya to her scheming. Gao had his hands full and his good days were fewer and fewer. But his short visit with China's director of propaganda had boosted his mood, quite by surprise. With Li Daiya's promise to fund Zulegen in a global marketing campaign around her son, Gao knew the company—and investors such as himself—stood to make a bundle. The timing was perfect. He would need some capital for the venture he hoped to pursue with Jewell Chan, whom he had recently rediscovered. His trip to the States, he hoped, would advance a number of pursuits.

...

On the morning of Christmas Eve Day, as Gao Cheng boarded his flight to California, his mood turned dark. A text from his office assistant reminded him of his part in accomplishing the latest dirty work of Li Daiya: the deception that began with his lie to Lilli days before at the photo shoot.

As the text confirmed, the letter Gao drafted the night before, per Li Daiya's instructions, had been delivered to the hotel where Lilli stayed. The letter, as Gao knew all too well, contained still a second, crushing lie. It was an especially low blow for Director Li who had long pushed for policies that protected her country's children. In this case, it seemed the woman felt justified in bruising a daughter of China in an effort to strengthen ties with a son.

Lilli read the letter three times and sobbed as if she lost someone she had known. She had not known her mother. Nor would she. There had been a "mistake," as the letter explained it, and there would be no meeting. She was going home having never met her mother. And she had been robbed of her one opportunity to be with Blu. For the remainder of the day, Lilli refused to speak, and she lit no tiles on her Glo-Me bracelet. None were black.

...

Christmas Day dawned. There were no Christmas trees inside or outside the training center. No comfort foods. No family. Still, Blu was thankful for the company of the reporter, James Wo, in from San Francisco, who sat poolside while he swam laps. Wo's company reminded him of home—the Y more specifically—and helped ease the sting of missing his much-anticipated meet up with Lilli the day before.

Instead, Lilli was to meet her birth mother, as Dwain reported back from his backstage visit. It followed, Blu reasoned, that they would also be together for the holiday. Blu was glad Lilli would have an epic Christmas. It didn't even bother Blu that Dwain was clearly crushing on her. Duh. She was awesome.

When he stopped to rest, Blu picked up his conversation with Wo. "So you sent out the photos of me in training here?"

"Yep. They went to my blogger friends and to the government news services," explained Wo.

"You told them I was passing up a spot on the U.S. team?"

"I only hinted at the possibility. The bloggers will understand that you are being *persuaded* to compete for China. The news services will simply report the happy news that you are loving China and open to the job of princeling."

"So what's in it for you?"

"Are you kidding? My flight here was paid for, thanks to the Professor, the paper is paying me for my stories, and I get an exclusive interview with you on New Year's. My resume is going to rock."

At the sound of shoes on the tile, the two turned their heads. "The bloggers are buzzing," announced the Professor, dressed in suit and tie. "You're earning your keep, Wo."

"If only I could cover the dance tour at home too," Wo mused. "Can't be two places at once."

"What dance tour—Lilli's doing a tour in the U.S.?"

"Zulegen's idea," the Professor answered. "We'll see."

The Professor had not intended for that information to be shared with Blu just yet. He made a mental note to remind Wo of the risk of distracting Blu with news of Lilli. In particular, he needed to protect Blu from learning of Li

Daiya's ruse to keep Lilli from seeing him. The Professor had done his own research of Lilli's parentage and turned up nothing.

"She's excited though?" Blu asked.

"I'm sure she's just excited to be on her way home tomorrow," the Professor assured him.

"Where's Jack?" Blu asked, satisfied that all was well with Lilli. "Surely he's not giving me Christmas Day off."

"Actually, he is taking some time to reconnect with an old friend today. He sent word that you are on your own."

"For real?"

The Professor nodded. "Apparently, Li Daiya has made it possible for Jack to move about with some freedom. You have given your coach quite a Christmas gift."

"Sounds more like a present for Blu," Wo laughed. "Hey, dude, I think the McDonald's is open on Christmas."

"Ho ho ho!" Blu pulled himself from the pool. "Will you take us, Professor? It's the holiday thing to do."

"You are determined to get me on Jack's bad side." The Professor smiled at his son. "Get into some dry clothes, and we'll pull together a feast of burgers and shakes. No camera, Wo."

"It's our secret!" Wo threw Blu his Zulegen towel.

# 59

On the afternoon of December 26, Jewell Chan sat on a bench by a fountain in the mall next to her coworker Derek Price. The scene overwhelmed her, having never experienced the shopping mayhem that followed the American Christmas. While the holiday was acknowledged in Beijing, elaborate Christmas celebrations abounded in more westernized regions such as Hong Kong. In her childhood, Jewell had poured over newspaper photos of Christmas festivities she believed she'd never see. This year, she had at last experienced the Christmas of her dreams. The day after, she was content just to spend time people-watching with Derek.

Her cell sounded in the back pocket of her jeans.

Derek watched her pull out her phone. "Uh-oh," he remarked, only half-joking.

"Don't let it be Beijing," Jewell wished under her breath. She was not expecting to hear from anyone. Her personal contacts hadn't grown much beyond the circle of her coworkers and Derek's family, the Prices.

"It's a text from the university," she announced, surprised, "from the automated system. There was a phone call for me."

"Who calls the school the day after Christmas?" Derek pried.

"Gao Cheng." She repeated his name, searching but failing to pull up a face for the name. "I don't know this man, but I think I have heard of him. I will do a search on him later."

"That's it? Just a message that he called?"

"No," she answered, concerned. "He asked if he could meet me tomorrow, regarding an urgent matter."

"Seems kinda pushy."

"He's Chinese."

"Oh, yeah," Derek bumped her shoulder good-naturedly. The two friends had survived many a cultural clash over food, money, and, most often, time management. "Lost time is never found again," he repeated the proverb she'd often recited.

"I'll tell him to be at the Starbucks early—before work," she decided happily, "then I can be sure no time is lost."

Derek loved Jewell's emerging sense of humor. Few people made him smile. But she did. "It's the perfect cultural mash-up!" he laughed.

...

The next morning, Jewell stepped out of the busy Starbucks, leaving behind her new acquaintance who had flown halfway across the world to meet with her. She pushed her hands deep into the pockets of the thick knee-length sweater she'd received as a Christmas gift from Derek's mother and turned toward campus. Her heart pounded, and her thoughts raced.

Since her arrival in the U.S., the Starbucks had been her boot camp for life in America. Hours had been spent there, mostly with Derek, discussing the Data Collection Project as well as comparing viewpoints on everything—family, friendship, politics, and their respective futures. And now, with the smell of coffee on her clothes and tea on her breath, Jewell faced a crossroads of sorts. Before her was an opportunity to proceed into new territory with her broadened perspective of life. In her estimation, the time she'd spent with the impressive and prominent Chinese businessman had not been wasted.

On the familiar route back to the Department of Social Sciences building, Jewell replayed the conversation with Gao Cheng. The man spoke to her in fluent English and, quite unexpectedly, as an equal. He admitted that many firms he owned, in full or in part, had benefitted from her Glo-Me technology. Without bitterness Jewell explained how it was that her invention had not secured her future. With knowing eyes, Gao expressed his apologies for the loss of what she rightly deserved. Then he had enlisted her help.

Both projects Gao Cheng described appealed to Jewell. The first project she would work alone. Gao was prepared to fund an effort to adapt her thermoelectric battery to treat the illness that threatened his life. The offer had awakened her love of invention. A second project, as Gao explained it, would put an end to the thievery she experienced with the Glo-Me, at the hand of her own government. Already, Jewell was ready to jump into this project, but she would need Derek's help to pull it off.

Jewell took the stairs to the third floor. It was still early, but the office door was already unlocked.

"Well?" Derek's impatient voice met her as she entered.

"You scared me!" Jewell scolded.

"Sorry. I'm the curious type." Derek braced for the worst. "So did he offer you a job?"

"No," Jewell took her time answering, enjoying Derek's concern that she might up and leave. "If you must know, he asked me to marry him, but I told him I am a high maintenance California girl now. So he passed."

"High maintenance, huh? A broke nerd like me won't have a chance."

"But you do have potential," she smiled.

"So, like, is everything okay?"

Jewell nodded thoughtfully. "Yeah, it's great." She seated

herself on top of the computer table they shared. Her face turned serious. "We do have an assignment though."

"We do?"

"That is, if you are up to some 'off the record' work."

"Sounds like the perfect way to kick off an interesting new year."

"For me too," Jewell sighed in resignation. "I love to work. Perhaps I am not high maintenance after all."

"Anything we need to discuss with Dr. Tan?" Derek was not interested in getting the boot for moonlighting while working the job that kept him in gas and coffee.

"Oh no," Jewell met Derek's eyes. "It's you and me and Gao." Jewell dropped to her chair and logged on to her computer. Derek rolled his chair next to hers.

"So what's this all about?"

"You remember the secondary search function my boss Wong Bao had me build into the Data Collection Project?"

"The one that found Blu?"

"Yes, but the list also included the names of fugitives or suspected enemies of the Chinese government. Remember?"

"Oh yeah."

"So we're going to do a little sub search through those names to see which of them might also have connections to Chinatowns in the U.S."

"And Gao Cheng wants this list, why?"

"He believes he'll find sympathizers for his cause."

"Which is—"

"Pressuring Beijing for economic change." Jewell worked quickly at the keyboard.

"Changing the rules of how people do business in a communist country sounds a lot like—"

"Yeah. I think you have the idea." Jewell's stomach flip-flopped. She wondered if she might be crossing some kind of line, one that would distance her from her life in China. Further, she wondered why she didn't care more.

"We need to add 'Chinatown' as a keyword in the

sub-search," she explained. "After we run a search, we'll have a list of those considered 'dangerous' to the Chinese government and having some association with Chinatown locations. When the search is done I'll download them to a flash drive, remove the keyword, and resume the search. Beijing won't even notice the brief interruption."

"Here we go," she said, hesitating momentarily. The coworkers exchanged a glance and Jewell hit the key that began the search. In silence, both turned their attention to their duties of the day. A short time later, the other members of the DCP team arrived. Stephen brought doughnuts.

While the day progressed like any other, the sound of the computers working reminded Jewell and Derek of what was happening in the next room. Like any other day, the program worked to collect and compile data on Asians in America. On this day, however, they also searched for soldiers.

# 60

Inside the Chinese Cultural Center, Lilli relaxed. In many ways the place she had frequented for years as a child felt like home. Bits of silver garland and wrapping paper littered the floor, and Lilli imagined the wonder and warmth of the holiday events that happened in her absence: Christmas lights glowing together with traditional Chinese paper lanterns, Santa surrounded by tiny carolers singing in Mandarin.

"Lilli! When did you get in?" Sarah Lu stepped into the lobby to meet the dancer. Sarah was dressed for cleaning rather than teaching, and they hugged like old friends.

"I came home yesterday," Lilli answered. "It feels like I was gone forever. I'm so excited to see you here."

"I'm pretty much a fixture," Sarah smiled. "It was a busy season."

"I remember Christmases here. You made them so special." Lilli's eyes filled, and she looked away.

"You're missing him."

Lilli wiped her eyes. "Yeah," she admitted, "my tour and his training, you know, it feels like everything's changed."

"Even his name, right? Blu?"

Lilli nodded, and Sarah continued: "It has changed but not so much because you both went away. It's just about growing up and how friendship evolves over time."

"What if Blu decides to compete for China, or that he wants to live there?" Lilli hadn't spoken her fears to anyone. "He has his birth mother now. It's possible. I mean, if I'd met my birth mother—who knows?"

"It's true. So many Chinese adoptees are connecting with their birth parents. It's on the news almost as much as the two of you."

Lilli leaned in to give Sarah a hug. "I was told I'd meet my birth mother," Lilli confided. "But something happened. There was a mistake, or maybe it wasn't even true. I don't know for sure."

Sarah stepped back, staring. "How'd that make you feel?"

Lilli tried to swallow the lump in her throat. "It felt like being left all alone—again."

Sarah had lived this moment with many teenage adoptees over the years. She took both of Lilli's hands. "You have so much to look forward to."

The teen cracked a smile. "You're right. Canyon is coming in April! Have you even seen my mom? She's huge!"

Sarah laughed.

"And I'll be touring again soon—here in the U.S!"

"Oh, I haven't heard a thing about that! Is it 'under wraps,' as they say?"

"For just a bit longer," Lilli shared. "I know for sure that Zulegen—the tour sponsor—was in touch with my mom the other day. She told me they were almost ready to release the tour dates and locations for the website."

"So exciting!"

"The guy working on the tour just handed off a huge list of new names for the fan database. Once those names are added we'll be ready to send the news out to the world!"

Sarah clapped in excitement. "Can't wait! Did you tell Blu?"

"I haven't even been able to talk to him, but I sent him an email through a mutual friend. I hope he gets it soon."

"Well, you'll see each other eventually," Sarah consoled Lilli. "I know you're going to have a happy New Year!"

# 61

It was early, and Blu longed to feel his body stretch while he did laps across the pool. Not this morning. It was New Year's Day, and he sat in one of two metal chairs set up under hot camera lights, waiting for his interviewer. A young attractive Asian woman stepped into the flood of lights and dabbed powder on his face with a small sponge. "Not pretty enough, huh?" Blu joked. The woman made him think of Lilli.

"Make face not—" the woman used her hands to demonstrate how Blu's face might explode on camera without her intervention.

Blu almost didn't recognize the young man in a suit who took the seat beside him. "I might need a little of that too," a spiffy version of James Wo suggested to the makeup artist. "After all, this interview is going to make me as famous as this guy." Wo straightened his tie. The woman smiled without comprehension, then reached over and applied some powder to the end of the reporter's nose.

"So this is the 'exclusive' the Professor promised you if you waited to tell the world I was coming to China to train." Blu felt underdressed in his khakis and navy blue pullover sweater. "Not only did the world find out anyway, but you ended up in China too."

"Apparently your mother-dearest had plenty of eyes on you and Jack," Wo responded, feeling a stab of guilt for his unconfessed leak.

"Hey, who's gonna see this interview anyway?"

"If we're lucky—everyone. The Professor is handling this one. Who knows where it'll make news? The more the merrier."

"So maybe it'll get back home to California."

"Oh!" Wo pulled a folded piece of paper from his suit jacket. "Speaking of home, I heard from your girlfriend."

"What?"

"Yeah, she used my work email."

"That's cool! What'd she say?"

Wo handed him the paper. "Here, I printed it out for you."

"Can you give me a minute?"

"Sure thing. Just don't take too long, dude. I'm ready for my fifteen minutes of fame."

Wo watched nervously as Blu stepped into the hallway. He knew he had taken a risk in passing along communication from Lilli to Blu against the Professor's wishes, especially in the moments before the cameras went live. But as a reporter, Wo also knew that an emotional or—better yet—controversial interview could make his big interview even bigger.

Once he was in private, Blu opened the letter.

> Thank you for the gift. It's perfect. Didn't meet my birth mother. There was a mix-up. Sure messed up our meeting, huh? So you'll be staying in China with your mother? Tell Jack hello for me. Canyon comes in April! Levi and Derek say hi! Your parents send love and a WAVE. My U.S. dance tour starts this week. Wish me luck. Write if you can. :)
> Lilli

Blu was crushed to learn that Lilli had not met her birth mother after all. Worse still, he suspected Li Daiya was to blame. It was then that it crossed Blu's mind to use the interview with Wo to expose his mother and to refuse her offer. Revenge would be sweet. Then he read the note again. WAVE. The word reminded him that a larger game—one he didn't fully understand—was being played out. There was too much at stake: he needed to protect Lilli, keep Jack, and take gold at the Games. With the note tucked into his pocket, Blu took a deep breath and determined to give Wo—and everyone else—something to talk about.

Back under the lights, Wo studied Blu. "You good?"

"Good to go," Blu responded.

"Alright then. Let's do this thing."

...

The Professor was sipping his morning coffee and watching students from his office window when the knock came. "It has arrived via courier," came the excited voice of his assistant, Waiyin.

"Come in, of course," replied the Professor. "Let's watch it together."

The woman handed her boss a flash drive, which the Professor plugged into his computer. "We'll see what kind of on-camera reporter Wo is," the man folded his hands and sat back, nervous, hopeful, aware that he could still stop the interview's release—if necessary.

"He's very handsome!" Waiyin remarked. Though she'd known of the Professor's son for years, she'd never seen him.

Together they watched the unedited recording. As cameras were adjusted, off-camera hands clipped lavaliere microphones to the collars of Wo and Blu, and the sound was checked multiple times.

"You gave him the words to say?" Waiyin asked, concerned.

"I did not," he responded. "I wanted it to be completely

natural. People respond to that." The Professor thought his son looked surprisingly relaxed.

The interview began with Wo introducing himself and his guest. Blu laughed when Wo asked the cameraman to pull in for a "close up" of the Olympic hopeful's signature blue eyes. As the interview proceeded, Blu talked passionately about his love for swimming and running and his struggle to overcome fear while cycling. He also expressed his great respect for Coach Bai Zhao Man.

"Some have called Coach Bai a dangerous man," Wo stated.

"He can be a bit pushy," Blu broke into a smile, "but he is not dangerous. Jack—I call him Jack—deserved empathy rather than prison for all that he has gone through."

"And what about the dancer Lilli Cohen? Is she your girlfriend, as it has been rumored?"

"Also not true." Blu winked at the camera. "I'm not anyone's boyfriend right now, but I'm pretty sure I am Lilli's biggest fan."

Waiyin laughed at this, saying, "Everyone will wish this boy good luck at the Games!"

After a few minutes of casual questioning, Wo straightened in his seat, a signal that he was transitioning to more serious subjects. "So this is your first trip back to the place you were born." Blu nodded and Wo continued. "What is your opinion of China? Is there any sense that you've come *home*?"

It was Blu's turn to shift in his seat. He leaned forward, resting his elbows on his knees. "I have been surprised by a kind of connection I feel here, a familiarity." He continued, "When I think of home though, I think of a feeling of being completely safe and completely myself. I have to be honest: I don't really feel that level of safety and acceptance. And I don't think I'm alone in that."

"That's an interesting perspective," Wo responded.

"And as far as being myself, I'm not sure I'm up to what's expected of me here. I'm just me—a jock with a not-so-impressive report card." Here Blu shared a chuckle with Wo before completing his thought. "Maybe it's just a matter of time before I relax into who I am here, but for now, I guess, the pool is still my home."

"You suggest others—like yourself—may not feel 'safe' in China. I'm wondering what observations you've made that lead you to that conclusion."

"I'm speaking as a newcomer, for sure. But in my time here, it has been my observation that there is a gap—like a rift—between the people and the government."

You don't think the Chinese government cares about the people?" Wo sounded more excited than incensed. His dreams were coming true.

"That's not it. It's more like, maybe, the passion of leadership is more about *how* to govern the people and less about the people themselves."

"And what do you think the people of China want?"

"Seems like they've made it clear what they want."

"Just in case the government isn't getting the message, what do you think the people are saying?"

"In my humble opinion, it seems like preserving Chinese culture is more important than the well-being of Chinese citizens. Why is that? I mean, I get how this is an amazing place, and every day I'm blown away by the history and the customs. But from where I sit, it seems like the people are saying they want to be heard, they want to make their own decisions about their families, their lives, and their work, and they want a sense of trust with China's leadership."

"You don't believe that the Chinese people are truly happy?"

"How could I say that?" Blu shrugged. "I'm just saying that it feels like there's an 'us against them' thing going on. I can't believe that it has to be that way. Maybe it's time to change things up, so people can find happiness without fear."

"So you're suggesting maybe there needs to be a change in focus?"

"Yeah, I guess that's it." Blu covered his head with his hands and spoke into the camera, "Don't hate me! I'm growing to love it here, really!"

Wo was quick to follow up. "When you say, 'I'm growing to love it here,' what does that mean for you going forward?"

"Would it surprise you if I said it meant Coach Bai and I will be going to the Games in July to compete—for China?"

Wo looked directly into the camera then back at Blu. "Yeah, in fact, I think that'll surprise more than a few people."

The interview ended and the Professor turned to a wide-eyed Waiyin.

"You did not tell him what to say?" she asked again.

"Every word he said came from inside him," responded the Professor, as if bragging on a star student. "What he has yet to learn is that honesty has a price."

# 62

Gao Cheng sat in his chair by the window of his hotel room when the interview landed on his personal laptop with a ding. He watched it through, twice. For him, the truth so plainly stated by Blu was cathartic, like an unburdening of the unspoken he had carried his entire existence. A text from the Professor followed. It read, "A reed before the wind lives on, while mighty oaks do fall." Gao smiled. It was good that he'd taken the morning to rest. The message was a green light to make their next move, and he worked more slowly than he once did.

His first phone call was to Zulegen executives. After his previous exchange with Li Daiya, Gao Cheng was able to convince them it was in the company's best interest to continue to sponsor Blu. Zulegen's marketing staff would be tasked with creating a campaign touting their Olympian, who was bringing countries on two sides of the globe closer together.

His second call would be to the Asian reporter from California. It was time to apprise the people of China and the world of all that had been taken from the esteemed Jewell

Chan. The news would also be released to a select group of Linda Cohen's "super fans," key persons in American Chinatowns identified by Chan's DCP. It was at these locations that the wave was expected to build to its greatest heights yet.

...

By the time Blu returned to his room after the interview, all he wanted to do was lie down and close his eyes. Tight. Judging by Wo's reaction to Blu's unexpected announcement, his world was about to get very—noisy. There would likely be a barrage of questions, commentary, and requests for additional interviews. That part of his surprise decision he had not considered. No sooner than Blu sat down on his bed, Feng was at the door. He held a phone out to him.

"Who is it?" Blu asked.

"Director Li Daiya."

Not yet. Please. More than anything Blu knew he needed to talk to Jack. Reluctantly, he took the phone. He waited until Feng was gone before answering.

"This is Blu."

"Son, I've just seen your interview with that American reporter."

"James Wo."

"You've made a very wise decision for yourself. Already I'm making preparations to get you the best possible training going forward."

Blu's heart skipped a beat. "You understand that Jack remains my coach."

There was a pause on the other end of the line. "If that's your decision. But I want you to know that I am giving you the Water Cube in Beijing as your training base. What do you think of that?"

The boy sat back down, his heart racing.

"Did you hear me?" Li Daiya persisted.

"I don't know what you mean. Why am I moving?"

"The Water Cube—built for the Beijing Olympics in 2008—houses the competition pool. It will be yours exclusively. You'll be the envy of every swimmer in the world." Li Daiya insisted. "Just ask Coach Bai."

"Jack can't be in the city! He's already been arrested. It may not be safe."

"That's in the past. Coach Bai has been free to go as he pleases. You know that. This isn't about him; it's about you!"

"No, it's not!" Blu was incensed. "We are a team. If you want us to train in Beijing, you're going to have to make good on your promise."

"What promise is that?"

"The Politburo needs to declare Jack to be free of all charges and suspicion in the death of Qin Ji. He must be at liberty to live and work in China—always."

There was another pause. "Bai's association with a known subversive—Professor Si—makes that difficult."

"Same for me! I have an association with Professor Si! He arranged for Jack and me to be here! He is my father!"

"I will do what I can."

"And I'll be right here until I know Jack is safe."

The mother of the princeling in training was not pleased. But she was impressed that the boy was gaining strength in the art of negotiation.

...

Li Daiya wasted no time in accomplishing her end of the bargain she'd made with her son. The next evening after dinner, Blu and Dwain sat on Blu's bunk and turned on the day's television recordings of note. Together they watched a broadcast aired on a government-controlled news station. In it, the reporter announced that Coach Bai Zhao Man had been cleared of any suspicion in the death of Olympic athlete Qin

Ji. Further, it was stated that the government had restored to Bai all the privileges of his citizenship, which had been under review. The story concluded with a teaser for the soon-to-be-aired interview with Bai's promising Olympian to be, the popular blue-eyed son of Li Daiya of the Politburo. It was also hinted that Blu would be training at the famed Water Cube in Beijing for the two months leading up to the Games.

"Who am I going to crush at chess when you leave?" Dwain asked at the end of the broadcast.

"Everyone," Blu smiled. "Hey, are the guys here going to be mad at me? I mean, is the dream team going to see me as a traitor for changing teams?"

"You don't get it yet, do you?" Dwain shook his head. "Everybody here, including you and me, are here to get the job done."

"And by 'get the job done' you aren't referring to taking gold at the Games."

"It's the bigger game, dude. Everybody here is pulling for you in the bigger game."

It was late when Blu finally turned in. The words of his buddy left him feeling pressure to accomplish something, but he didn't know exactly what. He reached for paper and pencil to jot off a note for Wo to email to Lilli. It was some comfort knowing, or at least believing, that Lilli was on the receiving end of his confused ramblings.

# 63

It was earlier than usual the next morning when Feng knocked then cracked open Blu's door. "They're coming to pack you up," he announced.

"What?" Blu sat up in his bed, his heart suddenly pounding.

"This morning."

"Where am I going?"

"You're going to the Water Cube. Don't you watch the news?" Feng said sarcastically. "Your stuff goes to your new apartment in Olympic Village. You and your coach will live in units there."

Blu looked at the clock. It was an hour before the morning meal.

"They'll be here to pick you up after you've dressed and eaten."

"That's big of them."

"Don't forget to dress for the press."

"You kidding?"

"It's your debut at the Water Cube. Reporters will be there. Get on it." Feng closed the door again.

For five minutes, Blu couldn't move. He hated change. He

hated the press. And he hated Li Daiya for pushing him. But he was the one who had given over the reins to her. At last he was up.

With little time to prepare for the events of the day, Blu made it his first mission to stash items he didn't want found or moved by others. The note he'd written the night before to Lilli was tucked and buttoned into the back pocket of his only pair of dress pants, the ones he'd wear that day to meet the press. Other correspondence letters—one from Candace and another from Lilli—his cycling glasses from Jack, and his laptop with his downloaded book were stuffed into his pool bag along with his goggles and towel. It was unlikely his movers would snoop there as they gathered up what little remained of the American life Blu had carried with him to China.

...

Blu had only seen the National Aquatics Center, more commonly called the Water Cube, on TV during the 2008 Olympics in Beijing. The massive three-dimensional structure, designed to resemble water bubbles, nearly took his breath. Beyond the Cube was the famed and equally spectacular National Stadium, or Bird's Nest, also constructed for the Games.

Then there were the people. Faces stared at him from outside the locked limousine that carried the driver, Blu, and the silent bodyguard who took his place at the boy's side in Beijing the minute he stepped from the plane. Even so, Blu felt anything but safe.

"She's beautiful, isn't she?" the driver gestured toward the Water Cube.

Blu was speechless.

"Twenty-five world records in swimming were broken here during the Olympics. Some say it is the fastest Olympic pool in the world," he added.

"It's so—big."

"Nearly eight acres in land space. Goes up over 100 feet too."

News reporters armed with microphones and followed by videographers pushed their way through the crowd to reach the vehicle.

"Your friend there will come around to your door," the driver instructed Blu. "Always wait for him."

"What about the press?" Blu felt dizzy watching the movement around the limo.

"The only press you need to talk to have been handpicked and are waiting for you inside."

"Ready?" The driver nodded at the guard. "He's coming to get you. Stay close."

...

The crowds cheered as the guard parted the sea of people for Blu to make his way to the Water Cube. Once inside, Blu saw James Wo standing among the press, his camera hanging around his neck. He relaxed a bit.

It didn't take long for Blu to suspect that the questions posed by the Chinese press had been prepared beforehand by the head of the country's Department of Propaganda, Li Daiya herself. *What did he think of the Water Cube? Would he break world records there too? Did he believe it was his destiny to bring home gold to his homeland?* Only Wo, the sole American reporter present, posed the question the world was actually waiting to hear. Wo leaned in with his microphone and asked, "Was your decision to compete for China in the Olympics a reflection of a change in your allegiance to the United States of America?" At the mention of "allegiance," Blu imagined himself standing on the podium with his gold medal as the anthem of China played. He felt sick. Instead of answering, Blu waved at the onlookers outside, thanked the press, then motioned for Wo to walk with him as he was escorted to the lockers.

With the doors closed behind him and his bodyguard out of earshot, Blu sat down to think.

"You okay?" Wo asked.

"I just need to get in the water," Blu responded. "Oh, one other thing." He reached into his back pocket and pulled out his note to Lilli. "Could you type this up and send it to Lilli? "Since you're going to read it anyway—my qualifying event is on May third."

Wo fingered the paper. "That's the day you officially earn your spot for the Games. Man, I love being a jump ahead of the rest of the press," Wo joked, then pulled out a folded piece of paper from his pants pocket and handed it to Blu. "This is her latest email to you."

Blu lit up. "Awesome."

"So what about my question, dude? There's a country on the other side of the world that wants to hear from you."

Blu sighed. No matter what he said somebody would be upset. "Okay, here goes."

Wo turned on his hand recorder.

"China has been kind enough to allow me to come here with my coach—Coach Bai—to live and to train," Blu began. "It has also been my honor to meet my birth mother and so many others who have filled in the missing pieces in my past and encouraged me to reclaim my heritage. In gratitude for this warm welcome, I have decided to compete under the name of China. That is my choice—as an American. My wish is that everyone could make choices freely and determine their own histories."

Wo clicked off the recorder. "Nice," he commented. "Hey, maybe you can get me in here, and we can hit the slides?" Wo tipped his head toward the other half of the venue that had been converted into a world-class water park following the 2008 Games.

"I bet over the next few months we can figure out how to make that happen." Blu was speaking, but his eyes were already on the pool where he hoped that he too would break a world record during his stay in Beijing.

Once Wo had been ushered out, Blu opened the print out of Lilli's email. It read:

> Your family is fine. Missing you. Last weekend was first stop on dance tour in San Francisco's Chinatown. Sold Out. WAVE of interest. Hoping for the same in Seattle, Chicago, NYC, Philadelphia, and the others. Last performance in Washington D.C. on May 3.
> Lilli

Chinatown? Blu wondered why Zulegen had chosen that location as a venue for Lilli. San Francisco was a short drive from their hometown, and he knew an appearance by Lilli Cohen could pack the largest concert hall in the city. Did it have something to do with the WAVE? And why finish on May third—the same date as his qualifying?

Earplugs. Nose plug. Goggles. A minute later, Blu was diving deep, deep into the blue, deep enough to leave the string of questions in his wake.

# 64

It had been just under a month since Wo released his exclusive interview with Blu to the world. Wo was still pinching himself that only months before he was the one to receive the tip on the young Asian athlete who was now headed to the Games and upsetting governments as he went. Then came the call from Gao Cheng. He couldn't believe his luck. A second story of interest to the world: the story of Jewell Chan, her contribution to technology, and the government that ruthlessly stole it. Chinese bloggers would send the story across their country and around the world; activists in Hong Kong would rail against the Chinese government and the Communist Party; and those who had emigrated because of disagreements with China would feel their wounds in a fresh way. Wo was also aware there would likely be repercussions for the messenger. For the first time in his relatively short career as a reporter, Wo was worried for his own safety.

By the time Blu sat down with his microwaved pizza on the floor of his apartment to watch the news, most of the world had already learned the story. Thanks to Wo, there was no corner of the world that had not heard the breaking news of how the rights to technology developed by fifteen-year-old Jewell Chan fell into the hands of the Chinese government. Just as Blu reached for the remote, he heard the beep of the intercom. The guard stationed outside his building announced the arrival of James Wo. Blu was glad for some company. Wo, on the other hand, was just grateful to be inside a secure building.

Blu cracked open the door and listened as Wo made his way up the metal stairs.

"Dude, I can't get you into the water park tonight," Blu said when the reporter arrived.

"Not interested in the water park," Wo answered, catching his breath.

Blu smiled. "Okay, so maybe I just need to start you on a workout plan."

"That may be just what I need." Wo entered the room and collapsed on the tiny couch near the television. "So I can make a quick getaway."

"In case you haven't noticed I'm the one with the paparazzi—which just so happens to include you."

"I'm gonna have a little trouble blending in after today." When Blu said nothing, Wo leaned forward. "You know, right?"

"Off the record, I know about swimming and running and just enough about cycling to pull off a triathlon. That's all I got."

"The news, dude. Have you heard it?"

"I was just about to watch the recordings left for me."

"What?"

"The Professor records news that he thinks I should see, so I don't come across as clueless as I am." Blu turned on the television. Three recordings had been left for him. He clicked on the first.

An American newscaster, a woman, began an only slightly altered version of the story Wo released just that morning as a result of the news tip he'd been given by Gao Cheng. A dated picture of Jewell Chan appeared on the screen as the newscaster recounted the facts of the young inventor and how it was that she had never profited from her revolutionary technology.

When the clip ended Blu turned to stare at Wo. "Are you kidding?" Blu began raking his hair and pacing. "Did you know about this—that Jewell was ripped off?"

"Not until Gao Cheng told me."

"Who?"

"The consultant dude with Zulegen. He set up Lilli's tour."

"So this is *your* story?"

"A humdinger, huh?"

"Why'd he call you with this?"

Wo shrugged. "Start the next clip. Maybe we can figure this out."

A second newscast from the U.S. followed. The scene was Lilli's dance tour in New York City's Chinatown. Before the outdoor performance, protestors waved signs for the cameras and shouted in the street.

"Please, let her be safe," Blu whispered.

"See the signs they're carrying?" Wo pointed at the screen. "Some are in English." Blu hit PAUSE on the remote.

"There! 'Justice for Chan!'—see it?" An Asian woman held the sign with an arm stacked with Glo-me bracelets. "And there! 'Stolen: American Olympian'—that's you!" While there were scores of women—young and old—in the crowd, Blu also noticed plenty of men on the scene, but segregated, just like on the tour in China. They were gathering in the U.S. too. According to the newscast, Lilli's stops in other U.S. Chinatowns had seen similar demonstrations.

"The Zulegen dude who tipped you off had to know this would happen!" Blu exclaimed.

"I agree. These are organized protests," Wo stated definitively.

"Why do this to Lilli?"

"It's not about Lilli," Wo assured his friend. "It's about taking the dance tour where many Chinese go to live and be free. It's the perfect—and safest—place for them to push for change back in China."

"You think Gao Cheng did this?"

Wo thought a moment. "I think a lot of people did this. Hit the last clip, would ya?"

Blu started the final segment. This one was a Chinese broadcast. The video was dated. Blu recognized the limo he'd ridden in the day he was brought to the Water Cube for the first time. His heart pounded.

"That was the day I started training here," Blu narrated the moment caught on video. "You were inside the Cube with the press." Blu remembered every moment of the scene he was watching. He did not, however, remember anything of what he read in the English translation of the story. According to the reporter, he had recently told the China News Agency that he was reclaiming his Chinese heritage and, after winning gold for China, would return to "the greatest country on earth" as a princeling.

"I never said that!"

The reporter went on to announce that the government was declaring May third a day of celebration for the "homecoming" of Blu, the same day the athlete would compete to secure his place on the Chinese Olympic teams at qualifying.

"How can they get away with this? I'm no princeling, and I don't want a celebration!"

"There's a tsunami headed this way," Wo remarked.

After a moment, Blu said, "I think I get it now."

"What?"

"I am the wave."

Wo responded, "That's how a tsunami starts, right?"

# 65

The water was no longer a place of escape for Blu. His mind wandered even as he pushed his way across the pool.

He was now four months into his trip and spending most of his waking hours in training. And yet his "exchange student experience," as the Professor called it, had yielded much. The China-born athlete had begun to understand his native country, to see the struggles of the peoples, and to hope for a legacy of his own. He struggled most with the latter. On the nights he read the account of the Tiananmen Square Massacre, he wondered about the legacy of those—mostly students—who had died there in the same city where he now trained. What had changed? Was it just a story of failed courage? Was winning gold for China even a legacy he wanted?

Blu's face emerged from the water to the unhappy voice of Jack. "Where is your mind?" Jack stood poolside red-faced, arms folded tightly. The swimmer wished for someone who would listen to all that was on his mind. He wished for Lilli.

"Again," ordered Jack.

Blu pushed off the side once more. As he did he consoled himself with the thought that he was now just two days away from his Olympic qualifying event. With the big day behind him, he would have some time off before the Games. His plan was to go into hiding. With his spots secured, he would have every excuse to politely refuse the demands of the press or anyone else—with the exception of Jack—for a time. A break was just what he thought he needed to shake off the relentless demands and unending questions that pummeled him into a worrisome state of numb. He would rediscover his competitive core and re-emerge a ready Olympian.

...

It didn't occur to Blu that the day before his qualifying event would be different from any other. But a crowd, later estimated to be about triple the average turnout, gathered that morning outside the Water Cube to greet Blu. In light of the numbers, Blu was instructed to stay in the car until a couple additional bodyguards could be rounded up to escort him inside.

The crowd was also at least three times as loud. "What are they saying?" Blu asked as he was bustled through the throng.

"Most wish you good luck," one guard answered. "Others ask you to bring change."

Inside the Water Cube, the press greeted Blu, as was their practice. Wo, however, was absent for the first time since Blu began training there. Instead, the Professor was present, dressed in a black suit and royal blue tie.

"So much excitement," the Professor greeted his son. "You should be happy for such support."

"Why are you here?"

"It is an important day, is it not? I enlisted an able graduate student to continue my classes."

"I swim like it's qualifying every day," Blu responded. Reporters keyed his words into their phones. "This is no different."

At this, the Professor smiled broadly. "Coach Bai has

prepared you well." The Professor fell in alongside Blu as he made his way to the locker room.

"Have you seen Wo?" Blu asked.

The Professor walked in silence until they were alone. Then he turned and met the boy's eyes.

"Wo has been—detained." The man looked away from his son's pained gaze. "He is accused of fabricating the story of China's injustice to Jewell Chan."

"I can't lose anyone else!" Blu dropped down on the bench. After taking a moment to process the news, he yanked his towel from his duffle and pulled off his dress pants to reveal his Zulegen jammers.

"He will be released eventually," the Professor said. "He is an American citizen."

"The people of China will never learn the truth."

"Does that matter to you?" the Professor asked.

Blu sat back down, the feeling of exhaustion overtaking him too early. "It hurts. I know that," he confessed. "But I'm not sure it matters."

"Every time the truth is told it matters," the Professor said.

"How can it matter if there is no change?"

"You stand with China now. The people are watching. Perhaps they will again dream of change."

"The world watched Tiananmen too."

"Ah, you've been reading."

"What can I possibly do that thousands could not?"

"No wave moves alone but with others: those that come before and after."

The Professor loosened his tie and sat down next to his son. "Have you been there—to Tiananmen Square?"

"No."

"I could take you there. We could go in the morning if you like. Perhaps it will give you strength to do what matters."

"Jack would have a cow," Blu started, then stopped and turned to the Professor. Blu realized that he actually did want to go there. And he wanted to go there with his father.

At Tiananmen he could honor those who had come before, those who had tried. It seemed the least—or most—he could do. "We'd have to leave early," Blu relented.

# 66

On qualifying day, Blu had a pre-dawn workout at the pool. He stood drying off next to his coach when the Professor arrived, dressed casually for a drive into the city. Jack looked up at the Professor but did not speak.

"I trust you've been informed that we're taking a short trip to Tiananmen Square this morning," the Professor addressed Jack.

"Yes," Jack answered without enthusiasm, zipping open Blu's duffle.

Blu felt a pang of guilt for slipping away on qualifying day. It was a day that meant as much to the coach as to the athlete. "You want to go?"

"I need to check your gear."

"That won't take very long," Blu insisted.

"There are other pressing matters to attend to this day," Jack responded as he handed Blu a change of clothes from the bag.

"I must meet with a friend." Jack exchanged a long glance with the Professor.

"The same friend you saw at Christmas?" Blu asked.

"Yes."

"Is this friend a *she*?"

"No," Jack answered irritated. "A former trainee of mine."

"Maybe he could come to qualifying?"

Jack looked at the Professor again before answering. "No," he said again. "But he will be following your progress."

"We should go," the Professor ended the exchange.

As Blu and the Professor moved toward the door, Jack called after them: "It is good for a man to stand in the place of courage."

With Jack's reluctant blessing on the trip, Blu felt released to embrace the experience he hoped would propel him to the finish line.

...

It was the third of May, and the sounds of fireworks accompanied Blu and the Professor as their driver made the half-hour long drive into the heart of Beijing. Along the way, banners bearing the Olympic rings hung from buildings. On others, the flag of China waved.

"A day of celebration in your honor," the Professor said.

While Blu would have preferred to ignore this fact, it was not possible. As the car drew nearer to its destination, Blu saw his face draped across ancient-looking buildings. The banners carried a line in Mandarin, which the Professor translated: "Good Luck, Blu."

"I'd have been cool with just a toothpaste commercial," lamented Blu.

"This success is yours," the Professor answered. "You remind the people of China to dream."

Since most tourists arrived at Tiananmen Square by public transportation—subway or bus—parking for cars was scarce. The Professor expertly directed their driver to the closest available lot. Once they were parked, the Professor opened up a map of the vicinity—designed for English-speaking tourists. Blu stopped his father, just as he was about to begin an explanation of the square.

"You know I've been reading about this place—a lot," Blu interrupted.

"Then we are ready?"

"I'd like to go alone," Blu said timidly. "Is that okay?"

"Of course, I will wait here," the Professor responded, unoffended. "I'll make some phone calls. Remember—there isn't much time."

Blu zipped his warm-up jacket and glanced at his watch. "Half an hour, okay?"

"I'll see you then, my son."

...

From where he stood by the car, Blu could see the Monument to the People's Heroes that he knew sat near the center of Tiananmen Square. From his reading, Blu knew the four-sided obelisk was built of marble and granite and had been the gathering place for the protesters at the Tiananmen Square Massacre in 1989. He headed directly for it.

The massive plaza was everything Blu had read about, yet beyond anything he could have ever imagined. He looked out over the 100-acre square, which was devoid of trees or even benches. It was indeed an ideal location for celebrations—or protests. Originally situated around the Forbidden City, home to early rulers of China beginning with the Ming Dynasty in the 1400s, the square was later redesigned, taking on its rectangular shape, and expanded multiple times. Tourists already mulled about the grounds, as well as a few guards, but no one gave the would-be princeling a second glance.

Upon arriving at the monument, Blu was awestruck. The centerpiece of the square stood ten stories high. He climbed two sets of stairs to reach the base with its elaborate carvings. From there he tried to imagine the space around him filled with as many as a million people on that day. It would have been warm, maybe hot, on the fourth of June 1989, the day when the protests turned bloody. Without cell phones, news of the student-led protest had grown in the weeks prior by word of mouth. Blu wondered how it was he had been summoned to this place.

From his centralized location, Blu saw the other buildings noted on his tourist map of the square. Behind the monument stood Memorial Hall, the mausoleum that held the body of Chairman Mao, the founder of the People's Republic of China and its first communist ruler. Beyond this, barely visible to the far South was the ornate Zheng Yang Gate. The walled structure was originally part of the extensive fortifications of the capital city. On the opposite end of the square stood a building called Tiananmen Gate—or Gate of Heavenly Peace—which served as an entrance to the Forbidden City. At the front, Mao's portrait is perpetually and prominently on display. On the east side of the plaza stood the Museum of Chinese History. To the west was the Great Hall of the People, a massive building marked by a red star on the roof, well known as the political hub of Beijing.

It was the monument, however, that captured the young American's attention. Blu stepped back from the perimeter of the structure and seated himself on the flagstone walk. From there he stared and thought and felt. Jack had been right. This was a place of courage. Admittedly, Blu had felt dull of late. His routine was burdensome. His purpose blurred. But in his aloneness with the heroes of the people—the students, none of whose names were inscribed on the monument—he was proud. Would they have halted their protests and gone home had they known they would not succeed that day? Blu knew they would not. They could not. Such was their legacy.

Blu checked his watch. Already he'd been on the square for twenty minutes. The number of visitors to the site grew by the second. They'd wonder why he didn't move out of the growing stream of sightseers. He didn't know himself.

After half an hour had passed, a small pair of sneakers stopped next to him. Blu looked up to discover a kid-sized version of himself.

"You are—Blu?" the child, who looked to be about eight, asked in broken English.

Blu nodded and glanced around, hoping no one else was listening.

At this the boy began waving his arms, jumping and yelling, "Blu! Blu!" The boy made sure everyone with working ears knew that the Olympic hopeful was sitting in the middle of Tiananmen Square. Passersby moved towards Blu and the exuberant boy with interest.

Now would definitely be the time to go, Blu told himself. But still he did not move.

From among the crowd, someone pushed through and dropped down on the other side of Blu. It was Dwain, the Olympic chess player.

"Are you kidding?" Blu said as the two bumped fists. "How are you even here? You're supposed to be in Kunming!"

"We're a team, right?" Dwain smiled. "A dream team. We should be together." One at a time, the athletes Blu lived among in Kunming seated themselves with him on the walk. The standing crowd backed away to make room as twenty more Olympic hopefuls emerged and sat together. The scene quickly grew noisy and crowded as those who had begun to congregate called others on their cell phones and posted pictures on social media.

There was a festive feel to the gathering, and the people freely approached Blu and the other athletes to wish them good luck and to shake their hands.

"I don't know what they're saying!" Blu complained to Dwain.

"Fine. I'll be your translator, mister celebrity," Dwain responded. "That man just thanked you for coming to China and said that meeting you here is a sign."

"A sign of what?"

Heads turned as a deep voice called to Blu, becoming clearer and louder as the speaker moved toward the athletes. By the time the Professor finally arrived on the scene, the noise of the crowd had dropped to near silence though the fireworks still sounded in the distance. When he stood with his dream team at last, the Professor looked at Blu but spoke so as to be heard by all those present: "Why are you still here?" the Professor asked in Mandarin, then continued: "You are expected at qualifying in a short time. If you miss this event you cannot compete in the Games."

Dwain translated the Professor's words to Blu. "Why is he speaking Chinese?" Blu demanded of his friend.

"He does it for *them*," Dwain explained. "Now answer him, and I will translate!"

His heart pounding, Blu rose to his feet. As he did, he understood why he had been unable to leave the square: he could not walk away from what mattered. From where he stood, he announced: "I wanted to swim for the people of this country, not for its government!" When Dwain translated for the crowd, they burst into cheers.

The Professor held up his hand, and the gathering quieted. He spoke again, and Dwain translated for his teammate: "Let your win today be for the people."

Blu shook his head decidedly. "The government will claim victory for itself, just as it did in this place, when the people stood for freedom." Blu turned and shouted into the crowd. "Just as it did when it falsely accused my coach—Bai Zhao Man, and when it stole the work of Jewell Chan!" Dwain translated Blu's response. Again the crowd erupted. Looking around him, Blu could no longer see across the grounds. Instead he saw children on the shoulders of parents, as well as cell phones used for taking pictures, and the tops of the buildings on the square.

"Son of Li Daiya!" the Professor called to Blu, and the crowd listened with interest. "Then you will give up your Olympic dream for a morning in Tiananmen Square?"

After Dwain translated the question, Blu paused. Was he prepared to give up all he'd worked for to make a statement? Now he heard encouragements from the members of his team: "It is time to make things right!" and "Will you take your gold medal and leave nothing behind?" Blu looked at Dwain, then at the Monument of the People. He faced his listeners and spoke with conviction: "If I cannot compete for the Chinese people," Blu gestured at his listeners, "I will stand here, in honor of those who came before, the students who put aside *their* dreams to demand freedom." As Dwain translated, there was movement in the crowd and a rumbling on the ground as uniformed men in lines parted the crowd until they arrived at the place where the dream team sat.

They were dressed in fatigues, and it dawned on Blu that they were not the Chinese police; this was the military. Like Tiananmen.

A voice in a megaphone shot across the crowd. Blu expected the people to scramble for cover. But they didn't. Dwain translated the soldier's announcement: "No one will be harmed here. These Americans are being escorted from the square." Blu searched the crowd for the face of the Professor, now lost in the crowd that filled the square and beyond. As panic threatened to overtake him, Blu felt Dwain's hand on his shoulder. "We are safe," he assured his friend.

How could he know such a thing? Blu stood, unable to move. Then a soldier stepped beside him, nudging him forward. There was no pushing. No shouting. No handcuffs.

In his peripheral Blu saw an angry rush of police at the edge of the square. But the soldiers halted their advance. As dream team athletes were escorted to waiting vehicles, other soldiers stayed behind with the crowd to keep the police at bay. Protestors ranted openly and the media, left undisturbed and uncensored, broadcast the chaotic scene to the rest of the world in real time.

# 67

As it turned out, Dwain was right. Upon his arrival at the prison in the Dongcheng District in Beijing along with the rest of the dream team, Blu learned they had not been taken there as prisoners as he had feared. Instead, the prison served as their safe house. Fortunately, Jack had arrived safely as well. However, what Blu had expected to be a one-night stay was extended by nearly a week.

Each day, Dwain interpreted the news for Blu as the athletes sat watching a small television. According to reports, the Chinese police had made numerous attempts to penetrate the border of military soldiers and break up the crowd that remained at the square day and night. On day five, the police had lobbed tear gas bombs into the crowd, and the scene turned riotous. At last, the announcement came, bringing an abrupt end to the squirmish: the government of the People's Republic of China had officially been disbanded.

At the news, Dwain and the other members of the dream team cheered and exchanged high-fives, while Blu struggled to comprehend the events that had taken place in the days they'd been safely tucked away.

"It is time to celebrate!" Jack gave his trainee a stiff embrace.

"How did this happen?" Blu asked, stunned.

"That is a question for the Professor," Jack responded, beaming. "What I know is that the soldiers that protected us in the square were not an isolated few." He continued, "Others were also in place to detain members of the Politburo. That made it possible for an interim governing body to step in, men and women who will be the first to lead the way to a democratic China."

"Were people"—Blu braced for bad news—"hurt?"

"No serious injuries have been reported," he replied. "The protest in the square as well as in the U.S. Chinatowns proved to be most helpful distractions in a swift yet bloodless takeover."

"Hey! They're already talking about a democratic constitution—and elections!" Dwain announced the news as it was released on a televised press conference. A fresh round of celebratory whoops followed.

It was then that the Professor arrived on the scene, looking tired but elated, slapping the backs of his athletes as he made his way to Blu. "You have done what mattered, my son," he said as they embraced.

"I only said what was on my heart."

"And on the hearts of billions, those in this country and so many more around the world. The second Tiananmen has come."

"You knew it would happen and that I'd be part of it."

"It was my dream that you would also want change for the people of China, but I could not make you care."

"On your feet, dream team! It's time to go!" Jack announced from where he stood near the front doors. Blu could see that an official of sorts had arrived and stood with Jack. The team members hurried to form a line, while Blu gravitated to the back. Each of the athletes shook the hand of both men as they stepped into a new China.

The Professor spoke to Blu, "I have much business to

attend to. Go with Jack and the others, and I will meet you later." Once at the door, Blu looked at Jack and his companion, a tall Asian man in military attire. The distinguished man met his eyes and said, "So this is the celebrity Blu!"

"Blu," Jack began, "I'd like to introduce you to an old friend of mine and the second in command of the Chinese military. By the way, he is also the man who saved our skins."

"Thank you, sir," Blu shook the man's hand.

"It was the work of many, was it not?" remarked the man with a presence even more commanding than Jack's. "There are soldiers, such as myself, who have remained loyal to our wise trainer." The man took Blu's shoulder and continued, "Through the years, many more have come to embrace his hope of completing all that was begun at Tiananmen Square and to distrust the government that wrongly accused him of a crime and drove him from China."

"Had your men arrived at the square even one minute later or failed at any point of their mission, the story would have ended quite differently," Jack said, returning the compliment.

It was then that Blu remembered that Jack's resume included his work with the Chinese Army. At the time, the information was superfluous.

"You've been separated from each other a long time, haven't you?" Blu asked, looking from the soldier to his coach. Blu thought of his own friends at home.

"Too long," the man turned to Jack. "But that needn't happen again. Ever."

...

Back in his apartment, which remained heavily guarded, Blu hosted his team members, along with Jack, the Professor, and a recently released James Wo. There was more popcorn than space available. Televised news blared behind the revelry as reporting related to the takeover continued day and night.

Cheers went up as a young male newscaster detailed the removal of the athletes from the square. According to the report, sources confirmed that the dream team was organized by Professor Si Zhen of Hong Kong University to promote and support China's freedom movement. Also highlighted was the fact that the athletes, who were also adoptees from China, represented tens of thousands more, like themselves, who hoped for change in the country of their birth.

Backslapping commenced, as Blu became the subject of the story that followed. Footage of Blu training at the Water Cube accompanied the story of the Olympian hopeful and son of Li Daiya, the former director of China's Department of Propaganda. It was reported that Blu's decision not to compete for the "government" of China sparked the protest at Tiananmen Square on the third of May. Thanks to texting, social media, and the underground news bloggers, the protest grew in size and intensity comparable to the 1989 student-led protest there that spanned nearly two months.

In the next story, listeners learned that the protest at Tiananmen occurred, not so coincidentally, while the President of the Central Military Commission was out of the country. Meanwhile, Jack's military friend had positioned "rogue troops" in order to accomplish the takeover.

Blu looked around the room for the Professor who had secured an end seat on the couch. Armed with a bowl of popcorn, Blu pushed his way to the Professor. "Popcorn?" he asked.

"Unlike you, I was not detained and enjoyed many fine meals with my comrades," the Professor said, patting his stomach.

"How many waves were in motion to do—this?"

The Professor understood his son's line of questioning. His son saw so little of the picture that spanned decades and nations. There had been educators like himself, immigrants like Candace, survivors of the first Tiananmen, and those who populated Chinatowns. These had held on to the dream for decades. Still others had come to dream more recently: ambitious young businesspeople like Gao Cheng; a new generation of restless Chinese students; and Chinese adoptees around the world.

"Scores," the professor replied simply.

"How long in the planning?"

The man paused, as if remembering both failures and triumphs. "As one works for any dream," he said at last, "one counts victories not years. Then the great day comes at last."

"When the celebration ends will I have one father—or two?"

"The celebration of freedom should never end," he answered. "Neither will I relinquish the place I have in your life. That being said, there is both mother and father across the ocean who welcomed you from China and now wait to welcome you home again."

"What will happen to Li Daiya?" Blu asked, though he wasn't sure he wanted to know the answer.

"Her proposals for policy change regarding the children of China are already being implemented," the Professor answered. "This will be her legacy, one far greater than giving China another communist princeling. Her work will be her healing and the way to finding her place in your life."

"Over here!" came a call for everyone's attention. It was James Wo. "You guys have to see this!" he pointed to the television. "Even I didn't know what was happening at home!" On the television were video clips of the protests that erupted in Chinatowns across the U.S. in the months prior to the takeover. The report confirmed Blu's suspicions:

> "According to anonymous bloggers in China's underground news network, the Zulegen-sponsored dance tour through Chinatowns in the U.S., featuring Chinese adoptee Lilli Cohen, also served as meeting places to address matters regarding the impending takeover. In addition, it

has been confirmed that the website for popular video blogger Linda Cohen, Lilli's mother, included a covert chat site for adoptees searching for their Chinese mothers. It is now believed that connections made on that site are responsible for the recent spike in the number of flights from the U.S. to China."

The reporter went on to say that a number of major corporations, both in the U.S. and China, had stepped up to provide funding for meetings between mothers and the children they were forced to give up due to China's one-child policy. The name of the prominent Chinese businessman Gao Cheng was mentioned among those leading the effort.

"More popcorn over here!" Dwain called from the kitchenette, his voice interrupting the next news story. Blu heard the name of Jewell Chan in the broadcast, but the rest was lost.

# 68

There was an undeniable sense of déjà vu for Blu as he again sat down next to Jack on the airplane to return home. Gone, however, was the dream of returning as an Olympian. In spite of his role in ushering in the wave, Blu yet felt the loss of his own dream. Surely Jack shared that disappointment.

Blu turned to his coach who was arranging his neck cushion for the long flight. "It still feels like failure," he confessed.

"Pure gold does not fear the furnace," Jack responded.

"What the heck?"

"Chinese proverb."

"What does it mean?"

"It means a real champion allows disappointment to make him stronger."

"Great—so better luck next time, right?"

"You were part of a winning team. Next time, different team, another win."

Getting no sympathy from his coach, Blu opened his laptop. It had been months since he'd been able to access his email. Maybe he'd been missed; perhaps he'd just been forgotten. He clicked the mail icon. A seemingly endless stream of emails appeared, all messages he had craved at the end of every long day of his trip. The most recent was entitled "For the Ride," and included an attachment. He opened it first:

> *Blu, check out the video your dad put together. Just wanted you to know we're all still here and can't wait for you to be home! Lilli*

Blu smiled thinking of the last video Lilli sent him—the one of them hip-hop dancing together.

With a click, the attachment opened, and Blu was face to face with the people he left behind in what felt like another life. "Hi, Blu!" came their unified greeting. While Blu didn't recognize the spacious room where they gathered, tears welled up as the camera began its scan of the familiar faces there. Seated on the far left of a big cushy white couch was his mother, waving. Next to her was Derek who had his arm around Jewell who held out her left arm and wriggled her fingers as the camera pulled in for a close shot. "Look what I received for Christmas!" Jewell gushed, and the group whooped and hoorayed.

"Oh my gosh!" Blu blurted out.

"What?" his coach asked, alarmed.

"Derek and Jewell are engaged!"

Back to the video, the camera was on Levi, who was seated on the arm of the couch. He waved and blurted out everything on his mind: "Yo, Blu, I killed it on the track team this spring! And guess what? There's a pool here, out back! Hey, do I have to call you Blu?"

Miguel's face moved into the shot. "Just call him home for noodles! Am I right?"

Blu laughed.

The camera moved to the floor where Lilli sat cross-legged

as usual, but with one arm around a huge gold-colored dog with an enormous—and somehow familiar—black snout. "This is my new dance partner. He's way better than Ben who, by the way, ditched me when he made it on *Dance Club*!"

"I'm here too," came the voice of Blu's father from behind the camera. This was the dad who had proved to be his biggest fan, even before he left for China; the same dad he had, for years, held at a distance for fear of disappointing him. Blu resolved to spend more time with him even if he had to sit through some documentaries.

Also making appearances in the video were Mr. and Mrs. Price and their three remaining offspring—Celeste, Victor, and Jana. Lilli's parents also stood in the room, Mrs. Cohen holding a tiny bundle in her arms. "Meet Canyon!" Mr. Cohen announced to the camera. "Babysitters wanted!" After this, the camera pulled back out to a wide shot. Blu paused the shot and elbowed Jack.

"Wonder who got a dog?" Blu turned the computer screen toward his coach.

Jack jumped to life. "That's Chum!"

"Who?"

"*My* dog!"

"You said you didn't own a dog," Blu reminded him.

"You know—he's my rental! I got an email that he'd been sold. I thought he was gone!"

"So this is *your* place?" Blu asked.

"It is not my home," Jack shook his head. "Perhaps it belongs to Ms. Chan."

"Oh, yeah, maybe it's a hotel or something."

Jack turned to Blu. "That's definitely not the Lunar Eclipse Hotel. You didn't hear the news story? She was fired from her government job when Wo's story about her came out. She has applied for U.S. citizenship."

"I missed that! So did the university hire her?"

"Don't know about that, but Gao Cheng—the Zulegen guy—"

"Yeah, I remember—"

"He's funding an effort to introduce new technology to fight cancer—he suffers from pancreatic cancer, I believe. Anyway, Jewell Chan is heading a team to develop an implant that releases the body's own electricity in pulses and stops cancer cells from growing. No one is going to steal her rights to it this time."

"So you think that's *her* house?"

"Likely the first of many she will own someday," Jack chuckled.

"Awesome."

So much had changed. Blu wondered what other news awaited him. His mother's painting came to mind: Was he at the beginning, middle, or end of a storm? The plane began to move into position for take off.

"Well," Blu shrugged and continued, "it looks like you have some dog sitters and a new place for Chum to hang when you're not around." Blu hoped that Chum was a permanent replacement for Ben.

"They can come around anytime." Jack's uneven voice betrayed his emotion. "I won't be traveling the world like I once did. The next four years are going to be very busy. It'll get hot—hot like a furnace—but in the end, I will give America pure gold."

# Reference of Chinese Names Used

(Listed Alphabetically)

### Bai Zhao Man
Athletic coach to internationally ranked athletes; also known as Coach Bai, Jack

### Dr. Tan
Head of College of Social Sciences, California State University, Fresno

### Feng
Dorm Attendant for Dream Team at the Sports Training Center in Kunming, China

### Gao Cheng
Businessman

### James Wo
Reporter for the *Seattle Asian Times*

### Jun
Bodyguard to Lilli Cohen in China

## Li Daiya
Director of Propaganda, member of the Politburo Standing Committee of the Chinese Communist Party

## Lien
Assistant to Director Li Daiya

## Mei
Assistant to Director Li Daiya

## Ming Ming "Jewell" Chan
Employee of the Center of Science and Technology in Beijing; Inventor of the "Glo-Me" technology and the program for the Data Collection Project

## Qin Ji
Olympic hopeful trained by Coach Bai who died before the 2006 Olympic Games in Beijing

## Si Zhen
Professor at the University of Hong Kong and founder of the U.S. Center for Adoption; also known as the Professor, Professor Si Zhen, Professor Si

## Waiyin
Assistant to Professor Si Zhen

## Wong Bao
Supervisor of Jewell Chan at the Ministry of Science and Technology in Beijing

# Glossary of Historic People and Events of China

(Listed Alphabetically)

**Chinese Communist Party (CCP)**—By 1921, the model of Russian Communism was being replicated in China. By 1949, the CCP was the founding and ruling political party of the People's Republic of China under its first Chairman, Mao Zedong. The CCP is the sole governing party of China today and is characterized by censorship and human rights infractions. In an effort to escape the fate of communism in Russia, the CCP restructured its economy to incorporate some measure of capitalism.
(Source: http://classroom.synonym.com/differences-communism-russia-china-5800.html)

**Cultural Revolution (1966–1976)**—In 1966, after the epic famine that resulted from Mao's Great Leap Forward initiative, the chairman introduced the Cultural Revolution of China, an effort to eradicate all that predated communism or was deemed reflective of capitalistic thought. The chairman believed the move would serve to buoy his own reputation as a leader and to move China's youth to a greater loyalty to Maoist thought. In response, between 1966 and 1976, youth,

later joined by others, formed Red Guards, which sought to purge China of the "Four Olds:" old ideas, old culture, old customs, and old habits.
(Source: http://asianhistory.about.com/od/modernchina/f/What-Was-The-Cultural-Revolution.htm)

**Hong Kong**—Once a dependent territory of the United Kingdom (1842), the island of Hong Kong has since been returned to China (1997) and enjoys prosperity under China's "one country, two systems policy." Hong Kong enjoys greater autonomy, including an economic system based on capitalism, with the exceptions of defense and foreign affairs. While the Constitution of Hong Kong guarantees human rights, freedoms, and a government with elected officials, relations between the two government systems are strained as many residents—including students—of Hong Kong push for greater democratic reform and independence from mainland China.
(Source: http://www.historyofthings.com/history-of-hong-kong)

**Mao Zedong (1893–1976)**—Mao Zedong led peasant soldiers to victory in the Chinese Civil War. Afterward he became the first chairman of the newly established People's Republic of China (1949) and leader of the Chinese Communist Party. While Mao is credited with casting a vision of China as an industrial power, Mao also directed radical reforms in China that resulted in the deaths of an estimated 20 million countrymen. Among the most devastating of these reform efforts were the Great Leap Forward (1958–1963) and the Cultural Revolution (1966–1976).
(Source: http://www.historylearningsite.co.uk/modern-world-history-1918-to-1980/china-1900-to-1976/mao-zedong)

**Ming Dynasty (1368–1644)**—The Ming ruled in the latter years of Imperial China and was responsible for building the Forbidden City and Tiananmen Square (1400s). Its reign

was marked by great art and exploration. The Ming Dynasty ended following a takeover by the Qing (1644–1911), which was the last Chinese dynasty.
(Source: http://asianhistory.about.com/od/china/p/ChinaProfile.htm)

**The Forbidden City**—Built to house the supreme or "divine" rulers of China, the Forbidden City housed twenty-four emperors of the Ming and Qing Dynasties. It is situated in the heart of Beijing, once considered the center of the world. On its 178 acres, the Forbidden City includes ninety palaces and over 900 buildings, many of which have been converted into exhibition halls. A three-story defensive wall surrounds the city, which remains a popular tourist attraction.
(Source: http://www.chinahighlights.com/beijing/forbidden-city/)

**The Politburo Standing Committee of China**—This elite, seven-member executive committee of China's Communist Party (CCP) is comprised of the most powerful figures of the larger 205-member Central Committee of the party. Its primary responsibility is policy-making, and its members include the head of the Chinese Communist Party (who is also chairman of the Central Military Commission), the premier of China, and the head of the National People's Congress. Appointees to this committee change with the leadership and have, in the past, included the head of the Propaganda Department.
(Source: http://www.businessinsider.com/china-politburo-standing-committee-2012-11?op=1)

**The Red Guards**—These were bands of youth (primarily) that organized across China as a result of a speech given by Chairman Mao Zedong introducing the Cultural Revolution (1966–1976). Red Guards turned fanatical, destroying religious writings and artifacts in response to Chairman Mao's challenge to destroy the "old China" in order to usher in a "new" China. As the number and power of Red Guards increased, there was infighting between groups, as well as betrayal of family members, neighbors, and coworkers. The Red Guards are responsible for the death or detainment of thousands.

(Source: http://asianhistory.about.com/od/glossaryps/g/Who-Were-Chinas-Red-Guards.htm)

**The Tiananmen Massacre**—This was one of the largest and well-known student protests in Beijing against the Chinese government. The event that grew to an estimated one million protesters over a two-month period was played out in Tiananmen Square in 1989. It ended on June 4, when government troops and tanks were summoned to the scene, resulting in the death of up to a thousand people. Protests began in April, following the death of an ousted government leader, Hu Yaobang, known to be a reformer. The government's refusal (later acquiesced) to give Hu a state funeral, together with its denial to meet with a delegation of students, fed the protests of the already disillusioned populous. Still today, the CCP censors all information related to this event.

(Source: http://asianhistory.about.com/od/china/a/TiananmenSquare.htm)

# Afterword

Reading was a welcome refuge for me growing up in rural North Carolina. The fiction I enjoyed in my youth grew my fascination of the temporal world I could see and the eternal one I could not (of note were the timeless works of Madeleine L'Engle). Here, at last, I offer my own effort. It is born of my adult experience as an adoptive mother, to give young people—particularly those born in one country and raised in another—a place where their experience is not foreign, where each can embrace his or her own story.

    The writing process for this book mirrored the building of our family. By this I mean it has been surprising, challenging, humbling, and dependent on a commitment to learn and keep on learning. I am privileged to be part of a growing community of parents who are openly navigating the international adoption journey. These parents are building different kinds of families and becoming different kinds of people—more compassionate, more determined people—in the process. I would like to express my profound thanks to those who have developed excellent resources that encourage growth and healing for families and equip educators and others to bring skilled empathy to those with early life disruption.

Why write a fictional adoption story? In this case, story is an ideal vehicle for both writer and reader to explore the challenges and unique opportunities of cross-cultural adoption through the eyes of both youth and parent. In addition, this effort gave me a place to express my deep passion for freedom. I hope for an end to the political oppression of the people of China, and I also hope for an inner freedom that extends to all people in all places. Both are gifts of heaven, releasing humankind to pursue worship, self-expression, fresh starts, and love of self and others.

# About the Author

Catherine Pike Plough graduated from the University of North Carolina at Greensboro with a degree in Communication Studies. She began her career as a news journalist, later freelancing for local and national publications. Along the way, she made her foray into fiction, taking first place in *Charisma*'s short fiction competition. *The Blu Phenomenon* is her first novel, birthed through the real-life experience of adopting a son from Hong Kong. Catherine and her husband live in their almost-empty nest near Charlotte, NC, where she is an avid student of China affairs and adoption-related topics.

Made in the USA
Lexington, KY
06 September 2016